Dear Reader:

The novels you've enjoyed over the past ten years by such authors as Kathleen Woodiwiss, Rosemary Rogers, Johanna Lindsey and Laurie McBain are accountable to one thing above all others: Avon has never tried to force authors into any particular mold. Rather, Avon is a publisher that encourages individual talent and is always on the lookout for writers who will deliver *real* books, not packaged formulas.

In 1982, we started a program to help readers pick out authors of exceptional promise. Called "The Avon Romance," the books were distinguished by a ribbon motif in the upper left-hand corner of the cover. Although every title was by a new author, and the settings could be either historical or contemporary, they were quickly discovered and became known as "the ribbon books."

In 1984, "The Avon Romance" will be a feature on the Avon list. Each month, you will find novels with many different settings, each one by an author who is special. You will not find predictable characters, predictable plots and predictable endings. The only predictable thing about "The Avon Romance" will be the superior quality that Avon has always delivered in the field of romance!

Sincerely,

THE BOOK WORM,
1743 COMMERCIAL DRIVE AT 2nd AVE
VANCOUVER, B.C. V5N 4A4

Walter Mead

WALTER MEADE
President & Publisher

MARIA LUISA YEE

WILDSTAR
LINDA LADD

▲ AVON
PUBLISHERS OF BARD, CAMELOT, DISCUS AND FLARE BOOKS

WILDSTAR is an original publication of Avon Books. This work has never before appeared in book form.

This work is a novel. Any similarities to actual persons or events is purely coincidental.

AVON BOOKS
A division of
The Hearst Corporation
1790 Broadway
New York, New York 10019

First Avon Printing, May, 1984

Printed in the U. S. A.

WFH 10 9 8 7 6 5 4 3 2 1

For Bill and my children Laurie and Billy

PROLOGUE

Colorado Territory, June 1862

The moonlight streamed through the wide mullioned windows, crisscrossing slanted squares of white light on the intricately patterned red Persian carpet. The room was dark otherwise, except for the ruddy glow of firelight from the small stone fireplace built against one corner. Its flickering threw shadows around the walls, vaguely outlining the massive four-poster bed draped heavily with crimson velvet. Beneath the richly crushed fabric of the huge canopy, atop satin sheets, a woman writhed beneath the muscular embrace of a man. Her moaning was soft and distinct in the quiet room.

The man was very big, his immense shoulders covering her body completely. His smooth muscles rippled fluidly as her hands moved up his back to hook over his broad shoulders. Her fingers curved and clenched, digging into his flesh as her scarlet nails clawed his bare back. His hands were large and strong, and he had them both entangled in the woman's long, silky hair. Her moans grew louder. He lifted his head and stared down at her as he held her face immobile, watching her half-opened eyes and panting, kiss-swollen lips. The dim light reflected on the hard, cleanly chiseled lines of his face, the shadows carving hollows in his high cheekbones and square jaw. He was an extremely handsome man, whose looks proclaimed his confidence in his own masculine strength and capability. His eyes, a brilliant azure, glowed like blue flames as he

1

looked down arrogantly into her passion-flushed face. His hair was a dark blond, sunstreaked almost white on top. It was long and shaggy and thick, and the woman brought one hand up to slide tapered fingers into it where it curled slightly at the back of his neck. His skin was dark, burned by the sun to a deep teak that contrasted sharply with the creamy whiteness of her shoulders and arms.

Everything about him exuded a sense of power. His hard biceps muscles tightened and flexed as he slid one arm under her shoulders and lifted her torso easily, sending her hair streaming down over his forearm in a coppery shimmer. He stilled his body as his eyes examined her writhing state of arousal with a self-assured, insolent gaze.

"Logan, don't torture me. . . ."

He laughed softly, deep in his throat, at her gasping entreaty. He dropped his mouth to hers, muffling her cries, and let the tip of his tongue slowly trace her parted, trembling lips. He lingered tantalizingly in the corners until she groaned beneath his probing invasion. He felt her tongue enter his own mouth and met it, feeling her shudder beneath him. Her hands moved to the hard muscles at his narrow waist, then grasped his hips to urge them down upon hers. Finally, he began once more to move within her, ravaging her senses and bringing her burning body to a fever pitch of excitement.

He inched his warm lips slowly along her finely drawn cheekbone and pressed his hot mouth into the curve of her delicate ear, where his tongue darted and licked at her earlobe and the sensitive hollow beneath it. His blond head moved slowly against her white flesh, down her throat, as she arched her own head back, flinging her red-gold hair from side to side, her breathing hard and fast. At the base of her throat, her staccato pulse raced beneath his mouth. He was purposely prolonging her release as he watched her pant and squirm, well aware that she wanted it that way despite her moaning entreaties to the contrary. He knew her well. He had been involved in a sporadic affair with Isabel Holloway Whitcomb since she'd come to Denver during the gold rush of '59. But he'd met her many years before that at the glittering soirées and balls of the St. Louis elite of which both their families were a part. Since then her father had lost much of his fortune through bad investments, forcing the cold-hearted, hot-blooded woman to make her own way in the world. She'd had too many lovers to remember their names; she knew the weakness in men, and delighted in teasing them with her exquisitely formed body. And she succeeded most of the time, twisting men around her long, slim fingers like loose twine.

Except for Logan Cord. He knew her too well to let her fool him or use him. He played her own game against her, holding his passion firmly in leash and forcing her to bow to him. It amused him, because it enslaved her.

He let his mouth trail slowly over the quivering softness of her flesh, his kisses moving teasingly until he drew a gasp of bittersweet pleasure from her. She moaned softly, and he drew back again.

"You're a devil, Logan," she said breathlessly through set teeth.

Logan smiled slightly, as his mouth sought the cord of her throat.

She groaned, molding her body to him as his hands moved with maddening slowness to stroke her gently.

"Please, please, I want you," she gasped.

Logan laughed softly, his lean hips moving over her softly rounded ones. His own pulse began to throb, her skin like hot velvet beneath him, her breath eager in his ear.

His passion accelerated, her fingers grasping the muscles at his waist and attempting to pull him closer as she rose to meet him. He used her roughly, because she demanded it that way. Although Isabel treated men like playthings, her own passion was aroused only when a man gave her no quarter. She was a violent lover, never sated for long, never failing to leave streaks of her passion across her partner's back.

The end was a consuming explosion of animal passion, and afterward they lay entwined, their bodies molded together as they regained their breath.

Logan moved first as he rolled away and stood up, and she watched his magnificent body in the firelight as he walked across the room. Isabel watched him, feeling the fire erupt in a hot throb in her loins, even in the aftermath of their furious lovemaking. His shoulders were broad, his chest hard, his arms and legs long and corded with muscle.

She watched him turn toward her as he drew on his buckskin breeches, and her eyes dropped as he buckled them across the flat, ridged muscles of his stomach. While she watched, he sat and drew first one, then the other knee-high moccasin over the bulging muscles of each leg.

She'd been married to Marcus Whitcomb for a year when Logan had gazed wickedly into her eyes and invited her into his bed. Her husband was twenty years her senior, and Logan was not the first man to propose such a thing to Isabel, nor was he the first she'd accepted. She'd married Marcus for his money, knowing that her voracious desires could never be satisfied by the old man. And now that he'd died, she hadn't been able to persuade Logan to marry her.

Damn him, he was arousing her now to near climax as she watched his muscles flex. She wanted him again, desperately now, even though she still tingled from their previous joining.

"Don't leave me, Logan. Not yet."

Logan glanced at her as he drew on his white linen shirt and began buttoning it over the blond mat covering his tanned chest, suddenly eager to be away from her. She kept her gaze on his bared flesh until the buttons hid it from view, disappointment written in her eyes.

"Sorry, Isabel, I've got things to do."

"To hell with them! I want you to stay!"

He ignored her commanding tone and shrugged on a fringed rawhide vest. "Not this time."

"You're cruel, Logan. I hate you." Isabel spoke sulkily.

"So you've said before." A humorless smile flashed across his lips.

He buckled his gunbelt and tied the gun snugly around his right leg, then positioned his large bowie knife on the outside of his lean left thigh.

Isabel wanted to slap him. She wanted to bend him to her will like all the others, but she knew it would never happen. Logan Cord would never be ruled by a woman. He used them as she used most men. As toys of pleasure. He used her that way. But he would marry her eventually. He had to. It rankled her deep into her core, but she swallowed her pride.

"Please," she begged softly. "Please, stay."

He was fully dressed now, and he turned to face her, his teeth white and strong in his dark, rugged face.

"I'll be gone a few months. I might look you up when I get back."

She sat up quickly in alarm and demanded harshly, "Where are you going?"

"That's something, Isabel, that doesn't concern you." He walked toward the bed.

"But, I have a right—"

Her shrill voice was cut off as Logan's mouth came down hard on hers. He pulled her body tightly against the rough leather of his vest, and, helpless to stop herself, she wrapped her arms around his neck, burying both her hands in his thick hair. He broke the kiss abruptly and pulled back, staring down into her breathless face, unaffected by her passion.

"You don't have any rights over me, Isabel, and you never will." His voice was flat.

She sputtered in anger, and he dropped her unceremoniously back onto her bed. He turned and strode out of the room and down the wide upstairs hall. The townhouse was silent; Isabel always banished her servants to their quarters for the duration of her trysts. Strident curses followed him down the curving staircase, and he sighed in relief as he stepped onto the porch and slammed the front door behind him.

The summer night was cool and he breathed in deeply, letting the fresh air cleanse his lungs. He was sorry he had let Isabel entice him into her bed. Although she was a beautiful woman and an accomplished lover he always found himself eager to leave her. She had no real feelings, no love or gentleness. She suffocated him after a time with her constant demands and cruel lovemaking. She drained him like a leech. Walking quickly to his horse, he swung into the saddle and pressed his heels into the stallion's flanks. Perhaps the meeting tonight would give him a good excuse to get away from the boring respectability of Denver for a time. He hungered for the mountains and the life of his Sioux friends. For the last few months he'd been dividing his time between the gold mine he owned near Central City, and his mountain estate, Woodstone, where he

caught mustangs to ship back east for sale. But both of his
businesses were managed by trusted friends, and Logan
didn't worry about leaving his business affairs in their
hands when he disappeared for a time.

He turned his horse toward the road and spurred him
into a gallop. The brisk night air rushed over his face, the
spirited stallion moving with powerful grace between Logan's thighs. John Walker had asked Logan to meet a man
named Huddleston in a saloon outside the small town of
Boulder. John was a good friend. He was the Indian Com-
missioner in Denver and probably the only honest man
connected with the Indian Bureau. Huddleston needed to
hire an expert tracker. Since Logan had gained a formidable reputation as the best white tracker in the area he was
the logical choice. Very few of his acquaintances in Denver
knew of his sideline or his Indian name, Tracker, and he
grinned now at the thought of his father's reaction if he
were ever to learn that his son was blood brother to a Sioux
warrior.

The thought of Two Bears brought an eagerness to Logan's heart. He would talk to Huddleston, then he would
travel on to the Sioux camp on Sand Creek. It would be
good to see his blood brother again.

Just after the war, when Mexico had ceded much of Colorado to the United States, Logan had been at loose ends,
not wanting to return to St. Louis to help run his father's
vast business enterprises. Then he remembered John Winstead from his unit of the Missouri Volunteers, and his
accounts of the beautiful, rugged mountains of this
new Colorado country. Logan's desire for adventure was
sparked. He'd learned how to trap and hunt, and had laid
claim to a beautiful valley high in the Rocky Mountains,
where John had died one harsh winter. After that Logan
returned to St. Louis only periodically to sell his furs. The
day he'd first seen Two Bears he had been running his
traps in the snow, when a nearby trail of fresh blood and
human footprints had aroused his curiosity. He'd followed
it, rifle in readiness, until he'd come upon Two Bears. A
huge grizzly had the sixteen-year-old Sioux trapped in a
tree. Half a dozen arrows protruded from the enraged
bear's thick fur.

Logan had dropped to his knees and fired, killing the

bear, but Two Bears had already been horribly clawed. He was barely alive, but Logan had managed to get him back to his cabin. He had nursed the young Indian back to health, but it wasn't until they returned together to the Sioux camp the following spring that Logan had learned Two Bears was the only grandson of the tribe's most revered chief. Logan had been welcomed as an adopted member of the tribe, becoming Two Bears' blood brother. It hadn't taken him long to master the Indians' language and their skill at stalking, and he had been honored by the Sioux with the name of Tracker.

Logan forced his thoughts back to the present and the business at hand when he finally sighted the frontier tavern. He had traveled hard for several hours to reach Boulder, and the hour was late. Logan drew up to the run-down building and slid from the saddle, looking around the dark street warily. The Stag's Head Saloon was a rough establishment, a place to be on guard. He tethered his horse, listening to the loud squeals of laughter and tinny piano music that drifted out of the brightly lit windows.

He moved through the swinging doors, his eyes sweeping the rowdy interior. Most of the men inside were dressed in buckskin or leather and carried guns strapped low on the hip. He quickly spotted a man who didn't fit in with the others. He was small, sitting alone in the far corner, anxiously scanning the room from behind wire-rimmed glasses.

John had described Huddleston as a greenhorn from St. Louis, and this little man fit the description well. Logan pushed the door open and walked to the rough-hewn bar at the rear of the room. In the mirror he could see the small man watching him. Logan moved to an empty table with his bottle and waited. Five minutes ticked by before the little man made his move. He stepped in front of Logan, looking nervous.

"Are you Tracker?" he asked, a hint of a tremor in his voice.

Logan looked up and took his time appraising the little man's appearance before he answered. He was dressed in a gray tweed coat and trousers, his high white collar crisply starched and fastened with a string bow tie. A small black derby perched atop slicked-back brown hair parted in the middle. His apparel would have been stylishly correct in Chicago or in Logan's father's lavish parlor on Lafayette Square in St. Louis, but here on the Colorado frontier, he looked ludicrous. He was ill at ease, his brown eyes wary under Logan's scrutiny. He twisted a gold watchchain nervously between his fingers.

"Who wants to know?" Logan finally said in a low voice.

The man looked startled at Logan's curt tone, then stuttered out an introduction.

"I'm Alfred Huddleston from St. Louis, sir. I represent the solicitors' firm of Bradshaw, Stern, and Watson. Here's my card."

He held out a small white card, and Logan watched him with an unblinking blue stare until Huddleston hesitantly laid it down on the table.

"What do you want with Tracker, Huddleston?"

"I have some business to discuss with him."

"What business?"

"An employment proposition. A lucrative one," Huddleston added quickly.

Logan searched Huddleston's anxious face a moment, his blue eyes piercingly intent as Huddleston continued.

"John Walker said Tracker would be the only one who could help me."

Logan raised his glass and drank, still watching Huddleston over its rim.

"I'm Tracker. Sit down."

Huddleston breathed easier, scraping out a chair. He perched timidly on the edge, as if ready to flee, and Logan suppressed a grin.

"All right, let's hear it."

Huddleston shifted uneasily and ran a finger between his neck and the stiff white collar. He took a deep breath.

"The firm I represent has been requested by a client to locate a man who knows the mountains around here. One who's friendly with the Indians." He paused as Tracker lifted an eyebrow.

"Who is this client?"

Huddleston squirmed, and Logan sensed he was reluctant to answer. "I'm not at liberty to say, Mr. . . . ."

He groped for a last name, but Logan cut him off.

"Tracker's enough. Seems to me that if you can't tell me

who you're working for, there might be a reason behind it. Maybe something illegal."

Huddleston looked up into Logan's narrowed eyes and watched his long fingers tighten around the glass.

"Oh no sir, I can guarantee that there is nothing whatsoever illegal here," Huddleston assured him. "Our firm is quite reputable. You see, the fact of the matter is that my client wishes to remain anonymous for his own reasons."

Logan reached for the bottle and poured another shot of whiskey.

"Go on," he said shortly, and Huddleston quickly complied.

"It's rather complicated, really. Back in 1847, Indians attacked a wagon train on its way to Oregon. It happened right in this area, as a matter of fact, in the South Pass. They took all the horses and supplies and killed almost everyone. There was a family along from St. Louis, a man with his wife and daughter. Both parents were killed, but the few who survived the attack saw the Indians take the child. She was three years old at the time. Her grandparents are very wealthy, and they've kept rewards for her return posted at all the forts and trading posts all these years."

Logan looked at him steadily, and Huddleston dropped his gaze.

"Recently an army scout sighted a blond-haired girl with light eyes with a band of Indians. The hair color is right, and she seemed about the right age. She was spotted in a village on the Crow Creek about eighty miles north of here."

Tracker took another drink.

"What tribe?"

"Cheyenne. And the wagon train was attacked by Cheyenne, which means it could very well be her."

Logan made a derisive sound. "That was fifteen years ago. If she's still alive, she'll be adopted by now."

Huddleston looked blank.

"What do you mean?"

"I mean, she won't remember her white family, much less want to be with them. She'll be Cheyenne through and through. She'll want to stay right where she is."

Huddleston frowned, considering what Logan had told him.

"It doesn't matter. The family wants her back."

Logan stared at him contemptuously. "Despite her wishes?"

"They didn't mention her wishes."

Logan shrugged. "What's in it for me?"

Huddleston relaxed for the first time as he leaned forward slightly.

"Twenty-five hundred dollars now and twenty-five more afterward."

Logan was surprised at the generous figure, but his blue eyes showed nothing to the little man watching eagerly for his reaction. Logan didn't need the money. His gold mine alone had already earned enough to keep him independently wealthy for the rest of his life. But taking the assignment would mean a chance to spend time with Two Bears. It would be his opportunity to leave the city of Denver and Isabel behind, and to feel the freedom of the open land.

Huddleston peered eagerly at Logan from behind the thick lenses that magnified his eyes. "Are you interested?"

Logan set down his glass and considered, staring into Huddleston's perspiring face. "What guarantee do you have that I won't take your money and forget the whole thing?"

Huddleston looked shocked, as if he hadn't thought of it.

"None, I suppose, but John Walker told me that you could be trusted. If this girl's the right one, her grandfather wants her back."

"It'll take time."

Huddleston showed relief. "How long?"

"Three months, provided she's in the village you say she is."

Logan paused, then gazed directly into Huddleston's eyes as he went on. "And I do it my own way or I don't do it."

"Of course, you'll be in complete control of the entire operation. We can set a date and a meeting place. I'll give you the first half of the money now and when you hand over the girl you'll get the rest."

Tracker nodded. "All right. Let's say the first day of October in Denver. The Cherokee Hotel. If I'm not there, wait."

Logan waited until Huddleston nodded agreement, then asked, "What else can you tell me about her?"

"Not much. Her most recognizable feature will be her eyes. They're supposedly of an unusual violet color."

"Purple eyes?"

Huddleston nodded and shrugged. "That's what her grandfather said."

"That should be easy enough to check."

Huddleston looked around the room, then quickly passed a heavy bundle beneath the table into Tracker's hands.

Tracker shoved the leather bag into his vest. Without another word he pushed back his chair and headed toward the door. When he looked back at Huddleston, the little man was wiping sweat off his brow with a large white handkerchief. One corner of Logan's mouth lifted in a half-smile as he pushed open the swinging door and stepped out into the dark night.

ONE

The girl sat cross-legged facing a huge bonfire, watching as the bright flames cast flickering shadows across the oiled bodies of the nearly naked dancers. They moved in a circle in front of her, writhing and contorting to the steady beat of a lone drum, their guttural chanting barely audible. She was dressed in the Cheyenne wedding attire: a soft and supple deerskin dress that fell just below her knees with long, beaded fringe at the hem and down each arm. Knee-high moccasins covered her legs, fashioned from the same snow-white deerskin as her dress. Both garments were beaded intricately in red and blue designs, reflecting hours of tedious handiwork.

The outfit clung to her slight build, emphasizing her full breasts and slim hips. Her blond hair hung past her waist, soft and straight and shiny. A white band, also beaded, encircled her forehead just above her finely arched eyebrows and held the bright hair in place. She turned her head slightly, and the firelight picked up the silvery tints in the pale blond tresses that shimmered down her back like a warm flash of lightning. Her eyes were downcast, her long black eyelashes lowered to form dark crescents against the soft, clear skin of her cheeks. Her nose was small and straight, her lips full and firm. When she raised her face to watch the twisting dancers, her clear violet eyes glittered like precious jewels. Her small, heart-shaped face was beautiful and sorrowful and she held her chin proudly, almost defiantly. Resentment smoldered in her eyes as she watched the ceremony dispassionately.

Starfire was angry with her father, Raging Buffalo. He had promised her to Lone Wolf against her wishes. She did

12

not wish to wed. Not Lone Wolf. Not anyone. She wished to remain a maiden, free to hunt and ride with her father and help her mother as she'd done all her life. She did not wish to become a man's slave. And besides that, she did not love Lone Wolf. She did not love any man.

She had argued with Raging Buffalo as much as she'd dared, but he'd stood firm, not allowing her to sway his decision. His words had been final: She would wed Lone Wolf. She would bear him many strong sons.

Starfire grimaced, her smooth brow furrowing into a frown as her vivid eyes found Lone Wolf. She met his gaze steadfastly, refusing to be intimidated by the intense black eyes fixed on her. She felt a shiver course down her spine as he stood, the hard muscles of his arms ridging as he folded them across his bare chest. He wore only a white loincloth, made from the same hide as her own dress. Her eyes lowered to the long muscled legs braced apart in an arrogant stance. His dark face was hard and handsome, with high cheekbones and a broad forehead. Long black braids hung on either side of his square jaw. He wore no headdress; he carried no weapon. It would not be a night of war, but one of love. He had awaited this night for many months.

Starfire lowered her gaze, knowing it would soon be time to go to him, to become his woman. Despite her inner resentment, she felt her insides quiver in anticipation. Lone Wolf was a brave and handsome warrior. He would be a suitable husband for her. He was so strong, yet he'd touched her hand with gentleness on the few occasions when he'd been alone with her. She glanced again at his hard, lean body and wondered what it would feel like to be possessed by him. She was yet a virgin, but her wedded friends had told her the experience was pleasant at times. She flushed and lowered her eyes. It would be soon. Lone Wolf paced impatiently now, his tall frame silhouetted against the night sky as he moved about restlessly.

Starfire looked at the row of chiefs where they sat in the position of honor in front of the dancers. Their wives sat behind them, and Starfire could see her mother, Gentle Reed, there among them. It was a joyous occasion for Gentle Reed, who had longed for grandchildren for many years.

Raging Buffalo watched Starfire solemnly, aware of her dissatisfaction with her wedding. Starfire forgot her anger long enough to smile at him, her teeth showing white against honey-tanned skin. He did not return her smile, but his eyes looked relieved as he turned his attention back to the ritual. Starfire stared at his granite-cut profile and the strong lines of his face. He looked so fierce sitting there in his full headdress among the other chiefs. Raging Buffalo was famous in many camps for his brave coups, but he'd never been anything other than kind and loving to her. It was Gentle Reed's barrenness that had prompted him to adopt Starfire so long ago. He'd loved his beautiful young wife too much to take another, so he'd taken the tiny white girl with the wondrous silver hair to be his only child.

Starfire knew Raging Buffalo and his warriors had killed her real parents when she was very small. He'd told her the tale himself. The white wagons carrying her parents and many others had crossed the sacred burial lands, defiling the spirits of the Cheyenne dead. Two Cheyenne had been killed as they tried to prevent the desecration. Starfire sighed. Although she'd tried many times, she did not remember her parents, nor did she grieve for them. All she could recall of that long-ago day was the fear. And the snake. A rattler had found her where her mother had hidden her among the rocks. She'd frozen as it had crawled over her, its long, thick body slithering across her skin. Raging Buffalo had found her and hacked it to pieces. He'd taken her in his arms afterward, and Starfire had clung to him, her small arms clenched around his neck.

A cold surge of horror inched up Starfire's spine as she remembered how the snake's blood had spattered on her skin. She shuddered. Even now, the sight of a snake still paralyzed her with a blinding, blood-chilling terror.

"Are you ready, my daughter?"

The soft voice jerked Starfire out of her fearful memories, and she stared up at her mother, who stood quietly at her side. Gentle Reed was as sweet and malleable as her name, and Starfire loved her as much as she could have any real mother. She despaired at the thought of leaving her parents, even though she knew Lone Wolf desired her and would be good to her. Had he not given Raging Buffalo six ponies in exchange for her? It was a generous and honorable gift.

Gentle Reed waited patiently, sensing Starfire's reluctance although her daughter hadn't complained since Raging Buffalo had made his decision final. Starfire sighed sadly and stood. Her eyes found Lone Wolf, and he watched her hungrily as Gentle Reed took her hand and pulled her into the darkness. They walked through the deserted camp slowly, not speaking, until they reached the marriage tipi. It was decorated with fertility symbols and set apart from the rest of the camp on the bank of the river. The newlyweds would be afforded complete privacy. For a whole day and night, they would remain in isolation. It was the sacred custom of their people. No one would dare intrude on them.

Gentle Reed smiled and embraced her warmly, her voice low beside Starfire's ear.

"You will bear many strong sons for Lone Wolf, my daughter. I know you will. He will be pleased with you."

Starfire nodded unenthusiastically and watched as Gentle Reed walked back toward the distant glow of red of the fire. Her eyes watched the fiery sparks ascend in the great cloud of gray-white smoke for a few moments, then she sighed again as she lifted the rawhide flap and entered the wedding tipi.

Inside, she stopped in surprise and looked around. It was very dark, the sides of the tent steeped in black crouching shadows. Starfire frowned and squinted into the dusky interior. She hesitated, then stepped closer to the center. Only a dim, reddish glow lit the ring of rocks on the ground. She could not understand it. The tent should have been readied by Gentle Reed before she'd come for Starfire. The fire could not have burned down in such a short time.

She knelt close to the rocks and looked at the logs. They were spread out and scattered, almost as if they'd been kicked apart.

She stared at the fire, puzzled. Suddenly a premonition of danger streaked through her like liquid fire and she whirled around, ready to run. She froze in shock as a man stepped from the darkness and blocked the flap. She couldn't see him well. His face and head were hidden in shadows as he towered over her slight height, seeming as huge as a grizzly bear in the small tent. He did not move toward her, and Starfire took one faltering step backward, her eyes huge and shocked. Then she panicked and tried to dart around his long legs. His powerful arms moved so fast that she barely saw them before she was scooped off the ground and held against an immense chest in a grip that took her breath away. One strong arm held her firmly around the waist and a huge hand clamped over her mouth tightly. She struggled furiously, jerking and kicking against his hold.

Starfire's violent movements caused Tracker to lose his grip, and she twisted out of his arms. Her terrified screech chilled his blood and he swore aloud, afraid she'd bring half the tribe down on him. He grabbed her again and tried to stifle her yell with his hand.

She was sobbing in terror but managed to sink sharp teeth into him. Tracker grunted, trying to shake her off, but she hung on stubbornly like a dog with a bone. He grabbed her hair and jerked hard, groaning again as her teeth ripped loose.

She started a strange, strangled yelping, and he clamped his hand back over her mouth immediately to smother her next hysterical shriek. He held her away from him, trying to dodge her feet as she kicked viciously at his groin. He was incredulous that such a tiny little thing could cause him so much trouble.

He carried her bodily to the entrance of the tipi, his grip so tight she could barely breathe. Their encounter hadn't exactly been quiet, and Tracker took a quick look out the flap. There were no signs of alarm, and he breathed easier. Now if he could just keep her quiet he could get the bridegroom. He'd have to tie and gag her. The girl was small but hard as hell to hold on to. He growled harshly in Cheyenne for her to hold still and shook her back and forth several times.

Starfire felt herself being jerked around until her eyes would no longer focus. She tried in vain to stop her head from spinning. Great waves of pain beat from side to side in her skull and her stunned limpness gave Tracker time to jerk his neckcloth off and wrap it tightly around her mouth. He then quickly tied her hands behind her back.

He couldn't take any chances with her. She fought like a demon.

Starfire grunted as she was shoved roughly to the ground. Tracker went down on one knee beside her and reached for her feet. She got her breath back quickly, and her anger came gushing after it. She aimed a hard kick at his face, while he fumbled in the dark with the cords. Her foot connected with his jaw with a loud crack, and when he groaned in pain she felt a grim triumph at hurting him.

"Damn it, hold still!"

Tracker's whispered curse was harsh and angry, and he mumbled a string of oaths under his breath as he tried to grab her flailing feet. He finally managed to lock them under one arm to tie them. She was still squirming furiously, and he could hear muffled sounds from behind the gag. He released her and took a deep breath, rubbing his aching jaw as he gently moved it from side to side. He felt as if he'd been kicked by a mule. She had spirit, that was for sure. And she was a lot stronger than she looked.

Tracker moved quickly to the flap. No one was coming, and he settled back into the shadows beside the entrance, hoping the bridegroom would be easier to handle than this little she-devil. He sat still, eager for the man to come so he could be out of the camp. It had taken himself and Two Bears a month to find the right village after heading to the vicinity Huddleston had described. Then another month had passed as they hid in the hills nearby waiting for the right moment to strike. For days, he'd focused his spyglass on the white girl as she rode upon a huge palomino, her fair hair billowing behind her. But it wasn't until Two Bears had hidden in a tree perch above the stream that they'd heard the Cheyenne women chatter about the forthcoming marriage. When Two Bears had told him of the isolation of the Cheyenne nuptial tipi, Tracker had known this would be the perfect opportunity to steal her. Now the time was at hand.

Starfire struggled impotently for a while, pulling desperately at the cords but succeeding only in tightening them across her skin. She exhausted herself and was forced to rest. Every time she moved, the rawhide bands sent jagged arrows of pain up her arms and legs. The corners of her mouth ached where the taut cloth stretched cruelly between her teeth. She turned her face, trying to see her attacker, but the fire was out now, and it was too dark to discern him.

She listened for his breathing, but all she could hear was the faint rushing sound of the river outside and the far-away, repetitious din of drums. She had not seen him up close, but she knew he was big, and incredibly strong. He had handled her like a child, picking her up and carrying her as if she weighed nothing.

Starfire laid her head back and closed her eyes. She lay helplessly in the dark, aware that he was waiting for Lone Wolf, probably to kill him. But why? What did this giant want?

Her blood turned icy and her stomach muscles knotted as a single word crystallized and froze its way into her brain. Pawnee! He had to be! Who else would try to steal her? A new fear gripped her. Pawnees were sacrificers. Stealers of virgins. She must have been chosen as a victim. Terror washed over Starfire in a violent shudder as the tales of their bloody sacrificial rites came back to her. Panic flared and blotted out reason, and she began to scream beneath the gag. She sobbed in despair when she realized all that was audible was a slight, muffled moan.

She tensed as she heard Lone Wolf softly call her name from the tipi's entrance. She tried to warn him, but her cry died in her throat as she heard the dull thud of metal against his skull. His heavy body hit the ground, and Starfire closed her eyes as Lone Wolf was dragged away and bound.

The big man came to her, and desperation flared as he leaned down and hoisted her over his shoulder. She lay unmoving for the first instant, then wrenched away with all her strength. He almost dropped her, and she heard a low laugh as he caught her and slung her back into place.

Tracker held his arm against the back of her knees and peered cautiously out the rear slit of the tipi. All was quiet, and he ducked out and started for the river at a fast trot, his slight burden not slowing him in the least. He made it safely to the bank and waded into the water. The swift current he felt would carry them quickly out of danger.

He felt the girl shiver as the cold water swirled around them, but he continued to walk deeper into the current. He let go with one hand to adjust his arm across her chest, and she wrested away from him. He cursed in exasperation as she disappeared into the dark water. He searched desperately and got a hold on her almost immediately, pulling her head above the water. He secured one arm around her waist as he drew his knife to cut off the gag. She immediately let out a hysterical shriek that echoed up the river.

He tried to stifle her yells, but she twisted away, still screaming. Tracker turned her quickly and gave her one short blow on the jaw. Starfire went limp, although he hadn't hit her hard. He didn't like doing it but he'd had to do something before she drowned them both or, worse, alerted the whole village.

Tracker held her tightly against his chest, letting the water carry them away from the Cheyenne camp. He floated in the darkness beneath the stars, his eyes constantly on the receding glow of the bonfire upriver from them.

About a mile downstream he reached the spot where he'd hidden his horse. He dragged Starfire into the shallows, slinging her up over his shoulder. The stallion was tethered in the bushes, and Tracker took the time to cut the ropes off Starfire before he wrapped her carefully in a warm blanket and lifted her into the saddle. He pulled her into position against his chest and cradled her as he guided his horse out of the tree cover. The way things were going, he was surprised he'd gotten as far as he had. But so far, so good. He was still alive.

TWO

Tracker rode with Starfire nestled comfortably in his arms, anxious to get to his destination. The cave where he was headed was high in the mountains about two or three days northwest of Denver. It was well hidden behind a waterfall, and it was far enough away that the Cheyenne would not be familiar with it. They had at least three more hours' ride ahead of them, and he was reluctant to stop even when the gray of dawn smoked over the trees around him. For miles the only sound he'd heard was the sporadic twittering of awakening birds and the muffled clops of his horse. When the sound of a stream finally came to him he nosed his stallion through the thick undergrowth toward it. It was fairly wide and slow-moving, and he reined up on a nearby grassy spot and slid out of the saddle with the girl in his arms. He laid her down gently, then sat down beside her. He was sore from his cramped position in the saddle, and he was chilled to the bone from the wet clothes he'd worn all night. His mood was not the best, and he was frowning darkly as he pushed the damp strands of hair off Starfire's face.

At that point, he got his first good look at Starfire, and his breath caught in surprise and pleasure. She was lovely. For some reason, he hadn't expected her to be. He let his eyes run over her beautiful face, examining the tanned skin and the thick black lashes against her cheeks. Her hair was a strange silvery color, like moonlight; he picked up a long lock and rubbed it between his thumb and forefinger. It felt soft and silky. Her lips were full and parted slightly, looking warm and soft. He felt a ridiculous urge to kiss her, which he banished quickly from his mind, feeling foolish. He watched her a minute, wanting her to open her eyes; then he would know she was the girl Huddleston had described to him. He stood up, staring down at her. She was so small, barely more than a child, yet he found it hard to stop looking at her. He saw the bluish discoloration on her chin and frowned, wishing he hadn't had to hit her. His horse waiting nearby moved restlessly and pushed a velvety nose into his back, bringing Tracker back to the business at hand.

He took the halter, led the horse down the rocky bank, and waded out a step or two, pulling the reins after him. The horse snorted and plunged his nose into the clear, cold water greedily. Tracker leaned down and scooped up a handful to drink, then dipped some more over his face and neck. It was cold and invigorating, just what he needed. He was dead tired. It had been hours since he'd slept. Days since he'd seen any kind of comfortable bed. And sleep was something he wouldn't get anytime soon.

He drank again, watching the woods around him, studying the terrain intently. The Cheyenne wouldn't be after him yet, but he was right in the middle of Indian territory. One look at Tracker with a captive girl dressed in Cheyenne wedding attire in his arms would bring an arrow ripping into his heart.

He turned his head sharply at Starfire's weak groan, then hurried back up to her. He was eager to see her awake, to talk to her.

Starfire was stirring, her lashes fluttering slightly as he leaned over her. He watched as she struggled to open her eyes. When she finally succeeded, Tracker stared into their clear violet depths and smiled, awed by the unusual color. She was squinting up at him now, trying to see him better, her delicate eyebrows drawn together in a small frown.

Starfire couldn't remember where she was. She was disoriented and confused, staring at the face above her. He was a stranger. She watched him closely, heard him tell her in a deep, pleasant voice not to be afraid. She examined him objectively, trying to remember who he was and why he thought she might be afraid of him. His hair was yellow like the sun, pale like hers. She'd never seen anyone else with blond hair. And even more surprising to her, there was hair all over his face. A great, thick growth darker than his hair covered his chin and jaw. It was a strange sight; her people did not grow hair on the face. Her thoughts muddled on as he leaned closer and fixed his strange eyes on hers. They were beautiful, she thought vaguely. The same color as the sky.

Blue eyes? Who was he? Her head ached, and her confusion made it worse. She closed her eyes against the pain that throbbed up behind her forehead and raised one hand slowly to the soreness on her chin.

When she touched the bruise, her memory came rushing through her mind like wind through a cave. Her lavender eyes flew wide and fastened on Tracker's surprised ones. He was taken aback by the wild fear that glinted out at him, and the next thing he knew she was up and running toward the river with the speed of a doe. It took him a few seconds to react. By the time he reached her, she was splashing up the shallows in a hard run, trying to reach a thick stand of woods about fifty feet up the bank. He grabbed her and got his arm around her slim waist, holding her carefully away from his body as he recalled vividly their little scuffle in the tent.

Starfire was breathless from the run, but fear gave her the strength to struggle desperately. She sobbed as she fought him, aiming her blows at his face and trying to kick him in the groin. If she could only reach the trees she could hide from him. She gasped as he suddenly locked her tightly against his chest, pinning her arms to her sides. She could not move, and her fear disintegrated into impotent fury. She cursed him bitterly through gritted teeth.

Tracker held her steady and waited for her to get tired as she graphically described the bloody things her father would do to him as soon as he found them. She was determined and angry, and he was amazed at some of the gory things she said were in store for him.

Finally, Starfire sobbed helplessly and hung limp, and Tracker swung her into his arms and started up the bank with her. He lowered her to the ground. Starfire tried again to twist away but his fingers bit into her shoulders. She flung back her head and glared up at him, her eyes darkened with hatred. She stiffened as he took hold of her shoulders and forced her to look at him.

"Now listen, you little hellcat," he said in Cheyenne. "I won't hurt you if you settle down and do as I say."

Starfire bared small white teeth and snarled at him. She looked so tiny but so ferocious that Tracker laughed and released her. His laughter infuriated Starfire, and her eyes went dark purple with rage. She drew back her fist and sent it against his face with every ounce of her strength.

Her attack was so fast that Tracker couldn't dodge, and her fist struck his jaw in the same place her foot had landed earlier. He grunted and grabbed the side of his face as pain streaked into his temple.

Starfire took advantage of his preoccupation, kicking his shin as hard as she could, then darting away toward his horse. Her hands were in its mane when three gigantic strides brought Tracker up behind her, grabbing the fringe on the back of her dress.

"Damn it, girl, you're beginning to get on my nerves!"

Tracker gave her a shake hard enough to fling her hair over her face in a silvery swirl, then pushed her into a sitting position. He was careful to keep out of kicking distance as he crouched and looked directly into her face.

"Look, you little devil, I don't like this any more than you do. But I'll be damned if I'm going to let you hit me again. Either stop your fighting, or I'm going to tie you up so tight you can't move. And if I do, you can ride slung over the saddle behind me like a buffalo carcass."

"You cowardly son of a dog," Starfire answered in a growl. "My people will cut out your white tongue, then they will tie you to a stake . . ."

"I've heard all that before," Logan interrupted harshly. "You're the bloodthirstiest little thing I've ever seen."

Starfire glared up at him, angry and frustrated, wanting to cut out his sky-blue eyes, wanting to kill him. He was so big though, and he looked at her as though he meant every word he'd said. He'd spoken to her in her own language, which confused her. She was thirsty and sore, and the hate roiled around inside her, simmering and ready to erupt.

Tracker saw her shift her cold eyes away from him to the stream.

"You thirsty?"

She refused to answer or to look at him. When she began

to rise, he grabbed her wrist. He didn't trust her. She did everything too quickly. It was hard for him to react as fast as she moved.

"Let me go, you rotten dog," she growled from between clenched teeth.

She looked so beautiful standing there, her bright hair all tangled and thrown back, her large eyes hostile and threatening. Tracker felt a familiar tightening in his loins, a deep throb in his veins. He wanted her. He wanted to throw her down and take her. The realization of just how strong his desire was shocked him. She was just a girl. It was ridiculous, and he shook off his thoughts in irritation.

"Not so fast. If you want a drink, we'll go together."

She tried to twist away, but this time he had his fingers wrapped around her wrist too tightly. He walked her to the water, ignoring her pulling and tugging, and kept his grip in place.

Her constant resistance was wearing on him, although he really couldn't blame her. He held on while she leaned down and dipped up a few palmfuls of water. He let her drink her fill, then dragged her back as she protested violently all the way. He pushed her down by the horse, then got a strip of jerky out of the saddle bag and tossed it to her.

She caught it, and to his surprise began to eat it. He moved to the horse, keeping a wary eye on her. He knew she'd run if given half a chance; his threats about tying her up didn't seem to bother her. He wouldn't do that unless she made him lose his temper, which was a distinct possibility the way things were going.

Starfire sat and glared at him, but she was hungry and she ate the beef. She studied him intently as he checked the saddle. He was dressed like an Indian, in tan buckskin leggings with fringe down each leg and high buckskin moccasins like hers. But his size was what amazed her. His arms bulged with great muscles as he bent to tighten the girth, and the breadth of his shoulders seemed incredible in the fringed tunic. She'd never seen such a giant. Even Lone Wolf would be small in comparison. But he was quick, for all his size. Starfire had always been a swift runner and had often beaten the other maidens in foot races. But he'd caught her easily with his immense strides.

She looked at him again as he moved around the big black stallion. His legs were long and powerful, with a gun strapped low on one. A long hunting knife in a buckskin sheath was buckled to his belt. Starfire shivered and looked away from him.

It would be hard to escape, but at least he wasn't a Pawnee, as she had originally feared. Despite his dark brown skin, he was a white man. She had not seen many white men, but had seen enough to know that their ways were very different. Why had he stolen her? What did he want with her? He would not get away with it! Her helplessness made her furious, and she ground her teeth in frustration, viciously tearing off a bite of jerky. Raging Buffalo would find them soon and kill the big white one for what he'd done.

She looked at Tracker, her eyes sparkling with malice. Her voice was hard and menacing.

"My people will find you and kill you. They will slice off your skin very slowly, then they will hammer hot spikes into your sky eyes."

Tracker looked down into her snarling face and tried to ignore her gory threat. She glowered maliciously at him, and her vicious words reminded him that they'd wasted enough time in one spot. He went to pull her to her feet, and sighed impatiently as she jerked away. The rest of the ride wasn't going to be much fun. She'd fight him every inch of the way. She was too damned obstinate. He'd always thought women were supposed to be afraid at times like this. He wondered where her fear was. Or if she had any.

She stood stiff and unyielding by his side until he boosted her up onto the horse. He swung into the saddle behind her, positioning his rifle crossways in front of her to hold her against him. He spurred his horse and picked his way through the trees, trying to ignore Starfire's low and angry tirade. He wasn't a fool. He knew he couldn't hide his tracks from experienced Cheyenne scouts. They could find him easily and would probably trail him to the ends of the earth for her. At least her bridegroom would. Tracker would if he'd been the one to have had her. She was a beauty. She sat ramrod-straight in front of him, leaning away as far as she could. He grinned, watching the way she was furiously gripping the saddle horn hard enough to whiten her knuckles. He suddenly wanted to know her name and interrupted a whole string of threats as he spoke.

"What's your name, girl?"

Starfire's mouth snapped shut abruptly. She was unwilling to tell him anything he wanted to know. He asked her again curtly, in a tone that brooked no refusal, and when he tightened the rifle against her stomach she spoke.

"Starfire." Her tone was sullen.

"Ah, for the stars. It suits you. You're as beautiful as they are."

He'd murmured his remark in English, more to himself than to her, but he felt her stiffen in the circle of his arms.

"Did you understand me, Starfire?"

She would not answer, and Tracker sighed. Of course she wouldn't remember English. She'd been captured when she was three years old. He felt a jab of disappointment, and wondered why.

Starfire held herself stiffly and contemplated his words. She'd understood him perfectly. She'd learned the odd, lilting language he used from Father Donegal, although the big man behind her pronounced some of the words differently. The priest had come from a place called Ireland and had lived with her people for a time, trying to teach them about his strange God.

Tracker's arms tightened around her, pulling her closer to him; she rebelled at once from the pressure, turning to scratch at his face. One sharp jerk of the gun against her ribs stopped her, and she clamped her lips together, her insides overflowing with frustrated hate.

Tracker rode faster now, knowing that Two Bears would be finished with his part of the plan. Tracker felt confident about that. Two Bears was his Sioux blood brother, the only man Tracker had ever completely trusted. He'd laid false trails out of the Cheyenne camp to delay the search party which would follow the missing girl. It would work for a time, but not long. Tracker had to reach the cave before they found his tracks. They would be safe from the search party only in this isolated, unseen place.

The cave was stocked for a month's stay, and now that he'd seen the girl and held her in his arms, he had to admit that things were looking better. Their stay there might not be as dull as he'd thought. She was too beautiful to be boring. Perhaps it would be a pleasant diversion to win her affection before he turned her over to Huddleston to return to her family in St. Louis. He leaned down and nuzzled the top of her silvery hair. It smelled clean and fresh and like wild flowers. He grinned as she jerked away in aversion, calling him something she definitely wasn't.

"Taming you should be interesting, girl. You sure as hell need it!" He'd spoken in English again, and Starfire sputtered in anger and turned to claw at him. He promptly cut off her breath; and she sat still after that, as cold and silent as a marble statue.

Their path wound among tall trees and huge rock formations, and they gradually gained elevation as they moved deeper into the mountains. Starfire refused to relax against him, occasionally cursing him, and Tracker said nothing, outwardly indifferent to her abuse, inwardly hoping he'd get away with her—and his scalp.

Starfire tired of talking after a time and remained silent for longer intervals. She grew tired of holding her back straight and relaxed her stiff posture as exhaustion set in. Tracker sighed in relief when she finally slept, feeling soft and warm and small in the circle of his arms. He looked down at her satiny skin and shining hair and pulled her closer to his chest, hoping she'd sleep for a long time.

THREE

Starfire drifted in a half-doze, lulled by the steady beat of Tracker's heart and hollow clop of hooves on rocky ground. She wasn't aware of the hard chest under her ear or the strong arms circling her so tightly, but lay peacefully, snuggled against him. When she opened her eyes dreamily, feeling so very comfortable and warm, it took her several minutes to realize that she was leaning intimately against her detested captor. Horrified, she sat quickly upright, humiliated by her unwitting surrender.

"Might as well stay comfortable," Tracker said reasonably.

Starfire ignored him and sat in haughty, cold rejection. He said nothing, and silence prevailed until her curious thoughts forced down her pride. Not looking at him, she asked haltingly, "Where are you taking me?"

Tracker glanced down at her lovely profile, surprised she'd condescended to speak to him. He debated telling her the truth about her white relatives, then decided against it.

"Where your bloodthirsty friends can't find us," he said dryly.

Starfire let out a low, mocking laugh. The underlying current of pure malice threading through it startled Tracker.

"There is no such place, son of dogs. You'll never escape them."

Tracker didn't answer, but her certainty about it was unsettling. He urged his horse on, keeping to the trees, watching for signs of Indian bands as they climbed slowly

28

through the thick pine forest, closer and closer into the shadow of the white-capped mountains.

Starfire's eyes darted and calculated, estimating distances and directions, planning to escape as soon as possible. She thought they were in Arapaho land and hoped they'd run into a hunting party. The Arapaho were strong allies with her people, and they'd kill this arrogant white man who held her against her will. And she'd help them. It would give her pleasure to plunge a knife deep into his heart.

Her hopes of being rescued dwindled as they rode on without seeing anyone. The man with her was very careful, and she doubted if he would be careless enough to be caught unaware. He moved with the surefooted caution of a Cheyenne scout.

She began to sense they were close to his destination when he turned his horse up a slight incline. She picked up a distant roaring that grew louder as they proceeded, until they came out upon a high bluff that overlooked a wide, fast-plunging waterfall.

He halted and dismounted, then looked up at her. She looked straight ahead, her chin high, completely ignoring him. One corner of his mouth lifted in amusement at the stony set of her jaw, and he reached up and pulled her off the horse. She didn't protest, so he let her body slide slowly down his own. As he'd intended, he could feel every soft curve, and he held her to him tightly, enjoying the warmth of her, the feel of her body, as he buried his face in the fragrance of her hair.

Outrage purpled Starfire's eyes, and she began a vicious protest inside his embrace. Her feet hung suspended about a foot above the ground, and although she tried to kick, she knew she had no chance to free herself. He was too strong, so it was like a cat teasing a mouse. Angry, she cursed at him with snapping eyes, but Tracker only knotted one hand in the luxurious silver tresses at the back of her head and kissed her hard on the mouth, quieting her by force.

Starfire could feel the steel-muscled arm flex as he tightened his hold on her waist, holding her immobile. She fought impotently, his head bending hers backward, his beard scratching her soft skin as his tongue forced her mouth open. The fury she felt was intense, uncontrollable;

but she could not move a muscle, could not stop him. She
was pinned, completely helpless against his immense
strength. She felt a horrified dismay when her skin began
to heat under the warmth of his kisses. Fierce, indescribable longings stirred somewhere deep inside her body. Unknown, confusing pleasures created an intense, sensual
ache in her loins. She began to tremble, unable to think of
anything but his lips searing her throat, her chin, then
again covering her lips. They scorched her, tingled her
flesh, fanned the fires of her sensuality alive for the first
time.

Tracker had wanted to kiss her from the first moment
he'd seen her; and now that he felt her softening under his
lips, it was almost impossible to stop. He fought the desire
to lower her to the ground, to possess her without another
thought, knowing it was foolish to stay in the open when
they was so very close to his sanctuary. Reason finally
forced down the tremendous need for her raging inside
him, and with a mental groan, he stepped back and stood
looking down into her flushed face, her eyes closed, her
skin reddened by his rough kisses.

She opened her eyes slowly, and Tracker saw the emotions play revealingly across her face. He saw the pleasure
first, changing quickly into confusion, then last of all, surprise. Tracker had to grin, knowing she'd expected him to
do much more.

Starfire stared up at him, trying hard to steady her ragged nerves and weak knees. The lovely feeling had ceased
the minute he'd taken his hands off her, and was replaced
by a wave of disappointment. Suddenly she was appalled
that she'd gotten pleasure from of his brutal, forceful treatment. She saw the knowing smirk on Tracker's dark face,
and it infuriated her that he knew she'd been affected by
him. Her jaw tensed hard as she gritted her teeth in embarrassment, in self-disgust. She wanted to strike him, to
wipe the smug expression out of his sky eyes. She released
her rage by kicking his ankle as hard as she could. It hurt
her as much as it did him, but it made him yelp, and that
made it worth it.

Tracker grabbed her up off her feet and gave her a few
violent shakes, muttering an oath under his breath. Then
he pushed her away and walked back to the stallion, try-

ing not to limp. She watched him in satisfaction, glad she'd hurt him, wishing she could do it again. She didn't understand what had happened to her. Why her body had burned as if a blaze had been fanned alive inside her. Lone Wolf's touch had not ignited such fire in her. Her eyes widened with sudden fear, wondering if the white man possessed some strange magic he used against her.

Tracker jerked loose the saddle bags and slung them over his shoulder. He was angry and trying without success to control his temper. He stalked furiously back to her and scooped her up in hard, capable arms. She didn't protest, intimidated by his black scowl. She stiffened warily as he strode with long, purposeful steps to a high point that jutted out precariously over the falls.

Cold spray spattered against them, wetting their clothes. Starfire gasped, and her heart pounded as he moved to the edge. The roaring was deafening at such close range, and Starfire watched with a clogged throat as his eyes probed the falls, estimating or searching. She was afraid she'd gone too far, angered him enough to throw her into the maelstrom below. She couldn't help the frightened cry that escaped her white lips, or the way she locked her arms around his neck in a stranglehold, determined that if she went into the raging water, he'd go with her. She heard a low rumble of laughter in his throat, but she was too frightened to care.

His arms grew tighter around her, and she screamed in terror and buried her face in his shoulder as he leaped off the ledge. The cold torrent hit them hard, a staggering force that drenched them in seconds, but Tracker held her securely to him. She screamed as the horrible sensation of falling took over. A moment later she felt a horrible jolt that shook her to her bones as Tracker's feet hit ground, not ten feet below the cliff.

She clung to him, paralyzed with fear, while he carried her out of the falling water. Starfire was afraid to look, her heart beating erratically, as he moved farther into a vast, cold darkness and set her down. She refused to let go at first, still afraid, but he gently disentangled her fingers and moved away from her. She opened her eyes and stared in disbelief at a small, crackling fire. Her eyes widened as she looked around, realizing they were in a cave behind the falls.

She began to shiver uncontrollably as she sat in her dripping clothes, her wet hair straggling over her face. She pushed it back, hugging herself for warmth, watching Tracker walk to a stack of supplies set against one corner. He tossed her a blanket.

"You'd better get out of those wet clothes. It's freezing in here."

She caught it, desperately wanting to fling it back into his face. She'd never wanted to do anything so badly in her life, but her chattering teeth stopped her. It was cold, and she needed the wool blanket. Despite her fierce pride, Starfire was practical. She took it silently, trying not to shiver as she looked at Tracker, suddenly more afraid of him. For the first time, she truly feared that Lone Wolf and Raging Buffalo would not find her.

His blue eyes shone in the firelight, fixed on the darkness behind her. Starfire jumped when a low voice spoke from the black shadows.

A tall Indian stood behind her, dressed in fringed buckskins like those of the big white man. He was handsome and stood casually, leaning against the entrance. He'd spoken in a dialect she didn't know, but it didn't matter what he'd said. If he was a friend of the white one, he was her enemy.

Tracker grinned at his blood brother in relief at finding him unharmed.

"Is everything set?" he asked in Sioux.

Two Bears remained impassive as he answered in the same low tone. "Yes, everything went well, and I saw no sign of pursuit."

Tracker's muscles relaxed for the first time since he'd entered the Cheyenne camp the night before. His smile widened.

"You bring good news, Two Bears. But they'll come, sooner or later. They won't let her go without a fight. She's too much of a prize."

Two Bears dropped his gaze to the girl, who was glaring up at him with the same poisonous look she used on Tracker. He looked back at Tracker, and his eyes gleamed faintly with amusement.

"She will be a hard one to handle, my brother. It is in the purple of her eyes."

Tracker's mouth lifted in a lazy smile. "She's a hell of a handful, but I can manage her. She needs some taming, that's all."

Two Bears didn't answer, but his intuition told him that Tracker's impressive experience with women probably didn't include one such as this beautiful, silver-haired captive. The girl looked wild and headstrong, and she wouldn't be an easy conquest. He glanced at her again and read the hatred in her face as she watched his white blood brother's every move. The obstinate slant of her jaw told him she wouldn't bend to Tracker's wishes as easily as most women; he knew that Tracker wasn't the type to be bested when he wanted something. It would be quite a contest, and Two Bears was almost sorry he would miss the battle.

"I wish you luck, my brother. How long will you keep her here?"

"Probably a month or so. Maybe more. The woods around here will be crawling with Cheyenne."

Two Bears stared hard into Tracker's blue eyes.

"Do they know of this cave?"

Tracker jerked a thumb at Starfire. "She didn't know about it, so I doubt if they've ever been this far west."

Two Bears nodded then said, "I will go now."

Tracker moved to him, and they looked affectionately into each other's eyes as they placed their palms upon one another's shoulders.

"May the all-spirit go with you, Two Bears."

Tracker's words were warm and so sincere that Starfire looked up, wondering what he'd said.

Tracker watched as Two Bears disappeared into the outer cave, then turned back to Starfire. She sat huddled by the fire, not looking at him. He hesitated, reluctant to leave her alone, but he had to check on the horses and the supplies in the other chamber. He ducked through the low ceiling into the next cavern, then hurried past the torch Two Bears had set against the wall to another opening. The horses were tethered inside, and he checked to make sure they could reach the food and water. He stood still a moment, listening. A steady drip of water from somewhere in the shadows of the cave was the only sound, except for the faint roar of the falls outside. He was satisfied, and he went back to Starfire, knowing she couldn't be trusted alone for long.

He walked in just as she dropped her wet shift from beneath the blanket she held securely around her body. His blood quickened as a vision of naked flesh invaded his mind with unsettling clarity. He made an effort to throw off his thoughts and walked toward the fire.

Starfire watched him covertly, shivering slightly when his hot sapphire eyes slowly raked over her. The kiss by the falls intruded into her mind. She recalled the way her body had blazed to meet his hard, searching mouth, despite her intense hatred of him. How could she be so attracted to her enemy, the man who had stolen her? She moved closer to the fire and refused to look at him.

Tracker knelt across from her and fed a few logs to the blaze, trying to give it all his attention and forget what he was thinking. When he did look at her, she was huddled down into the blanket, staring into the flames. He lounged down on his side and propped his head up in the palm of his hand. Starfire glanced at him warily, then lowered her eyes again, not comfortable under the strange, unwavering blue gaze, feeling an intuitive alarm. He looked at her as Lone Wolf had so many times. She wrapped her arms tightly around her chest, trying not to shiver.

Tracker studied her, examining the flawless skin, the exquisite bone structure of her face. He'd always enjoyed beautiful women, and she was the most beautiful he'd ever seen. She threw out an aura—one of sensuality, of hot blood and warm response. But she was so young, not much more than a child.

Starfire was unaware of his thoughts, but she was cold, and nervous with him sitting so near. She leaned closer to the warmth of the fire, and as she moved, the blanket fell apart. Tracker's eyes dropped immediately to the exposed curve of her body. His breath caught, his mind changing in mid-thought. Starfire was not a child. She was a woman, a woman he wanted. He could not take his eyes away, and he felt the desire rising with such force he couldn't block it.

Starfire saw his dangerous expression, then quickly followed his intent stare to her naked breast. She gasped and pulled the blanket together quickly, cursing herself for being so stupid as to undress in his presence. She jerked her head up as Tracker sat up suddenly, his unwavering stare pinning her where she sat.

"Don't come near me," she warned harshly through her teeth.

His laugh was arrogant, and it created a fury in her that jabbed like a spear to the core of her pride. He was contemptible, he was insolent. He held her at his mercy and laughed about it. She hated him.

"I hate you, you dirty wasichu, white man," she gritted passionately, her violet eyes slits of venom.

Tracker's eyebrows drew together in a dark frown, and Starfire pulled back quickly from the terrible, fierce expression.

Tracker was angry. For some reason her words bit into him, ate at him like acid. He didn't want her to hate him. He didn't want her to be afraid of him. He didn't know exactly what he wanted, but now he could see the fear and uncertainty in her eyes. The vulnerable look killed the storm about to erupt in him. She was trying to hide her fear now, but he'd seen it.

Starfire watched his anger dissolve and the now familiar, taunting grin take over his features. Her anger ballooned until she was livid with rage. Her fingers found and curled around a large heavy rock near her hand. She got a grip on it, then hurled it across the fire at him with all her might.

Her action caught Tracker unaware, and the rock struck him on his left temple, stunning him for an instant. Like lightning, Starfire was out of her blanket and at his side, jerking his long knife from the scabbard at his thigh.

Tracker rolled back and deflected the blade with his forearm as she brought it plunging down toward his chest. The sharp steel cut into the back of his tensed muscle, and he groaned as it opened a long, bleeding gash. He fought to disarm her, knowing she was savage enough to cut out his heart if she could.

He grabbed her shoulders and threw her down beside him, then swung his leg over her until he straddled her. Starfire stabbed at him desperately, hysterically, but for all her efforts, she was unable to wound him again. He grabbed her wrist and squeezed it until her whole hand went numb and the knife fell free.

Tracker was furious, a blind rage ruling his mind. His temple bled and ached, and he could feel the hot rush of blood over his forearm. He ignored the pain and pinioned her wrists above her head as he locked her kicking legs between his knees.

"I underestimated you this time, you little hellcat, but it won't ever happen again."

Starfire fought him wildly, her teeth bared in a fury that matched Tracker's immense wrath. She finally gave up and lay panting, knowing it was futile against his strength.

Her violet eyes locked with his angry blue ones as she spoke calmly and bitterly. "I'll kill you next time, white dog. You'll have to kill me first to stop me."

Tracker lowered his eyes to her naked breasts, wanting to teach her a lesson, wanting to humiliate her. He looked back into her eyes.

"No, I won't ever kill you, love, you're much too beautiful and worth too much money, but there are things I could do, things you wouldn't like."

He touched her with his finger, and Starfire intensified her struggle.

"Leave me alone," she gritted, hating him with every fiber of her being.

Tracker only laughed as he lowered his head. Starfire stiffened in despair as he began to nuzzle her throat, and she tossed her head to prevent it, but his lips moved to her shoulder, causing a shiver to run over her limbs. Starfire was horrified, hating herself for reacting to his touch. She tried to go numb, to forget what his strange powers could do to her.

Tracker felt on fire, her skin was so soft, so smooth. He lifted his head and stared into the amethyst of her eyes, seeing the bewilderment and confusion in them. He was giving her pleasure, but she snarled and called him a name. He smiled, sliding his hand down the velvety warmth of her skin, and Starfire squeezed her eyes shut. She tried desperately to free herself, but Tracker brought his face back to hers, holding her immobile as he stared into her eyes.

Starfire began to feel weak and fluttery as his hand continued to caress her, her insides alive with a craving she could not explain. Her body moved her in one direction, but her mind rebelled. She refused to look at him, knowing his eyes would have the same mocking amusement in them. The thought turned her blood cold, and she refused to give in.

Tracker wanted her as he'd never wanted another woman. He knew she was ready for him, and he knew she detested him for what he was doing to her. She was aroused but fighting it, and his passion began to control his actions. He'd have her. He couldn't wait, didn't want to wait. He moved over her, the blood drumming in his temples.

Starfire felt his hard body against hers and became frantic, her voice high and shrill.

"You're a filthy animal, a wasichu! I hate you, I hate you!"

She was sobbing, her panic-stricken tone cutting through Tracker's lust and rage and making him sickeningly aware of what he was doing. His mind winced, appalled at his own actions. He'd never forced a woman. And the girl was a virgin. Wild and beautiful and untamed, but an innocent. He cursed inside, forcing himself to release her. It took every ounce of self-discipline he had. He'd never wanted anything as much as he wanted her.

He rolled away from her quickly before he could change his mind, and got to his feet. He felt shaky and a little sick. And ashamed. He leaned down and got his knife and walked quickly away without looking at her.

Starfire lay unmoving, afraid to believe that he was really gone. Her mind was jumbled, confused by conflicting emotions. She'd wanted him to stop, but her body had reacted to his brutal touch. A terrible, frightening sense of danger rolled over her. She was no longer afraid of him, but of herself.

She had to escape. She had to get away from him, before something else happened. She jumped up, slipping her dress over her head on the way to the opening. She peered out, and when she didn't see him, she ran into the waterfall. It felt like a frigid shower, and she hesitated, trying to see through the torrent.

His low voice behind her sent her to the very edge of the

cliff. She could see the water far below, roiling and gushing as the falls rushed into it. She stared back at Tracker, her hair plastered over her face, her outspread hands in front of her, as if to fend him off.

"Don't be a fool, Starfire. You can't escape that way. It will kill you!"

As he spoke, he inched toward her, thinking she wouldn't have the courage to jump. The leap was far too frightening, too dangerous. He wouldn't even attempt it.

Warily, Starfire watched him approach, determined he would not touch her again. She knew now that his magic was too strong to fight. She could swim well, and the falls were her last chance for freedom. She glanced down into the teeming water, more afraid of the white man than of the river. She gave him a defiant look, then Tracker's eyes widened in horror as she leaped out into the plunging, roaring water.

He stood for a shocked second, not believing that she'd actually done it. Then the danger of her action brought him to his senses, and without another thought, he followed her at a run.

Starfire felt herself hurled furiously into the deep water, the slashing falls pounding her under. She fought her way to the surface, her lungs straining from the pressure. When she broke into the air, she gasped for breath as she was slung through the rapids in a violently twisting course. She tried to control the immense push of the current, fighting frantically to ward herself from the jutting rocks on either side.

Tracker hit the water moments behind her and surfaced, trying to see through the blinding spray. He had little power against the current, and his heart clutched in panic when he thought of Starfire's chance against the torrent. He kept his eyes riveted in front of him as he let the force of the water carry him along. When he saw her, he only caught a glimpse of her head, buffeted and swirled by the river, but relief flooded him. He renewed his fight against the current, anxious to reach her.

Starfire rode with the water until she felt herself being washed out of the rapids into a gentle stretch of the river. She had gashed her head against a rock, and the hurt overrode any other concern. She could see a sandbar through the red haze of pain over her eyes, and she splashed toward it, spent and exhausted. By the time she reached it, she was too tired to move and lay with her cheek against the sand, her eyes closed.

Tracker's initial concern was rapidly giving way to anger as he made his way toward her. Sloshing up behind her and pulling her to her feet, he wanted to shake her for her stupid recklessness.

"Damn it, you little fool, are you trying to kill yourself?"

He'd yelled it into her face breathlessly, furiously; but Starfire was too exhausted to answer him and only stared up at him out of glazed, pain-filled eyes.

Tracker saw the blood running in red streams in her wet hair, saw the pain in her dull eyes. His anger fled him, and he quickly enfolded her in his arms, holding her tightly. Emotion swelled in his throat, and an overwhelming tide of protectiveness rolled over him. She was safe, she was in his arms. But he had to admit that it was he who had driven her to such a drastic action. Feelings he could not explain touched his heart, and he closed his eyes and breathed hoarse words against her hair.

"Please, Starfire, please don't ever do anything so foolish again. I won't touch you, I swear it."

Starfire closed her eyes weakly, not really hearing what he said, or caring, only sickeningly aware that he had caught her, that she was his captive again.

FOUR

Starfire opened heavy lids, blearily watching dark shadows twist in grotesque shapes on the ceiling of the cave. Weariness sent the dark, heavy lashes fluttering downward, hopelessness welling as elusive visions of her plunge into the cold falls and recapture flitted through her mind. Wood burned near her, crackling and snapping as waves of warmth fanned her cheeks. She turned her head quickly, and regretted the swift action at once. Hot arrows of pain jabbed viciously into her right temple. She moaned indistinctly, raising slender fingertips until they touched the cloth bandage wrapped around her forehead.

"Does it hurt?"

The warm, masculine voice startled her, accelerating the penetrating thud in her skull as she jerked toward it. She winced in pain, eyes riveted on the big white man. He sat across from her, one buckskin-clad arm dangling over his bent knee, his azure eyes glowing like blue flames. Starfire stared in fascination at his strange eyes, until he smiled slowly, his teeth flashing white. The grin seemed mocking to her, but she was too groggy to dwell on it. She let her eyes drift slowly closed when he rose to kneel at her side. Aware of his closeness, she kept her eyes squeezed tight, not wanting to look upon his dark and handsome face.

"Come on now, Starfire, open those eyes. Two days is long enough for anyone to sleep."

Two days! Startled violet eyes flew wide, and she struggled weakly to raise herself on one elbow. The pain intensified, and she groaned, lowering her head feebly to the ground.

"Here, let me take a look," the voice ordered from above her, and Starfire flinched away from long fingers that tenderly smoothed away the silky white-blond strands around her face. But his touch was gentle, and she didn't have the strength to resist him. She lay still as he slowly unwound the bandage, watching out of resigned eyes as he carefully applied a greasy salve to her temple.

"It'll be sore for a while, but it's healing nicely," he said quietly.

The hurt in her head had settled into a muted throb, but Starfire still found it difficult to think rationally. She stared up at him, unable to take her gaze off his glittering eyes.

"Your eyes are like the sky," she murmured half to herself, then wondered why she'd said such a thing.

Tracker darted a surprised look at her, but it was the first encouraging sign from a very hostile girl.

"And yours are as clear as priceless amethysts."

Starfire studied him uncomprehendingly, and Tracker tried to explain in Cheyenne.

"Amethysts are precious purple jewels. Valuable to the white man." Starfire's blank expression greeted his words, and he added, "Someday, I'll show you one."

Starfire pulled her attention away from him, confusion swirling her mind into a turmoil of contradictions. The big white man smiled now and touched her with gentleness. But before, he'd been brutal, his kisses as hard as his lean body. She shivered under vivid images of his warm mouth on her bare flesh, and the unknown fires he'd sent spiraling into her core.

Tracker saw the long shiver that almost didn't stop, and he stood, looking down at her, silently admiring the way the silver tresses framed her delicate features. He moved away, not wanting to frighten her again, but unable to keep his eyes elsewhere. He leaned against a saddle, greatly relieved that she was finally awake and well. He'd been worried about her; her delirium had lasted much too long. But he'd have to double his guard now, because she would try to escape as soon as she was strong enough. He had no doubt about that.

"I am thirsty."

Her voice was low and husky, and she did not look at

him. Tracker reached for his canteen, dropping to one knee beside her.

Starfire tensed as his strong arm slipped beneath her and lifted her easily. The worn buckskin of his shirt felt soft under her bare shoulders, and Starfire gasped, realizing she was naked beneath the blanket. She clutched it to her, frowning accusingly into Tracker's face. He shrugged with a half-smile and raised the cup to her dry lips.

"You were shivering with cold, and your clothes were wet. I had to get you warm," he said calmly.

He didn't deem it prudent to tell her how he'd done it. But her soft body pressed against his own had warmed him much faster than it had her.

He let her drink her fill, then lowered her easily to the blanket. She seemed very tired then, and Tracker returned to his place by the fire, watching her as she dozed fitfully. When she finally slept, he left her to check the outside entrance for sign of Cheyenne pursuers. He'd kept a close lookout, and so far he'd been lucky. They'd eluded the Cheyenne search party, but it was just a matter of time until the Indians closed in. He hurried back to the cave, knowing Starfire was too unpredictable and headstrong to trust alone for long—even with a head injury.

When he entered the dark chamber, Starfire was awake and sitting. He could not risk frightening her into trying another reckless escape, and he proceeded cautiously, not wanting to startle her. He chose a spot a safe distance away, and she avoided his gaze.

"Feeling better now?"

Starfire ignored his softly uttered question. She did feel better, and although she was still a little woozy, the pain in her head had disappeared. Only when she moved too quickly would a dull ache erupt in her temple. She was fully aware of his sky eyes watching her, but she tried not to think about it. She shifted uncomfortably beneath the blanket, feeling the grit of sand upon her skin and in her hair. Her eyes dropped to the kettle of water near the fire, and when she raised them to Tracker, his breath caught as they gleamed with their own violet brilliance in the firelight.

"I am not clean."

"The water is warm," he answered in Cheyenne, noting

how her fist clutched the blanket tighter, a trace of fear flashing in her shrouded eyes. He added quickly, "I'll wait outside."

Starfire watched his broad back stoop to leave the cavern, and she marveled at his size, thinking even Lone Wolf did not stand so tall. The thought of her betrothed furrowed her smooth brow. The wedding feast seemed long ago now. It seemed she'd been with the white man for a very long time. An apprehensive quiver ran up her spine, and her eyes sought the entrance distrustfully.

She waited a few cautious minutes, then swayed dizzily as she stood. She wrapped the blanket carefully under her arms, dipping one end of it into the warm water and rubbing it slowly over her face and neck, sighing with pleasure. It felt wonderful, and she scrubbed her skin until it tingled.

She caught sight of the filthy bridal dress she'd worn, thrown in a tangled heap against the wall. She picked it up distastefully, eyeing the torn and bloodstained garment. She was reluctant to put the tattered dress upon her clean skin.

Starfire didn't notice that Tracker had ducked into the opening, and she whirled to face him when his deep voice emerged from the shadows. She had forgotten how stealthily he moved, and she took one involuntary step backward. His expression was intense but unreadable, which made her uneasy.

"There's a clean shirt in my saddlebags. You can wear it if you want."

His offer was uttered brusquely, then he was gone as silently as he'd entered, leaving Starfire staring after him. She hesitated, her eyes going to the leather saddlebags. She did not want to wear his shirt! She wanted nothing from him!

She looked down at the dirty dress in her hand, and her pride fought with her reluctance to don the dress. Her desire for cleanliness won out, and she moved to the bags, lifting the fringed flap to draw out the shirt. It was white, and very soft, softer than anything she'd ever felt. She rubbed it wonderingly between her fingers, then raised it to her cheeks, delighting in its silkiness.

She could not resist the temptation to wear it, and she

slipped her slender arms into the sleeves, sighing at the feel of it upon her skin. It was much too large, the cuffs hanging almost to the ground while the tail was well below her knees. The white man was a giant, she marveled, and she searched for the laces. She could not find them and frowned, wondering how it fastened.

When Tracker returned, Starfire stood by the fire, swallowed in his huge silk shirt, her finely arched brows drawn together in bafflement, as she tried to force a button into a buttonhole far too high on the other side. The corner of his mouth lifted at her intense concentration; but when she became frustrated and stamped one small foot angrily, he laughed aloud.

Starfire's head jerked to him in alarm, and she backed away, gripping the shirt closed. Tracker's smile faded when he read the uncertainty in her expressive eyes, watching the distrust grow as he moved nearer. She was trembling slightly now, and when she nervously caught at her full lower lip with her teeth, shame dug sharp spurs into him as he realized she expected him to attack her.

He halted knowing he would first have to calm her with words. He kept his voice low and said, "Don't be afraid, Starfire. I won't hurt you. I just want to show you how it fastens."

Her eyes were wary, and she stood poised for flight, like a beautiful wild creature. She didn't move away, and Tracker reached out slowly and touched the shirt. Her slender body stiffened against his fingers, her face upturned to his, her lips parted with quickened breaths. He was aware of the high rounded breasts just inches from his fingertips as they heaved beneath the fabric, and desire whipped at his nerve endings, but it was the softness of her mouth that captured his gaze, forcing him to fight against bruising it under his own hungry lips. But he did not move, did not give in to the tremendous urge to pull her close. He'd sworn not to frighten her again. He restrained himself with difficulty, aware of the hoarseness in his own voice.

"Here. You have to push the top button on one side through the top hole on the other side. See?"

Starfire watched intently as he demonstrated, tensing slightly as his hands paused where her womanly curves strained against the shirt. She looked up expectantly, no longer afraid, for his touch was soft. It surprised her when a look almost like pain passed over his dark face, and she watched with puzzled eyes as he walked away and out of the cave. As an innocent, she did not understand his plight, her own desires awakening only when he touched her flesh or pressed his lips against hers.

She struggled with the rest of the buttons, watching the cave door for his return as she tied a lace from her shift around her tiny waist. Her attempts to roll the sleeves stopped abruptly, her mouth sagging slightly as he reentered the cave. He was soaking wet, his clothes dripping water on the floor of the cave, his yellow hair plastered away from his forehead. It was as if he'd stood beneath the cold falls intentionally. Starfire looked at him as he moved to the fire, amazed at the strangeness of white ways.

Tracker turned suddenly and ran impatient fingers through his wet hair. Their eyes met and locked across the fire, and Starfire's heart sped out of control. He seemed as huge and bronzed as the sun god of Cheyenne legend, and goose bumps rippled down both arms, her fear of him returning.

Tracker watched her expression change, wondering what had caused her wariness to return. He set about preparing their meal, trying to ignore her, but despite the cold shower in the falls, her small and exquisitely formed body haunted him. He'd never been so aware of a woman, never wanted a woman so strongly that his loins burned with desire. But he'd vowed he wouldn't touch her unless she was willing. Which was a very remote possibility, he thought glumly.

He glanced to where she sat cross-legged on the blanket. Her eyes had followed him, but her lashes lowered immediately at his gaze. He finished cutting the rabbit into the pot and slid his knife into the scabbard. Things were not going at all as he'd planned. When he'd first seen her, he'd thought to amuse himself by taming her. But she'd shown him that she was brave and spirited and proud, and she'd earned the right to be treated with respect. Although he wanted her with a passion he'd never dreamed possible, he would never again frighten her. The month he planned to be alone with her in the intimate confines of the cave threatened to be a slow torture, and the thought of turning her over to Huddleston no longer set well with him. Perhaps he'd escort her to her family in St. Louis himself, just to make sure she got there safely.

He decided suddenly to try to talk to her, tell her about her grandparents, assure her that he would take her to them himself. It might relieve some of the tension between them. He crouched in front of her, and when she didn't look up, he reached out with one finger and turned her chin to face him. She did not recoil at his touch, and her large eyes were like soft blue-violet pools of velvet. He stared down into them, feeling like a fool as he forgot what he was going to say.

"How's your head?" he said gruffly.

Starfire sat still, feeling more secure with him now that the hungry expression was gone and a frown had taken its place. Despite his dark look, his fingers did not hurt her as he checked the healing cut. She didn't answer, becoming uneasy as he remained so close to her. She could smell the clean, leathery man scent of him and the thought entered her mind how pleasant it was. She gritted her teeth in self-disgust, then looked at him as he spoke.

"Starfire, I want to tell you why I took you."

He used Cheyenne, but he wasn't as fluent in that dialect as he was in Sioux and found himself groping for the right words. It was very important that she understand what he was about to say. He frowned to himself, muttering in his own language, "Damn, I wish you could understand English."

He tried again to put the right Cheyenne words together, then was stopped in midsentence by Starfire's soft voice.

"I can understand your words."

She'd spoken in an oddly lilting English, almost an Irish brogue, and he was so obviously astonished by her admission that Starfire smiled, two deep dimples framing her small white teeth. Tracker's surprise rapidly turned to awe as the fleeting smile enhanced her beauty. Her smile quickly disappeared as fires flared in the blue depths of his eyes, turning them dark with passion. Her eyes darted to the door, seeking escape, and furious with himself, he spit out harshly in her language. "I'm not going to touch you, so quit looking so damned afraid of me."

The fragile line of her jaw hardened as she clamped her teeth together and set her eyes on the fire. The soft moment of her smile was gone forever, and he cursed himself for his inability to handle her or the situation as calmly and sensibly as he should. He sat back on his heels and stared at her finely chiseled profile.

"I was paid to bring you home. Your white family wants you back."

Starfire's brilliant eyes flew to him, the look so wild that Tracker was startled. Her words came at him through clenched teeth, deadly low.

"I will never go. You have stolen me away and stopped my marriage to a brave chief. I hate you! I hate all wasi-chus!"

At the mention of Lone Wolf, a great, billowing cloud of anger roiled up inside Tracker, one he didn't dare analyze. "I'm taking you back whether you like it or not," he told her in a tight voice. "You can't stop me, so you might as well get used to the idea."

Starfire burned with rage, venom coloring her eyes a deep purple. "You'll never take me there, never! I'll kill myself first!"

Her words were laced with a steel resolve that made Tracker sit straighter. It had never occurred to him that she might harm herself, and it was a frightening thought.

"Over my dead body you will, my sweet," he said harshly.

Starfire's eyes caught fire at his threat, and her words were razor-sharp. "Yes, that is the way I want it to happen, you skulking stealer of women. I would like it that way."

The hairs at the nape of his neck lifted and waved at her calm hatred, and he stared into her challenging amethyst eyes, noting how her fingers curled in upon her palms, whitening her knuckles. He'd be lucky if he made it back to Boulder with her, as determined as she was not to go. And he was beginning to believe she just might manage to escape, if he wasn't very, very careful with her. So his thoughts ran; but Starfire remained unaware of his doubts as he grabbed her by the arms, speaking coldly into her glittering eyes.

"You will not harm yourself, Starfire, and you will not escape. And if you try either, I just might forget my promise not to touch you again."

Starfire trembled slightly at his threat, staring after him in hopeless hatred as he moved away.

They ate his savory stew in a stony silence, and afterward, Starfire sat with her arms hugging her shoulders, cold eyes on the big white man. He leaned comfortably against the wall, completely relaxed, although she kept her frigid violet glare upon him. To her inner chagrin, he remained oblivious to her, saying nothing, acting completely uninterested unless she moved toward the outer cave. Then he was on his feet with incredible speed and agility.

Starfire finally gave up and turned her gaze to the fire. She felt much better now. The food had given her strength, and her headache was gone. She spent most of her time contemplating various plans of escape, but had discarded one after another because of his constant watchfulness.

Her only hope was to wait him out. He'd have to sleep eventually, and she vowed to be ready when he did. Encouraged, she glanced up at Tracker to find a mocking grin on his face.

"Since you're waiting for me to go to sleep, I guess I'll oblige you by turning in early."

His teeth flashed briefly at her startled expression.

"I'm going to turn in now, as a matter of fact." He paused, watching the disappointment extinguish the hope in her eyes. "And so are you."

He pulled her to her feet, expecting her to jerk her hand away. She didn't disappoint him and resisted his grip all the way across the cave. He stopped alongside a low natural rock shelf, holding her wrist securely as he spread the blankets, then pushed her down on them. She immediately backed as far against the wall as she could, her eyes scorching him as he stretched out beside her, effectively blocking any possible escape route.

Starfire's fists doubled, and she sat as rigid as stone, while he settled himself comfortably, crossing his long legs and placing both hands beneath his head.

"Goodnight, sweet. Sleep well."

Starfire gritted her teeth in fury at his taunting words. "I hate you, you dog, you . . ."

Tracker turned his head slightly, arching a blond eyebrow, as his mocking eyes raked over her furious face.

"Starfire, I really need some sleep, but if you keep that up for long, I'll have to think of some way to keep you quiet."

His eyes strayed to her soft mouth, trembling with rage, and lingered there with a very real desire to do just what he threatened.

His arrogance infuriated her, but she believed his threat, because she saw the banked fires in his sky eyes. She bit back her ire, rolling over to face the wall. Presented with a cold view of her back, Tracker chuckled, incensing Starfire further.

She lay tense and unmoving for a long time, listening to his breathing. She had to get away. Get out of the cave and hide from him. Raging Buffalo had taught her to walk without snapping a twig; if she could make it into the forest, he'd never find her. Barely breathing, she slowly turned over until she could see him. He lay very still, his eyes closed, the thick blond eyelashes resting against his tanned face. His profile seemed carved in granite, and her eyes strayed to the curve of his mouth. The fire burned on the other side of the cave, and the thick growth of hair upon his chin and hard jaw glowed golden against it. She wondered how it felt, resisting with disgust the urge to touch him. It was so very different from Lone Wolf's smooth cheeks and long black hair. And his sky eyes were so very beautiful. Against her will, she was fascinated by the white man, who looked so different, but acted much like a Cheyenne warrior. Yet his light eyes and yellow hair were like her own. For the first time, Starfire found herself considering the fact that she was white, like the big man beside her. Always before she'd known it, but the Cheyenne had accepted her, and the strangeness of her skin and hair had not been important.

Her gaze moved lower to the crisp furring of blond hair at the open throat of his shirt, and she felt small shivers course through her, remembering the hard molded muscles of his chest and thighs as he'd held her so tightly. He was so strong, and he'd shown much courage to come into her village and take her away. If he were Cheyenne, he would be a great chief with many coups, she decided, then quickly forced away her traitorous thoughts, appalled at any admiration of him, however reluctant. He had not moved a muscle, and she moved stealthily down the shelf. She stole another look at him, her heart racing as she slowly inched one arm over his legs.

"Don't try it, Starfire."

Starfire groaned aloud, darting a despairing look at him. He did not open his eyes, but lay relaxed as if bored with her. Seething inside, Starfire threw herself against the wall, muttering curses under her breath. A long time later, Tracker smiled to himself when he heard her soft, even breathing as she finally slept in exhaustion. He checked to make sure his rifle was propped in position at his side before he closed his own eyes for some much-needed rest.

FIVE

For the next few days, Starfire tried without success to find a way to escape. The big white man outguessed her every move, until she wanted to scream and scratch out his sky eyes in fury. She had almost given up on catching him unawares. His warm blue eyes watched her incessantly, but he'd been gentle with her, not touching her except to change the bandage. She'd been extremely grateful that he left her to bathe in private each day, even if he remained on guard just outside the entrance.

And he'd begun to talk to her often, telling her wild and hard-to-believe stories of the whites. At first, she'd walked away, covering her ears with her hands until he'd stopped. She had not wanted to hear of it; the very thought disgusted her. But it became harder not to listen to his deep and pleasant voice, and against her will, she felt the first stirrings of wonder at some of the things he said, disbelieving such marvelous things could really exist.

Eventually, Starfire's vibrant curiosity began to rise, many questions on her mind about the huge white man who captured women and held them captive. As time went on and he did not touch her, she lost her fear of him and began to examine her captor, unable to stifle the growing admiration of his masculine strength and handsome features.

One night as she watched him turn meat upon a spit, she realized that she did not know his name.

"What do your people call you?"

Tracker looked up at her, his blue eyes glinting in the firelight, and she wondered if he could really be pleased by her question.

"I'm called Tracker, Starfire."

He smiled warmly at her, his eyes lingering on her in a most pleasant way, and she almost smiled back before she caught herself and turned away, trying to act indifferent. He laughed and handed her a plate.

Tracker felt triumph at her question and sat down with his own plate, watching her eat.

"The whites dine on long, shiny tables," he said casually, as he took a bite of meat. "And drink from crystal glasses as clear as mountain water."

"I do not care what white men do! I am Cheyenne!" Starfire cried defiantly. She was proud of her people and their ways, she thought, lifting her chin, and nothing he said would make her want to live among the whites.

"And there are many different foods to choose from," Tracker continued calmly, as if she hadn't spoken. "So many that you could never sample them all. And when white men travel, they don't have to walk and lead travois; they ride in great iron horses that take them long distances."

Starfire raised her fine eyes and listened raptly in spite of herself as Tracker told her more of the white man's trains. Then, as was his custom, Tracker left her to check the horses, leaving her a time of privacy before he led her to the makeshift bed against the wall. She had behaved herself so far, but he still did not dare leave her unattended while he slept.

He'd tried hard to entice Starfire into accepting her role in the white world. He had exulted at the sparks of interest she could not hide in her vivid violet eyes when he'd first told her of houses bigger than a hundred tipis that gleamed as light as day in the dead of night. Her eyes had grown round and intrigued at his description of the beautiful velvet gowns the woman wore, and he found himself growing eager to return to town and introduce her to all she'd missed during her life with the Cheyenne.

They had reached an uneasy truce, and even the fact that he'd found signs of Cheyenne presence nearby did not unduly worry him as he returned and led Starfire to their bed. She'd been most cooperative the last few days, even smiling at him on occasion, but he was not foolish enough to let down his guard. She was too smart to take lightly and too savage to underestimate. He'd found that out the hard way.

Tracker watched her obediently stretch out on the bed, moving over to make room for him. His breath halted when his eyes discovered the open throat of her shirt, where the full swelling of her breasts had been too much for the buttons. One soft pink peak was offered to his view, and he was unable to force his eyes away from the satiny skin, or the way her long hair fell over her shoulders in a shimmering mantle of silver. He wanted to touch it, touch her, and his hand moved toward her of its own accord, stopping when Starfire turned her innocent gaze upon him. He could not move, did not trust himself to speak, and his silent stare unsettled Starfire. Her mouth suddenly went dry, and she nervously ran the tip of her tongue over her parted lips. The totally provocative message it sent undid the man above her.

Tracker muttered hoarsely to himself, leaving Starfire staring after him, perplexed by his strange behavior. Outside, he walked straight to the falls, lifting his face into the spray. The frustration of having her near and being unable to touch her was an agony invented in hell. Any other woman he would have taken long ago, but Starfire was not like the other women he'd known. She had strength and courage he'd never found in any other woman. Her spirit was as free and wild as the Cheyenne she loved so much. He wanted her for his own, wanted her to want him.

If he vented his passion for her now, it would destroy what little trust he'd managed to win. But the constant restraint tore at him more each day, more each time he lay sleeplessly beside her warm body. But he refused to give in to his desires, not wanting her to fight and claw at him in hatred but to wrap her silken limbs around him and open her soft red lips for his pleasure. His vivid fantasies did not help, and he stood miserably for a long time, hoping the frigid water could calm his lusty thoughts and soothe his feverish body.

It did not work, and when he went back into the other chamber where Starfire slept in peaceful repose, her silvery hair spread upon his side of the ledge, he slumped down against his saddle by the fire, not trusting himself to approach her. He dozed fitfully until just before dawn, making love to Starfire in dreams so real he could almost smell the fragrance of her.

He finally arose, muttering an oath under his breath, and left the chamber to check the horses. They stood quietly at their picket, and Tracker walked past them and out the back opening of the chamber where he could scout the area for Cheyenne. The sun was just beginning to rise, and he climbed the steep rock ledge that rose on either side of the entrance to the cave. He moved along the cliff, looking toward the forested hill at the end of the passage that led into the cave. He dropped at once to his belly when the whinny of a horse drifted up to him. He crawled to the far edge of the cliff, keeping low, his heart pounding.

Two Cheyenne bucks, their hard faces streaked with yellow and black war paint, picked their way over the terrain below him, passing within feet of the camouflaged opening of the passage. He sucked in his breath, his rifle in readiness, but they did not detect his presence. He watched them until they disappeared into the trees, then hurried to the cave for his spyglass and a supply of ammunition.

Starfire still slept, and he did not wake her. He hurried back to his position atop the rocks, and within an hour, saw twenty painted ponies come into view. Tracker watched them closely as they scouted out the area thoroughly, then divided, half the war party moving toward the falls while the others set up camp among the trees about fifty yards from Tracker's position. They sat around a campfire, awaiting their meal, and Tracker lay very still, praying Starfire would not awaken.

Starfire came awake suddenly, sitting upright and blinking away strands of sleep. She looked around for Tracker in the darkness of the cave. Tracker had never allowed the fire to dwindle beyond a blaze, and she swung her slim legs over the edge of the shelf, knowing instinctively that something was wrong. She walked swiftly to the entrance and peered cautiously into the outer chamber.

Her heart began to hammer in excitement as she realized her long-awaited chance had come. Tracker was nowhere in sight, and she moved cautiously, oblivious to the roaring water as she tried to remember how they'd first entered the cave. She searched the shadowy walls and easily found the passageway, her hopes rising with each footstep away from her detested cell.

A horse whinnied softly when she entered the other cavern, and Starfire moved toward it quietly, stroking its velvety muzzle, murmuring soothing Cheyenne syllables. Horses! She was confident now she could escape, but petrified that Tracker might return. She quickly loosened the bridle from the picket and led the horse down a slight incline toward a soft glow of light. Hooves rang against the rocky floor, sending amplified echoes through the silent chambers, and Starfire increased her pace. She breathed easier when she ducked out into the warm sunshine, squinting from the bright glare, her eyes unaccustomed to the sun after days inside the dim, cool cave. She raised her face to the sky, shielding her eyes as she breathed in the fresh air. Her confidence rose as she started through the rocky crevice.

Tracker saw Starfire the minute she emerged from the cave, and he swore under his breath at her bad timing. He had to stop her. He glanced quickly at the stand of trees behind him before he followed in a low crouch on the rocky ledge above her. If she should clear the passage or even let out a yell, the Indians would be upon them in minutes.

Desperate to stop her before she unwittingly warned them, he trod soundlessly above her. She was moving slowly and carefully, picking her way around rocks, giving him ample time to jump her. He hung his rifle over his back, taking one last look at the Indian camp before he leaped down, grabbing the unsuspecting Starfire from the side, then rolled with her, protecting her body with his own. The horse reared in fright, thrashing his front legs in the air, neighing loudly as he backed away in panic, his hooves clattering like bells on the stones.

Tracker uttered a string of oaths, jerking Starfire upright, one palm tightly pressed over her mouth. She hung limply against him, not struggling. He realized he had knocked the breath out of her and counted himself lucky. He got one arm in a steel band around her waist and edged to the hidden opening. The Cheyenne warriors still relaxed around the fire, and Tracker headed back to the cave before Starfire could recover from her shock.

But Starfire knew help was near, and she began to scream under the huge hand, her legs kicking viciously as she clawed the back of his hand with her fingernails. He'd learned his lesson with her the last time, and his grip tightened brutally. Although she struggled furiously, she was helpless against his enormous size and strength.

Tears of despair welled in her eyes as the darkness of the cave swallowed the warm sunlight, and Starfire ceased fighting as he carried her into her prison.

Tracker knew what he had to do, and he didn't like it. But he had to get back outside, and he didn't have much time. If the Indians did find the opening, his only chance would be to pick them off from his hiding place atop the rocks. He jerked his scarf from around his neck and wrapped it around her mouth, trying not to look at her violet eyes as they glared at him in fury.

"Sorry, Starfire, I just can't take any chances," he muttered, lowering her to the ground. He tied her hands behind her back, making sure the cords were not tight. He hated himself for what he was doing, knowing she'd never forgive him, but he had no choice. He avoided her eyes as he fashioned a rope into a narrow loop and slipped it around the fragile column of her neck.

"Now listen to me, Starfire, and listen good." He tried to ignore the hatred in her glittering eyes, his voice growing gruff.

"This won't tighten any more unless you pull too hard. And if you do, you just might choke yourself to death. So it wouldn't be too smart to try to get loose."

While he spoke, he knotted the other end tightly to a rock outcrop. "You'll be fine here, as long as you stay near the fire and behave yourself. I won't be gone long."

He threw several logs on the fire, then gave the rope one last tug to make sure it was secure. His eyes went to Starfire, where she knelt by the blazing fire. Tears shone vividly in a violet gleam before she turned her face away. Tracker frowned, feeling guilty, before he headed back to keep watch over the enemy.

Alone, Starfire let the hot tears roll down her cheeks, giving vent to her disappointment. She'd almost succeeded, had been just a few feet from freedom when the white devil had grabbed her. After a few moments, she shook away her self-pity and scrambled up, walking until the rope tightened dangerously around her throat. She stopped at once, then moved to the other end, trying to pull it free from the rocks. It was impossible to loosen, and she sank to the shelf, heartsick.

She stared into the flames, the tether around her neck stretching out tautly in front of her. She was uncomfortable, the bindings cutting into her wrists, the gag making it difficult to breathe. She wondered who he had seen. Was it Raging Buffalo? Or Lone Wolf? They were so close! If she could only get to them! But it was impossible. She could hardly move, and she knew Tracker would leave her tied until they were gone.

After a long time, she lay on her side, depression settling heavily on her heart. Tears filled her eyes again as she thought of her mother, Gentle Reed. She would be worried about her, grieving her for dead. She missed her so much, missed the long rides in the sunshine with her good friend, Tree Winds. Tracker was cruel to take her away from everyone she loved, to tie her in a dark cavern like an animal when her people were so close. The fear that she would never see the Cheyenne again tightened painfully around her heart, and she wept softly at the agony of her helplessness.

In time her eyes grew heavy, and she dozed, awakening much later, shivering against the chilled air. The fire was nearly out, and she rose awkwardly, then moved toward it, but drew up abruptly as a slight scraping sound caught her attention. She turned her head slowly, cold chills undulating in a slow crawl from the base of her spine. Then she saw it.

Horror heaved her stomach into a forward roll, and she watched out of terrified eyes as a snake as thick as her arm slithered toward her, creating ghastly designs on the dusty floor, its deadly rattles held slightly erect. Buried memories oozed out of the hidden corners of her mind until she relived the long-ago terror when serpents crawled beneath her childhood skirts, their heavy coils weighing upon her legs.

She stood paralyzed as the huge serpent touched her foot, ripple after ripple of cold fear going through her as its cold body encircled her ankle, its flat, triangular head nudging its way slowly up her calf. She squeezed her eyes shut, her mind rebelling in abhorrence, as the viper coiled upon her, sucking all warmth from her flesh, until she was left as cold as the deadly parasite clinging to her legs.

Later, when the serpent slowly unwound and slid to a warmer spot near the fire, it took long moments for Starfire's shock to recede; then she was left trembling so violently that her teeth chattered audibly in the silent chamber. It took every ounce of will for her to back away, her wide, fearful eyes glued on the ugly, slit-eyed stare of the rattler. When the backs of her knees touched the stone shelf, she lay slowly upon her side, inching toward the wall until the rope around her neck drew tight. She lay frozen in abject terror then, her eyes never leaving the rattlesnake, moving lazily and at will around the fire, until the flames died and all was dark.

SIX

Tracker lay high on the rock cliff, his rifle loaded and resting across his forearm, as he intently studied the terrain below. He peered through the long spyglass, magnifying the Cheyenne braves as they moved among the dense copse of blue spruce and aspen trees below. It was a small regrouping camp, and he could make out some men resting their mounts while others scoured the surrounding woods. Scouts returned at short intervals, and Tracker decided with foreboding that they'd tracked him this far and were trying to pick up his trail again.

As he watched, a group of ten rode in, sliding with confident grace off their ponies, to seek out a tall, powerfully built man whose appearance clearly identified him as the chieftain. Each group reported to the same man, and Tracker focused the spyglass on him, wondering if he could be the one he'd bound in the nuptial tipi. He was startled to realize how curious he was to see the man Starfire would have wed.

The buck was taller than the others, with a strong, tightly muscled physique. He wore a dark loincloth, his muscular torso was streaked with yellow war paint, and long jagged black marks coursed down each lean cheek. Even from his perch in the rocks, Tracker could detect suppressed rage emanating from his erect stance and frustrated gestures. The intensity of his stern face assured Tracker that this was Lone Wolf, infuriated that his beautiful silver-haired bride had been stolen from him. An aura of unrequited injury surrounded the tough, good-looking warrior. He'd be a formidable opponent in his fury of vengeance, and Tracker would face his wrath if the cave was discovered.

A sudden flurry of activity arrested his attention, and his eyes narrowed as the Cheyenne kicked out the fires and swung bareback upon their mounts, then moved off to the east. He breathed easier, but remained where he was, watching and waiting while darkness slowly descended upon the landscape until it had swallowed the last vestiges of day. He was anxious to return to Starfire; she would be uncomfortable by now, bound as she was. He had left her alone for a long time, but he had had to make sure the Cheyenne were gone for good. He couldn't risk being surprised in the cave.

The cricket's strident song was loud and steady and the moon a pale crescent of gold over the trees when he moved surefootedly atop the high rocks. He dropped soundlessly at the opening of the cave and made his way quickly to Starfire's chamber. It was shrouded in darkness.

"Starfire? Where are you?" he called out anxiously.

He frowned as his voice faded with an eerie loneliness. She should not have allowed the fire to burn down. There had been an ample supply of wood, and she could have kicked pieces of it unto the fire. He paused uneasily, the first flickerings of fear licking at him. Unless she was gone. Panic surged, and he moved quickly toward the ashes. He threw a handful of sticks on the glowing embers, trying to kindle the fire, peering into the shadows as he fanned it into a small blaze. He saw the tether then, stretching into the dark recess of the shelf. She must have fallen asleep. She was still with him. Much relieved, he took the time to put a log on the fire. When the flames rose higher, Tracker saw her and froze.

Starfire lay rigid upon the shelf, glazed eyes focused unblinkingly on a huge rattlesnake lying beside her. The diamond-patterned coils nearly touched her cheek, and Tracker swallowed hard, standing motionless. His eyes sought Starfire where she lay as still as death, and his gut clenched painfully at her danger. He inched forward, easing his gun from his holster as he thought quickly. A shot would bring Cheyenne from miles around, or even cause a landslide. He slid the revolver back in place and slowly withdrew his knife from the scabbard on his thigh. He glanced around, afraid any wrong move on his part would cause the snake to strike.

A blanket lay on the shelf, and Tracker began to move his hand toward it. The movement caused the rattler to raise its head warily, alert to danger as it wound itself into a posture to attack. The deadly rattles began their death music inches from Starfire's frozen face. Tracker hesitated with bated breath, then moved like lightning, flinging the blanket over the snake and hurling it off the shelf with one quick jerk.

Tracker was after it at once and lunged at the snake's head as it darted from beneath the blanket. It struck at him with one deadly whipcord stroke, but he dodged its bared fangs and desperately grabbed for its head. He caught it too low but brought his blade down against the head as the thick, muscular length entwined itself around his arm. He hacked at its head over and over, until the coils finally loosened, then he threw it from him, sinking to shaky knees as he watched the serpent writhe obscenely in the throes of death.

He was at Starfire's side moments later, slitting the cords from her wrists, speaking to her soothingly in a low voice. He cut away the gag, then swept back the silky hair to remove the loop from her neck. He winced at the ugly bruise on her tender nape and murmured softly, "I'm here now, Starfire. It's all right. You're safe."

He gathered her small body close, pulling her onto his lap. Her eyes were open, unfocused horror frozen into their blue-violet depths.

"Starfire, listen to me. It's gone."

Tracker gave her a gentle shake, then held her tightly, smoothing her hair with his palm, crooning soothing Cheyenne words. He rocked her for a time, until her cold skin gradually warmed and her slender body began to tremble.

Tears welled, and she gave a pathetic little sob that wrenched Tracker's heart. He held her as tightly as he could without crushing her, and she clutched at him desperately, her soft cheeks wet with tears. She wept into his shirt, her words smothered and incoherent.

"They were on my legs . . . and Mama screamed . . . then there was blood . . ."

Tracker cradled her shuddering body, sick that he'd left her to endure such suffering.

"Did it crawl on you, sweet? Did it hurt you?" he asked, his mouth pressed against the soft silver at her temple.

Her words were breathless as she jerked with great wrenching sobs. "Raging Buffalo killed it . . . Mama had an arrow in her neck . . . and my white apron was all red . . ."

Her voice rose close to hysteria as she relived forgotten memories of her capture, and Tracker sought to comfort her.

"It's all right now, my love, you're safe," he whispered. "I'll never let anything frighten you again. I swear it."

Starfire raised tear-drenched lashes, staring into his dark, compassionate face. She never wanted to be alone in the dark again, never wanted to be afraid again. He'd saved her, he would protect her. At that moment, her fear of him slipped away and she forgot he'd taken her from her people, she forgot he was her enemy. He was the one who'd killed the snake, who wouldn't let anything ever hurt her again. Her slender arms moved slowly around his neck, her eyes like warm pools of lavender as she looked at him with a new soft trust.

Tracker stared in fascination at her lovely eyes, the long, black eyelashes spiky with tears, before his gaze dropped to her lips, shining red and moist in the dim light. He could not stop himself, and his mouth dropped to hers, caressing the incredible softness. He'd wanted to kiss her for so long, so very long; and now as her lips parted willingly, his blood raced. One large hand went to her hair, long brown fingers sliding into the soft, silvery tresses, as the other lightly touched her naked thigh, then slid slowly up the silken flesh to the curve of her hip.

She was soft, felt so unbelievably good, and his mouth moved across her fragile eyelids to one dainty, shell-like ear. He pressed gentle kisses into the hollow below, then moved slowly along the cord of her neck. As his eager mouth explored her smooth shoulder, somewhere deep in the farthest corners of his mind, conscience gnawed, warning that he was taking advantage of her vulnerable state.

But she moaned weakly as his warm lips intruded into the throat of her shirt, and he knew then he would not stop this time, not unless she made him.

Starfire drifted in a vague cocoon of pleasure, feeling his strong arms lift her easily and take her down with him. She clung to the manly strength, her loins throbbing with a life of their own, as his fiery mouth dropped nibbling kisses across her collarbone to the staccato pulse at the base of her throat. She wanted to be held, to be comforted, to be safe in the circle that his steel embrace offered. She wanted to block away for good the obscene feel of the rattlesnake as it had writhed upon her cringing flesh.

"Hold me, hold me . . ."

Her Cheyenne words were low, murmured huskily into his ear, and he groaned and found her waiting mouth hungrily. Starfire tingled all over, letting the lovely unknown tide of desire rule her actions, breathing shallowly as his gentle hands caressed her satin skin beneath the shirt. She began to quiver as his fingers released one button after another, then gently pushed the shirt aside, baring the silken perfection of her body to his pleasure.

"You are so very beautiful," he whispered in gruff awe, his eyes darkened to royal blue with the passion she aroused in him.

He lowered his head to her throat, and Starfire closed her eyes, sliding her slender fingers into the thick blond hair as his mouth pressed hot and gentle kisses along the honey flesh of her breast. She was enthralled by each new sensation, not believing such pleasure could be had from the touch of a man. She cried out in a bittersweet shock when the warmth of his lips took the rosy peak of her breast. She pressed her small body into his urgently as long ripples of reaction raced over her slowly fraying nerve endings. It was then that she began to lose touch with reality, victim of his gentle, persuasive lovemaking, groaning in protest while holding supplicating arms out to him when he rose to remove his clothes. Moments later his long, hard length was beside her, her palms against the crisp blond furring of his chest. The hardness of his desire was like a brand against her soft hips, but she felt no fear, sliding her arms around his waist, then up over the rippling, sinewy muscles of his broad shoulders. His breath caught hoarsely in her ear as she lowered her mouth trailing warm kisses across his shoulder then arched against him, sensuously moving the fullness of her breasts against his chest.

Her willing passion turned Tracker to flame, every nerve and fiber in his body craving her, aching for her, but his mind warned urgently of her virginity, shrieked at him to proceed with gentleness. Starfire's body was in a fever pitch of excitement, his expert lovemaking building the tension until she felt she could not bear the pleasure he created. She shivered all over as he moved atop her, his hips moving forward, his lips upon her brow and hair.

Starfire bit her lip at the first tingle of pain, surprised he hurt her. She began to struggle, suddenly afraid, but he held her in a gentle band of steel, whispering hoarsely into her hair, "It won't last long, sweet, and I'll never hurt you again. It's the only way. . . ."

The sudden pain was sharp, but her cry was muffled by his warm mouth upon hers, kissing her until the hurt faded. Tracker's hard body moved with hers, both his huge hands tangled in the silvery mass of her hair, his lips upon hers with a gentle forcefulness that reeled her senses. She instinctively moved with him, her small palms sliding over the iron-hard, rippling contours of his back, her grip tightening as the exquisite delight built until her fingers dug into his back as the explosion of ecstasy ripped its way through her blazing body. She arched to meet the pleasure again and again, her cries of bewilderment muffled against Tracker's wildly beating heart as they soared to infinity, starbursts of pure rapture fusing them into one.

Afterward they lay entwined, Starfire's small fingers clutching his thick hair, his arms tightened around her in fierce possession. After a time, Tracker turned on his back, pulling her tightly against his side, until she nestled comfortably in the curve of his arm.

She slept at once, warm, content, sated; but Tracker lay

awake for a long time, half awed by the passion he'd awakened in the tiny, lovely girl. She pleasured him more than any other woman he'd ever had, and the knowledge that he was the first to lie with her filled him with a special tenderness toward her. He gathered her closer, intoxicated by the sweet fragrance of her hair where it spread out in a silky, shiny swirl upon his broad chest. He closed his eyes, a smile playing at the corner of his mouth. He'd been sent to capture her, and instead he'd been captured by her. He hoped she would now be able to reconcile herself to going back with him. He intended to help her in the months ahead of them, to be with her through it all, because he'd found a treasure in this dark cave, hidden in the mountains. A treasure he meant to keep.

Starfire awakened later, her small body safely snuggled alongside the long, hard length of the big white man. She lay against his chest and could hear the strong, even thud of his heartbeat beneath her ear. She moved her palm idly over his chest, thinking of what had happened between them. He'd made her his woman, as Lone Wolf would have done if Tracker had not stolen her away. He was her enemy, a white man, but he had touched her with gentleness and awakened pleasures she could never have imagined.

It was shocking to think that she'd wanted him so desperately, but she did not feel regret and smiled at the current of warm affection which spread through her body. She raised her head and dared a quick look at his face. He was sleeping peacefully. She realize with a start that it was the first time she'd ever seen him completely relaxed. His face no longer seemed hard and forbidding, and she raised herself on one elbow to study him closely. His arms immediately tightened around her, his blue eyes open and on her face.

They stared at each other a moment, and Tracker looked at the honey skin, the long dark lashes surrounding clear violet warmth, and could not prevent his hand from reaching for her, and he traced her soft cheek with his finger.

"I'm sorry I hurt you, Starfire," he whispered.

Her eyes darted to his in surprise. The pain was already

forgotten, but she could not never forget the way his touch turned her skin to fire.

"You gave me much pleasure," she answered softly, her violet eyes showing their wonder. "What is this magic you work upon me?"

Tracker smiled at her innocence, his teeth white against his bronzed face, and she returned his smile shyly. He drew her down beside him and pulled her close. She came willingly, and he said softly, "You are my magic, my sweet, the only magic I'll ever want."

They lay together quietly, Tracker running his hand slowly over the supple curve of her back, wondering at her thoughts. He propped his head up on his hand and gazed down into her expressive eyes.

"What are you thinking?"

Starfire spoke truthfully, her delicately arched brows drawn together slightly.

"I am thinking that I am not sure I wish Raging Buffalo to cut out your sky eyes after all."

Tracker leaned back his head and laughed.

"I'll take that as a compliment."

She smiled, and he grew serious, afraid of her reaction to his next words.

"I still have to take you back, Starfire, but I'll be with you. I won't let anyone hurt you."

She was silent, her eyes downcast.

He watched her carefully and asked, "Will you trust me and go back?"

She did not answer at once; and he waited, afraid her hesitation meant she still did not trust him.

"Yes, I will trust you," she whispered.

Tracker breathed easier, but she had not promised to stay with him.

"Will you promise me you won't try to escape?"

She was silent much longer, conflicting emotions flickering across her lovely face, and he feared his hopes were too hasty, until she said in a tone so low as to be inaudible, "No, I will not escape."

Tracker's smile was quick and triumphant. They would be together, and he would make her happy, as he showed her everything she'd missed in her years with the Cheyenne. The future would be good for her; he would make sure of it. His blue eyes searched hers before he was pulled irresistibly to the softness of her lips. His mouth lowered to take them in a gentle caress that slowly exploded into the rocketing desire she ignited in him so easily.

SEVEN

Starfire watched Tracker move around the big stallion, pulling the girth tight, then checking the saddlebags. Her heart was very heavy, for it was time to leave her beloved mountains. She shivered. The many things Tracker spoke of were strange, incomprehensible, but worst of all was the knowledge that she might never see Raging Buffalo or Gentle Reed again. Or her friend Tree Winds. Tears glistened in her eyes as she wrestled with the doubts that assailed her.

Tracker finished strapping their gear, eager to be on their way. They had been in the cave for almost a month, and there had been no sign of Cheyenne in over a week. It was already early September, and he wanted to leave before early winter snows trapped them. In a way, though, he regretted having to leave the mountain hideaway. The last weeks had been good, hidden away with Starfire. He'd been amazed at her passion, and the discovery that she stirred his blood as no woman ever had. One touch and she came into his arms eagerly, her hunger rivaling his own. He smiled, glancing over to where she sat by the entrance. His grin faded when he saw the glitter of tears in her eyes.

He went to her, cradling her small face in one large palm.

"What is it, my sweet?"

She raised great amethyst eyes, the vivid violet depths brimming with sadness.

"I do not want to go."

Fear squeezed icy fingers around Tracker's heart. He had thought that as they grew comfortable with each other she'd resigned herself to leaving with him. The thought of forcing her to do anything she didn't want to do was now repugnant to him.

"Please, trust me, Starfire. I'll take care of you."

"What if I hate the way of the whites? What if I am lonely for my people?"

Her face was miserable, and her eyes begged him to understand.

Tracker could not bear her distress, the warm tears rolling down her cheeks.

"If you are not happy, I will bring you home," he said on impulse, desiring to reassure her.

Her eyes darted to his face, alive with a great vulnerable show of relief.

"Is it so? Do you promise?"

The thought of willingly returning her to Lone Wolf and the Cheyenne was totally inconceivable, but he nodded, certain she would not choose to come back after a taste of civilization. He would introduce her to every convenience, overwhelm her with luxury. He would teach her white ways so that she'd never wish to return to the hardship of Indian life. He'd never kept a woman before, never found one he wanted badly enough to even consider it. But Starfire was different. She would be his treasured, pampered love, with jewels and fine clothes and servants to wait on her. And if her white family didn't like it, they could be damned. Starfire was his now, and he'd never let her go.

Starfire smiled tremulously, and Tracker lifted her in his arms, his lips seeking her softness, as always the smell of her, the touch of her, arousing him until he could not think. The kiss was long and leisurely, until he lowered her to her feet, muttering hoarsely, "You make me forget everything but you, sweet. But we must go, so come."

He lifted her easily to her saddle, and she straddled the horse gracefully, ignoring the reins as she grabbed the mane with small, sure hands. She had a lot to learn about white ways, and they might as well start now.

"You must learn to guide him with the reins."

She obediently picked them up, lifting her slim nose disdainfully as she guided the horse skillfully with her knees.

He swung into his own saddle, grinning, as he preceded her through the narrow passage. It would not be easy to teach his love white ways.

The mountain air was crisp and clean, the rugged, tree-spiked terrain breathtakingly beautiful. It would take about three days to reach his house in Denver, and Tracker kept them moving at a brisk pace, still wary for war parties. He knew the Cheyenne would not give up easily, especially when the treasure was Starfire.

They made good time, and Starfire never complained about the long hours in the saddle, but cuddled against him happily as they lay on soft buffalo robes beneath the stars at night. On the last day out from town, snow threatened and the air grew colder. Great rolling dark clouds indicated snowfalls in the higher elevations, but they were nearly out of the mountains, where they were less likely to run into Cheyenne. Starfire's tribe rarely came so far south but kept to the north or west of Denver. Tracker began to relax a bit, although he knew Lone Wolf still searched for his beautiful bride. But Tracker was equally determined that no one would ever take her away from him. He glanced back at her as the wind whipped her cloak and swirled her hair off her shoulders.

She looked up and smiled at him, and Tracker felt his loins tighten, amazed what she could do to him with one soft look. They followed a small, angry stream, the rushing and gurgling water loud in their ears. They carefully picked their way along the rock-strewn bank, until Tracker pulled back on his reins, squinting at the gray cloud bank on the horizon. They'd reached a point where they could ford the stream safely, and he motioned for Starfire to wait. She nodded and sat her horse patiently while he urged his stallion into the cold water. The current was swift but shallow, and he waded his horse across, spurring him up onto the opposite bank. Now sure that Starfire could cross safely, he turned to wave her forward, but froze when he saw movement downstream. It was a band of Cheyenne, riding parallel to the river, and his eyes riveted on them as they continued to move in the opposite direction. The war party had not seen them, and they were on the other side of the river,

Starfire's side. He turned in sudden dread to see if she had spotted them.

Starfire sat upon her mount, gazing at the dark hills huddled in front of the snowcapped peaks of her beloved land. She was sad, her heart still crying to see her Indian mother and father again. Leaving with the big white man was the most difficult decision she'd ever made. It gave her quivers of uncertainty even now to think of leaving her whole life behind. It especially saddened her to think she could not even say goodbye to them. They would be so very worried about her.

She stared despondently at the rippling water as it cascaded angrily over rocks and snags, then raised her eyes, idly looking down the stream.

Tracker watched, his throat clogging as she caught sight of the horsemen. She suddenly straightened and leaned forward, her eyes intent on the distant Indians. Tracker could never cross the stream in time to catch her if she galloped to join them, so he sat stiff and tense, watching. He knew the moment that she realized they were Cheyenne, because pure joy lit up her lovely face, then immediately afterward, her smile faded as she slowly turned her eyes to him.

Their gaze met and fused, blotting out the rush of the current and the rustle of the trees in the wind. Time stood still, all reality dissolving beneath his silent appeal and her tortured indecision. Starfire could not move, could not break his hold on her, until her horse shifted restlessly beneath her. She tore her eyes from him and sought the riders in the distance.

Tracker held his breath, reading in her face the intense desire to join them. She was frowning, both hands gripping the saddle horn, torn, as her desire to stay with Tracker warred with her need to return to her people. He was suddenly afraid, sure she would leave; and he jerked his horse's head toward the water. He could not let her go. He halted as her face turned to him again, the tension draining away to be replaced by a sad resignation. She cast one last wistful look at the far-off band of Indians, then waded her horse into the creek.

Relief streaked through the man across the water, exhilaration painting a wide smile across his handsome features. He swung off the horse exultantly, waiting as she slowly came to him. Unshed tears darkened the violet eyes, and he pulled her down into the steel cradle of his arms. She was shivering, and he held her close, his warm lips upon her hair.

"You won't regret it, sweet. I swear you won't," he promised her.

After the encounter with the Cheyenne, Tracker rode more slowly, feeling secure in the knowledge that she had willingly chosen to stay with him. She had had her chance to leave him, and she had trusted him. He was elated, but regretted that he couldn't break through her silent melancholy. But his own spirits soared high, because they were nearing Denver and the end of their journey.

"Tonight you'll sleep in a real bed," he told her with a smile, and she looked blankly at him. His words meant nothing to her, for buffalo robes spread upon the ground were the only bed she'd ever known.

Tracker frowned slightly and asked, "Have you never seen another white man? Not in all the years with your tribe?"

Starfire gazed innocently at him. "No one but Father Donegal," she replied.

"Your tribe did not trade with the whites?"

It was hard to believe she was so inexperienced about the world.

"Our chiefs met wasichus at times. But Raging Buffalo kept me hidden away. He was afraid they would try to take me, and he did not wish to kill a wasichu."

Tracker stared at her delicately chiseled profile, knowing exactly how Raging Buffalo had felt. But he knew her total ignorance would make her adjustment to civilization more difficult. He smiled tenderly at her, vowing he would do everything in his power to make it easier for her. And with her beauty and intelligence, she would be accepted quickly, and her childhood with the Indians would become part of the past.

Denver was a young town, founded a mere five years before, and the wide, deeply rutted streets proclaimed its youth. The town slept as Tracker's horse clopped through the silent darkness. Starfire had grown weary of the journey, and not wishing to stop for the night so close to town,

Tracker had taken her on his stallion in front of him. She now lay nestled in his arms, feeling tiny and warm and sleepy.

He walked his horse slowly through the night, his destination a large house on a rise on the eastern perimeter of the settlement. He was glad the moonless night cloaked their arrival. It would spare him from answering questions about the beautiful girl slumbering so peacefully in front of him. He was not ready to share her. Not yet. Not with anyone.

Weary himself, he drew up before the dark house, then held her securely as he slid off his horse. She was exhausted, and he wanted her to sleep as long as possible. She'd been through much in the last weeks, and as they rode through the silent town he had resolved to shield her from further unhappiness. He walked up the wooden stairs, his footsteps soundless in his moccasins. The carved front door was locked, and he kicked at it a few times, then waited.

Minutes later, light appeared at a window on his left. Holding Starfire's slight weight easily, he waited for the door to open, then grinned at the little man dressed in a long white nightshirt who was grumbling crankily as he raised his lamp.

"A man can't even sleep the night through anymore without somebody having to come and disturb him . . ."

Tracker smiled as the light shone upon his face, and James Parker's sleepy eyes widened. He began to stutter then, as Tracker pushed past him.

"Sir . . . sir, we had no idea you were coming. We didn't get a message to expect you."

Tracker hesitated just inside, the dim light illuminating a circle around them in the darkened hall, the gilt-edged tables and velvet chairs only vague outlines in the deep shadows around the walls.

"I didn't send one, Parker. But it doesn't matter. Just get the master suite ready. We have a guest."

The servant's eyes dropped for the first time to the small bundle in Tracker's arms, his eyes widening as Starfire stirred, turning her face toward Tracker's chest. Her long, silvery tresses fell free, tumbling over Tracker's arm, and Parker tried to hide his initial shock. He was accustomed to his young employer's female companions, but never before had he brought an unconscious, scantily clad one home with him in the dead of the night.

"Is she ill, sir?" he asked falteringly.

Tracker's teeth gleamed white for an instant, and he gave a low laugh.

"She's just asleep, and I want her to stay that way, so you'd better hurry up and get the room ready."

He started for the wide staircase at the rear of the hall, and Parker hurried after him.

"Which guestroom do you want for her, sir?"

Tracker's blue eyes glinted amusement.

"I made no mention of any guestroom, Parker. I said the master suite."

"But . . . sir, I . . ."

Tracker cut him off abruptly, ignoring his offended sense of propriety, as he started up the steps.

"Never mind the sermon, Parker. I don't intend to hold her in this chilly hall all night, so I'd appreciate it if you'd do as I say."

The old man shook his head, appalled at Tracker's intentions, but he rushed past him up the steps to do as he'd been instructed. His young master was never one to be overly worried about appearances, but at least when he'd had other female houseguests, a guestroom had been prepared, even though the bed was never used.

He shook his head as he hurried across the landing and threw open the doors of the master bedroom. He moved to the large brass bed and pulled back the coverlets. The room was cold, so he went directly to the marble fireplace and lit the fire that was always laid in readiness for just such an occasion.

Tracker lowered Starfire gently to the bed, covering her carefully with the silken linens. She moved slightly, opening sleepy violet eyes long enough to breathe his name, before she closed heavy black lashes and slept again. He bent to brush the soft hair away from her temples, staring tenderly down at her, entranced at her innocent beauty.

He was sharply brought back to the present when Parker cleared his throat in embarrassment, and he turned, feeling a bit foolish.

"That will be all, Parker. Thank you."

"Very good, sir. Goodnight."

Parker backed out the door, glad that his master was safe at home again, despite his reservations about the young lady in his bed. He wondered how long either one would stay; his employer wasn't known to keep one woman in his bed for long, or stay in town for any stretch of time.

Starfire opened sleepy eyes slowly, her head cradled upon Tracker's bare shoulder, his strong arms holding her slim body possessively close. It was not the first time she had awakened in his arms, and she smiled dreamily, snuggling closer to him. She was still drowsy, and her thick lashes drifted together again, and the steady thud of Tracker's heart lulled her back into a half-sleep. She dozed contentedly until the faraway sound of a woman singing snapped open her eyes. She glanced around quickly, her fragile jaw dropping a degree.

The bedroom was large and resplendently decorated, and Starfire's eyes widened at the rich draperies of royal blue velvet, hung with gold tassels. Her gaze moved slowly to the huge fireplace and paused at the golden, fan-shaped andirons. The place was full of strange and beautiful objects, with many more upon the walls. She stared hard at everything, then sat upon her heels, her long silvery hair tumbling around her naked shoulders. She sat unmoving, her eyes sweeping the room again, awe suffusing her beautiful face.

Forgetting the woman's voice, she looked down at Tracker, who slept on his back, one arm flung over his head, and the other outstretched where it had fallen when she'd moved. They were atop a large, shiny metal rack, and she peered over the side to find they were several feet off the ground. The white man's bed, she mused wonderingly, and ran her small hand across the gold threads embroidered into the red satin coverlet. It felt so good to her fingers that she brought it before her eyes for a closer examination.

Everything was so very pretty, with more colors than she'd ever seen before. Except in the glory of the autumn trees. She inched toward the edge of the bed, shocked when the mattress moved with her. Oblivious now of Tracker, she climbed down, her eyes still moving over the wondrous place. She looked down as her feet touched the thick Persian carpet. It felt soft to her bare feet, even softer than buffalo fur, and she knelt to touch it, marveling that it covered all the floor.

She had no idea where she was, but everything was new and exciting to look upon. Her curiosity sent her to each foreign object. She touched the gold brocade wingback chairs, then gazed into a picture of a wide river in the mountains. She ran her fingers over the marble mantel, then jumped, whirling around, when the tall grandfather clock in the corner hollowly bonged the hour.

Starfire eyed the frightening contraption warily, noting with a hint of trepidation the swinging pendulum in the lower glass case. Suddenly afraid of it, she ran quickly to the bed, scrambling into Tracker's arms.

Tracker was alert to her fear at once, raising himself on one elbow and drawing the other around her as she pressed close to him.

"What is it, sweet?" he asked.

She shivered, burying her face in his shoulder, muffling her words. "There is something in the corner. It lives, I think."

Frowning, Tracker sat up and looked around the room. "Where?"

Starfire sneaked a hesitant glance over her shoulder, pointing an accusing finger at the silent clock.

"What? The clock?"

"Clock?"

At her confused expression, he looked at the corner again, realization dawning. He threw back his head and boomed out a laugh, then cut it off abruptly at her startled look.

"It won't hurt you, Starfire," he explained, trying hard not to smile. "It can't move, it just tells you the time."

Starfire was not convinced, watching the pendulum skeptically.

"But it did move, Tracker! It still moves! And it spoke loudly."

He laughed again, and she stared into his eyes, twinkling in amusement, then moved away, hurt by his light treatment of her fears.

At once regretful, he drew her back into his arms, feeling a prickle of shame. He must watch himself and be more sensitive to her feelings, or he might lose her.

"I'm sorry, Starfire, I didn't mean to laugh at you."

Pacified and feeling warm and safe in his strong arms, she snuggled close, completely unaware of the wide grin that still split Tracker's face above her head. A moment passed while he feathered soft kisses along her temple, lips still curved in indulgent amusement, until Starfire sat up, distrustfully pointing at the tall timepiece.

"If it doesn't live, why is it moving?"

"It moves because . . ." He was suddenly at a loss of words. How could he explain the intricate mechanism of a clock to a girl like Starfire? He floundered momentarily, before he finished vaguely, "It has to move to keep the correct time."

"But why?"

"So white men will know exactly what time of day it is."

Her delicately arched eyebrows formed a thoughtful V as she considered his words.

"Why can he not look into the sky at the sun, like my people?" she asked seriously.

He looked down at her tenderly, knowing that she would never understand why white men lived by regulated time, not after the free and easy existence of the Cheyenne.

"Ah, Starfire, it really isn't that important. Some men just act as if it is."

She looked dubious, and he spoke, wanting to ease the furrow of confusion on her smooth brow.

"Enough about the clock, Starfire. How do you like my house?"

Her eyes scanned the room, not sure what she thought about it.

"I do not know. It is strange and hard to understand."

At the apprehension in her voice, Tracker squeezed her small hand. "It will be better in time. When you get used to everything, it will be easier to understand. I'll teach you myself."

He spoke earnestly, with warmth in his blue eyes; and Starfire shrugged off her fears, endowing him with a brilliant smile that took his breath away. He stared at her fragile beauty in wonder, smiling at her, as he leaned close to her, murmuring softly against her lips.

"And I'll begin now, my sweet, by teaching you the most enjoyable use of the white man's bed."

He pressed her gently backward into the silken pillows, but Starfire smiled wickedly to herself, deciding she would teach Tracker a lesson for laughing at her fears.

"No," she said, pulling away and crouching at his side. "You will suffer for laughing at me."

Logan frowned slightly, surprised Starfire would deny him. It had never happened before; she was usually as eager as he for their lovemaking. He looked at her sensuous smile, at her violet eyes, half veiled by long black lashes, and the totally seductive look in them sent his heart into a faster cadence. He lay back and smiled as Starfire swung one slim leg over him, taking his wrists in her hands as she held them on either side of his head.

"You are at my mercy now," she said softly, leaning forward until the softness of her breasts brushed teasingly against his furred chest. She smiled, rubbing silky skin slowly over him, tingling his nerves and Logan gasped as her lips began a fiery descent at the middle of his chest.

Starfire savored the role of seductress as she tightened her naked thighs against his sides. Her own body was warm and ready, but she continued to kiss him, enjoying the taste of his heated skin. Logan groaned, his blood beginning to pulsate.

"Enough," he muttered thickly, and Starfire's laugh was low and throaty as he broke her hold and captured her wrists, imprisoning them behind her back. He rose to his knees, and Starfire stared into his eyes, her soft breasts touching the molded steel of his chest. He raised her slowly, until their lips nearly touched.

"Now you are at my mercy," he breathed in her ear. "What should I do with such a lovely captive?"

"I am yours, my Tracker," she murmured. "Do anything you wish with me."

Her violet eyes glowed with undisguised love, and something in the way she'd said her words made Tracker swallow hard. He released his grip, and Starfire slid soft arms around his neck. Their lips sought each other, warm, hungry, loving, as Logan crushed her slight weight against his chest, then rolled with her upon the silken coverlet, all thoughts gone in their eagerness to give all their hearts, all their souls to the spiraling pleasure of their love.

EIGHT

Much later, Tracker led Starfire into the dining room, standing back to view her reaction. She walked along the polished table, then gazed up in awed wonder at the intricate crystal chandelier, until Parker pushed through the swinging doors that led to the kitchen.

"Good morning, sir, Miss."

Starfire looked startled, then darted a questioning look up at Tracker. He put his palm beneath her elbow reassuringly and led her to the table.

"Starfire, this is my butler, Mr. Parker. Parker, allow me to present my guest, Starfire."

"I'm pleased to meet you, Miss Starfire."

Parker tried not to reveal his shock at her sole garment, a huge, soiled gentlemen's shirt. His eyes were a wee bit sympathetic, but friendly, and Starfire caught his honest warmth, rewarding him with a dazzling smile.

Quite disarmed by the tiny girl's loveliness, Parker pulled out a chair for her, mentally chastising his young master for allowing the beautiful child to wear such rags.

Starfire looked blankly at the chair being held for her, then to Tracker for help.

"Sit down, Starfire," he instructed, and as Parker gallantly pushed her close to the table, Tracker suppressed a grin at her startled expression.

"Parker, I'd like a word with you. I'll be right back, sweet."

They left her gazing eagerly around the room, and Tracker paused in the hall and spoke in a low voice.

"We'll be here about three weeks, Parker, but it would

be better if no one knows we're in town. I hope you and Mrs. Parker will be discreet about our presence."

Parker nodded solemnly.

"And another thing. I'd like Mrs. Parker to prepare both of us a bath while we're dining. We've been on the trail for days."

"Yes sir."

Parker stood waiting, and Tracker hesitated, then answered the unasked questions hovering on Parker's face.

"She's lived with the Cheyenne since she was three. Everything is new and strange to her, and I would appreciate it if you and your wife would help her adjust in any way you can."

"Yes sir, we'd be delighted. She's such a lovely little lass."

Tracker grinned, agreeing wholeheartedly, then paused at the door. "And Parker . . ." He grinned sheepishly. "Make that a bubblebath for her, if you will."

Before Parker could respond, Tracker left him and entered the dining room. Starfire held a silver fork close before her eyes, turning it over as she examined it in detail.

Tracker smiled at her absorption.

"That's a fork, my sweet. You eat with it."

It seemed ridiculous to her. Why would one need such a thing? With five fingers on each hand it seemed so useless. "Why?"

Patiently, Tracker tried to explain. "White people do not eat with their fingers. It's not good manners."

"What are manners?"

Tracker took a deep breath, realizing Starfire's education would take a very long time. There were such gaps in her experience that only time would fill. He was phrasing an explanation of the fork when Mrs. Parker backed through the doorway, carrying a silver tray loaded with dishes.

"Hello, sir, it's good to have you home again! You and your little guest."

She smiled engagingly at Starfire, who took in her benevolent face with instant liking. Agatha Parker was a tiny woman with a stocky, maternal build and snow-white hair pulled severely into a bun at her nape. Her wire-rimmed spectacles were perched upon a small pug nose, and the lively blue eyes behind them took in every detail of Starfire's appearance.

"And what a lovely child you be, dearie. I do hope you like eggs and biscuits."

Starfire returned her bright smile, wondering what eggs and biscuits could be. Tracker leaned back, his smiling blue eyes on Starfire's face, as she watched Mrs. Parker's every movement while she served them bountiful portions of her excellent cooking.

Mrs. Parker bustled out, and Starfire listened carefully as Tracker told her the name of each dish. She stared skeptically at the mounds of strange, yellow food, reluctant to put any in her mouth. Tracker grinned at her hesitation.

"It's very good, Starfire. Look, this is how you use a fork," he urged.

He showed her how to use it, taking several bites of scrambled eggs.

"See, it's not hard."

She watched him closely, then carefully dipped up a bite of the eggs, watching in surprise as they slid from the fork, landing with a wet plop in her lap. Tracker threw back his head and laughed at her frown.

"It takes some practice. Why don't you try the spoon? It's easier."

Starfire took the spoon he held out to her and tried again, this time managing to deposit a morsel into her mouth. Her expression of concentration changed to pleasure, and glowing eyes found his.

"It is good," she exclaimed with her mouth still full, scooping more into her spoon.

The meal was a success, with Starfire exclaiming with delight over each new taste, but adamantly refusing to touch the strong black coffee.

"It is bitter. I cannot drink it."

Tracker poured her a cup of hot chocolate and was rewarded as her violet eyes closed in ecstasy.

"It is wonderful, Tracker." She drank more, and one corner of Tracker's mouth lifted at the brown mustache it left under her dainty nose. "I have never had anything like it."

"It has sugar in it, Starfire. That's what makes it taste so good," he explained.

Things were turning out even better than he'd expected. Even at this early stage, she was adjusting well, seeming to welcome and enjoy each new experience. It would just take time, as much as she needed, which was something Tracker was more than willing to give her.

After three more cups of chocolate, Tracker led her back upstairs. At one side of the bedroom there was a draped bathing alcove, and he drew back the curtain for Starfire. She gazed down at the huge hip bath, bewildered by the curious white foam that bubbled up over the edge.

"This is a bathtub, sweet, and I think you're going to find it quite enjoyable."

He scooped up a handful of the scented foam and held it under her nose.

"It's like flowers," she said happily.

"You get in it to bathe. Here, let me help you."

Starfire stood docilely, smiling up at him, as he undid her buttons, then pushed the shirt away, letting it fall around her feet. His eyes roamed at will over her slim, high-breasted body, and she met his eyes without embarrassment, her exquisite eyes soft with love. His breath quickened, and he put one arm around her small waist, lifting her against his chest, their lips meeting hungrily.

She twined her arms around his neck, and his lips went to the side of her throat.

"Woman, I'll never get anything done with you in this house," he whispered hoarsely, before he swung her into his arms and lowered her into the bath.

Starfire gasped, then sank to her shoulders in the warm bubbles, losing herself to the lovely, relaxed feeling. She leaned her head against the padded back, emitting a long sigh of pleasure.

Tracker sat back in a chair, captivated by the sight of the satiny flesh of her breasts where they broke the surface of the water in provocative mounds. Starfire opened contented eyes, and happiness forged the purple depths into sparkling amethysts.

"This is very wonderful, Tracker. I think I shall like your house very much."

Every hardship he'd faced since his first meeting with Alfred Huddleston was made worthwhile by the loving expression upon her beautiful face. He bent and grazed her lips, unable to resist tracing one fingertip over the wet flesh to touch the soft pink crest that was only partially hidden by the bubbles. It sprang to life under his gentle caress, and he leaned close. Starfire's hands went around his neck immediately, and she lifted herself up against him. Tracker was pleased at her quick passion, kissing her lightly as he stood.

"You're a temptress. I'm already fighting the urge to get in there with you."

She smiled, and he gave her one last lingering look, then left her alone to enjoy the newfound delights of bathing.

Starfire leaned her head back, closed her eyes, and thought. The white man's bath was wonderful, the water so warm and fragrant. At home, she had bathed in cold river water in the summers, and in melted snow during the long, hard winter. Tracker had told her the truth. The white man's life was most wondrous. Everything was so soft and clean and easy. Never had she eaten food that Raging Buffalo had not killed in a hunt, but Tracker's food was brought to him on shiny trays. She sighed, her initial fear of Tracker almost forgotten, eagerly anticipating the next remarkable surprise that Tracker would show to her.

Downstairs, Tracker entered the kitchen in time to catch the end of the Parker's conversation about Starfire.

"Such a wee little girl, Jamie, but a lovely one, she is. I do hope he will treat her better than his other women."

Before her husband could answer her, Tracker spoke from the door. "I have no intention of mistreating Starfire, Mrs. Parker. I am not the monster you seem to think."

Mrs. Parker gasped in dismay, then, seeing the glint of amusement in his eyes, she scolded him affectionately with the familiarity of an old and trusted friend.

"I declare you move about like a savage, and I don't care, the little one upstairs is an innocent. I just know she is. She shouldn't be hurt any more. Growing up with the Indians was horrible enough," she clucked.

"You can rest easy on that account, Mrs. Parker. Hurting her is the last thing I'd ever do." She smiled, and he went on, "But now I'd like you to do something for me, if you will."

Mrs. Parker untied her apron, reaching for the serviceable black bonnet hanging on a brass hook by the door.

"Glad to, sir. What you be needing?"

"Starfire needs some clothes." Tracker hid a smile at their quick nods of agreement. "Spare no expense and get her everything she'll need. Can you estimate her size?"

"Yes sir. She's as little as a minute, she is."

"Good." He spun on his heel, then turned and tossed over his shoulder, "Oh, and, uh, Parker, you might as well go with her. I won't be needing you for a while."

Tracker watched the door close after them, knowing he could trust his two loyal friends. He grinned suddenly, and with a hoot, headed upstairs, fully intending to join Starfire in the sudsy bath.

Starfire sat in the deep tub, luxuriating in the perfumed water, entirely relaxed. She curved her lips slightly at Tracker as he entered the room, and he dragged a chair to a spot near the tub, where he could feast his eyes on the tiny droplets of water glistening on her smooth, golden skin. He turned it around and straddled it, bracing his arms on the back, his gaze intent on the loveliness before him.

"Do you know how very beautiful you are, Starfire?"

She met his eyes, answering without guile.

"I've never seen myself, except in the river water, but Lone Wolf told me many times that I pleased him greatly."

She swiveled to retrieve the cloth in the water, missing the sudden tension to Tracker's square jaw. She turned to face him then, and continued speaking, unaware that her innocent words had cut deep.

"I do not like my white hair, though. I wish it were as black as midnight, as Tree Winds' is."

Tracker tried to ignore the hard coil of jealousy hardening inside his chest, but when Starfire stared sadly at the surface of the water and whispered, "I miss them all," Tracker stiffened.

His blond brows met in a massive frown, and Starfire
looked up quickly when he rose in one swift, angry movement and glared down at her.

"I have sent for clothes for you," he said coldly. "I'll see
you after you're dressed."

Starfire watched him leave, perplexed at his sudden,
unprovoked anger, then shrugged and sank deeper into
the lovely warm water.

Tracker strode to his library, grabbed a bottle of
brandy, and took it to the guestroom where his own tub
had been prepared. He took a long draft straight from
the bottle, then tossed off his fringed deerskin shirt and
leggings and eased into the warm water, thinking jealously of the tall, lean Cheyenne that Starfire had wanted
to marry.

Grimacing, he took another deep swallow, then rested
his head against the rim and closed his eyes. He was surprised by his reaction. He'd never before experienced the
rush of emotion which filled him. He'd always scorned men
who let a woman rule their actions, but even the thought
of Starfire with another man brought a tide of fury expand-
ing against his chest. He tried to calm himself, knowing
full well that she had done nothing to warrant his burst
of ire. She'd mentioned a name and he'd overreacted to it. He
would have to work to control his possessiveness, he decided with a self-mocking smile. After all, Starfire had
been a virgin when he'd first made love to her, and no man
had touched her since. Or ever would, he vowed. Lone Wolf
had not been intimate with her, and if she'd wanted to return to him, she'd had the chance at the river. But if mere
thoughts could provoke such anger in him, what would the
actual attention of another man do to him? The thought
was unsettling, and he thrust it out of his mind, thinking
instead how good her skin would smell when he pulled her
into his arms.

He was still thinking about it when he lathered his face,
eager to shave off the long winter's growth of beard. It was
the first bath he'd had in months, and he felt invigorated
as he put on the unaccustomed white man's clothes. The
white silk shirt and tan breeches felt very strange after
months in buckskins, making him wonder how Starfire
would like her new clothes. Something told him her re-

sponse would be negative, but he could already envision her in clothes complementing her great beauty.

Suddenly anxious to see her, he started toward the bedroom, but stopped on the landing when Mrs. Parker entered the hall below, both arms full of boxes. He changed course and went to meet her, and she laid most of her purchases on the hall table.

"There you are, sir. Everything's all taken care of."

"Did you have any trouble?"

Mrs. Parker shook her head as she pulled loose the strings on her bonnet. "No sir, not a bit."

"Good. Now I have to ask you one more favor. Would you take those up and help Starfire to dress? She's still in the bath, I'd imagine. She's finding it most delightful."

"I'd be happy to, sir. I'm looking forward to seeing the little lass in decent clothes. And you look a mite better yourself, if I might say so," she observed tartly.

Tracker laughed, then retired to the den to wait. He found himself pacing impatiently, eager to see Starfire again, and the half hour that passed seemed more like half a day. He turned quickly when Mrs. Parker finally spoke from the hall door. She gave a little shrug as she glanced down at the articles in her hands.

"I'm afraid I couldn't persuade the little one to wear these, sir. Although I did try to explain."

She held a corset in one hand and a pair of high button shoes in the other. Tracker broke into a grin, not the least bit surprised at Starfire's refusal. If Mrs. Parker had managed to get her to wear the rest of it, she was doing well.

"You did fine, Mrs. Parker. She doesn't need a corset, anyway."

His housekeeper's face darkened under a crimson blush, but his thoughts were upstairs, and he took the steps two at a time. When he opened the door, he found Starfire staring out the paned window.

"Starfire?"

She turned slowly, refusing to look at him, her face solemn and unhappy. Her gown was pale lavender silk with a low square neckline, and its bodice was tight, trimmed with a soft white ruffling. Lace edged the cuffs and hem, and the color complemented her blond beauty to perfection. Tracker's breath caught as he realized she was even more exquisite than he'd imagined. He closed the door softly, his eyes moving over her figure in open admiration.

"You look beautiful, Starfire."

She faced him then, her face angry, but her expression faded as she saw his clean-shaven jaw. She stared at his lean, smooth cheeks in astonishment, thinking he looked very handsome, but very different.

"Where is the hair upon your face?"

"I shaved it."

She didn't speak, studying him as if she didn't really know him.

"How do you like your dress?"

His beard was forgotten then, as she spit out with low, rebellious venom, "I do *not* like it! It is tight here." She gestured to her bodice, and Tracker's eyes noted with pleasure the soft swelling of her satiny breasts above the lace. "And all this makes it hard to walk."

She showed him, taking a few angry steps down the room, then viciously kicking at her long skirt and petticoats. Her fragile chin tightened into an obstinate slant.

"I hate them. I will not wear them."

Tracker walked across the room and pulled her resisting body close.

"You'll get used to them, sweet, and you look lovely."

At her baleful look, he said, "Come, I have a present for you."

She allowed him to pull her beside him on the bed, her eyes on his naked face, noting for the first time a small cleft in his chin. She resisted the urge to touch it as Tracker spoke.

"Do you remember, Starfire, when I compared your eyes to amethysts?"

Starfire nodded sullenly, pulling petulantly at the tight buttons of the bodice. She stopped, her eyes widening as he took a small velvet case from his pocket, opened it, and raised a slender golden chain before her eyes. On it hung a large amethyst, set in beautiful swirling scallops of gold filigree. She touched it with one finger, staring in fascination as it caught the light and flashed purple fire.

"It is very beautiful."

Tracker smiled, opening his closed fist to reveal a matching amethyst ring. He took her hand and slipped it on her tapered finger.

She gasped at its beauty, admiring it as she lifted wondering eyes to Tracker.

"Do my eyes really glow with the same fire as these?"

He could not speak, nearly losing himself in the depths of the shining orbs she described, then uttered huskily, "Yes, but these stones are not nearly so lovely."

He fastened the slender chain around her throat, following the large amethyst in fascination as it settled into the shadowed softness between her swelling breasts.

"Come, I'll show you."

He stood, then led her into the adjoining dressing room, where he guided her to a bench before an ornate golden-framed mirror. Starfire sat down; staring at her reflection in awe, lips parted. She reached out and touched the glass with the tips of her slender fingers. "How can this be, Tracker? I am here, and I am there?"

Not waiting for his answer, she lifted the heavy jewel to a spot near her eyes. After a long moment's comparison, she faced Tracker, where he loomed in the mirror behind her.

"You are right. They are exactly the same."

Her words were simply honest, and Tracker smiled fondly before he leaned down and drew her into his embrace, as always intoxicated by her sweet warmth.

The three weeks passed much too quickly, and when Tracker sought out Starfire, he was more than reluctant to take her to the scheduled meeting with Huddleston. He found her in the front parlor, and he paused at the door to admire her where she sat quietly beside the fire, her eyes on her folded hands. She was dressed in deep rose, the velvet skirt draped becomingly over a pale pink underskirt of satin. Mrs. Parker had artfully arranged the heavy silver hair into fashionable ringlets, then pinned the shining mass behind one ear, and after a good bit of cajolery, Tracker had persuaded her to wear the small white shoes.

His eyes dropped to the satiny flesh of her breasts, soft

and tempting above the lace insert. Much more bare skin than he wished other men to see. She always wore the amethyst necklace, and the heavy stone rose and fell with each rapid breath, alerting Tracker of her anxiety about the coming meeting.

"Are you ready, Starfire?" he asked gently, already regretting that she had to be shared now with others. They'd spent the last weeks wrapped in the wonder of each other's company, Tracker leaving her only occasionally to check on the status of his business. Even then he had rushed back to her eagerly, jealously guarding their time together.

Starfire had not heard him enter the room, and she looked at him quickly, clasping trembling hands tightly in her skirt. He stood at the doorway, big and handsome, and a slight tremor ran through her as she took in his immaculate appearance. Since they'd come to his house, he no longer wore the fringed garments of her people but dressed like a white man. He had told her the names of all his clothes, and she tried to remember them now. But he'd taught her so much in the last weeks she'd begun to wonder if she would ever learn it all.

His coat was a rich blue, with a shorter satin one beneath it. The short one was called a waistcoat, she recalled, and it was the same azure color as his eyes. His pants were dark blue, like his coat, and he wore tall, shiny black boots instead of his knee-high moccasins. His eyes radiated the warmth they so often possessed.

He smiled, but she could not return it. Not with her stomach twisted into painful knots of fear.

"I am very afraid."

Tracker came to her at once, drawing her up against his broad chest. She slipped her arms around his muscled waist and pressed herself against him.

"There is nothing to fear, I promise. I'll be with you all the time."

Shivering, she laid her cheek against his coat and closed her eyes.

"You will protect me, for I am your woman," he heard her whisper fiercely.

It was the only real comfort she had, and Tracker smiled against the top of her soft hair.

"Yes, love, I will. For you are most definitely my woman," he promised.

Outside, it was near dusk, and he lifted Starfire into the carriage. Despite his reassurances to her, Tracker was loath to return her to her family. Even though he would remain with her, a vague uneasiness plagued his mind. Perhaps he was just reluctant to share her with anyone else. The last few weeks had been most enjoyable. Even the Parkers hated to see her go, though in the past, Tracker admitted to himself ruefully, they had usually been glad to see the last of his lady friends.

They headed for the Cherokee Hotel, which was located next to the Criterion Saloon, a rowdy establishment frequented by a wild band of young bloods called the Bummers. Both places were owned by Charley Harrison, a man Tracker did not like or trust. As they approached, Tracker wished he'd insisted upon a more genteel rendezvous point; he didn't like the idea of taking Starfire into the seedier sections of town. He still wished she were safe at home with the Parkers, but Huddleston would need to see her with his own eyes before he would reveal the identity of her grandparents. Tracker frowned, tempted greatly to turn around and keep her for his own, and Huddleston be damned. But she had a right to know her own family, and he tried to resign himself to that fact as they drew up before the hotel.

When they alighted, Starfire was still trembling slightly, and he said reassuringly, "I won't let anything happen to you. Ever." He took her arm and led her across the porch, their footsteps clomping hollowly upon the wooden planking. Tracker held the door open for her, then kept her close by his side, one arm protectively around her waist.

There were several men inside the lobby, and Tracker was suddenly glad for the long velvet cloak that hid her delectable figure from their view. Even now, they stared with gaping mouths at Starfire's beauty, until they noted the forbidding glare of the giant with her. Despite Tracker's fierce appearance, most hazarded a second look, believing Starfire well worth the risk.

They approached the desk, Tracker already annoyed at the young clerk, whose eyes did not leave Starfire's face, even when Tracker spoke to him.

"Is there an Alfred Huddleston registered here?" Tracker repeated harshly.

"Yes sir," the clerk answered automatically, smiling vacuously at Starfire, until Tracker's eyebrows hunched together in a thunderous scowl.

"He's in room three, upstairs on your right." He paused, losing his train of thought as Starfire lifted her incredible violet eyes to him. At Tracker's obvious anger, he went on quickly, making a determined effort to keep his eyes off the beautiful lady.

"Are you Tracker?" Tracker nodded curtly, and he finished, "He's been expecting you, sir."

Tracker took Starfire's arm and propelled her quickly up the stairway, aware of the masculine eyes following her every movement. Room three was halfway down the second-floor corridor, and he banged on the door, louder than he meant to, still irritated by the lascivious attention Starfire had given rise to below. Jealousy was a new sensation to him, and he was beginning to find he did not handle it well at all.

The door opened, and a tall, impeccably dressed man gazed inquiringly at Tracker. He was handsome in a fragile, effeminate way, his black hair oiled and combed slickly back from his broad forehead. His skin was pale, almost pasty, as if he never saw the sun. He seemed too oily and smooth, and Tracker loathed him on sight.

Tracker watched the man's small black eyes linger on Starfire with obvious appraisal, and he sought to draw them back to himself.

"I'm looking for Alfred Huddleston," he said in a sharp voice.

Recognition sparked deep in the man's eyes, and Tracker's blue eyes narrowed.

"You're Tracker, of course. Please, come in. We've been waiting for you."

He stepped back for them to enter, and Tracker hesitated, some gut instinct warning wariness. When he moved forward cautiously, Starfire was close beside him. The little attorney, Huddleston, was not in sight, and the other two men in the room were strangers. Tracker eyed them distrustfully. One was very dark, both skin and hair, and his small eyes darted around nervously, while the other man was blond and grotesquely obese with triple chins hanging over his cravat. They sat in chairs near the fireplace, and both regarded Starfire with the same lewd appreciation she'd received in the lobby.

Tracker's uneasiness mounted, and he kept his back to the door, his hand on Starfire's arm.

"Where's Huddleston?" he snapped.

"He was called to St. Louis on a family emergency. We were sent to close the deal for him. I'm Carl Rankin, and these are my associates, Mr. Smythe and Mr. Haynes."

Tracker glanced briefly at the two men, who nodded a silent acknowledgment. Tracker still did not like the situation, some intense premonition gnawing at him.

"Won't you please sit down? Smythe, why don't you take the lady's cloak?"

The dark one with a tiny pointed mustache came forward. He was small but built like a wrestler, his anthracite eyes gleaming as Tracker removed Starfire's cape. He led Starfire to a small sofa, and Tracker watched for a moment, then sat down at the table with Rankin, missing Smythe's eyes as they raked over Starfire's body with a slow, insulting stare that made her lower her gaze uncomfortably, only secure in the fact that Tracker sat so near.

Tracker kept cold blue eyes on Rankin, suddenly anxious to find out the name of Starfire's family and get her away from the three men watching them so intently.

"Let's get this over with, Rankin. Are you aware of my agreement with Huddleston?"

Rankin shot a sidelong glance at Starfire, whose eyes never left Tracker's face. He leaned forward, lowering his voice slightly.

"It might be best if the young lady did not hear all the details right now. Perhaps you'd allow Smythe to pour her a cup of tea in the dining room?"

Tracker hesitated. He didn't particularly want her to hear everything that was said; there was no need to upset her unnecessarily. He glanced into the dining room, making sure she would remain in sight, then nodded tensely.

"Starfire, go with Mr. Smythe. He'll get you a cup of tea."

Her face showed alarm, and he said gently, "It's all right. I'll be right here."

She hesitated, then obeyed, and Tracker watched until she sat at the table in the next room. He made sure Smythe kept his distance, then turned hard eyes back to Rankin when he spoke.

"I must compliment you on a job well done. Although I'm sure you enjoyed it. The girl is more than beautiful," he said, smirking.

His insinuation angered Tracker, but before he could answer, Rankin pulled an envelope from his inside coat pocket and pushed it toward Tracker.

"Here's your money. Twenty-five hundred. You can count it if you like. You've done a good job, but we can take her from here."

His smile was unctuous and false, and Tracker ignored the envelope, his blue eyes so dangerous that Rankin tensed.

"She's not going anywhere with you," Tracker said, his voice low and deadly.

Rankin's gaze dropped to Tracker's hand where it rested on his right thigh near the revolver beneath his coat, then at the fat man beside the fire. He smiled again, but his eyes were watchful, sensing the big man across from him could be ruthless if the need arose.

"You have nothing to worry about. We'll take good care of her."

Tracker leaned forward, his huge hands curling into tight fists, but he restrained himself from yanking Rankin out of his chair. But he froze then, at Starfire's terrified scream, jerking toward the dining room, where he got a brief glimpse of her struggling with Smythe before the door was slammed, blocking his view.

Tracker's chair skidded backward, crashing into the wall, rage contorting his handsome features into a mask of black fury. He started for her, but Rankin made a grab for his arm. Tracker drew back his fist, slamming it into Rankin's face, sending him sprawling in a heap in the corner. Tracker instinctively felt movement behind him and tried to turn, but something hard and heavy swept the air close to his temple, connecting with a terrible thud that echoed with hard and steady reverberations inside his skull. Then the darkness came over him quickly and completely, like a heavy black blanket.

NINE

"You'll never guess who's back in town, Henrietta. Logan Cord!"

The matronly dowager had spoken behind her ivory fan, and her companion on the red velvet settee leaned closer for yet another juicy tidbit of gossip. They completely ignored the dancing couples whirling past upon the polished ballroom floor, unaware of the flame-haired beauty behind them, or how she moved closer at the mention of the man's name.

"Oh, he's a handsome devil, to be sure. Will he be here tonight? Or have all these eager mothers towed their daughters along for naught?"

The other lady twittered in amusement, shaking her elaborately coiffed gray head. "Those blue eyes would melt the heart of the coldest virgin, 'tis true. And I know a few husbands who'll not be so happy to have him back. They say Logan's bedded nearly every woman in Denver."

"If only we were young," returned her companion. They both sighed wistfully, and the young eavesdropper moved away, pumping her fan vigorously as two high spots of color reddened her cheeks.

Isabel Holloway Whitcomb was angry. But even more, she was excited that Logan was back in Denver. Her green eyes roamed the milling crowd eagerly. The Palace Hotel with its polished floor and crystal chandeliers was the grandest establishment in town, but nothing compared to the ballrooms she'd enjoyed in St. Louis. But it would suffice to quell her boredom, especially if Logan showed up.

Her lovely face drew into a frown, and she snapped her fan shut angrily. The last time she'd seen Logan he'd made violent, passionate love to her, then walked out on her, and she hadn't heard a word from him since. Damn him. She moved agitatedly into the arched doorway, where she could search the other rooms.

A string of lovers had satiated her passionate nature in the last few months. They'd satisfied her in bed and remained at her beck and call until she tired of them. But Logan Cord was different. When he enfolded her in his steel embrace, he took her to the heights of ecstasy. She experienced pleasures with him she could not come close to attaining in the arms of any other man.

A long shiver ran down her limbs as she remembered his strong and powerful body astride her own and the way his huge hands looked running across her ivory skin. The fan came open and began to move in an attempt to cool her heated face as her gaze traveled hopefully over the crowded room. He'd used her and tossed her aside, like a common strumpet. For eight months, she'd waited eagerly for his return—just to slap his handsome, arrogant face.

Her vicious thoughts fled her mind then, chased away like leaves in the wind, when she saw him. His incredible height distinguished him as he stood a full head above most of the men in attendance. Her body froze, her fan stilled in midair, as her heart beat a fast, erratic cadence. He moved through the other guests, mingling easily with the social elite of Denver, his finely carved face surveying the people around him with a detached, polite interest. He looked better than she'd ever seen him, his skin darkly tanned, making vivid blue jewels of his eyes. His tall, virile build was clad resplendently in a dark brown frock-coat that fit to perfection across his wide, muscular shoulders. He was a magnificent figure of a man, from the snowy white cravat at his neck to the fawn breeches molding the iron muscles of his thighs.

Isabel kept glowing eyes on him as he stood idly, observing the dancers, his hands clasped behind his back. As she hurried toward him, she hoped, despite her earlier anger, that his azure eyes searched for her.

Logan Cord's gaze ran derisively over the glittering room with its glittering people, barely able to conceal his contempt. He had just fully resumed his other life as one of the wealthiest men in Denver, owner of the Marietta Lode

gold mine and many square miles of land. He was finding
it hard this time to take up the reins of his business and assume the boring respectability that even the brash young
town of Denver expected. He'd much rather leave his work
in the hands of his friends and go back to the free and easy
existence of Tracker. The good people now smiling and trying to foist off marriageable daughters on him would be appalled to learn of his close association with the savages.

He frowned darkly and took a glass of champagne offered by a passing waiter. The last four months had been a
living hell. His long brown fingers curled dangerously
around the fragile goblet as he remembered regaining con-
sciousness to find Starfire gone. Pure rage had possessed
him that night as he'd staggered downstairs and nearly
killed the clerk, trying to find out where Rankin had taken
her. His jaw tightened in frustration, a tic appearing in his
lean cheek, as he focused his eyes unseeingly on the dancers. It had taken four men to pull him off the man, and he'd
searched every inch of Denver in a murderous, methodical
rage, his worry for Starfire overshadowing his fury at
being duped by Rankin.

His mind had taunted him cruelly during the long
months when he rode from town to town with Two Bears,
searching, asking questions, following every lead, stopping only to fall into a few hours of exhausted sleep. But
that was the only time he could sleep, the only time he did
not relive the sight of Starfire being manhandled by
Smythe, the sound of the fear in her voice as she'd
screamed his name. The echo of her cry haunted him incessantly. Every waking moment he heard it, until he felt
he'd go mad. His stomach turned and twisted, and he became oblivious to the laughing people around him. He
gritted his teeth, his eyes darkening to royal blue. He'd
kill them! All three of them! He'd make them pay for the
hell he'd endured. And what of Starfire? Sweet and trusting Starfire, where was she? What had they done to her?

He tossed off the drink, his stomach churning like
windswept waves. He'd not found a trace of her, although
he'd posted rewards in every town and fort they'd traveled
through. It was as if Starfire and her three abductors had
been swallowed by the earth.

"Hello, Logan."

He turned quickly at the low voice, staring down into Isabel Whitcomb's flushed face. She could not suppress the shiver as Logan's hard blue eyes attacked her, a mocking half-smile playing upon his sensual mouth.

"Hello, Mrs. Whitcomb. How are you?"

It was a pleasantly uttered, innocuous question, one he'd ask anyone in the room. Suddenly the pent-up frustration, the aching urge to touch him, to have his hands caress her flesh, overwhelmed her. She wanted him to throw her on a bed and take her, hard and hungry, the way she craved it.

"How am I?" she spit out in a hissing whisper. "Just how the hell do you think, Logan? You've been gone for months. You owe me an explanation!"

Logan's eyes glinted like sun off an icy field, but when he spoke, his voice was low and impersonal.

"I told you once before, Isabel, I don't owe you a damn thing."

She caught his sleeve as he turned, a note of desperation creeping into her voice. "Please, Logan, don't go . . . I'm sorry, it's just that I've missed you so. You know how much you mean to me."

Logan smiled mockingly at her anxious face, and Isabel relaxed, realizing with a flush of wicked pleasure that she had to have him again, and that she would lie down right here in front of everyone if he asked her to.

She ran her palm up the front of his shirt, and her whisper was husky as she leaned wantonly against his legs, not caring who saw them. "Come to me tonight, Logan. I want you. I've wanted you since you left. I've waited so long."

He smiled coldly, ignoring the well-practiced seductive quality of her voice.

"Tell me, Isabel, how is your poor excuse of a brother? Still the lowest snake in Colorado?"

"Brent's in St. Louis. For nearly four months now."

"What's he doing there?"

"I don't know, and I don't care. I heard he's seeing some woman. I haven't heard two words from him since he found out you and I were lovers. You know he hates you since you stole his mine."

Logan's eyes narrowed dangerously, and she felt the powerful muscles of his arm go rigid beneath his fingers.

"Stole?"

"Well, you know what I mean! He says you cheated at cards and he was too drunk to catch you."

Tracker snorted. "I didn't need to cheat. And if Brent was stupid enough to mix liquor and cards, he deserves what he got."

"You really hate him, don't you?"

Logan studied her face, his voice curt when he spoke.

"Brent's the filthy coward who got my brother killed in Mexico. He's a rotten, crooked bastard, and you know it as well as I do, sister or not."

Isabel dropped her eyes. She did know it, but Brent was not worth thinking about. She set her gaze on Logan's hard lips, her own lips parted invitingly.

"I've missed you, Logan, can't you see that? I've been lonely since you left."

Logan cocked a skeptical brow, placing sardonic eyes on her eager face.

"Don't tell be your bed's been cold, Isabel. Not with your legion of lovers."

"You know there have been others, but they aren't like you. You know how good it is between us."

"Do I?"

"You devil! How can you goad me when you know how I feel about you?"

He moved closer, towering over her until she was forced to tilt her head to look at him. His voice was relentless, his blue eyes hard. "You don't have any feelings, Isabel, and you never have. Like Brent, you don't care about anybody but yourself; and you're only happy when there's a stud rutting between your legs."

Isabel gasped at his crudity, but couldn't stop the streak of erotic fire that stirred her to the depths of her loins. She moistened dry lips, and Logan could easily read the passion in her green eyes. He gave a short, contemptuous laugh.

"Logan, please—tonight."

Logan smiled coldly. "Perhaps, Isabel, perhaps, but now I have better things to do."

For the next hour, Logan avoided Isabel and danced with the usual assortment of shy virgins pushed in his direction by glittery-eyed mothers. He'd expected it, because it always happened. Rich, eligible bachelors were hard to find in Denver. But it was worth it, because he had been able to make discreet inquiries about Rankin. So far, he'd had no luck, but sooner or later, he would pick up the trail. He had to.

The brown-eyed beauty in Logan's arms wondered at his sudden frown, but he remained oblivious to her as they danced, his mind planning his next move, in the event he couldn't find Rankin. He'd have to try St. Louis after all, he decided. He'd posted a letter to Huddleston in St. Louis as soon as Starfire had been taken, hoping he'd know something. Then after the first blinding waves of rage had settled into a slow burn, he'd been convinced that Huddleston had been tricked as well. Perhaps the little lawyer was too timid to risk Tracker's wrath, and had ignored the letter. But now, since his search in Colorado had proved futile, he regretted he hadn't left for Missouri immediately. He'd been so sure at the time that Rankin would steer away from there, knowing Tracker could trace him easily. Now he wasn't so positive.

"The waltz is over, Mr. Cord."

The quiet words brought Logan back to his partner. He'd been so engrossed with thoughts of finding Starfire that he hadn't heard the music stop. And he'd virtually ignored the young girl as they'd danced. Embarrassed by his lack of manners, he smiled down at her warmly.

She blushed prettily, then lowered her lashes as he escorted her back to her beaming mother, distinctly glad she was off his hands.

He was tired of the gathering, tired of dancing. He'd go to the cardroom and try to pick up information from some of the men, and if that didn't work, he'd leave. Two steps into the lobby, he froze in his tracks, his eyes riveted on a woman standing at the door. His breath caught as he glimpsed the long silvery hair beneath her hood. Starfire's beautiful face drifted painfully across his mind, but his heart fell as she turned, returning his stare with interest. Disappointment cut into him sharply, and he turned away from her. He needed to get out, he needed to breathe in some fresh air, and he changed his course and moved out of the French doors into the shadows of the garden. The early February night was still, and he stood motionless, listening to the faint strains of the orchestra filter out of the brightly lit windows. He inhaled the cold air, raising his face to the vast sparkling blanket of stars in the ebony sky.

Starfire's eyes had sparkled with the same brilliance when she'd been happy and laughing and when she'd run into his arms and pressed herself against him eagerly. Her hair had always smelled of flowers, so silky and shiny that it begged a man to touch it. He squeezed his eyes tightly shut, unable to bear the memories. Oh God, where had they taken her? What had they done to her? The helpless frustration hit him then with such force that he desperately fought the urge to drop to his knees and sob out the agony of his loneliness. She had become the love of his life, and without her he was lost.

"I greet you, my brother."

Logan whipped around at Two Bears' low voice, and the Indian separated himself from the night shadows, moving like a dark wraith to his friend. They locked their wrists in a strong clasp of friendship. Two Bears had continued the search, while Logan took time to attend to his business affairs and make inquiries in Denver and Central City. But the Indian's presence in town meant he'd found something, and Logan questioned him eagerly.

"What have you found?"

"The ring of purple and gold."

Logan's eyes glowed in the silvered moonlight with deadly intensity.

"Rankin?" Logan's teeth clamped and held, his fists clenched at the thought of catching up with Starfire's abductors.

"He is not one of them. He is not tall, but very powerful. He wears the ring on his finger and plays cards now at the Criterion."

Logan moved away at once, and the Sioux moved surefooted and silent at his side. He had never known his blood brother to be so enraged for so long. He was certain that the three white men who had taken Tracker's woman would soon regret the day they saw Tracker's silvery-haired captive.

The saloon was packed with a boisterous crowd, and Logan pushed open the doors, his eyes taking in the loud men and laughing saloon girls, seeking out his objective. Four men played at a table near the back wall, and Logan moved casually toward them.

"Mind if I sit in?"

The four cardplayers glanced warily at him, shifting uncomfortably as he stood beside the table. Something about the set of his jaw made each uneasy, but unwilling to rile the big man, they nodded. Logan chose a chair against the wall, facing the man with the amethyst ring, and the game resumed.

They played poker, and it did not take Logan long to learn that the man's name was Will Nichols. He played nervously, drinking whiskey from a bottle on the table. He was a drifter of no account, and a wariness in his dark eyes and a tendency to lick dry lips when his hand was bad made it easy for Logan to maneuver him into betting the ring.

Logan's eyes narrowed as Nichols removed it from his grimy finger and laid it upon the green baize tabletop. None of the players saw the slight hardening of the big man's jaw as he leaned carelessly back in his chair, one hand resting on the pile of coins in front of him. Nor did they see the cold look of murder in his eyes as he stared at the family heirloom he'd last seen on Starfire's slender finger. He dealt with steady hands, his blue eyes unreadable, as the three other men checked their cards and threw them on the table, leaving Logan and Nichols facing each other.

Will Nichols squirmed in his chair, bloodshot eyes darting from Logan's impassive face to the cards in his hands. Since the big, tanned man had joined them, he'd lost steadily. The ring was his last chance to recoup. He watched the blond giant, trying to see a chink in his composure, but Logan sat completely relaxed, leisurely smoking a cheroot. His eyes were unwavering, and the relentless blue stare began to unnerve Nichols. He began to perspire, wiping his upper lip with the back of his hand. He took a deep breath, then reached out with trembling fingers and turned over his cards.

"Three jacks."

Logan didn't move, and Nichols' eyes flickered to the five cards lying face down in front of his opponent. Logan smiled slowly, reaching down to flip over three kings, one at a time. He took his time raking in and stacking the large pot, then picked up Starfire's ring last, clenching it tightly in one huge fist for an instant before he pocketed it.

Nichols scraped back his chair angrily, frowning darkly, thinking the big man must have cheated him, but too much of a coward to accuse him of it. Something told him the man who'd won the ring was lethal under his gentleman's veneer.

Logan allowed Nichols to get out the swinging door before he stood and pocketed the rest of his winnings. When he stepped out the doors, Two Bears materialized from the ebony shadows of the alley, moving along with Logan as they kept a safe distance behind Nichols' retreating figure. Two streets away, he entered a sleazy boarding house, and moments later the two men moved silently through the dark and shabby lobby, past the dozing night clerk. They took the steep stairs without a sound, and Two Bears leaned against the wall, indolently watchful, while Logan stepped to Nichols' room. One vicious kick sent the door banging open, and Logan had the astonished Nichols by the front of his coat.

"What . . ." Nichols' words were cut off as he was jerked around by the lapels and slammed into the wall. Tracker gritted out between set teeth, "Where'd you get that ring, Nichols?"

Logan saw all color drain from Nichols' face as fear dilated his eyes almost black.

"I . . . don't remem—"

Logan got him by the throat with one hand, then drew back, slamming his fist into Nichols' horrified face. His body catapulted across a table, overturning it. Logan ignored the tinkling of breaking glass and rolling bottles and was on him immediately, pulling him to his feet, as he glared into wide, frightened eyes.

"Where'd you get the ring?"

Two crimson streams ran from his nose, and his eyes went sick with horror as Logan's steel-knuckled fist doubled and drew back again.

"Wait . . . please . . . I'll tell you . . ."

Logan dropped his arm slightly, holding Nichols upright with one hand.

"Talk, damn you."

Terrified by the black rage in Logan's eyes, Nichols slurred his words through puffy, bloodied lips.

"I bought it." Logan's grip tightened against Nichols' Adam's apple, and his eyes protruded as he half croaked, half sobbed, "Smythe was his name, I swear it."

"Was there a woman with him?"

"No, no, he said he had to get to St. Louis, that's all I know, please . . ."

Logan let go abruptly, and Nichols slid down the wall, staring fearfully at Logan's retreating back as he moved soundlessly into the hall.

TEN

Isabel Whitcomb tossed her coppery curls and gripped her riding crop with white fingers as she drew to a halt in front of Logan's townhouse. She lifted her knee from around the sidesaddle and slid gracefully to the ground, then took a moment to smooth the skirt of her brown velvet riding habit as she stared at the closed front door with grim green eyes.

The arrogant devil hadn't shown up. After leading her to believe he'd come to her. Damn him, he enjoyed making a fool out of her, making her pursue him. She hurried up the wide steps and jerked hard on the bell pull. The faraway chimes had not faded when she yanked it again. She kept up the same procedure, all the while tapping an impatient toe, until Mrs. Parker pulled open the door, exasperated at the persistent caller so early in the morning.

"I am here to see Logan," snapped Isabel curtly. Mrs. Parker made a futile attempt to block her entry as the younger woman forced her way into the hall, looking around imperiously.

"Mrs. Whitcomb, please. Mr. Cord is not receiving visitors!"

"Well, he'll receive me! He'd damn well better!"

Mrs. Parker's mouth dropped ajar, appalled at such unladylike language, and Isabel headed toward Logan's library, impervious to the disapproving glare given her by his tiny housekeeper. She did not knock, but thrust open the closed door to find Logan standing behind his desk. His blond head was bent over a letter, and he looked up sharply, a fierce, thunderous scowl compressing his handsome features.

"What the devil do you want, Isabel?" he snapped.

His dark frown dwindled her own wrath instantly. Lazy amusement usually met her angry outbursts, and she was momentarily abashed in the face of his anger. Her eyes dropped to the paper in his hand, and she asked falteringly, "What is it, Logan?"

His square jaw clenched dangerously, as if he were forcing down rage, and his eyes remained as hard and cold as metal in winter. Isabel couldn't stop a long shiver that undulated slowly up her spine as he slowly tightened his fingers, deliberately crumpling the letter inside one huge, sun-darkened fist.

"It seems that I am a married man. I have been for more than a month."

Isabel gasped, and Logan barked a short, humorless laugh, then added contemptuously, "Obviously, the groom's presence wasn't a necessity."

He stopped, his lean cheek working to control his temper, then continued in a tight voice, "There's even a wedding ball planned at my mountain estate. So I can meet my blushing bride."

Isabel was too stunned to speak, and bitterness oozed like snake venom from his next words.

"You're invited, of course, Isabel. That is, if I'm allowed to invite anyone."

Isabel's mind was barely able to register the invitation as his words hit home. One well-manicured hand went to her throat.

"It can't be legal, can it?" she said slowly. "You must do something about it!"

In a sudden burst of fury, Logan hurled the paper into the fire, watching as flames ate a ravaging line of ash along the edges.

"You're damn right I'm going to do something!"

He moved with two long strides to the oaken sideboard, splashing a liberal amount of brandy into one of the goblets. Isabel watched him out of wide and disbelieving eyes. Logan—married? She couldn't believe it, wouldn't believe it. She was to be his wife someday; she'd been confident that given the time she could entice him into matrimony. They were meant to be together, but now Logan was already married!

She sank slowly to the large leather chair behind her, fixing worried green eyes on Logan, as he tossed down another drink.

"But how, Logan? How could such a thing happen?"

Logan twisted his head slightly, looking at Isabel's dismayed face. In the past, he'd always considered her quite beautiful, despite her cruel and selfish nature. But after beholding Starfire's youthful, innocent loveliness, Isabel seemed dull and artificial. He frowned again, tortured that he'd lost her. And because of his own stupidity. He gripped his glass tighter. His sanity was already near the breaking point trying to find her, and now on top of that worry, the damnable marriage contract had come up.

He set down the glass and clasped his hands behind his back as he paced agitatedly before the fire. He stopped and braced both hands on the mantel, staring down at the ashes of his father's letter. Vivid images of Starfire taunted from beneath the dancing flames, her lovely trusting violet eyes, her soft mouth parting willingly beneath his own; and he could not suppress his anguished groan at his torturous thoughts.

"Logan, tell me, please, how can such a marriage be legal?"

He turned and faced Isabel.

"Because, Isabel, I signed a betrothal agreement before I went off to the Mexican War. And it's still binding under the law."

He startled Isabel by uncoiling from his indolent posture and slamming his fist so violently on the oaken mantelpiece that the clock rang with discordant chimes.

"Why on earth would you sign such a thing?" she asked hesitantly.

Logan sighed, leaning one elbow on the mantel as he massaged tired eyes with his thumb and forefinger.

"At the time, my grandfather and a friend of his decided they wanted their families joined by marriage. I don't even remember why. But I would have done anything for Grandfather at that age. The girl was just a newborn then, and I haven't seen her or even heard of her since."

Frustration proved too much, and one of Logan's hard fists pounded into his open palm.

"And I'll be damned if I know why Father let this happen! He knows I never intended to marry."

He turned, staring into the grate, oblivious now to Isabel as he spoke softly, his vow honed in steel. "But he sure as hell won't get away with it."

Isabel had listened to it all, white-faced, her fantasies of being Logan Cord's wife slowly shriveling, but at the determination in his last words, hope raised its head in her heavy breast.

"But what can you do? You said yourself that it's legal."

Logan stood straighter, his mind made up.

"When I'm in St. Louis, I will go to my father's house and confront him. I can get it annulled. I was leaving for there anyway."

He smiled grimly at her heavy sigh of relief.

"Don't worry, love, I may be legally married at the moment, but I won't be for long. You can count on that."

Again wavery images of wide, blue-violet eyes and silvery tresses invaded his heart, pain burning harshly. Driven by an overpowering urgency to erase the agony of losing Starfire, he moved swiftly to Isabel, pulling her into his arms, feeling the need to bruise her lips until the sparkling amethyst eyes no longer haunted him. But as Isabel responded passionately, pressing against him eagerly, he released her abruptly and stepped away, knowing that it was useless, because his body and soul continued to crave the smaller, sweeter softness of Starfire.

It was nearing the end of February before Logan arrived in St. Louis. He'd made the long, tiring trek upon horseback as far as Independence, Missouri, then he'd managed to catch a riverboat for the rest of the journey. He was dirty and travel-stained but did not take the time to bathe or shave before he sought out Huddleston. He'd pushed hard, anxious to talk to the lawyer, and he wasn't going to put it off any longer than necessary.

He walked his horse along the riverfront, wearily watching the steamboats and military gunboats anchored along Laclede's Landing. The bricked waterfront was busy as slaves grunted over heavy cotton bales and fashionably dressed ladies strolled upon gentlemen's arms. St. Louis had grown rapidly, even since his last visit home, nearly three years ago. Many buildings were new, many others under construction. It was a teeming metropolis now, dwarfing the infant city of Denver.

He reined his horse to the side, allowing a detail of blue-coated soldiers to tramp past. For the first time in months, his thoughts touched on the war still raging bloodily between the Union and the Confederacy. It meant little in Denver, with the wide prairie he'd just traversed insulating it from the conflict. And it meant nothing to Logan.

His immediate concern was finding Starfire and annulling the travesty of a marriage engineered by his father —in that order.

He'd had his fill of the army in the Mexican War. Ugly memories burrowed up from mental trapdoors, and he frowned blackly. He and his brother Justin been young and brash and had joined the Missouri Volunteers, eager to fight. And Brent Holloway had been with them, their trusted friend. They'd fought all right, for survival in a humid, dirty godforsaken country. For a whole year, they'd fought the impossible odds of rattlesnakes, scorpions, and bloody battles. Justin had died at Chihuahua, when the Mexicans outnumbered the Americans four to one. Died because Isabel's brother, Brent, had run when he could have warned them. Justin died with a bullet in his head, because Brent Holloway was a rotten yellow coward.

Logan's jaw flexed to granite, his palm resting lightly on the long, jagged scar down his thigh. He'd been bayonetted in the same skirmish, a wound that had gotten infected and incapacitated him for months in a hot and filthy peasant's hovel in the middle of nowhere. And Brent's punishment? A dishonorable discharge.

Logan had sworn over his brother's dusty, lonely grave that Brent would pay. Even when John Winstead had persuaded him to travel to Colorado, the desire for revenge lingered. It had taken ten years before he could wreak his vengeance, but he'd finally done it. When gold was discovered on Cherry Creek and Denver was born, Logan owned much of the land in the area. His own mine was farther in the mountains, but it yielded a high profit from the very beginning. And Brent Holloway had fared as well when he followed the smell of gold and staked claim to the lucrative

Santino mine. It had become the core of the Holloway
wealth, until Logan had won it in a poker game. And he'd
managed to humiliate Brent further with Estelle Bow-
man. Logan's mouth curved into a cruel smile, remembering how Brent's lovely mistress had given up the fancy
Holloway townhouse for a whirlwind affair with Logan.

But now as he clopped along the bricked streets of St.
Louis, searching every open carriage, every pedestrian for
a glimpse of silvery hair, thoughts of Brent seemed incon-
sequential. She was the only important thing now, and he
wouldn't rest until he found her.

Logan found the firm of Bradshaw, Stern, and Watson
on Olive Street, one of the oldest, most prestigious streets
of the city. The tall and narrow red brick building of three
stories reeked of expensive, upper-class respectability. He
dismounted and tied his horse to the hitching post, then
climbed the curved brick steps to the stained-glass doors.
Inside, the foyer was large and quiet, and an efficient-
looking male secretary glanced up, then watched as Logan
walked toward him. The man behind the desk was young
and blond, and his gray eyes crawled over Logan's dirty
buckskin attire with a condescending look that lingered on
the gun strapped on his hip. His voice was carefully polite,
but still managed to sound patronizing.

"May I help you?"

"I'm here to see Alfred Huddleston."

"Do you have an appointment with him, sir?"

"No."

The secretary gave a small, businesslike smile, placing
his pencil carefully on the paper in front of him.

"Then you'll have to make one and come back. I'm sorry,
but . . ."

His words hung in midair as Logan parted the little gate
beside the desk and walked to the door behind it. The clerk
recovered from his first shock, jumping to his feet and following the big man at a run, just as Logan hauled up his
boss by the lapels.

"Where's Huddleston?"

The commotion brought men from several other offices,
and Logan relaxed his hold, allowing the man to fall
limply into his chair, as a voice spoke close beside him.

"I'll be glad to talk to you about Alfred, Mr. . . . ?"

"Cord," Logan supplied tersely.

"I'm John Watson, and if you'll come this way, I think we can straighten this out."

Logan ignored the whispering men who lined the hall, following Watson into a large paneled office. The man gestured to a large gold brocade chair across the desk from him, and Logan sat down, waiting while the other man lit a long cigar. He was tall and slim, his dark hair a distinguished gray at the temples.

"Would you like a cigar, Mr. Cord?"

Logan shook his head, in no mood for pleasantries.

"Let's talk about Huddleston. Where is he?"

Watson exhaled the smoke slowly, looking at Logan carefully. "That's what I want to know, Mr. Cord."

Logan's blue eyes narrowed, but Watson didn't give him time to speak.

"He was on assignment in Denver, but we haven't heard from him in six months. Neither have his wife and family. I thought you might be able to tell me something."

Logan's last remaining hope plummeted, sure now that Huddleston was dead and that the letter he'd sent to the lawyer's office immediately after the kidnapping had gotten lost. He cursed silently, furious at the time that had been lost. Huddleston *had* been tricked, too. But why?

He quickly explained his association with Huddleston, and Watson shook his head, saying thoughtfully, "What do you think happened to him?"

"I haven't found that out yet, but I will. Have you ever heard of the others?"

"No, Alfred didn't mention them after he came back from his first meeting with you. He must have gotten involved with them on the second trip."

"What about the girl's relatives? Surely you have records on the case."

Watson shook his head. "I'm afraid not. Huddleston's client insisted on complete confidentiality. I'm not even sure Alfred knew the client's name. I didn't even know the particulars of the case until you told me a moment ago. I'm sorry, Mr. Cord. I know I'm not much help."

There was little else to say, and Logan gave Watson his address in Denver in case of any word of either Huddleston or Starfire. He walked past the now wary secretary, then mounted his horse, furious at reaching another dead end. Everywhere he turned led into a brick wall, and time was running out. What if Rankin had taken her back east? How would he ever find her? What if she was somewhere nearby—in one of the houses he now passed? How would he ever know?

The despair mounted, and his mood grew blacker. By the time he reached his father's house, he was enraged all over again at his helplessness, ready to take out his pain and frustration on the lesser of his two dilemmas. The one he could resolve.

The Cord mansion was on Lafayette Street, near the north border of Lafayette Park, a great, imposing Georgian structure of sandstone with tall Doric pillars across the front portico. He took the front steps two at a time, not bothering to lift the heavy silver knocker. He strode in unannounced, scaring the wits out of a freckled young maid in a white cap who stood dusting a polished table near the door.

"Where in the hell's my father?"

Logan hadn't meant to yell at her, but his pent-up anger and frustration drove him unmercifully. To the terrified maid, he seemed immense and terrifying, and she quailed back from the angry man, shaking and clutching her dust mop tightly in both hands. Her mouth opened but she could not speak, and she was luckily saved from Logan's wrath by the entrance of his father from the library.

"What's going on out here?"

Michael Cord took in the young girl's frightened face, then his eyes went to the dirty, heavily whiskered Logan, who was glaring at him.

"Logan! Where did you come from?"

"Never mind that, Father, I want some answers!"

Ignoring the weeping maid, they entered the library. Michael shut the door softly, then turned to face his furious son.

"Good grief, Logan, you look terrible," he said, frowning. "Where in the devil have you been?"

Logan looked stonily at his father, ignoring his question.

"What do you mean by honoring that marriage contract without my permission?"

Michael winced mentally at his son's harsh words, knowing from past experience that Logan would calm down after he had all the facts. But he'd cause a hell of a row until he did. Since he was a boy, Logan's temper had been quick and violent enough to get him in trouble. For a long time, though, Logan had managed to control it, and Michael hadn't seen him in such a rage for years.

Father and son stared at each other in silent confrontation. Although Michael was not as big as his son, he had the same handsome, cleanly chiseled features. His slate-gray eyes met the angry blue ones steadily.

"All right, Logan. I'll tell you all about it. But I think you'd better fix yourself a drink first."

"Forget the drink. All I want is an explanation."

Michael took his own advice and poured himself a shot of bourbon, dreading the argument that was bound to follow.

"Thomas Pennington presented the document himself, Logan. It's completely legal. I couldn't do anything to stop it." He lifted his glass as Logan sneered cynically.

"And it wasn't worth the effort to notify me. I might have been able to buy them off! Money's probably what she's after."

Michael fought down his own annoyance, controlling his temper with difficulty.

"I wrote you as soon as Thomas talked to me. But you were out on one of your jaunts among the savages and couldn't be reached."

At Logan's ugly look, he went on, "Anyway, Thomas was insistent that his granddaughter be wed as soon as possible."

Logan turned from his restless pacing.

"What kind of ugly crone is she, if her grandfather has to force someone to marry her?"

"On the contrary, she's quite lovely. As a matter of fact—"

Logan interrupted, speaking harshly with a tight jaw and cold eyes. "I don't give a damn what she looks like—I'm going to buy them off and get an annulment. Or did my proxy see fit to consummate the ceremony with the little gold digger?"

"Logan, for God's sake, be sensible about this! She's anything but a gold digger. Her grandfather is Thomas Pennington, and if you'll think about it, he owns about half of the city of St. Louis!"

His son's words were black with bitterness, uttered through clenched teeth. "And you own the other half, which makes it a nice little arrangement. What a clever idea Grandfather and his friend had—provided she's capable of giving you an heir to the Cord-Pennington empire."

He stopped, both fists clenched. "How hideous can she be that no one will have her, even with the Pennington dowry? I'm going to stop this, and nobody can stop me," he vowed.

"Logan, there's nothing you can do about it. Marriage by proxy is legal in Missouri, and it has your signature, observed by witnesses! And Thomas won't be bought off, because he wants this marriage."

Logan stared at him, then asked mockingly, "Whom do I have to thank for standing in for me, anyway?"

Michael hesitated and avoided Logan's eyes.

"You won't like it."

Logan's look was frigid. "Who the devil was it?"

"Brent. Thomas insisted on it, because the girl knows him."

Logan stared at his father incredulously.

"Holloway? The one man I most despise on this earth? He might as well have murdered Justin himself."

Logan did not see the pain flicker on his father's face at the mention of his younger son, and he hardly listened as Michael continued, running weary fingers through his graying hair.

"Logan, you haven't even seen the girl yet. She'll be here soon, and you can meet her and make your own judgment. I daresay you'll be in for a pleasant surprise."

Logan's expression was derisive. "Where is she, Father?" he asked mockingly. "Out spending my inheritance?"

His father ignored the sarcasm and braced himself for his son's next reaction. "Brent took her to the doctor."

Logan's blue eyes widened in disbelief. "You don't mean to tell me that you've saddled me with an invalid."

"No, don't be absurd. She's healthy enough physically."

"Physically?"

"She's been having a little trouble remembering things, so Thomas insisted on her seeing a physician."

Logan stared at him for a long moment without speaking. "A little touched in the head, is she? No wonder no one will have her. I can see now why Thomas was in such a hurry to marry her off."

The thought of being trapped with such a wife was infuriating enough to bring on another white-hot blast of fury.

"I'll stop this travesty, if it's the last thing I ever do," he thundered.

He was halfway to the door when his father called after him desperately, "She's not crazy! She had an accident; she's just lost her memory. You've got to wait and meet her. She's expecting to return to Denver with you."

Logan glowered at his father from the door.

"I'm not taking her anywhere! And if you like the woman at all, you'd better advise her to get an annulment or expect to have a damn miserable life."

Michael shook his head sadly, his voice low and pleading. "Give her a chance, son. None of this is her fault, and she's prepared herself to go home with you."

Logan turned back, his hand on the doorknob, his voice cold and deliberate. "I don't really care if she has or not. It's not my problem, and I have more pressing matters on my mind at the moment. She engineered this whole mess without my help, and she can get out there by herself. Or you can take her, Father. But if you do, don't expect any welcome from me."

Michael Cord watched the door slam behind his son, dreading the moment he'd have to relate Logan's message to his lovely new bride.

ELEVEN

The room was very quiet and almost dark. Heavy brocade draperies were drawn over tall, paned windows, allowing only a narrow band of afternoon sun to escape across the polished floor. A myriad of golden motes hung suspended in the bright shaft of light, reflecting dusty images in the glass bookcases lining the walls. A single candle burned, casting a yellow glow upon a thin, elderly man who sat hunched over a curved velvet couch. He moved slightly, his craggy face intent upon the woman before him, then spoke softly to her, his words gently rhythmic in a heavy French accent.

The woman was beautiful, and she lay still, her slender hands folded upon the voluminous folds of her skirt. The shimmery fabric glowed beneath her creamy skin, and her long blond hair was pulled back in a heavy chignon at her nape.

Across the room, nearly hidden in one dusky corner, Brent Holloway's eyes gleamed as he watched the gentle rise and fall of soft, satiny curves above her bodice. He was very handsome, with straight features under dark, curling auburn hair, and his eyes were green, darkened by brown flecks in the iris. They did not waver from the woman as he absently stroked one finger across his immaculately trimmed mustache, his lips curved in a self-satisfied smile.

Brent was amazed at just how much he wanted Elizabeth. And he'd wanted her since the first moment he'd seen her. He could vividly remember that night in Denver, when Rankin and Smythe had brought her to the shabby boardinghouse on the outskirts of town. They'd dragged

117

her into the room, kicking and snarling like a small wild thing. Now, dressed as a lady, she was exquisite, but of that first night all he could remember was her silvery hair and purple eyes. All his life he'd craved fiery, passionate women, and she was like a hellion in her fury. He liked women to fight him. His loins tightened with desire, and he awkwardly shifted his long legs on the oriental hassock.

She'd hurled vicious curses at her captors in a strange guttural language, her bright hair tangled and thrown over her shoulders, and Brent had wanted to step from his hiding place behind a screen and fling her upon the bed for his pleasure. Subduing her in such a rage would have been immensely satisfying. But he had not. It would have ruined his scheme to hold her for ransom. A scheme he'd taken a lot of trouble to set up.

It had started the night he'd run into an old friend from St. Louis at the Criterion Saloon in Denver. His name was Alfred Huddleston, and they'd met several years back before Brent and Isabel had made the move from St. Louis to gold-rich Denver. Huddleston was already well into his cups by the time Brent had joined him, and he'd mumbled for some time about his homesickness for his family before he'd mentioned Thomas Pennington. Brent had come alert at once, aware that Thomas Pennington was one of the richest men in St. Louis. When Huddleston had gone on to say that Pennington wanted his granddaughter back before he died, Brent had plied his lawyer friend with liquor. His tongue had loosened considerably after that, and Brent had found out that someone named Tracker was to steal the girl from a tribe of Cheyenne, then meet Huddleston at the Cherokee Hotel on the first of October.

Brent had seen the opportunity at once to make a great deal of money by abducting the girl and holding her for ransom. After all, the hard part was being done for him; the girl was to be delivered on a silver platter. All he had to do was get rid of Alfred and take the girl away from the man called Tracker. But in order for it to work, he knew he'd have to hire others to do the actual abduction. Brent knew Thomas Pennington too well and might be identified by the girl later; Brent's mother was a distant cousin of the Pennington family.

It hadn't taken him long to persuade Carl Rankin, a dishonest cardshark, to join in the scheme. He'd been Brent's partner for a time in a gambling con and was totally unscrupulous. Carl hadn't batted an eye when Brent had told him to kill Alfred Huddleston.

All had gone well from that point, and Rankin had paid off his two friends the night the girl was abducted. They had left for St. Louis that very night, but the girl had remained wild and savage, refusing to speak or even tell them her name. They'd been forced to keep her inside the covered wagon during the entire six-week journey. But it had been just as well, because Brent could not afford to let her see him. He remained out of sight, permitting Rankin to keep her in line when they let her out of the wagon. But he'd made sure that Rankin had not violated her in any way. She was to be his and his alone.

He frowned suddenly, his heavy brows forming a harsh slash above his eyes. When they'd arrived in St. Louis with the girl, Rankin had sent the ransom note to Thomas Pennington, keeping Elizabeth in a sleazy hotel on the waterfront. Brent had made it a point to be with Thomas when he received it, so he could act as intermediary for him. Thomas had never suspected Brent was involved, much less that he was the engineer of the whole plot, and Brent had managed to ingratiate himself with Thomas, becoming fifty thousand dollars richer at the same time. And he was certain he would have won Elizabeth too if her fool of a grandfather hadn't insisted on dredging up the damn betrothal contract. Now she was legally married to Logan Cord. The scowl deepened, compressing Brent's features, as an angry tic jumped in his clenched jaw. His hands curled into hard fists, and he sought to relax his ire, transferring his eyes away from Elizabeth to the windows. His only consolation was that Logan wouldn't have Elizabeth for long. If everything went as planned, the lovely lady would ask that her marriage be annulled. Brent was determined to marry her, and as her husband control the fortune she'd inherit from her grandfather.

He grinned, returning his regard to where she lay upon the couch. He'd made great progress already at poisoning her mind against Logan, and it had been even easier than he'd expected. She'd become exceedingly receptive to suggestion since Dr. Petaire had mesmerized her. His eyes sought the elderly doctor. They were halfway through the session now, and Brent listened intently as Marcel droned the familiar words.

"Elizabeth, my dear," the slow, whispery voice was saying, "you must listen carefully and obey me. You must forget all that has happened to you before you came to live with your grandfather. You must forget the Cheyenne, you must forget your childhood with them. You will remember nothing of the abduction, of being held for ransom. Your life will begin anew, your past forgotten. You have lost your memory in a fall. You were born Elizabeth Pennington Richmond, and now you have married Logan Cord. You grew up in Boston with your Aunt Margaret. You will be receptive to all new experiences, Elizabeth. You will diligently learn everything taught to you about white people and their ways. You must learn to be gentle and ladylike in all that you do. . . ."

Brent quit listening, having heard the identical indoctrination session every day for almost four months.

He'd continued to win gratitude from Thomas by suggesting mesmerism to control the girl's behavior. Even after Elizabeth had been returned to her grandfather, she had remained savage, refusing to wear white clothing or acknowledge Thomas as her kin. It had broken her grandfather's heart, especially since he was ill with tuberculosis without long to live. The fact that Elizabeth hated him and blamed him for her misery ended his reluctance to take her to Dr. Petaire. He wanted her to love him, to allow him to love her before he died. He would have done anything at that point to make her accept her new life. When Thomas saw the success of the initial treatments, he decided that Michael Cord and his son need never know the real reason for Elizabeth's sessions with Dr. Petaire, preferring to hide her experiences with the Cheyenne. He prefabricated the story of a fall and a memory loss, and through mesmerism Elizabeth had come to believe it; Michael Cord had no reason to question his own father's friend.

Bringing Elizabeth to Marcel Petaire had been a stroke of genius on Brent's part, and since the process of mind control was a new concept in America, it was fortunate that Brent had met Marcel in Paris, where he'd traveled some years earlier, and become interested in his work.

Their friendship had encouraged Marcel's move to St. Louis, and it had been easy enough to persuade the good doctor to work on Elizabeth. Marcel had been intrigued by her case.

They'd had to resort to drugs during the first session to gain her cooperation, but then once she was in a trance, they'd found her to be an excellent subject, very easily indoctrinated.

Brent sighed and crushed out his cigar in the bowl beside him as Dr. Petaire's voice repeated the same words over and over. He stood and stretched, wishing the session would end. He moved to the window, watching the street below, but his thoughts remained on Elizabeth. It had never occurred to him that he might wish to marry Thomas' granddaughter. From the beginning, when Alfred Huddleston had let slip his mission in Denver, Elizabeth had been nothing but a pawn in Brent's plot. But after he'd seen her, he'd known he had to have her.

He regretted that Huddleston had had to die, since they'd been friends for so long. He felt a twinge of guilt when he thought of Alfred's wife and three daughters. But the lawyer could have incriminated Brent, and Brent couldn't let that happen. Nothing could tie him to the plot, nothing could make Elizabeth hate him as she hated the man called Tracker.

Brent turned to face her. It was working according to his plan. At first she'd hated this Tracker for betraying her. She'd cursed him and Thomas over and over. That was before the mesmerism when she'd fought against anything that tied her to the life of the white man. Now she seemed to have forgotten a man named Tracker ever existed. Brent drew another cheroot from his breast pocket and lit it. The plot had worked beautifully from beginning to end. Now all he had to do was woo Elizabeth until she was so in love with him that she would defy her grandfather and refuse to stay married to Cord.

A door opened behind him, and Brent turned, as a white-clad nurse entered quietly and whispered urgently to the doctor.

"Is there a problem, Marcel?" he inquired, and the doctor nodded, openly dismayed by the interruption.

"Yes, there's an emergency downstairs. Some kind of warehouse explosion at the docks."

Dr. Petaire paused, casting a worried look at the sleeping woman. "I suppose I must bring her out of the trance early, but it is not good to vary the treatments."

"I'll sit with her, Marcel. Perhaps it won't take long."

The doctor frowned in indecision and at his hesitation, Brent continued persuasively, "Go ahead. I don't mind waiting, especially when it's for Elizabeth's sake."

The nurse cleared her throat anxiously. Marcel glanced at Elizabeth again, then warned Brent to watch her until he returned.

Brent nodded, anticipation glittering deep in his eyes. The door closed behind them, and his teeth flashed briefly as he stared down into her beautiful face. The need to touch her hardened in a tight knot of desire, his eyes traveling slowly down the fragile column of her throat to the soft curves above the neckline. He trailed one finger slowly over the satiny mounds, savoring the warm velvety feel of her skin, then lowered it into the deep valley between her breasts. His breath accelerated, and he wetted dry lips as he intruded his hand farther beneath the green silk until he cupped her breast. He tightened his fingers cruelly.

She would have cried out in pain if she'd been awake, and his loins reacted to the thought. More than anything in his life, he wanted to tear the thin bodice apart and feast his eyes on the perfection hidden from him. He'd wanted her for so long, and she was so very helpless lying before him. But it would be stupid to molest her now, and Brent Holloway was not a stupid man.

He slipped his hand away and rearranged her gown, just as Dr. Petaire entered. Brent leaned back, surveying Marcel out of innocent eyes.

"It's very bad. Many are hurt, and I fear I must end the session."

Brent stood back silently and watched Marcel lean over Elizabeth.

"I will count backwards from five, Elizabeth, and when I reach one, you will open your eyes. You will remember my commands and obey them. Five, four, three, two, one. . . ."

Elizabeth opened her eyes, their violet depths dark with confusion. An unnamed fear arose within her and tightened like a heavy leather strap, as she struggled to remember what had happened. Dark green eyes loomed above her, and Elizabeth stared up into their warmth, the panic receding as she recognized Brent. Brent loved her. If Brent was with her, she was safe. He smiled down at her, a tender, loving smile, and his voice was soft and reassuring.

"I'm here, my dear. Everything is all right."

She remembered Dr. Petaire then, and turned her head, knowing the old French doctor would be nearby. He smiled and patted her hand.

"And how do you feel, my dear Elizabeth?" he asked gently.

Elizabeth smiled shyly, now that the first wave of suffocating fear had left her.

"Did everything go well?" she asked him. She wanted so desperately to regain her memory, the memory Grandfather said she had lost in a fall, to fill all the voids she could not understand.

"The session was most satisfactory, Elizabeth."

"But will I remember soon?"

Hope trembled in her voice, and Dr. Petaire's eyes met Brent's briefly before he answered gently, "In time you will, my dear. I promise you."

He took her small hand and squeezed it, then helped her to her feet. "The day will come when you will remember everything, so just relax and empty your mind of worry. Let things happen as they will. Anxiety will only impede your progress."

Elizabeth nodded, and the doctor turned to Brent. Both men missed the disappointment etched so vividly across Elizabeth's lovely features as she stood quietly beside them. It was a terrible way to live, remembering nothing of her past, of her parents or childhood. She looked around the dim room dejectedly. Her memory began in this very room. She had not known Brent or Dr. Petaire for long, but they were her friends now. Knowing she could count on them helped soothe the savage, terrifying nightmares of naked, painted bodies and dark caves and serpents and circles of blue that haunted her nights.

She squeezed her eyes shut, trying to block out the images that awakened her screaming.

"Elizabeth? Do you feel well?" Brent said as he slipped

one hand around her slender waist and pulled her close to him.

"Don't worry, my love. You'll remember eventually. I know you will."

Elizabeth nodded and leaned gratefully against his tall strength, wanting to believe him. He'd been so good to her, and he'd been there for her whenever she needed him.

"I must go now, Elizabeth," said Dr. Petaire with a warm smile. "Please try not to distress yourself. You must trust us. Brent and I have your best interests at heart."

"I do trust you, Doctor, you and Brent."

And it was true, they were her only two friends, except her grandfather.

"I must get downstairs now, my dear. Do take care of yourself."

Brent placed her velvet cape over her shoulders as the doctor hurried from the room. He gripped her arms lightly, then slid his palms slowly down her arms. He turned her to face him, his lips touching her brow with the lightest of kisses, and Elizabeth allowed it, leaning slightly into the circle of his arms. Her eyes drifted closed as his mouth brushed against her fragile cheekbone. He was always so gentle with her, Elizabeth thought despondently. If only he could have been her betrothed. How wonderful it would have been to marry him, instead of a stranger she'd never met. Brent had found her lips, his kiss deepening, and Elizabeth placed her palms against his chest and turned her head away.

"Please, Brent, I cannot. I am a married woman now."

"You should belong to me," Brent murmured, as he pressed a warm kiss against the side of her throat. Elizabeth slipped from his grasp.

"Please. Logan Cord is my husband."

"Damn Logan Cord to hell!"

Elizabeth jerked away, shocked by his viciousness.

"You're too good for him! He's a brutal rake, never satisfied with one woman, and he'll make life hell for you!"

Elizabeth gasped, fear of the unknown rising until she could not breathe. Brent had told her many times that Logan Cord was a cruel man who would treat her badly, and her heart now became like a lump of ice in her breast.

Brent enfolded her in his arms, satisfied at the fright so

evident in her large, expressive eyes. Her fear of her husband would serve Brent well. And he would make sure it grew until Logan could not touch her without her quaking with terror. He murmured softly against her fragrant hair, "It's just that I love you so, my darling. I want you with me, so that I can take care of you."

Suddenly the thought of leaving Brent and traveling far away to the Colorado Territory with an unknown husband overwhelmed her. Her throat constricted, and her whisper was hoarse.

"I cannot bear the thought of leaving you, Brent."

It was the first time she'd admitted any feeling for him, and Brent fingered an escaped tendril of silver.

"Then don't go to Cord. Tell Thomas you want an annulment."

Elizabeth broke away, and Brent watched, hoping she'd agree this time. She turned to face him, her words tortured, her eyes beseeching him to understand.

"I can't, Brent. You know Grandfather is too ill. He would be terribly upset if I disobeyed his wishes."

Brent frowned, wishing the old man would hurry up and die. But he still believed that if Elizabeth insisted, Thomas would relent and agree to the annulment. She was the only living member of the Pennington family, and Thomas had paid a small fortune to get her back. He couldn't last too much longer, and then Elizabeth would become a very rich heiress. It galled Brent that Logan Cord would control the Pennington fortune. Cord had already stolen the Holloway mine. And Estelle. Brent's teeth clenched, but none of the suppressed rage showed as he took Elizabeth's arm.

"When Thomas sees how you suffer at Cord's hands, he'll realize his mistake in forcing you to marry him."

Brent's words sent more shivers of apprehension over Elizabeth's skin, and she moved silently at his side, her mind flitting uneasily from one thought to another. No matter what Brent said, it was too late to stop her marriage. Logan's father, Michael, had already written his son informing him of the marriage contract, and she'd already moved out of her grandfather's house and into the Cord mansion. Michael was in the process of making arrangements for her to return to Colorado when her husband came for her. But each day that Logan Cord did not arrive was like an answer to her fervent prayers. She could not contemplate a life with a man like Logan Cord. If Brent held him in such contempt, he must be a terrible man. Brent would never hate without reason.

Dr. Petaire kept his office in the Sisters of Charity Hospital at the south end of Fourth Street, and as they stepped outside the hospital foyer, the rumbling of wagons and carriages was loud after the quiet corridors inside. Elizabeth waited as Brent motioned to their coachman, and she took a deep breath, enjoying the fresh air. She always felt better out of doors, especially when she took long, solitary walks on the grounds of the Cord estate.

The carriage was drawn by two high-stepping grays that pranced impatiently as Brent helped her into the cushioned seats.

He climbed up, ignoring the seat across from her as he settled very close, resting one arm behind her. His fingers touched her shoulder, and Elizabeth looked quickly at the driver. Her father-in-law frowned upon her friendship with Brent, but fortunately Michael had not forbidden her to see him, and until he did, she would not voluntarily give up the pleasure of his company.

"Why do you frown so, my darling?"

Concern threaded Brent's voice, and when Elizabeth kept her face averted, he raised her small chin with a gloved finger. His breath caught as she raised her long black lashes.

"I am so very frightened of meeting Logan Cord."

A glimmer appeared in the dark green eyes, and he squeezed her hand consolingly.

"I know, Elizabeth. That's why you must refuse to go with him."

"You dislike him, don't you?"

Brent's answer was quick and unequivocal. "That's a mild way to put it. I despise the man."

Elizabeth swallowed hard at his hatred. All the days after her memory loss, Brent had come to her grandfather's house to see her, had been understanding and kind, insisting on driving her daily to see Dr. Petaire. He was a good man, and the only time Brent was anything but kind and gentle, she thought with foreboding, was at the mention of her husband. She sighed deeply as they passed the

gates of Lafayette Park, and she set her eyes on the tall
sandstone portico of the Cord mansion ahead. She caught
sight of a tall man running down the steps, and she leaned
forward slightly.

"Is that Michael leaving the house, Brent?"

Brent followed her gaze, hoping it was. Michael Cord
made no pretense of liking Brent's relationship with Elizabeth.

Elizabeth watched Brent's intent gaze turn slowly into a
black frown.

"That, my dear, is Logan Cord himself. It looks as
though your new husband has finally come for you."

Elizabeth's heart stopped in midbeat, her eyes riveted
fearfully on the rider in the distance as he galloped away
in the opposite direction. They reached the graveled drive
at the front of the house moments later, and Brent helped
her down, his face set in hard, angry lines. He stood stiffly
without speaking, and Elizabeth looked down the street after Logan Cord, half afraid he'd seen them and would turn
back.

The road was empty, and she breathed easier as she
moved up the steps. The carved entry doors stood ajar, and
Elizabeth paused at the threshold. Her maid, Amanda,
stood in the center of the wide marble hall, sobbing hysterically into her stiff white apron, while Michael Cord stood
patting her shoulder in an awkward attempt to calm her.

"Come now, Amanda," he was saying in an exasperated voice. "There's nothing to cry about. Logan's gone
now. . . ."

His words trailed away as he caught sight of Elizabeth's
white face in the doorway. Brent Holloway stood behind
her, watching mockingly as Michael gave Amanda a push
toward the kitchen.

"What has happened to Amanda?" Elizabeth asked at
once, and Michael avoided her intent eyes and shrugged.

"Nothing, really. She's just high-strung."

He smiled, but Elizabeth persisted. "But she's so frightened. Surely something must have happened to make her
take on so."

Michael hesitated, unwilling to tell her about the ugly
scene between Logan and him. Especially in front of Brent
Holloway. He more than shared his son's low opinion of

Elizabeth's friend, and it was damned unfortunate Elizabeth had grown so fond of him. Michael tolerated his presence only for her sake, but this was a private matter, and he'd be damned if Brent would be included.

"This concerns our family, dear. If Brent will excuse us, I'll explain it all to you."

He looked pointedly at the other man and saw something ugly move in the dark green eyes.

"Wasn't that Logan we just saw?" Brent asked with a malignant smile, lounging indolently against the door frame. "We saw him as we turned the corner, and he rode off as if the hounds of hell were after him."

Michael fixed cold eyes on Brent as he finished his deliberate taunt. "Could it be he's not exactly thrilled with his arranged marriage?"

Elizabeth's body tensed as Michael uttered an oath beneath his breath, then answered tightly, "It was Logan, and that's why Elizabeth and I need to talk. Alone." The last was emphasized, and Brent inclined his head with a polite smile.

"Of course, Michael. I understand."

His words were studied, his smile false, and Michael was only too aware it was all for Elizabeth's benefit. Brent turned to Elizabeth, drawing her slim fingers to his lips. He ignored Michael's dark scowl and lingered over her hand.

"I'll call again tomorrow," he whispered.

Elizabeth nodded, quickly withdrawing her hand when she caught sight of Michael's disapproving frown. Brent smiled and bent in a slight bow, then left, closing the hall door quietly behind him, pleased that Logan opposed the marriage. His feelings would work nicely in Brent's plan to take Elizabeth away from him.

TWELVE

After he'd left, Michael and Elizabeth stared at each other in silence, Michael dreading to relate what had happened earlier with Logan. Logan's irrational behavior put him in a most difficult situation, but he would not hurt Elizabeth if he could help it. She'd been charming and agreeable during the eight weeks he'd known her, and he'd grown very fond of the beautiful young woman. She had enough to cope with since she'd lost her memory, and he wanted to shield her from further pain. She waited warily, her delicate brows dented in a small frown. It was suddenly important to Michael to ease the worried furrow and bring back the warm glow of happiness to the soft violet depths. But most often, that particular look was reserved for Brent Holloway, and Michael found that most disturbing.

"Come into the parlor, Elizabeth, and I'll tell you about Logan."

Elizabeth followed him dutifully, watching as he walked across the room to stand before the marble fireplace. The front parlor was small compared to the other rooms in the Cord mansion, but it had become Elizabeth's favorite since she'd been in residence. The dark green Victorian furniture and gold brocade wallcovering reminded her of a warm summer day. She hesitated just inside the door, until Michael looked across at her.

"Please sit down, Elizabeth."

She did as he bade, gracefully spreading her skirts upon the nearest curved sofa. Michael stood, his back to her, facing the ornate golden mirror above the mantel. She watched his reflection worriedly, and the silence soon became uncomfortable enough to cause Elizabeth alarm. It must be very bad news if Michael was so hesitant to begin.

When he finally looked at her, it was easy to read the uncertainty in her eyes, but he still hesitated, inwardly cursing Logan for walking out and leaving him in such a predicament. He took a deep breath.

"Logan's very angry, Elizabeth. Brent was right—he doesn't want this marriage."

Elizabeth sat very still. Inside, deep in her heart, the first stirrings of hope fluttered alive. Perhaps Logan Cord would dissolve the marriage himself, leaving her free to marry Brent. She waited with bated breath as Michael continued.

"I tried to explain the legalities to him. There's no question your marriage is binding. But he's so damn stubborn, Elizabeth, I just couldn't make him see reason. I'm afraid he's on his way to confront Thomas."

Elizabeth's alarmed eyes darted to him. "He must not upset Grandfather! He is too weak!"

Michael's voice gentled, his eyes drawn to the nervous fidgeting of her fingers in her lap.

"I'm sure the doctor won't permit Logan to see Thomas, dear. You're the only one they've allowed in his bedchamber since he worsened."

Elizabeth thought a moment, then asked the question that had been hovering in her mind. "Please tell me why Amanda was so upset."

Michael ran an impatient hand through the thick waves of gray over his temples. "Oh, Logan was angry, and he stormed in and ranted around a bit. Nothing really to warrant such fright in her. As I said, Amanda is easily upset. I understand she grew up with a brute of a father who often took a whip to her."

Elizabeth shivered. Brent had described Logan as a brute.

Michael turned away from Elizabeth's obvious anxiety and paced to the windows, staring unseeingly into the sculptured gardens below. Only the tick of the clock broke the silence until Elizabeth said quietly, "I would not oppose an annulment if your son wishes his freedom."

Michael turned quickly to study her.

"You know that's impossible, Elizabeth. Thomas wouldn't

hear of it. He's convinced this marriage to Logan is in your
best interest. It's done now; there's no turning back."

Elizabeth looked down at her hands, and Michael sighed
as he walked back to her. Slowly he sat down beside her,
silently studying her finely boned profile. Finally he spoke
the question that was hovering between them.

"Is Brent the reason you want to end the marriage?"

The question hung suspended between them. Elizabeth
gathered her nerve to reply truthfully, and Michael sat
very still, afraid of what her answer would reveal. She
avoided his questioning gaze and spoke so low that he
barely heard her.

"I fear I am falling in love with Brent."

Michael groaned in dismay and stared at her. It was the
very worst thing that could have happened. But he'd seen
it coming. He sighed heavily and laid his hand over hers.

"Elizabeth, you must never let that happen. You are Logan's legal wife, whether the two of you like it or not. A
relationship between Brent and you would have repercus-
sions I shudder to think about."

Elizabeth raised her eyes at the seriousness of his tone,
and Michael went on, anxious to impress on her the danger
of the situation.

"There's bad blood between Logan and Brent already.
Logan blames him for my son Justin's death. And if there
is any hint of scandal, there's no telling what Logan would
do."

"Nothing has happened between us, Michael. You must
believe that." The innocence in Elizabeth's face left no
question of her guiltlessness. "But Brent wishes me free so
that we might wed."

Michael stiffened with anger, thinking Brent Holloway
was a self-serving scoundrel, and if the truth were known,
Brent was after the Pennington fortune. Michael had
heard rumors that he'd fallen on hard times out in Denver,
but he seemed to be doing well enough at the present. Elizabeth was well worth any man's attention, but her grandfather's vast estate made her doubly attractive to men like
Holloway.

He watched Elizabeth, as always struck by the perfection in her small face. If her feelings for Brent were genu-
ine, they were all in trouble. But if it was only an

infatuation, separating them was Michael's highest priority. They'd already planned a trip to Colorado for the wedding ball, and there she'd be out of Brent's reach. The sooner Logan saw her, the sooner he'd come to his senses. Women had always found his son irresistible, and Elizabeth would probably be no different.

"We'll leave soon for Colorado, and things will be better. Brent has been your only friend since your accident, and it may be that your feelings toward him are based on gratitude."

Elizabeth didn't agree, and he felt obligated to warn her of the dire consequences of seeing Brent again.

"Being with Brent will only lead to tragedy, dear. Please believe me. I know how Logan feels about that man. A confrontation between them would be most unpleasant."

Elizabeth looked unconvinced, so Michael tried again.

"When you and Logan get to know each other, I'm sure you'll be happy. My son is a fine man, Elizabeth. It's just that damnable temper of his that gets him in trouble. He needs to settle down and raise a family. And I'm sure he'll be most pleased with you. Any man would be."

None of Michael's words raised Elizabeth's spirits, which had sunk to new lows. Brent was lost to her forever, and her face reflected her sorrow.

"Will Logan be back soon to meet me?"

Michael winced but answered truthfully, "No, he's already gone, my dear."

"Gone?"

"Back to Denver. We'll be following as soon as I can finalize the arrangements. I've decided to escort you myself, and by the time we get there, Logan will have calmed down."

Despite Michael's fears of how Elizabeth would accept the news of Logan's departure, Elizabeth felt nothing but relief. She listened while Michael told her about their journey to Colorado, appalled to learn that he planned to leave before the week was out. More upset by the prospect than she wished Michael to detect, she excused herself as soon as she could and fled the parlor. She stood in the hall below the crystal chandelier and listened to the soft tinkling of the glass prisms in the gentle breeze from the transom over the front door. The sound was happy and at direct odds with her mood as she climbed the curved oaken staircase with leaden footsteps. She found sanctuary inside her bedroom, tossing her cape upon the white silk bed. She moved to the wide window and stood looking out, trying not to think about her future. Her eyes came alert as Amanda rounded the side of the house, carrying a market basket. Elizabeth waited until she entered the house, then pulled the embroidered bell pull. She had to know what Logan Cord had done to frighten her so much.

Moments later, Amanda appeared at the doorway. She was about Elizabeth's size, only a bit taller. Her carroty hair that curled in bouncy ringlets peeked from beneath her cap, but her almond-shaped brown eyes lacked their usual cheerful glint. Her small freckled face still bore traces of weeping, and Elizabeth put a comforting arm around her thin shoulders.

"Tell me what happened downstairs, Amanda." Her voice was steady, but her heart beat in a staccato rhythm. "Did he strike you?"

Amanda O'Neil looked at the sympathy in Elizabeth's eyes, and her heart twisted to think her sweet little mistress was married to the huge, scowling giant. His long legs and massive chest brought to mind vivid memories of her own father in his rages. Her young face whitened and her voice shook pitifully.

"No, ma'am, but he might have if Master Michael hadn't come."

Elizabeth's face took on an ashen hue at her words, but Amanda was too excited to see the alarm that had surfaced in Elizabeth's eyes.

"Did you do anything to provoke such anger, Amanda?" she asked quietly. "Did you disobey him?"

"No, ma'am, I swear I didn't! I was just standing in the hall, dusting, and the door flew open hard enough to bang against the wall! And he came in, cursing like a . . ." She strove for a fitting comparison, then found one that did not soothe her mistress's anxiety. "Like a huge and wicked devil!"

Elizabeth's slender hands went to her heaving breast as she visualized the scene. "What did he look like?" she whispered.

Amanda wasted no time, for Logan's furious visage was burned like a brand into her young, impressionable mind.

"He is huge, much bigger than Master Michael, or even Mr. Holloway. He's the biggest man I've ever seen. His hair is blond, and his shoulders like this." She held out her arms to their full capacity. "And his eyes were blue, I think, but they looked black because he was frowning."

Elizabeth sat very still, as her mind dipped back and picked up an elusive picture from her shrouded memory of a tall man with massive shoulders. His face was obscured in the shadowy confines of her mind, and something about him had frightened her. She was sure of it! Excited by the possibility of remembering someone from her past, she tried very hard to bring the wavery image into clear focus. She frowned in frustration as it suddenly vanished.

"I was so scared, I couldn't open my mouth, Miss Elizabeth," Amanda was saying. "Then he and Master Michael went into the library, and I could hear them yelling at each other just before he came out again. He said there would be no welcome for you in his house."

Her thin shoulders began to quake, and with a stricken expression, she fell to her knees, clasping her arms around Elizabeth's skirts.

"Oh, Miss Elizabeth, you are too good and kind to be married to such a man."

She sobbed into the shimmering green silk, and Elizabeth stood like stone, trying to control her own reaction to Amanda's description of her husband. Brent had been right. No matter what Michael had said, Logan Cord was a frightening man. She patted Amanda's red curls, her hand trembling slightly, and it took several minutes for Amanda to calm herself. After her maid had left to fetch tea, still sniffling into one of Elizabeth's handkerchiefs, Elizabeth sank limply before the mirror of her dressing table, staring miserably at her reflection. A frightened face looked back at her, the light violet eyes dark and troubled as she contemplated the horrid sufferings she would endure in Denver at the hands of her cruel husband.

Three days later, Elizabeth stood outside her grandfather's bedchamber. Michael waited downstairs to take her to the railway depot after she'd bid Thomas goodbye. Regret at leaving him tore at her heart as she turned the knob and entered the room. She looked across the long, shadowy room toward Thomas Pennington's immense bed set against the far wall. The massive canopy was hung with lustrous scarlet satin, embroidered with golden dragons by a Chinese hand. The dark wood of the walls emphasized the rich gold-and-black Persian carpet, and Elizabeth's feet made no sound upon its softness as she moved to the foot of the bed.

The Sister of Mercy sat silently and held her rosary tightly as she prayed for the shell of a man lying upon the wide bed. Thomas lay very still, but as Elizabeth watched, his dark, sunken eyes opened. He smiled slightly when he saw her, then said huskily, "Come closer, my dear."

At his words the nun arose at once, her black-and-white habit a stark shadow against the crimson finery of the bed, before she moved wraithlike to the door.

Elizabeth rounded the thick carved bedpost and approached the old man who'd been so good to her. His face had lost its color, and his long, frail hands lay limply upon the red satin coverlet, his skin as cracked and wrinkled as ancient parchment. Elizabeth took one between her palms and rubbed it gently, wishing to warm the cold skin.

She smiled down at him, a tide of emotion swelling her heart. "How are you feeling, Grandfather?"

He nodded wordlessly, a dry, hacking cough preventing him from speaking. Elizabeth watched in concern until the spell subsided and he tried to speak again.

"Open the drapes so I can see you. They keep it too dark in here."

Elizabeth obeyed, going to the wide casement windows that overlooked the lawn. She reached out and grasped the dark velvet curtain, flooding the room with the bright sunlight of late morning. Then she unlatched the window, wishing to rid the room of the stuffy odor of medicine.

Thomas lay still, half awed by the beauty of his only grandchild. She was dressed in pale yellow, a gown of the finest satin and Venetian lace. He'd chosen it himself just after she'd come back to him. The thought of sending her away after so recently finding her twisted painfully at his heart, but he forced down the grief that threatened to overwhelm him.

"Come, my child, sit beside me."

Elizabeth moved gracefully to the bed, the satin rustling prettily, conjuring elusive memories in Thomas' mind of long ago, when his wife and daughter added their beauty to his life. Elizabeth stepped upon the footstool and smoothed her skirt as she settled herself beside him.

"You are so like your mother that sometimes I forget and think that you are Anne."

Elizabeth fought her tears at the forlorn quality to his voice. "I wish I could remember both my parents."

He looked at her pityingly. "You never really knew them. They were taken from me so very young." Sadness permeated his voice as he looked out toward where the roses bloomed in summer. "They both loved flowers. I built the rose garden for them. Your grandmother ordered different varieties from all over the world. And Anne was the same way until she married Aaron and went away."

He looked at Elizabeth, knowing she didn't remember that her parents had died in a Cheyenne massacre. She didn't remember anything—and he didn't want her to. He searched her lovely face, appalled to think of what he'd done to gain her affection.

Elizabeth watched him, her eyes tender, but he had learned her moods in the last months, and he knew she did not want to go to Colorado. And it pained him to have to send her into such a wild place. His only consolation was that she went to Logan Cord. Logan would protect her.

"Would you like me to read to you, Grandfather?"

He nodded, and she picked up the Bible beside the bed. It still amazed him how much she'd learned since Dr. Petaire had begun his treatments. He'd never have believed it if he hadn't seen it himself. He listened as she began, haltingly but with amazing skill for the short time she'd been tutored. He did not understand this new mesmerism, but he thanked God that Brent had suggested it. She had been so filled with hatred when she came back to him, and he'd had such a short time with her.

He sighed, bringing Elizabeth's eyes to him briefly before she read on, carefully tracing the line with her finger. At times he was despondent, afraid he'd done the wrong thing. Erasing her past life, all her memories, good or bad, was cruel, but then he thought back to how wild she'd been when Brent had rescued her.

Elizabeth quietly closed the Bible, knowing Thomas was not listening to her. Since he'd become so ill, he often lapsed into his own world, where his wife and daughter still lived and laughed. She sat patiently, still holding his limp hand, knowing she must leave soon. Thomas had been so very good to her, so understanding when she'd first awakened without a memory. She'd been alone then, so terribly alone, and he'd held her close and told her stories of her family until she slept. Tears burned suddenly, and she fought them, hiding their brightness under her lashes. Thomas roused at her movement.

"Your hair catches the light and makes it gleam with silver. Like Anne's when she was a little girl. But her eyes were gray, like mine."

Elizabeth nodded, having spent many hours in front of the portrait in the sitting room. She did resemble Anne Richmond, but try as she might she could remember nothing about her mother. Everything in her past was like shadows of velvet, and if she tried too hard to remember, her head would pound until she gave up.

"Is it today that you leave?" Thomas asked suddenly.

Elizabeth nodded, thinking how frail and weak he appeared. The tuberculosis had eaten away at him for years now, and the doctors feared he would not live much longer. Elizabeth refused to give up hope, however, and she only wished she did not have to leave him.

"Please let me stay until you're better, Grandfather, I cannot bear to go away when you're so ill," she pleaded.

Thomas reached up and wiped her tears away, but the small gesture tired him and his hand dropped weakly to the bed.

"No, my sweet darling, you belong with Logan now. He is your husband."

"But you need someone here to take care of you," she protested.

"The doctor takes good care of me, and Albert has been my valet for many years. I will be well taken care of, and I can rest peacefully now knowing Logan will protect your interests after I'm gone."

Elizabeth raised her hand to wipe her tears away, and Thomas spoke again.

"Do not cry, child. It saddens me to see you unhappy. Is it Logan that frightens you?"

Elizabeth could not meet his eyes, and her voice was subdued.

"I have not met him, yet I am his wife."

Thomas was distressed by the unhappiness in her voice. Her hands were clasped tightly in her lap, and he laid his palm over them.

"Listen to me, child. There is nothing to fear. I have known Logan since he was a boy. He is a fine, strong man, and he'll take care of you. Do you really think I would send you to a husband who would mistreat you?"

Elizabeth shook her head, but a confused expression flickered briefly across her face. He hated the pain he was causing her by sending her to a husband she had not met, but he trusted Logan, and even though Logan had balked at the marriage, Thomas knew Elizabeth was better off with him than with any of the unscrupulous young men who would surround her when she inherited his money. The marriage contract he'd arranged with Logan's grandfather had been a godsend, and although Logan was furious now, he'd come to love Elizabeth. Thomas had no doubt of that. She was so very beautiful, and so very easy to love.

"I have to talk to you, Elizabeth, before you go. Please listen to me. You must understand that everything I've ever done for you has been because I love you. You are so dear to me. . . ."

His voice broke, and his eyes grew watery. Elizabeth leaned forward in concern, thinking her fears had upset him.

"Grandfather, please, don't upset yourself so. I will go to my husband, and I'll try to be a good wife to him."

"No, no, I must tell you this before you leave. There may come a day when you'll regain your memory. And you won't understand some of the things I've done, but I've only done them because I love you. I cannot stand the thought of you hating me."

Elizabeth spoke soothingly, alarmed at his agitation.

"You have been nothing but kind to me. I'll always love you."

Thomas fell back weakly, completely exhausted. They sat silently for a time, until Thomas turned his head upon the pillow to look at her.

"You mustn't be unhappy. Go to Logan, give him a chance. Promise me you will. Please."

Brent's warm green eyes glowed inside Elizabeth's mind for an instant. She had not seen him since her conversation with Michael, although he'd come calling at the house every day.

"I promise, Grandfather."

He smiled then, and relaxed. The strain in his face dissolved, and it was not long until he slept. She sat for a time with him, then leaned down and kissed his lined cheek. She moved to the door, pausing to look back one last time, knowing with great sadness that she'd probably never see him again.

Downstairs, Michael paced impatiently in the foyer, anxious to be gone. He turned quickly when he heard her on the steps and smiled fondly at her. Her face bore evidence of weeping, and he slipped his arm around her shoulders.

"You must not worry. Perhaps Logan will bring you back to see Thomas soon."

Elizabeth nodded, but her chest was heavy as she gazed around the lavishly appointed house for the last time. Her eyes lingered on the grandfather clock beneath the stairs as it chimed the noon hour. A similar clock superimposed itself over the polished mahogany case, and she stared at it thoughtfully, as a flashing glimpse of a room from her past and warm male laughter absorbed her mind until Michael took her elbow.

The elusive memories haunted her daily, but when she became anxious and tried to force them back, her head would pound, forcing her to give up the battle to remember.

The servants were lined up outside to bid her farewell, and many wept openly as Michael assisted her into the carriage. Elizabeth turned and waved to them, glad to see that Amanda had lost her fear at the prospect of going with Elizabeth to live with Logan Cord. Now she sat atop the baggage wagon, her full, smiling attention on the handsome driver.

The streets were jammed with horse-drawn conveyances, the city bustling with noonday activity. The train had not arrived at the station, and their driver drew up to steps that led to a high platform beside the tracks. Michael took Elizabeth's arm as they climbed to the top, then threaded their way through the crowd of Union soldiers who were congregated in small groups or dozing against cotton bales as they awaited their orders. Many of them turned admiring eyes upon Elizabeth as Michael led her to a bench that ran along the building. It was near the ticket window and protected by the overhang of the roof, and he thought it safe to leave her there for a few moments.

"The train should arrive any minute, but I must see to the baggage. Would you mind waiting here for me? It won't take long."

She nodded, watching him hurry toward the wagon that was being unloaded at the far end of the platform. The train would take them to Jefferson City, where they would board one of the Pacific Railroad's fleet of riverboats for the voyage up the Missouri River to Independence. From there, they would book passage on a stagecoach across the wide plains. Michael had made the trip before and had told her the scenery was most beautiful at times, but Elizabeth could not become excited about any of it as she stood staring at the tracks remembering her last view of her grandfather. She heard a faraway horn blare, and the engine came into sight. Elizabeth watched in fascination as it neared, its smokestack belching great billowing clouds of black smoke.

The soldiers began to stir as it chugged in alongside the platform with a great deal of clanging and hissing. A sergeant bellowed orders, and Elizabeth watched as they gathered their gear and slung long rifles over their shoulders. Another train pulled in next to the first one, and the station soon became a mass of confusion as travelers rushed past her and baggage handlers yelled at each other over rumbling carts filled with trunks and boxes. She stepped out of the way, a little intimidated, and tried to see Michael and the others. She could barely make them out through the crowd, and a little hesitant to remain unescorted in the midst of the milling soldiers, she turned and began to walk toward them.

She gasped as strong fingers closed around her arm and jerked frightened eyes to the man beside her. Brent Holloway smiled down at her.

"I couldn't let you go without saying goodbye," he said, drawing her with him behind a post. Elizabeth couldn't hide her pleasure at seeing him again, and smiled brilliantly up at him.

"Michael asked me not to see you," she said. "But I wanted to say goodbye."

Brent pulled her against his chest, and although she knew she should not, she allowed it, hoping Michael Cord was still too preoccupied to come searching for her.

"I know, my love, but you mustn't worry. Things will work out for us," Brent promised.

Elizabeth pulled back, realizing the danger they were in. Her eyes sought Michael, where he still supervised the servants, then looked back at Brent pleadingly, a picture of her grandfather flashing in her mind.

"No, Brent, I've promised Grandfather I will try to be a good wife to Logan. We must not see each other again."

She missed the flash of anger that crossed Brent's face at her words.

"Don't forbid me to see you, darling. I couldn't live with the thought of never seeing you again."

"But we can't change it, Brent, and I'm going away. I may never come back, never see you," she said, her resolve weakening.

"But you will, my love, and very soon. I'm leaving for Denver within the week."

Elizabeth's eyes caught his, and he smiled at the pleasure he read in them.

"Can it be true? You will be close to me."

"Yes. My sister, Isabel, has a house in Denver. I want to be near you, even if all we can be is friends. Surely you will not deny me your friendship."

He leaned down then as if to kiss her, but Elizabeth's head jerked up as she heard Michael's voice above the din.

"I must go, Brent. He can't see us together!"

Brent grabbed her to him, pressing a quick kiss upon her lips, then Elizabeth pulled away, appalled he'd done such a thing with Michael so near, but he caught her arm as she tried to leave, whispering against her ear.

"Remember how much I love you, darling. And if you need me, I'll be in Denver."

Elizabeth fled from him with tears in her eyes, and Brent watched from behind the post as Michael took her arm and assisted her onto the steaming train.

"Ah yes, my rich and beautiful little heiress," he murmured to himself, "I'll make it a point to be close to you."

Elizabeth paused on the platform as the train began to move, and Brent smiled with triumphant eyes at the way her eyes searched wistfully for him before she followed Michael into the car.

THIRTEEN

Logan reined up and looked out across verdant fields dotted with yellow dandelions and white lacy wildflowers. His mountain lodge set nestled at the far side of the meadows with dense thickets of spruce rising in tall green spires behind its immense chimneys of gray fieldstone. A lake lay glittering in front of him, the clear turquoise water mirroring the majestic, white-capped peaks that circled the valley. It was a breathtaking scene, but he'd chosen the site for its convenience as well as its beauty, since it lay only a day's ride from Denver.

Zeus pranced sideways beneath him, eager to reach the stables of Woodstone, and Logan let the black stallion have his way. It was good to be home, despite the unpleasant business that awaited him there. It had been nearly two months since he'd had the heated argument with his father in St. Louis. After he'd left him, he'd spent several weeks on a variety of steamboats on the Missouri River, inquiring after Starfire with everyone from boat captains to riverfront tavern owners. Neither Carl Rankin nor his two men had booked passage on any of the larger boats, nor had they ridden on any of the stagecoach lines. He'd even given their descriptions everywhere he went, thinking they might have used false names, but no one had seen them, no one knew them. It was a frustrating, unrewarding trip, topped off by the news that had awaited him in Denver. His mine outside Central City had caved in. No one had been killed, but it had put the Marietta Lode's production behind schedule. He'd gone there at once to help his foreman, William Timbers, oversee the digging-out operation, but Two Bears had continued the search for Star-

fire for him, and Logan was anxious to know if he'd
learned anything in the mining towns down south.

He grimaced, thinking of the letter that had been waiting for him at his house in Denver when he'd returned
from the Marietta. It had contained more bad news. His father and his wife had arrived in Woodstone and were waiting for his arrival.

He shielded his eyes as he rode on, searching the long
veranda hugging the front of the house. Pots of scarlet
geraniums were set upon the railings, vivid against the
weathered gray wood, but no one stirred there that he
could see.

He shifted his gaze to the corrals, hoping to see one of the
boys. He grinned as he saw Aaron clinging to the back of a
wildly bucking mustang, while his twin brother, Jacob, sat
watching him from the top rail. Logan stood in the stirrups
and gave a long whistle. Jacob's head came up to peer
across the fields, and when he saw Logan, he scrambled to
the ground.

Logan watched the boy mount and ride toward him at a
hard gallop, wondering how the Winstead family, the farm
managers, had taken to their unexpected guests. According to the letter in his vest, Michael and the blushing
bride had arrived in mid-March, almost three weeks ago.
Logan grimaced, hoping the ugly heiress hated the isolation of the mountains enough to demand an immediate return to St. Louis. He looked toward the lodge again as
the alarm bell pealed out over the valley and saw Maria at
the bell pole. He raised his arm in greeting to the old
black cook, and she returned his wave as she yanked on
the rope.

Jacob arrived in a cloud of dust and flying turf, and Logan
grinned at the fifteen-year-old's exuberance, holding Zeus
firmly as the other horse danced close beside him.

"You've finally come!" Jacob shouted, his sunburned
face split by a delighted grin. "Mother's been wondering
when you'd get here."

Logan looked at the boy, thinking he'd grown a lot in the
last year. His shaggy black hair was windblown from the
wild ride, and his dark eyes sparkled as he waited for Logan to answer.

"How is your mother?"

"Fine. She's down at the lake. Zack took the womenfolk to pick wildflowers. Aaron's gone to get them."

Jacob pulled his wide-brimmed hat down to shade his eyes as he turned his horse to walk alongside Logan's mount.

"Is my father with them?"

"No, he's at the house. Mother and Rachel went with the mistress and her maid."

Logan frowned. The woman probably couldn't walk two steps without a maid to fan her face. Jacob misinterpreted Logan's dark look and added quickly, "But don't worry. Zack's got his rifle."

Logan darted a quick look at him. "Has there been Indian trouble?"

"Not in the valley, but the Cheyenne have been raiding south of here. We've been real careful, especially since your missus came." Jacob grinned again. "We sure were surprised to find out you were married."

"Not as much as I was," Logan muttered sourly under his breath, ignoring Jacob's puzzled look as he glanced down toward the lake.

"How does Lily like her?"

"Mother loves having another woman in the house, and so does Rachel. Zack hasn't said much, but I think he's sweet on the maid. Her name's Amanda, and she's got red hair and freckles."

"What makes you think he likes her?"

"Because he goes down to the creek every night and washes!"

Jacob made it sound like such a bizarre habit that Logan laughed.

"It looks like he's kept you and Aaron busy. Both holding pens are full."

"We've already caught enough mustangs for the army contracts," Jacob told him proudly. "Now all we have to do is break them."

"Good work," Logan said, and Jacob grinned with pleasure at his praise. "I'm surprised Lily would take time off to pick flowers," Logan commented, as they reached the drive that skirted the front of the house.

"It was the mistress' idea for her to go. She said Mother works too hard."

"And Lily agreed?" Hard work was Lily Winstead's philosophy of life, and Logan found it a little hard to believe an afternoon of idle pleasures fit into her agenda.

"Everyone tries to please your wife, she's so sweet," Jacob said, and Logan didn't answer, frowning as he spurred his horse into a faster gait.

At the stone steps that led to the wide, shady veranda, Logan dismounted and handed his reins to Jacob. Michael opened the front door as Logan removed his rawhide gloves, and they looked at each other, remembering the angry encounter in St. Louis. By now, Logan's rage had dissipated into indifference, but the despair at losing Starfire remained like a suffocating weight inside his chest.

"Hello, Father," he said, climbing the steps and extending his hand. Michael gripped it and smiled with relief.

"I'm glad you've come, son. It's good to see you."

His gray eyes showed his relief as they entered the house together. The wide, airy room that ran along the front was cool and dim and felt good to Logan after a long ride in the sun. Immense beams as big around as a man's waist crossed the ceiling, and a wide central staircase led to a landing at the back. A rock fireplace adorned each end of the room, each with a raised hearth beneath a long mantel. A long dining table was set before one fireplace, and at the other end, massive couches and chairs of brown leather were set before the hearth. Logan walked toward the latter, and Michael followed him.

"I'd almost forgotten how beautiful Woodstone is, Logan. The scenery alone is breathtaking."

"I've missed it," Logan said, pouring himself a brandy at the sideboard. Michael sat down as Logan drank it, and neither spoke, both hedging the subject that was on their minds. Logan turned finally, deciding to get to the point.

"Well, here I am, Father. I got your letter in Denver, while I was away at the mine and it sounded more than urgent. What's so important?"

"I wrote you when we arrived here, and you know exactly what I want. I want you to meet your wife."

Logan drank again, without answering.

"It's been over three months since the wedding," Michael continued in the wake of Logan's silence. "You can't put it off forever."

Logan let silence fill the room, then spoke calmly. "You can rest your mind, Father. I came here to meet her."

Michael studied his son's impassive face.

"I can appreciate how you feel, Logan. But once you meet your wife and get to know her, I think you'll see things differently."

Clear violet eyes burned briefly in the depths of Logan's mind, and he looked down at his drink. Meeting his wife would make no difference. There was only one woman on earth he wanted. And she was gone; he was ready to accept that now.

Logan suddenly felt tired, too tired to think, and he dropped heavily into a chair across from Michael.

"Tell me about her illness," he sighed, closing his eyes. "What's wrong with her?"

Encouraged by the first spark of interest Logan had shown in his wife, Michael was quick to reassure him.

"It's nothing serious, really. She stumbled on the stairs, and a blow to her head affected her memory."

"She can't remember anything?"

"No. She couldn't even remember her name at first. Or her grandfather. And no one could help her much, since the doctor insisted that she should regain it herself. He warned Thomas that pressuring her to remember her past could be quite detrimental to her health. I suppose it's better for it to come back a little at a time, but it's been very hard on her," he mused.

Logan didn't comment, and Michael's hesitation was fractional. "She's been under a terrible strain with all that, and not having met you and all, I hope you'll be understanding of her reticence in certain matters."

Logan opened his eyes. "What are you trying to say?"

Michael's gaze was steady. "I've promised her you'd give her time to get to know you before you consummated the marriage."

Logan snorted derisively. "That's a little presumptuous on your part, isn't it?"

His father frowned, and Logan gave a short laugh.

"Don't worry, Father. That's the last thing she has to worry about. I still want an annulment."

"Maybe."

Michael's comment was cryptic, and Logan stood, pacing across the wood-planked floor to open the doors to the veranda. He wished the women would come back, so he could have it done with. He'd already decided to be honest and tell her about Starfire. No woman would want a husband who could never love her. And if she was foolish enough to stay at Woodstone anyway, she could live the life of a widow. As soon as Two Bears returned, he planned to leave for Mexico. It was his only hope now. Rankin had to have taken Starfire south.

"Tell me about Lily Winstead."

His father's question jerked Logan out of his thoughts, and he turned around and stared at him.

"What about her?"

Michael avoided his eyes, and Logan took note of it.

"She just seems like such a young woman to have four grown children. And she's so quiet. She hasn't spoken ten words to me since we've been here, and it's very hard to persuade her to dine with us."

"Her real name is Lily on the Water, and she's one of the heathen savages you've always held in such contempt. She's Ute."

Michael shot him a startled look, thinking uncomfortably of the disparaging remarks he'd made about Indians in her presence just the night before.

"Her husband was John Winstead." Logan went on. "He was my partner after the war when I was still trapping. Lily was only thirteen when he bought her."

"Bought her?" Michael frowned.

"He offered a horse and a buffalo carcass in exchange for her."

"That's barbaric." Michael's outraged disapproval brought a laugh from Logan.

"That's the way the Ute do it, Father. Running Water thought it was an honorable trade. Horses are valuable to Indians."

His father shook his head. "If Zack's twenty, she couldn't be more than thirty-three."

Logan nodded and took his seat again. "Why are you so interested in Lily?" he probed.

"Just curious, I guess."

"Could her long raven hair and soft dark eyes have anything to do with it?" Logan suggested, and Michael's silence answered his question.

But Logan was more interested in his own problems, and he abruptly changed the subject.

"Is this woman aware that I intend to have an annulment?"

"Her name is Elizabeth, Logan," Michael said in annoyance. "And yes, I told her, and she didn't seem particularly upset by it."

Logan waited until his father continued, "As a matter of fact, she was in favor of it."

Logan sat upright. "Then why didn't you arrange one?"

"Because Thomas refused to allow it. Not even Brent could change his mind."

"What the hell does Brent have to do with it?"

"Since you saw fit to ride off and leave Elizabeth alone, Brent took advantage of the situation."

Logan's jaw hardened. "What do you mean?"

"He did quite an effective job of courting her in your long absence."

"How effective?" Logan inquired acidly.

"She's very fond of him."

Logan made a derisive sound. "And Holloway's just as fond of her money, I'm sure."

"No doubt," agreed Michael. "But on the other hand, Elizabeth is very lovely."

"That may be true, but she can't be too discriminating, if she's taken with Brent Holloway."

"He can be charming enough with the ladies."

"I'll consider myself lucky if he's charming enough to take her off my hands. I'd even pay him for that favor, since money appears to be what he's after."

"I daresay you'll change your mind about that soon enough."

Logan frowned, irritated by the smug look on Michael's face. "What the hell's keeping her?" he said, impatience rising to the surface. "I don't intend to wait much longer."

"You don't mean to tell me you're leaving today?" Michael said incredulously.

"That's exactly what I mean. You asked me to meet her, and I will, but I sure as the devil didn't come here to court the woman."

Michael bit back a retort as his son paced restlessly. Despite Logan's stubbornness, he still believed his son would change his mind about Elizabeth within the hour.

"I just hope you'll remember that Elizabeth is a lady and treat her with respect. She's gone through a lot in the past few months."

"I'll do my best to be gallant," Logan said mockingly, sitting down and massaging tired eyes.

Michael sighed. "Well, I hope so. I have enough on my mind with Cassandra."

Logan looked up quickly at the mention of his beautiful younger sister. "What's she done now? I thought she was in finishing school in London."

"She was until she decided to come home to, in her words, nurse the heroic men wounded for the glorious cause of the Confederacy."

Logan laughed. "That crazy girl. I'm surprised you let her."

"I didn't. She sailed home with her roommate to New Orleans, then wrote to tell me where she was."

Logan shook his head, thinking it sounded like something Cassie would do. But right now, he had other things on his mind, namely disposing of an unwanted wife.

Elizabeth sat high on the wagon next to Lily, holding to the seat as they lurched along the rutted path. She shivered, despite the warm sun on her head. When the alarm had echoed out over the water, Zack had grabbed his rifle and gathered the women around him, until Aaron had arrived at a gallop, shouting that Logan was home. The news had filled the Winsteads with excitement, but a cold glaze had crusted over Elizabeth's heart.

She reached up, absently removing the crown of wildflowers she'd fashioned earlier, oblivious to the giggles of Rachel, as Amanda flirted with her oldest brother. For her, all the fun had gone out of the day. She set dull eyes on the lodge in the distance, then shifted her gaze to the purple haze of distant peaks. Since she'd first seen the magnificent Rocky Mountains from the wide prairie, her fears of traveling to Colorado had dimmed and a strange peace had descended upon her. When she'd arrived at Woodstone, she'd loved the peaceful valley on sight, and except for missing Brent and her grandfather, she had been happy the last few weeks with the Winstead family.

"What causes the shadow in your eyes?" Lily asked in her soft voice, and Elizabeth turned to her. She thought her friend was very beautiful, especially her shiny black hair that she wore braided and coiled on top of her head. It was hidden now beneath a blue sunbonnet, but Lily's warm brown eyes watched her in concern.

"I am frightened to meet Logan."

Lily smiled. "That is to be expected, but your fear will not last long. Logan is a good man. You will learn to care for him as I did for my husband."

"What is he like, Lily? I have heard he is terrible when he is angry."

Lily heard the quiver in her voice and tried to reassure her. "He is very strong and sometimes stubborn, but I have never seen him lose his temper. When John died, he gave my children and me a home here. I owe much to him."

Elizabeth nodded, but her eyes were full of dread.

"It will be over soon," Lily said with a quiet smile, as she guided the horse through the tall meadow grass.

Elizabeth looked down at the simple blue cotton dress she wore, wishing she'd had time to change. The hem was muddy and her hair had come loose. She tried to tuck it back into the neat coil, but many of the pins had disappeared, and she finally gave up, letting it flow unhampered down her back.

Lily drove the wagon to the back of the lodge and stopped near the kitchen entrance. Elizabeth took her time untying her apron and smoothing the wrinkles out of her skirt. Lily waited patiently, but when Elizabeth continued to procrastinate, she smiled.

"You must go now, Elizabeth. They are waiting for you," she urged gently. "There is nothing to fear from Logan, I promise."

Elizabeth's smile was wan, but she climbed from the buckboard, watching as it rumbled off toward the stables. She walked through the kitchen, halfheartedly returning Maria's greeting. The old Negress hummed happily as she prepared special dishes for the master's homecoming. Everyone's delight at having Logan Cord back home did help to bolster her flagging courage, however, as she moved through the narrow hall that ran behind the staircase. She paused at the threshold of the great room when she heard the low buzz of masculine conversation. She stood still, an internal battle raging as she fought the overpowering desire to run. Back to the wagon, back to St. Louis, back to Brent.

It took several minutes for it to pass, and she waited it out, then steeled herself with a deep breath. She'd promised her grandfather she'd give Logan Cord a chance, and she would. Perhaps Brent had been wrong about him. She stepped resolutely into the room, her hands clenched tightly together to stop their shaking.

Neither man saw her at first. Michael was looking at Logan, and Elizabeth slowly moved her eyes to the tall man who stood by the windows, his huge, sun-darkened hands clasped behind his back. His wide shoulders seemed to block the opening completely, and he looked very fierce in a fringed tunic with his long, powerful legs encased in deerskin. A shiver undulated down her spine as the sight of him brought images boiling into her mind. She'd seen such garments before. But where? And when? She jumped when his deep voice shattered the quiet of the room.

"What in blazes is keeping the woman?"

Elizabeth blanched at his angry tone and grasped the back of the nearest chair for support.

"Be patient, Logan, she'll be here in a minute," Michael said, his own irritation fading when he noticed his daughter-in-law. Her eyes were huge in her white face, and he went to her at once, draping a comforting arm around her as he drew her into the room.

"Here she is now, Logan. This is Elizabeth."

Michael felt Elizabeth's slender shoulders stiffen, and he watched expectantly, eager to see his son's expression upon first sight of Elizabeth's exquisite beauty.

Logan took a deep, cleansing breath, hoping the woman would be reasonable. He was not in the mood for an ugly scene. He turned, barely glancing at Michael, as his eyes went straight to the tiny woman at his father's side.

Too stunned to move, his eyes locked for an eternity with Starfire's beautiful violet ones. He could not speak, staring openmouthed at her beloved face, the lovely features that had haunted his every waking thought and invaded his dreams for months.

He gave a low groan and shut his eyes, afraid his mind was playing a cruel trick on him. It couldn't be Starfire. Half afraid he'd seen another woman, he looked again to find Starfire watching him warily. His heart began to pound, and Michael frowned, having expected surprised pleasure from his son, but nothing like the total astonishment suffusing Logan's handsome face. When Logan moved, it was so swiftly that it caught Elizabeth and Michael by surprise.

He suddenly loomed before them, his great height dwarfing Elizabeth's petite figure, and she gasped as one strong arm folded about her waist. Then she was pressed against steel muscles, as burning azure eyes devoured her shocked face. The intense blue eyes penetrated the dark and hidden corners of her mind, causing dormant memories to stir, and the burning blue circles of her dreams became reality. But further recollections fled abruptly as long brown fingers knotted in the luxurious mane of her hair, and his mouth came down upon hers with a hunger that sent her mind reeling.

"Starfire, Starfire," he muttered thickly, crushing her against him, his heart constricted by a joy so great as to cause pain.

For several seconds, Michael watched helplessly, astonished by Logan's behavior. Then, as his senses returned, so did his voice.

"Logan! Are you mad? Put her down!" he bellowed in outrage, horrified at his son's insensitive treatment of his new bride.

Logan was completely oblivious to his father, and Elizabeth could not think at all as she hung limply against him, his kisses searing into her lips over and over. When he finally lowered her to her feet, she would have fallen but for Logan's firm grip upon her waist. It was only then that Michael's enraged words filtered through to them.

"How dare you treat her like that, Logan! She's a lady, not some strumpet brought here for your pleasure!"

Elizabeth's mind began to function again, and she raised trembling fingers to touch her kiss-swollen lips, staring up into Logan's handsome face.

Logan smiled down at her, a glad smile he could not stop, but to Elizabeth's wounded sensibilities, it seemed mocking, as if he'd meant to humiliate her. His expression changed abruptly as she pulled away, lifted her skirts, and flew toward the front porch. He started after her, but Michael caught his arm.

"Let her go, damn it! Can't you see what you've done? I warned you about treating her like that. She can't cope with it yet."

"I can't let her get away again," Logan said, his eyes on the door where Elizabeth had disappeared.

Michael frowned and released his grip. "Then you'd better start treating her with the respect she deserves as Thomas Pennington's granddaughter!"

Logan turned confused eyes to him. "She's not Thomas' granddaughter."

Michael gave him an incredulous look. "Have you lost your mind, Logan? Of course she is!"

Logan moved to the French doors and watched as Elizabeth ran toward the creek that fed the lake. Every fiber in his body urged him to follow her, but after the first shock of seeing her had receded, he realized she had not recognized him. He couldn't explain it, couldn't understand any of it.

"She's Thomas' granddaughter? Elizabeth Richmond?" he asked slowly, remembering suddenly Elizabeth's amnesia. Michael stared at him a moment, then nodded his head.

"Yes, I just told you she was! What in heaven's name is the matter with you?"

Logan didn't answer. He was unable to wait any longer; they'd lost too much time already. He'd sort it out later, but right now, he had to find Starfire and hold her in his arms.

"I'm going after her," he said, moving toward the door.

"I'm warning you, Logan . . ." Michael threatened, but Logan was already halfway to the point where Elizabeth had entered the trees.

FOURTEEN

Elizabeth ran along the bank of the creek, ignoring the vines and branches tearing at her unbound hair like bony, grasping fingers. All she wanted was a place to be alone, a place where Logan Cord could never find her. Angry tears coursed down her cheeks, and her lips felt bruised from brutal, relentless kisses. She stumbled toward a shallow sandbar that lay across from a small wooded island, then raised her skirts and hurried across the partially submerged stones. In her haste, her heel slipped from a moss-slickened rock, painfully twisting her ankle. She lost her balance, and the current tugged at her sodden skirts, but she managed to regain her footing and limp to the sandbar, where she sank to the ground.

Her wet petticoats clung to her legs, but she pushed them away and took off her slipper. Her ankle had already begun to swell, and she fingered it tenderly, wincing at the sharp stab of pain. Something about the pain and the sound of the water made her touch the small scar hidden beneath the hair on her temple, intuitively sure that she had injured her head near a river. But she wasn't in the mood to think about the past. She was too angry to think about anything.

She gritted her teeth and looked out over the stream, her fists clenched tightly with fury. Brent had been right all along. Logan Cord did not want her for his wife, and he meant to make her life miserable with his cruel kisses and harsh treatment. He'd grabbed her up without any regard for her feelings. And who was the woman named Starfire he'd mentioned when he had kissed her? Probably his mistress! She hated him! She could never be happy with such a man. She hugged her knees against her breast, her eyes flaming from indignant fury such as she'd never known before. She would have the marriage annulled, she vowed. She would go to Brent in Denver and persuade him to take her home to St. Louis. And Logan Cord could not stop her!

Logan tracked her easily. She'd rushed in headlong flight through the trees with none of the Cheyenne stealth Starfire could use so adeptly. He followed her trail along the creek, trying to decide just what the devil was going on. Huddleston had told him at the first meeting that Starfire had wealthy grandparents in St. Louis. That much fit, but it was a hell of a coincidence, one he wasn't sure he could accept. And even more strange, Michael obviously had no idea of Starfire's past with the Indians.

He knelt where the small footprints ended and scanned the bank for her. He didn't see her until he let his eyes move out over the water. Her silvery hair caught the sun with a brilliance that stopped Logan's heart, and emotion swelled tightly within his chest. He had to get to her, had to have her safely in his arms again.

He waded into the water, his eyes never leaving the small figure huddled upon the island. He was almost to her when she raised her head, and when she scrambled away from him in alarm, he stopped.

"Don't be afraid," he called out, still standing knee-deep in the rippling icy water. "I won't hurt you."

She looked like a small, cornered animal, watching a predator advance, and Logan ran his eyes caressingly over her face, the desire to touch her again nearly staggering him. He tightened his jaw, gathering every ounce of his willpower. She tensed but did not move as he lounged down several feet away from her.

Elizabeth watched him warily as he stared at her with his piercing blue eyes. He was big and arrogantly handsome, his skin bronzed to a deep teak. His blond hair was longer than was stylish and rather shaggy, she decided. But his eyes were what unsettled her, and she looked away, her wrath rising again.

"I'm sorry if I frightened you. I was just so glad to see you."

She did not look up, her fine brows drawing together in

an angry frown. He'd raged over their marriage, insisting upon an annulment, refused even to meet her for months on end, and now he professed to be happy to see her. She looked up at him, eyes cold.

"Glad to see me? Pray tell why? I would think you'd be happy never to set eyes upon me," she snapped.

Logan's eyes had been moving admiringly over her face and hair, trying to detect any change in the months they'd been apart, but at her angry words, he looked up in surprise.

"But now I have seen you, and it makes all the difference," he said, smiling.

Elizabeth tossed her head, sending the silvery tresses swirling over her shoulder. "Perhaps to you it does," she retorted. "But I still intend to have an annulment."

Logan frowned darkly at the contempt in her violet eyes.

"An annulment is totally out of the question, of course," he said, with an arrogant finality that sent Elizabeth livid with fury. Her eyes hardened.

"And my feelings don't matter in the least?"

Logan's frown remained in place, as he realized he wasn't handling the conversation well, but it was hard to remember she didn't know him anymore. They would have to begin again, he resolved. But just then he was more than distracted by the way her angry breathing was moving the wet bodice. He reached out and lifted a soft, silvery lock where it lay upon her shoulder, and Elizabeth jerked it away and tried to stand.

She groaned as her injured foot took her weight, and Logan was up, his hands supporting her waist. "What is it?"

"Nothing," she gasped, allowing him to assist her down. "I twisted my ankle."

"Here, let me see," Logan said, and she watched, aghast, as he swept her petticoats well past her knees. He tugged loose the ribbons of her garter before she could move, and she gasped as he began to roll down her white silk stocking.

"Stop that at once!" she cried, but Logan barely heard her as he feasted starved eyes on her sleek white thigh.

"You have no right . . ." she sputtered, but her protest died in her throat as his palm slid slowly up her bare leg to the back of her knee, while he looked up at her, dark azure fires burning deep inside his eyes. She could not move, and a long moment passed before Logan spoke huskily.

"It's not too bad, but you shouldn't walk on it."

His hand continued to caress her leg gently, and Elizabeth stared at him, while muscles twitched furiously in Logan's cheek as he worked to keep from kissing the moist lips so close to him. But she did not know him, he reminded himself, and her face was still flushed from anger. He'd worry about that later. Right now he was only glad to have her back with him.

He smiled, deciding her twisted ankle was a very good excuse to get her in his arms. "I'd better carry you back."

"No, that's not necessary. I . . . ."

Logan took her into his arms, shutting his eyes as the warm softness of her body put an inhuman strain on his self-control. He waded into the creek with her, and Elizabeth froze, as a memory came back to her with powerful strides, so vivid as to reel her senses. She felt herself being held tightly in the cradle of steel arms, the smell of buckskin and trees and the roaring of water all coming together with such reality that her breath caught.

Logan was unaware of what was going through her mind, absorbed only by the feel of her body against his as he carried her toward the house.

The unnerving sensation gradually left Elizabeth, and she rode rigidly in his arms, piqued by his disregard for her wishes. Brent Holloway's dark green eyes came into her mind, and Elizabeth's chin hardened. Why couldn't it be Brent holding her? She frowned determinedly. It would be Brent soon. She'd never submit to the rude giant who already acted as if he owned her.

Michael and Lily stood together upon the veranda watching as Logan carried Elizabeth across the front lawn. Michael was still upset with Logan, but Lily's dark eyes searched Elizabeth's stormy face.

"Logan, I warned you . . ." Michael began, but Logan cut him off.

"Elizabeth twisted her ankle crossing the creek, and I'm merely carrying her upstairs."

Lily hurried to open the door, and Elizabeth remained stiff in his arms as Logan strode purposefully across the great room. Amanda hovered at the top of the staircase, but one look at Logan, climbing the steps with Elizabeth in his arms, sent her scurrying down the back stairs to the kitchen, and caused Logan to frown at her strange behavior.

"I assume you're using my bedroom," he said, and Elizabeth's voice came back coldly.

"No, I am not. I'm in Cassie's old room."

Logan paused before his own room, giving it a longing look before he turned toward the one across the hall.

"I'll have your things moved then, before tonight."

"You'll do nothing of the kind," Elizabeth retorted, infuriated at his presumption, as he entered her bedroom and crossed the rose-hued carpet to lower her gently onto the lace-draped bed.

Elizabeth stiffened as he sat down beside her and subjected her to an intense scrutiny that eventually brought a warm crimson stain beneath her skin.

"Is it too much for a husband to ask his wife to share his bedroom?" he asked quietly, his eyes on her mouth.

"It is if an annulment is forthcoming!"

Logan looked at her, his blue eyes delving into hers until they seemed to probe into her very soul.

"We are married," he said evenly. "And we're going to stay that way."

He arose quickly as Michael entered the room behind them. "Lily's preparing a poultice for your foot, dear. She should be up with it in a moment," he said, glancing nervously from Logan to Elizabeth. Michael didn't understand what was going on, but he was determined to protect Elizabeth from any more of his son's embarrassing behavior.

Lily arrived moments later and immediately set about mixing her dressing, and when Logan gave no sign of leaving, Michael cleared his throat.

"Elizabeth would probably like to get out of that wet dress and bathe before supper, Logan."

Logan was reluctant to let her out of his sight, especially if she was going to bathe, but he finally lifted Elizabeth's fingers to his lips, disregarding her frigid stare.

"Until tonight," he said with a smile. "When we can get to know each other better."

Elizabeth gritted her teeth as he left with Michael, and Lily smiled encouragingly at her.

"It appears that Logan is most pleased with you."

"He is the only one pleased," Elizabeth said bitterly, surprising Lily.

"Michael told me what happened. I'm surprised Logan did such a thing when he first met you. It is not like him," she admitted.

"I think it is very like him. Rude and arrogant. He even expects me to share his bed this very night."

Lily looked at Elizabeth's smoldering eyes, thinking it had not taken her long to lose any fear of her husband.

"You are his wife," she reminded quietly.

"Only in name, and that will not be for long."

Lily remained silent. She'd known but a few men in her many years among the whites, but even she had seen the desire for his young wife in Logan's blue eyes. He would not let her go easily. It did not bode well for the young couple, especially with Elizabeth's determination to end the marriage. She applied the thick poultice to Elizabeth's foot, hoping her friend would not be unhappy.

"This will help the swelling and take away the pain," she told Elizabeth. "Now let me help you undress, so you can rest before supper."

It was nearly dusk. Michael sat at one end of the great room, watching his son pace. Logan's hands were clasped tightly behind his back. He stopped before the stairs for the hundredth time.

Michael shook his head at Logan's impatience. "For heaven's sake, Logan, stop that infernal pacing and sit down. She'll be down in a minute. You're acting as if she's giving birth up there."

Logan stopped in midpace.

"How long did you say you've known Elizabeth?"

Michael cradled his pipe in his palm, smiling at his son's sudden avid interest in Elizabeth's past life. After all the angry accusations about the arranged marriage to Elizabeth, Logan now seemed obsessed with his bride.

"I met her right after Thomas presented me with the betrothal agreement."

Logan considered his answer, then moved back to the hearth.

"You've been good friends with Thomas for years, Father. Haven't you ever wondered why you haven't met her before, at a ball or a soirée?"

"No. As I understand it, her parents were killed when she was a child, and she was raised by an aunt in Boston."

Michael put a lit taper to his pipe, puffing it into flame.

"None of that is true," Logan said in a low voice, and Michael held the wick poised in midair as he raised astounded eyes. Logan watched him intently, and Michael decided he'd heard him wrong.

"What did you say?"

"I said that none of that is true. Elizabeth was raised by the Cheyenne Indians some miles north of here, until I stole her away from them last year."

Michael's jaw dropped as if unhinged, and silence prevailed until he found his tongue.

"Logan, that is undoubtedly the most absurd thing I've ever heard. Have you completely lost your senses?"

Logan smiled humorlessly. "I've wondered the same thing in the last few months."

He paced back to the center of the room for another look up the staircase. He was growing increasingly uneasy. Starfire had been out of his sight too long, making him want to doubt that the whole unbelievable situation had really happened.

Michael put down his pipe, his brows drawn together in concern. "Son, I'm truly beginning to worry about you. You've been acting strangely for months now, and this nonsense about Elizabeth . . ."

"It's not nonsense. Her name is Starfire, and we were lovers. She was taken from me last autumn in Denver by three men, and I've nearly gone mad these past months trying to find her. Why do you think I was so dead set against the marriage?"

"But it just can't be. Thomas—"

Logan interrupted him, running both hands through his hair. "Perhaps she is Thomas' granddaughter, I don't know. I was hired by a solicitor named Alfred Huddleston to get her back for her white family, and he wouldn't tell me their name."

Michael tried to keep his disbelief out of his voice.

"There's just got to be some mistake, Logan. You've seen Elizabeth. She couldn't have grown up with savages. She's a lady." He gave a short laugh at the preposterous idea. "Perhaps Elizabeth just resembles this girl you knew."

He stopped at Logan's mocking laugh, but the sound died abruptly as Logan spoke seriously. "Do you honestly think, Father, that I could ever forget a woman like Elizabeth, even if I'd seen her but one time?"

Michael thought of Elizabeth's exquisitely formed face and knew it would be impossible for any man to forget her.

"I'm just finding this a bit difficult to believe."

"So am I. Especially the fact that she doesn't recognize me."

Michael steepled his fingers and looked over them at Logan.

"I told you about her memory loss. But even if all this is true, why didn't Thomas tell me about it?"

"I don't have the slightest idea," Logan said, sinking into a chair where he could see the steps. "And I'm not sure I care, as long as I have her back. I've gone through hell on earth looking for her."

"But she doesn't remember you."

"She's my wife, now," Logan said flatly.

"Still, you're a stranger to her, and she'll need time to get to know you."

Logan's eyes grew dark. "She acts as if she hates me."

"Well, grabbing her and kissing her as you did this afternoon didn't help any. If your story is true, I can at least understand your motives. But since I told her she'd have until the wedding ball to get to know you, you'll have time to work things out."

Logan's voice was low. "I don't intend to wait. If anything will bring back her memory, a night in my bed will."

"But Logan, I promised her . . ." Michael's voice died away under steady blue eyes, and he finished lamely, "I can't help but think you're making a mistake trying to force her to remember you."

Logan shrugged and took the steps two at a time, unwilling to wait any longer.

Upstairs, Elizabeth sat in a rocking chair by the fireplace, her small fingers clenched hard on the carved arms. She turned her head and stared dispassionately at her reflection in the mirror upon her dresser. Amanda had arranged her hair in an upswept mass of shining curls, then threaded it with dark blue ribbons to match the cording on her pale blue gown. But Elizabeth did not care how she looked. All she knew was that she didn't want to go downstairs.

But if she didn't, she had no doubt that Logan Cord would carry her down, whether she liked it or not. The idea incensed her, and she limped to her dressing table, where she picked up a lace shawl. She would not give him the opportunity to touch her again, and if he expected her to sleep with him, he would be very disappointed. She had already refused to let Rachel move her things into his bedroom.

She whirled as Logan opened the door without knocking, and was overwhelmed by his size alone as he came toward her. He'd shaved and dressed for dinner, and Elizabeth reluctantly admitted that he was a very handsome man in his dark green coat and buff-colored waistcoat. The well-tailored clothing emphasized his immense shoulders, and his legs looked very long and muscular in his snugfitting breeches. She watched him cautiously, but he only smiled at her, his eyes dropping to her lips. His absorption with her mouth disconcerted her, and she turned away.

"Is your foot painful?"

She glanced up, then away as his eyes scorched a hole into her face. She hated the way he made her feel, like some prize animal he'd bought. Resentment roiled and rose, and her words were clipped.

"It is much better, thank you."

She raised her slim nose and swept past him with as much dignity as she could muster with a pronounced limp. Logan laughed, and the next thing she knew she again rode securely in the steel cradle of his arms. Pride kept her from protesting, but an angry retort burned on her lips, as Logan strode down the hall, the fragrance of her hair conjuring intimate memories that heated his blood.

Elizabeth continued to fume silently as Logan walked past Michael. Lily stood quietly waiting beside the dining table, where tall silver candelabra glittered over delicate crystal and the finest of English china. Logan put her down, and to her chagrin, did not move away, but stood behind her, his eyes upon the satiny mounds swelling above the blue-corded silk. She leaned forward, intentionally blocking his view, and Logan moved reluctantly to his chair.

Maria had prepared a sumptuous feast for Logan's return, but he was too engrossed in the pleasure of having Starfire beside him to pay much attention to the excellent fare, and his constant warm regard put an end to any appetite Elizabeth might have had. Michael made several valiant attempts to relieve the tension, but more often than not, his remarks were met by complete silence, or at best, desultory replies. As Maria served a cobbler, Michael decided to broach the subject of the wedding ball, hoping to draw Logan's fascinated eyes off his wife, if only for a moment.

"The invitations to the ball went out several weeks ago, Logan. I've invited a great many people from Central City as well as Denver. Lily was good enough to help me with the guest list." He smiled at her, and she lowered her eyes. "I'm hoping the gathering will give Elizabeth a chance to make some acquaintances out here."

Logan frowned. The idea of Denver society descending on Woodstone just when he'd found Starfire again definitely did not appeal to him, but if the plans had already been made, there was little he could do about it.

"Is everything in readiness?" he asked without really caring.

"I'm hoping Lily will help me with the preparations," Michael said, looking at Lily for her reaction.

"I will be more than glad to be of service to you, Mr. Cord," Lily murmured.

"Call me Michael, please."

Logan had lost interest in their conversation already, his eyes on Elizabeth as she picked uninterestedly at her dessert. It had been only months ago that he'd taught her the use of a knife and fork, he thought, remembering that delightful morning when he had feasted his eyes on her half-nakedness at the dining-room table. Now her manners were beyond reproach, and he wondered how she'd become so accomplished in so short a time.

To Elizabeth's heartfelt relief, the meal finally ended, and she stood, determined to keep Logan Cord away from her.

"Michael, may I lean on your arm, please?" she asked, triumphant at Logan's frown.

Michael glanced at his son, thinking Elizabeth didn't seem to be overly impressed with him, although he couldn't fault Logan's manners during the meal. He offered Elizabeth his arm, and Logan followed with Lily to the other end of the great room.

Michael lit his pipe and opened a book, pausing now and and again to admire Lily, where she sat quietly near the undulating fire. Logan stood, one elbow resting on the mantel, and Elizabeth felt she'd scream if he did not stop looking at her. His bad manners were astonishing, and his blue eyes continued to rattle her composure. It enraged her to think that she was legally bound to this stranger, that he had the power to disrupt her life, to trap her into a loveless marriage with him. Why would he want a wife who did not love him? She fumed. And now he watched her, his blue eyes seeming to strip away her clothes. She took up the sampler she'd begun for her grandfather, so she wouldn't have to look at him, and Logan marveled, amazed she'd even attempt needlework.

He moved to stand behind her chair, hiding a grin at the uneven row of stitches slanting across the fabric. It gave him a perverse pleasure that Starfire had not mastered everything. Elizabeth jabbed the needle in and out of the fine linen, piqued by his proximity. He unnerved her completely, and she could not concentrate with him so close. When his warm hand settled unexpectedly upon her bare shoulder, she jumped, stabbing the sharp needle into her finger. She cried out, dropping the hoop, and Logan immediately had her hand in his, examining the wound. He raised his eyes to hers, then placed the fingertip between his warm lips.

A jolt ran up Elizabeth's arm, tingling her flesh, and she stared into his eyes as indescribable longings flickered alive deep inside her. Her lips parted, and she jerked her hand away, frightened by her own response.

"Logan?"

Zack's voice was hesitant, and Elizabeth breathed easier

as Logan turned toward the boy. "I'm really sorry to bother you, sir, but I'm leaving early in the morning to round up a few strays, and I need to talk to you."

Logan hesitated, looking down at Elizabeth.

"I'll be there in a minute, Zack," he said, then turned to Elizabeth. "I'll be back shortly to carry you to bed."

Elizabeth averted her face, thinking he'd never get the chance. She meant to spend the night safely behind a bolted door, regardless of what he wanted. She barely gave him time to leave the room before she stood.

"I'm really very tired. I believe I'll go on up."

"Can I help you, dear?" Michael offered at once, but Elizabeth shook her head.

She climbed the steps as fast as she could. Her ankle was throbbing by the time she reached her own room, but she smiled as she slid the bolt firmly into place. She undressed quickly without ringing for Amanda, donning a thin gown and robe. She looked down at the sheer fabric with its delicate lace, wishing for a less revealing gown than those furnished for her trousseau.

But the door was safely locked, and she was certain that Logan Cord would not be so crude as to force himself upon her. Or would he? She found herself pacing the floor, each step worsening the pain in her foot. She froze, her hands clutching each other, as a low knock sounded at the door. She looked around in desperation, thinking she would pretend to be asleep.

"Let me in, Elizabeth."

There was no mistaking who stood outside, and by the tone of his voice, he meant to gain entrance one way or another.

It rankled her to the core to have to let him in, but she would not cause a scene for everyone in the house to hear. She slid back the bolt, then quickly moved away.

Logan stepped inside, having removed his coat for the comfort of shirt and breeches. He closed the door and leaned against it, but Elizabeth did not give him time to speak.

"Why do you deny me an annulment?" she said angrily. "Surely you cannot want a marriage without love!"

The irony of the situation was not lost upon Logan, as she used the very argument he'd planned to use himself.

He stared at her, realizing that the woman standing before him with angry violet eyes was not the Cheyenne maiden who'd won his heart. She was a completely different person now. He would have to get to know her all over again, but perhaps if he tried, he could bring Starfire back. Elizabeth or Starfire, he wanted her, he needed her, and he'd never let her go.

"Do you think it's impossible that I could love you?" he asked, his eyes running over her lightly draped figure.

Elizabeth answered coldly, "I think it's possible that you desire me, but that has little to do with love."

Logan smiled. "If you only knew, my sweet." He paused, then said softly, "If I told you that I love you more than life itself, would you believe me?"

Her answer was a contemptuous toss of her head.

"Can you deny then," she challenged coldly, "that more than anything else, you want to take me into your bed this night? Even though Michael promised me you would wait."

It was one thing Logan could not deny, and his voice was steady.

"No, I can't. You are my wife, and I want you."

"Then that is very unfortunate, because I love another. And after I am granted an annulment, I will marry him."

Logan's face went rigid, his voice under steely control. "And whom, if I may ask, are you in love with?"

Elizabeth watched him approach her, tremors racing across her flesh as she remembered stories of his violent temper. He waited, and Elizabeth swallowed hard, thinking he could be very dangerous.

"Brent Hollo—"

She got no further, because he had her in his grip, his fingers biting cruelly into her arms. She gasped, for the first time truly afraid of him. He stared down at her, his eyes so dark with anger and anguish they no longer looked blue, then he released her abruptly, one angry swipe of his arm clearing the top of her dressing table, sending her crystal bottles of perfume and oils tinkling and shattering against the wall.

Elizabeth sank down upon the bed, shaking uncontrollably as Logan moved across the room with long, angry footsteps. She hugged herself, terrified, as he braced both arms

against the mantel and stared into the fire. The soft crackling of the logs was the only sound until he gained control
and turned to her, the firelight making glittering sap-
phires of eyes. His voice was deceptively calm.

"Regardless of whom you think you love, I am your legal
husband."

Their eyes locked, and Elizabeth could not breathe as he
continued, "But I'm willing to give you time to get to know
me, if that's what you want."

Relief washed over Elizabeth like a cool wind.

"But only until the ball. If you have not come to me by
then, I will come to you."

"You will force me?" Elizabeth managed to ask.

"If need be." His quiet admission astounded her, and she
stared at him, realizing he meant it.

"And in the meantime, you will deny me nothing else
that I ask of you."

Elizabeth considered it, but afraid of his reaction if she
refused, she nodded slightly.

Logan's grim face relaxed somewhat, and she watched
him move to the rocker by the fire and sit down.

"Then right now, more than anything else, I wish the
pleasure of holding you in my arms."

He waited, but Elizabeth didn't move. Then afraid his
temper was about to erupt again, Elizabeth moved slowly
to stand in front of him. His azure eyes held hers relentlessly.

"Put your arms around my neck."

His voice was hoarse, but brooked no refusal, and she
hesitantly obeyed. She gasped as his arms came around
her, one swift movement turning her until she lay across
his lap. Her gown caught around her hips, exposing satiny
thighs, and her hair fell in a silken cascade over his forearm. Her heart began a wild and fearful cadence as he slid
long fingers beneath the soft silver and knotted a handful
at her nape. His lips went like a heated brand to the side of
her throat.

"No! You promised . . ."

He groaned and slid his open palm along her warm
thigh, and she struggled to escape. An unintelligible protest came deep from within his throat, and Logan held her

in a gentle band of steel, his words muffled against her hair.

"Just let me hold you for a time, then I'll leave."

Elizabeth did not relax as he pillowed her head against his shoulder. They sat quietly, Elizabeth tense and wary as he cradled her, and it took a long while for her pulse to calm. When it beat normally again, she hazarded a glance at him from beneath the dark veil of her lashes.

He stared into the fire, his face like carved marble, but he made no further move against her. After a time, Elizabeth's muscles gradually lost their rigidity, and her slender body softened against his hard chest. Her ear lay upon the fine fabric of his shirt, and the steady thud of his heart lulled her mind and calmed her ragged nerves. The day had been very long for her, filled with anger and stress, and she found to her surprise that lying so intimately against Logan Cord was not so terrifying as she'd imagined. His arms held her warm and secure, and as the fire began to die away, her tiredness took its toll.

She drowsed in a lovely netherland closer to dreams than to reality, and the way his palm gently stroked her hair was almost pleasant. She was only vaguely aware of the soft kisses he pressed with utmost tenderness upon her brow and she snuggled closer against the molded contours of his chest as misty strands of sleep entwined over her mind, wrapping over and around until she sank into dark blue peace.

Logan sat holding her close long after she slept, never having experienced such exquisite, bittersweet torture as having his beloved Starfire in his arms at long last, and being unable to possess her.

FIFTEEN

Elizabeth awoke, and reassured by the familiar white lace canopy above her, she snuggled deeper into the downy softness of her satin comforter. It had been almost a week since Logan Cord had come to Woodstone, and each night he'd held her in the rocker by the fire until she slept. But every morning, true to his word, she'd find herself alone in her own bed.

She sleepily pondered the stranger who was her husband, a perplexed frown marring her brow. He was so hard to understand. He'd made her so angry that first day, but since then, he'd behaved like a perfect gentleman, courteous to her in every way. Only that first night, when she'd mentioned Brent, had his terrible anger showed itself. Now when he held her at bedtime, his gentleness was infinite.

She closed her eyes, and hazy recollections of his mouth upon her neck brought an inexplicable thrill of pleasure. Logan Cord's touch sent ripples across her flesh and strange stirrings deep inside her body. She thought of the way his blond hair looked moving lingeringly across her breasts, the soft texture of his hair between her fingers.

Suddenly she sat bolt upright. But he'd never done such things to her! She'd never run her fingers through his hair! It was so strange and confusing that she frowned deeply, until a soft tapping brought her attention to the door. Although Logan had made no demands upon her, he entered her chambers as he would, regardless of her dishabille, and Elizabeth had not dared to lock her door against him a second time.

Amanda's freckled face peeked around the door, and

Elizabeth smiled and lifted her long hair in a luxurious stretch. Amanda carried the tray to the bedside table, glad to see her young mistress did not yet share the blond giant's bed, despite the fact that Rachel laughed at her fears concerning him. She propped a pillow behind Elizabeth and handed her a cup and saucer.

"How nice of Lily. I love chocolate," Elizabeth murmured, savoring the sweet-tasting beverage.

"It wasn't Miss Lily who sent it up. It was Master Logan. He sent Zack all the way to Central City for a supply of it."

Elizabeth turned to Amanda, her cup suspended in her hand. "But how would he know it is my favorite?"

Amanda shrugged, and Elizabeth contemplated Logan's thoughtfulness as Amanda tied the heavy damask drapes aside to reveal a breathtaking view of the lake as it glittered like millions of diamonds under the morning sunshine.

"This is the day of the picnic," Amanda reminded her, opening the double doors of the cherrywood armoire. "What will you wear?"

"The white gown with the pink ribbons, I suppose. It's cool."

Amanda pulled out the dress and hung it upon the door, then reached for the matching hat, while Elizabeth dreamed out the window, remembering how warm Logan's blue eyes became when he looked at her. She had found in the last week that he was not the cruel and heartless monster she'd first thought. In fact, he could be most charming at times. She smiled and swung slim legs over the side of the bed. She lifted her gown and examined her ankle, pleased that the swelling was gone. She stepped down, gingerly trying her weight. It was no longer painful to walk, and perhaps now Logan would not be so inclined to sweep her into his arms at the least provocation.

She moved to the dressing table, bathing her face in the basin of water, then raised her brush, absently pulling it through her tousled hair. Her mind was elsewhere, on strong arms that held her on a warm, masculine lap and blue eyes that darkened and lightened according to mood. A small smile curved her lips, and she nearly dropped her brush when her gaze collided with the blue eyes in question. He had come up silently behind her, and she could not move as he lifted a silvery strand of her hair and smoothed it carefully over her shoulder with a touch so gentle it took her breath. His slow smile caressed her face, then moved to her low-cut gown.

"Good morning, my love," he said, and the endearment sent a warm blush into her cheeks. He moved to a chair behind her, and she saw that he wore snug black breeches and a white linen shirt. He'd left it unbuttoned partway, and her eyes touched on the crisp blond fur covering hard, sunbrowned flesh, and her heart quickened alarmingly. She jerked her eyes away, nerves on edge as she fingered one crystal bottle of perfume, then another on the mirrored tray before her.

She wished he'd speak; his interest in her every movement disconcerted her completely. For something to do, she chose a bottle, touching the fragrance to the hollow of her throat. Logan's eyes followed her slender finger, his breath catching as it trailed downward toward her soft and mounding cleavage. Elizabeth replaced the perfume, but Logan's eyes lingered upon her swelling breasts. Her own pulse reacted, and she stood, uncomfortable in the sheerness of her gown.

"Your foot seems much better," he noted as she drew on a diaphanous dressing gown.

"Yes," Elizabeth answered, pulling the sash about her waist. "There is very little pain now."

A silence followed as his attention was drawn to her body so tantalizingly veiled from him.

"Is there something you wish from me?" Elizabeth said finally, hoping to alleviate the uncomfortable quiet.

Logan laughed. "There are many things I wish from you, my love, but you continue to refuse them to me."

Elizabeth's mouth went dry, and she moistened her lips nervously, bringing Logan's gaze to them.

"I only wish for time to know you better."

"And do you know me better now?"

"I am beginning to, I think."

"Then I am content to wait."

His hot eyes said differently, and Elizabeth walked to the window.

"I came to tell you that we've decided to picnic in the high meadows . . ."

Logan's voice stilled as the bright sunlight created a halo around her, revealing every delectable curve of her body. It wasn't until she moved toward the bed that he could find his voice again.

"Maria fixed a lunch, and Lily and the girls are going."

"That sounds very pleasant," she said truthfully. "It shouldn't take me long to dress."

She waited for him to take his leave, but when Logan only smiled, Elizabeth realized he could very easily remain during her toilette. He looked into her wide eyes, as if aware of her thoughts, then stood.

"Hurry then, sweet, and I'll wait for you downstairs." He strode from the room, chuckling, his mood lightened.

The pleasure she felt in anticipation of the day with him disturbed her enough to crease a frown between her brows, and she puzzled over her feelings as she slipped on the lace-trimmed white dress of the softest lawn. Pink ribbons were sewn across the midriff, leaving her shoulders soft and bare above a wide eyelet ruffle. She fashioned her hair in loose curls atop her head, then picked up the wide-brimmed hat designed to protect her creamy skin from the sun. A long pink plume decorated the low crown, and she set it in place, tilting her head for the effect. Satisfied, she tied the ribbons beneath her chin and went to meet Logan.

When she entered the great room, Logan's slow and thorough admiration sent a becoming rosiness into her cheeks. He came forward and extended his arm.

"Come, they're waiting outside for us."

Elizabeth returned his smile shyly. She put her hand upon his arm as he led her outside. Lily and Michael sat upon the wagon seat with the girls in the back alongside two gigantic wicker hampers. The three boys were mounted, their rifles in sheaths upon the saddle, and Logan had to grin at their openmouthed appreciation of the pink-and-white vision that barely reached his shoulder.

Elizabeth started toward the wagon, but Logan's hand detained her.

"No, I would like you to ride beside me."

Elizabeth stared in dismay as Jacob stopped in front of them with Logan's black stallion and a lovely bay mare.

"But I have never been upon a horse," she protested quickly, and Logan looked down at her. Fleeting memories of Starfire racing like the wind upon a wild palomino filled him.

His laugh brought puzzled violet eyes to him, and he smiled down at her. "Something tells me you'll catch on quick enough."

Elizabeth looked at the flaring nostrils and twitching tail of the mare and wasn't convinced.

"Lady is very gentle," Logan said, stroking the mare's velvety nose. He looked at Elizabeth when she stepped back, realizing she was truly afraid.

"Then come ride on Zeus with me," he offered. "And I'll show you how to handle the reins."

The idea of sitting atop the huge black stallion with Logan was even more disquieting, but she did not protest when Logan lifted her onto his saddle, then settled behind her as he took up the reins.

Elizabeth felt very small within the circle of Logan's strong arms, but the way he held her caused faint nibblings at the far edges of her mind, as if she'd experienced it before. The disturbing sensation took flight quickly as Logan's warm breath fanned her cheek.

"Don't be afraid, sweet, you're safe with me."

Elizabeth felt anything but safe with the steel wall of his chest so close behind her that the heat of his body penetrated her thin dress. Her pulse sped dangerously as Logan spurred his mount, one large hand securing her to him, the other controlling the spirited stallion.

The little caravan began to move, and Logan led the wagon, the lake glistening beside them as a brisk wind ruffled sparkling whitecaps across the water. The day was beautiful and warm for late April, the air fresh and invigorating. They traversed the mountain-rimmed pastures toward the far side of the valley.

Halfway through the meadows, Logan galloped ahead, and Elizabeth clung desperately to her hat as the wind tore the ribbons from beneath her chin, but never once did she experience alarm while in her husband's firm grip. She felt exhilarated and free during the fast ride, and when a sudden gust of wind whipped her hat out of her grasp, she laughed as it rode the air currents like a graceful white bird, then settled upon the tall green grass as if it were nesting there. Logan reined up, and Zeus reared slightly and pranced sideways.

"Do you want it?" Logan asked her, and Elizabeth turned in the saddle to look up at him, surprising him with a dimpled smile.

"No, I do not. I've often wished to toss it into the wind myself!"

Logan laughed, pleased by the happiness upon her face.

"Then there it will stay. And you might as well get rid of these as well."

His fingers went to her hair, carelessly discarding pins and combs until the heavy silver tresses tumbled across his arms.

"Now I can touch it." His words had been husky, his lips teasing the sensitive spot behind her ear, and gooseflesh rippled down both her arms.

He urged Zeus on, and she fought for control of her own pleasure as they flew ahead. Elizabeth's hair blew in the wind like silver silk, the sweet fragrance intoxicating the man behind her.

The fields rose gradually to dense forests of gigantic spruce, and Logan took them into the coolness of the sun-dappled shade. Elizabeth smiled, happier and more care-free than she'd ever dreamed possible in her husband's company. When the wooded ridge leveled into a rocky ter-rain spotted with great rust-red boulders, Logan halted Zeus, then turned the stallion to give Elizabeth a breath-taking view of the sprawling valley.

Woodstone was but an insignificant dot against the roll-ing hills, and far below, the wagon left parallel tracks in the tall meadow grass, waving and rippling in the breeze.

"Will they be able to find us?" Elizabeth asked breath-lessly, looking around the dark and quiet trees.

"Not for a time," Logan answered, then added under his breath, "If we're lucky." He was determined to have some time alone with Elizabeth for a change. And what better place than in the mountains she loved?

Elizabeth twisted and peered over her husband's wide shoulder at her friends far below, but the steep incline soon forced her to relax back into the cradle of Logan's arms. But she found that she did not really mind it, and leaned her head intimately against his chest.

"Surely a wagon cannot come this way," she said, as Logan nosed the horse through a narrow path between tall trees.

"No, but Zack knows another way. This is quicker."

A swift-running brook materialized before them, the clear water rippling softly over smooth, emerald-crusted rocks.

"Do you like it?" Logan asked, and Elizabeth's answer was awed.

"Oh, yes."

Logan smiled. "I thought you might."

He walked the horse across the sandbar, then urged him up a small slope. He dismounted in a grassy clearing surrounded by thick-boughed spruce trees, then looked up at Elizabeth through eyes as clear and blue as the summer sky. Memories stirred anew behind the velvet curtains that held her prisoner, and she strained to remember.

"What is it?" Logan asked in concern, but Elizabeth shook her head as he lifted her down, holding her for the briefest of moments, and Elizabeth did not even think to protest. He spread a blanket upon the ground for her, and Elizabeth sat watching as he unsaddled Zeus. Powerful muscles ridged in his arms as he swung the heavy saddle to the ground with no show of effort.

He smiled down at her, and her smile came easily.

"Come, I want to show you something."

He extended his hand to her, then laced her small fingers in his as he led her to an opening in the trees. She waited as he held back a branch to reveal graduating rock cliffs in the distance, where the river cascaded in roaring, rushing waterfalls.

"It's lovely," Elizabeth breathed, pleasure lighting her face, and Logan watched intently, hoping the falls would trigger memories of their time together in the cave.

"Have you ever seen a waterfall, Elizabeth?"

"Oh yes, but it was much bigger—" She stopped abruptly, turning astonished violet eyes upon him. Logan smiled and encouraged her gently.

"Tell me about it. What do you remember?"

Elizabeth shut her eyes and saw it very clearly.

"It was very loud with a great roaring, and there was a river far below with angry, twisting rapids." Her brows came together as she tried to concentrate. "And I was afraid. . . ."

Logan waited with bated breath, daring to hope she would remember the rest of it. He was tired of waiting, tired of holding himself in iron restraint when he was near her.

"Think, Elizabeth. Why were you afraid?"

The image of the falls slowly disintegrated as sharp pain pierced into her temples, and Elizabeth let it go.

"You must try to remember. Concentrate very hard."

"I cannot!" she cried, stepping away from him, her face dark with frustration. "It hurts when I try."

She pressed her fingers over her eyes as pain throbbed behind them, and Logan frowned, putting his arm about her slender shoulders.

"I'm sorry. Let's go back."

He led her back, then lounged down on the blanket, watching as she sat, arranging her skirts modestly. His hand trembled with the desire to touch her, and his voice was unsteady when at last he spoke, but he was struggling to understand the strange memory loss which kept her from him.

"Is it often that things come back like that?"

"A headache usually drives them away," she admitted.

"It must be very frightening at times."

"It is terrible," she murmured. "And I have awful dreams I don't understand."

"What is the first thing you can remember?"

"Waking up in the doctor's office with Dr. Petaire and Brent."

Logan's jaw tightened, enraged at the thought of Brent's enjoying her company during the long months he had searched for her in vain.

"And you didn't remember Thomas at all?"

"No." She smiled wistfully. "It was as if I had no life before that moment."

She shuddered, remembering the first days and nights when she'd felt so alone and afraid. Logan watched her put her fingers against her temples and press.

"Does your head still hurt?"

She nodded, and Logan sat up. "Turn around and lean against me," he ordered. "So I can rub it for you."

She looked at him, a little wary, but as another streak of pain stabbed into her temple, she moved in front of him, sighing as his long fingers slid up beneath the silkiness of her hair. The gentle circular motion he worked upon her temples relieved the pain almost at once, and the tension in her body began to ebb away. His lean fingers moved to her shoulders, and Elizabeth laid her head against his shoulder, letting the rippling water and twittering birds soothe her until she floated in dreamy contentment. It took her several minutes to realize that his lips had replaced his fingertips upon her temples, and she sat forward. His words were husky, uttered close beside her ear.

"Is a kiss so much to ask, when I've denied myself everything I desire?"

Elizabeth was intensely aware of their isolation in the leafy bower, and when Logan leaned closer, her heart accelerated wildly.

"A kiss, Elizabeth, that's all I want. I'll take no more than you're willing to give. I swear it."

She looked into his handsome face, thinking a kiss was little for a husband to ask, and she could take comfort from the fact that he'd held her close in the privacy of her bedchamber without violating his word. Brent's face flickered for a guilty moment, then was banished from her mind as she leaned toward him. The lightest of kisses would not endanger her. Perhaps she would even find it pleasant.

But her good intentions were swept away like smoke in the wind from the instant his firm lips pressed warmly against her soft red ones. Fingers of fire shot into the deepest core of Elizabeth's soul as Logan's arm folded around her waist, pressing her backward upon the blanket. His mouth slanted across hers, hot and demanding, and she could not move, could not protest as his warm lips took total possession of her thoughts, swirling them into a boiling, leaping maelstrom of sensation.

His lips worked upon hers, twisting, burning, subjugating her until she had no will of her own. His tongue touched hers, and the shock that coursed through her sent her world spiraling. She barely heard the groan wrenched from Logan as her silken arms slid around his neck. His breathing became ragged as she offered him the parted sweetness of her lips, and like a man starving, he traced the satiny cheekbone, one hand knotted in the silky mane of silver, the other molding gently the full swell of her breast.

Elizabeth's body flamed higher, gasping as his mouth found and explored the fragile cord of her throat, then dropped a molten trail along her smooth, bare shoulder. His mouth muffled her murmured protest as his hand quit the silkiness of her hair to ease along the back of her bodice, releasing buttons until her swelling bosom fell free.

"No . . ." she whispered, but her breathless murmur lacked the conviction needed to give Logan pause in his thundering passion. His hand intruded beneath the soft layers of her skirt, and she moaned beneath his mouth as his fingers touched bare skin, then moved slowly up her naked thigh.

"Starfire, Starfire, surrender, my love. . . ."

His kisses robbed her of reason, and she could no longer resist, as his caresses grew bolder, drawing her hips against him until Elizabeth could not deny his masculine need.

"Logan! Are you up there?"

It took several seconds for the voice to carve a path into the swirling mists of their passion, but when it did, Logan froze, groaning like a man near death. He held Elizabeth's trembling body for as long as he dared, then rose to his knees, his shaking fingers working to fasten the gaping bodice.

Elizabeth stared at him helplessly as he straightened her skirts and pulled her to her feet. Every inch of her burned with unfulfilled desire. He crushed her limp body against him.

"I'm sorry, sweet, so sorry."

Michael called again, and Logan muttered an oath under his breath.

"Up here," he yelled, still unable to bring himself to release her. He cupped her face between his palms, his eyes searching hers.

"Elizabeth, please, listen to me. I couldn't stop myself. When you began to respond, I . . ."

Elizabeth did not give him time to finish, but pulled

away. Logan watched her go, helpless to stop his relief. A great burden had been lifted from his heart, for even if Elizabeth's mind did not remember him, her body did. He'd won Starfire's love long ago in the darkness of a cave, and given the time, he would win Elizabeth's as well. He knew he would. Smiling, he quickly saddled the horse and followed Elizabeth's hasty scramble down the hill.

For the rest of the day, Elizabeth avoided any but the most casual contact with Logan, and he was careful not to upset her further. The encounter in the shady glade above the brook haunted Elizabeth's every thought, and Logan's attention rarely left his beautiful wife. They ate the lunch of ham and sweet bread that Maria had provided, and afterward, Elizabeth and Lily removed their stockings and joined Rachel and Amanda where they waded in the shallows.

"You're very quiet," Michael commented to Logan as they sat together beneath a tree watching the women. "Did you and Elizabeth have a falling-out?"

Logan shook his head. "We did all right until you got here."

"I had a feeling we showed up at the wrong time."

"That's an understatement."

Michael grinned at his son's despondent expression.

"Is she any closer to remembering you?"

Logan shook his head.

"Perhaps it won't be long now," Michael said, and Logan watched as Elizabeth lifted her skirts to wade deeper. His throat dried as the water washed over her legs, wetting her thighs.

"It had better be soon, because I won't last much longer," he groaned, and Michael laughed at him.

Logan's voice was low. "She's just so damn beautiful. It's been this way since the first day I saw her. And when she was taken from me . . ."

His voice dwindled, as if he could not put his pain into words. They lapsed into silence then, and Michael's gaze rested almost as exclusively on Logan's Indian housekeeper as his son's did on Elizabeth. He was admiring the way her ebony hair glinted blue in the sunlight when he turned at Logan's low laugh.

"If the expression on your face is any indication of how

you feel about Lily, you have woman trouble as bad as I do."

He grinned at Michael's sigh. "I can't seem to get her to talk to me. Even when I try, she makes excuses to get away from me."

"I know how you feel," Logan said glumly, and they turned their attention back to the women splashing in the water.

The sun hung low in the sky when they packed the wagon, and Elizabeth did not dare trust herself to ride upon Logan's steed. She insisted upon mounting the mare, and Logan untied it from the wagon and lifted her to the saddle. Even the casual contact sent a tingling through her, and she rode close to the rear of the wagon, where she could listen to the girls excited chatter. It did not take her long to realize she'd definitely ridden before. She handled the mare instinctively with sure, capable hands, feeling at home in the saddle.

Logan rode behind her with the boys, watching her slim hips sway with the gentle movement of the mare, wondering if she'd ever let him touch her again. The thought was depressing, and he was growing less confident he could last until the ball.

By the time they reached Woodstone, it was nearly dusk, and Logan dismounted in front of the house, then lifted Elizabeth down. He wanted to talk to her, but she avoided him and stepped away as soon as he released her.

"Logan, look," Zack called from his horse, and Logan turned to see a horse galloping down the road toward them.

"Who's that?" Michael asked, and Logan frowned when he recognized the rider.

"It looks like Parker."

Seconds later, the lathered horse reached them, and Logan grabbed the bridle, frowning as Parker nearly fell into his arms. His face looked gray with exhaustion, and Logan supported the old man as Jacob led the horse away.

"What's happened, Parker?"

"Fire," Parker gasped out. "Denver's on fire!"

His words brought gasps all around, as Logan questioned him quickly. "What about the house?"

"It's right in the path of it. I tried to get enough men to move the furniture out if it gets to us."

"Is Agatha all right?"

Parker nodded. "Yes, she's with friends. I came as fast as I could."

"We'd better get you inside."

Parker nodded tiredly, then smiled weakly as he saw Elizabeth.

"This is my wife, Elizabeth," Logan said to him quickly. "She came out from St. Louis with my father."

Parker looked confused, but Logan's warning had registered, and he said politely, "It's a pleasure, ma'am."

Elizabeth nodded, sensing undercurrents she couldn't explain, but there was no time to dwell on it as Lily sent Rachel and Amanda running for food and drink for the weary traveler. Elizabeth followed the men into the house, listening as Logan assisted Parker into a chair.

"It's a bad one, sir. The whole main street is already gone. The wind kept changing directions, and the sparks ignited everything for miles. It's been so dry that water is scarce, and we just couldn't put it out."

Logan poured him a stiff shot of whiskey, and Parker drained it gratefully. Logan poured more as Parker continued.

"It's terrible, just terrible." His eyes grew watery with emotion, and Logan laid a comforting hand on the old man's shoulder.

"It might be best if you stay here tonight, Parker. Zack and I can take care of things. You need some rest."

Parker shook his head obstinately. "No, I don't want to leave Aggie there alone. If our home goes, I want to be with her."

Lily brought food for him, and Elizabeth watched as her husband gave orders with quiet authority, making preparations to leave. Her feelings were still in a quandary, but the thought of Logan's going to Denver without her caused a pain within her heart she did not understand.

When Zack brought the horses around, Elizabeth stood quietly in the shadows of the veranda while Logan talked quietly to Michael. She was aware his blue eyes had often sought her during the past hour until it was time for him to leave, and she tensed as he moved close behind her. His hands closed upon her bare arms and turned her.

"I hate leaving you," he murmured softly, caressing the softness of her cheek. "I wouldn't go if I didn't have to."

He gathered her close, his face buried in her flowing hair. He held her back and looked down at her.

"I want to give you something before I go."

He handed her a small velvet box and stood watching as she opened it. She stared at a beautiful amethyst ring set in delicate scallops of gold filigree. A vague recollection haunted her as she turned it, and it flashed purple in the lanternlight. "It's lovely."

"It's my wedding present to you." He slipped it on her finger and smiled down at her. "I hope it will make up for my waiting so long to meet you. That's something I shall always regret."

Elizabeth smiled up at him, and every fiber in Logan's body rebelled against leaving her.

"Take care, my sweet. I'll be back as soon as I can."

He started to leave, but stopped when Elizabeth gingerly touched his sleeve.

"Please, be careful," she said softly, and Logan grinned, crushing her in one last embrace.

Parker and Zack sat waiting upon their horses, but it was a long moment before Logan stepped away from her again. He leaned down, his lips touching hers with a gentleness that bore no resemblance to the ravishing kisses of the afternoon, and Elizabeth watched with a heaviness around her heart as he strode down the porch and swung into the saddle.

She moved to where she could see the road and watched him until his broad back was swallowed by the night. She sighed, leaning her cheek against the rough wood of the pillar as she stared unseeingly into the darkness, unable to explain the tears upon her cheeks.

SIXTEEN

Heavy boots echoed hollowly over the wood-planked side-walks of Central City's main street as miners trooped before the newly painted storefronts, eager to spend their gold. Brent Holloway leaned against a corner post in front of a busy saloon, indolently observing the activity around him. Central City was only twenty-eight miles west of Denver, and drifters and gamblers were arriving daily, uprooted from the chaos of the fire-damaged city. And many other Denverites, like his sister, Isabel, had preferred the comfort of a hotel while her house was being rebuilt.

Brent removed a thin gold case from his breast pocket and drew out a slim cigar, raising one eyebrow at a trim-hipped young woman who accompanied her mother. She turned to look back at the handsome man eyeing her, and her mother scolded her soundly and pulled her away.

Brent smiled, clipping his cigar carefully. His dealings with the Indians had gone very well since he'd arrived in Colorado, evidenced by the thick wad of bills in his pocket. With the help of his old partner, Carl Rankin, he'd managed to make several trips into the mountains with rifles. The time was ripe to make a profit with the white man encroaching more and more of the Indian hunting grounds, and he'd made contacts with the Sioux and the Arapaho. Rumors of an angry young chieftain named Lone Wolf meant the Cheyenne would pay a pretty price for ammunition for their rifles.

He'd leave again soon, but not before he'd seen Elizabeth.

He flipped his cigar into the dirt at his feet, his expression ugly. Thomas Pennington had continued to worsen since Elizabeth had left St. Louis, and it wouldn't be long before the old man died. Elizabeth would inherit an immense fortune, and it galled him that he had not yet gained control of it.

He grimaced, looking toward the Teller House Hotel, wondering if his sister had returned from the dressmaker. Isabel insisted that Logan would be the one to annul the marriage, but Isabel had never met Elizabeth. Logan was much too fond of beautiful women to ignore his lovely bride.

A well-fitted carriage rolled past him and arrested his attention as he recognized it. It swayed to a stop in front of a millinery shop, and Brent's eyes narrowed as Michael Cord emerged, then turned to help Elizabeth out. Brent's breath caught at the sight of her. He hadn't seen her in weeks, and in the expensive dress and jacket of dark red, she turned the head of every man who passed. To Brent's delight, Michael strode off, leaving her looking into the shop window. Brent let him get a good distance away, then stepped down into the street.

Elizabeth looked around, welcoming the excitement of the bustling boardwalks after the quiet of Woodstone. The ball would be held the next day and Lily had been much too busy with last-minute preparations to come for supplies, but Elizabeth had been eager to accompany Michael on the ten-mile ride, wanting something to occupy her mind besides her husband's return. Logan had been gone two weeks, and in his absence, she'd wandered aimlessly about the lodge feeling unexpectedly lonely without him.

It had taken several days for her to admit that she truly missed him. The time in the cool, leafy glade was on her mind often, as she remembered how his touch had turned her to fire. A blush rose even now as she relived the tingle of his hands upon her naked flesh. Deep longings stirred, and she smiled dreamily, wondering if it could really be possible that she was growing to love the husband thrust upon her by her grandfather.

"Elizabeth!"

The masculine voice brought her out of her reverie, and she turned to see Brent Holloway making his way across the wide and rutted street. The shock of seeing him faded rapidly as he stepped up and took her hand.

"Brent! What are you doing here?" she said delightedly.

"Looking for you." He smiled down at her as he brought the back of her hand to his lips. "I've thought of you every day since we've been apart."

Somewhere deep inside Elizabeth, the fact registered that Brent's lips did not burn her skin as Logan's did, but he was her good friend and she was glad to see him.

Brent looked down at her smiling face, trying to read her thoughts, as she drew her hand out of his grip. He could sense a change in her, and it put him on his guard.

"Are you all right, darling? I've been worried about you."

Elizabeth smiled. "I'm fine, truly. Michael's here with me."

"What about Logan? He hasn't mistreated you, has he?"

Elizabeth looked away from his searching eyes. "No, he has been more than kind," she murmured softly, and Brent frowned.

Which meant that Cord did not oppose the marriage as much as Isabel had thought. He hid his annoyance from Elizabeth, realizing how much more difficult it would be to marry her if Logan wanted her, too.

"Has he bedded you?" he asked bluntly, and Elizabeth gasped, her eyes shocked.

She did not answer, and Brent read her embarrassment and tried again.

"Please, forgive me, but I still hope for an annulment. You know how much you mean to me."

Elizabeth looked up at him, guilty for her lack of feeling toward him. He was so nice and gentle and had been so good to her.

"He agreed to wait until the night of the ball, so that I could get to know him better. But he refuses to consider an annulment."

So it was not too late, Brent gloated silently. Logan was very stupid to delay. Perhaps with Isabel's help he could make sure their union was never consummated. A glimmer of a plan was born in his mind as he smiled down at her.

"Where has Michael gone?"

"He had some errands to take care of, but I'm to meet him at the Teller House Hotel within the hour."

"Good, that's where I'm staying. My sister, Isabel, should be back there soon, and I'd like you to meet her."

He took her elbow, propelling her quickly toward the Teller House. It was just down the street, a narrow, three-story structure built of brown mountain stone. Brent stood back and let Elizabeth precede him inside, then took a moment to search the street for Michael.

The lobby was lavishly decorated, the one haven of elegance in an otherwise rough-hewn town. Brent led Elizabeth past the marble-topped desk to the velvet-draped entrance of the dining room. It was midafternoon, yet most of the red-draped tables were full, and the male diners present took immediate note of Brent's beautiful companion.

"We can have tea while we're waiting for Isabel," Brent suggested as he led her to a secluded table and held her chair as she sat. "She should return anytime now."

Elizabeth sat quietly while Brent ordered from the waiter, then smiled at him when he looked back at her.

"What have you been doing since you arrived?" she asked, and Brent's answer was silky.

"Waiting for the opportunity to be with you again."

Elizabeth lowered her eyes, and Brent's mouth hardened into a tight line. "Where is Logan, anyway? I'm surprised he allowed you to come here without him."

"He went to Denver because of the fire."

"That's why we're here. Isabel lost her house."

Elizabeth raised her brows quickly. "Do you know if Logan was able to save his house?"

A muscle jumped in Brent's cheek at the concern in her voice.

"No, I don't know." An idea flashed out of nowhere, and he went on, "But Isabel stayed on after I left, and I'm sure she'll know about Logan."

He avoided her eyes as if embarrassed, and Elizabeth frowned slightly. Brent caught sight of Isabel passing through the lobby and arose at once, wanting to talk to her alone before she met Elizabeth.

"There's Isabel now. Excuse me, and I'll bring her in to meet you."

Out in the lobby, Isabel Whitcomb was smiling up into the eyes of a handsome young miner, thinking he'd do nicely to amuse her in bed that night, when Brent took her arm and pulled her away with him. She jerked her elbow away angrily but followed him into a draped alcove where they wouldn't be overheard.

"What in the hell do you think you're doing, Brent? I was talking to him!"

"Logan Cord's wife is in the dining room," Brent said without preamble, and the anger dissolved from Isabel's fair face. She looked toward the door.

"Is Logan here with her?" she asked quickly, and Brent sneered at her hopefulness.

"She said he was in Denver."

Isabel smiled triumphantly. "Then he's not living with her. I told you he'd find a way to get out of that betrothal contract."

"According to Elizabeth, Logan won't hear of an annulment."

Isabel's brows knitted. "I don't believe it. He was furious about the marriage."

"He hadn't seen Elizabeth then. Any man would want her."

Sparks flared in Isabel's clear green eyes, and her chin hardened.

"But that doesn't mean he'll get her," Brent said. "There are ways to remedy the situation. It's not just her money I want. I intend to have Elizabeth as my wife. And since Logan has been good enough to postpone the consummation of the marriage until the wedding ball, we have time to make a few plans. But we must move quickly, because after tomorrow, an annulment will be out of the question. I'm depending on you to make marriage to Cord seem less attractive to her."

"What do you mean?"

"Use your imagination, sister dear. What do you think Elizabeth would do if she knew Logan had been with you in Denver for the past few weeks."

"But I've been here. . . ."

Isabel's face dissolved into a slow, comprehending smile, and Brent took her arm.

"Now, let's go meet Elizabeth."

Elizabeth looked up as Brent entered the dining room, escorting one of the most beautiful women she'd ever seen.

Brother and sister shared the same aristocratic features and green eyes, but Isabel's hair was not dark auburn like Brent's, but a rich copper color that glowed against the emerald-green gown she wore.

Brent smiled down at Elizabeth, handling the introductions as he assisted Isabel into a chair.

"Elizabeth, please allow me to present my sister, Isabel Whitcomb." He turned to Isabel. "And this is Logan's wife, Elizabeth. I know how much you've wanted to meet her."

"How do you do, Mrs. Whitcomb."

The green eyes watched her with an expression that made Elizabeth uncomfortable.

"So we finally meet. Logan mentioned you just the other day."

Isabel's voice was low and husky, and Elizabeth looked up quickly. "Then you did see my husband in Denver?"

A small, awkward silence followed, as Brent and Isabel exchanged meaningful looks. Elizabeth looked from one to the other questioningly until Brent leaned forward, his expression grave.

"Forgive me, Elizabeth, for being the one to tell you this, but I feel you have the right to know."

Dark, foreboding intuition worked to prepare Elizabeth, but nevertheless, her face paled slightly as Isabel interrupted her brother.

"Logan and I are lovers. We have been for years."

Elizabeth could not speak, wanting to put her hands over her ears, but she struggled to retain her dignity.

"I cannot expect my husband to have been chaste before we met," she said in a low voice.

Brent frowned, and Isabel spoke again.

"I'm glad to see you are so understanding, because Logan doesn't want to end our relationship. He gave me this necklace just yesterday when I left Denver. As a token of his love."

Brent looked at the amethyst set in gold filigree that she held up for Elizabeth to see. It was the one Rankin had sold to Brent in St. Louis, and Brent admired Isabel's cleverness in using it to convince Elizabeth of her husband's infidelity.

Elizabeth stared at the swirling scallops, her heart like lead, as she realized it matched the ring upon her gloved finger. Isabel had told the truth; there was no doubt now. A great hurt ballooned against her chest, and Isabel's eyes glowed victorious as she read the pain in the violet depths.

Satisfied, Brent said gently, "Logan and Isabel were to be married, my dear, until he learned that he was already married to you. That's why he opposed it so much."

"Then why won't he grant me an annulment?" Elizabeth asked, her pride making her lift her chin.

Isabel was startled by the question, but Brent's answer was smooth. "Logan's made some bad investments, and I'm afraid he expects your inheritance to offset his losses."

Elizabeth swallowed hard, not quite believing the explanation, but Brent pressed on, encouraged by her distress. "Don't you see, my darling, he's only using you. But if you leave with me now, I can take you back to St. Louis. Thomas will understand when he knows how Logan feels about Isabel. Then we can be married."

Elizabeth looked at his face, her throat constricted with indecision.

"I cannot just leave. Michael is here with me."

Brent's grin was triumphant, and Isabel breathed in relief.

"Then tomorrow night. I am invited to the ball. We could slip away and be gone before Logan even knew it."

Sickness grew in the pit of Elizabeth's stomach at even the thought of it. "No, I couldn't."

"Please, darling. It's our last chance at happiness."

Elizabeth looked away from him, grateful when she saw Michael at the doorway, searching the tables for her. She had to get away where she could think. She stood, grasping her purse with white knuckles.

"I must go."

Brent grabbed her arm. "Think about it, Elizabeth, and tell me tomorrow night."

Elizabeth did not answer or look at Isabel as she turned from them and rushed toward Michael, who smiled and raised his hand in greeting.

Brent watched them leave, then turned to his sister and smiled.

"The barb of distrust is set, my dear, and something tells me that Logan will find it most difficult to dislodge."

* * *

It was the same night, but very late, when Logan walked his horse up the rocky drive of Woodstone. The stars were hidden by looming clouds that lumbered across the moon, turning the night into heavy black velvet. When he reached the stable, he slid off tiredly, then pulled the horse inside. When they'd arrived in Denver, his house had been aflame, and they'd joined the fight to bring it under control. Parker's arm had been broken in the process, but between them they'd saved most of the structure. The whole town had been rebuilding, and it had taken him several days to find enough carpenters to go to work on his house. He was paying them four times their usual wages, but it was worth it. They'd gotten a good start by the time he'd left for Woodstone, and he hoped it would be finished soon. Besides that loss, his mining office downtown had burned to the ground, and the mustangs the boys had herded to Denver for the army contract had been set free when the fire neared the corrals. He'd slept an average of two hours a night the whole two weeks, but he'd gotten most things in order. And through it all, Elizabeth had controlled his thoughts, her beautiful face ever with him.

He sighed, thankful he was finally home, then unstrapped the saddle and rubbed the lathered horse with a handful of straw. He'd ridden hard all day in his eagerness to be home, only stopping once to rest his horse. But the ball was tomorrow night, and Elizabeth waited for him. He walked outside picturing Elizabeth sleeping, her silver hair spread over the pillow. He hastened his footsteps, crossing the back veranda to the kitchen.

The house was dark and quiet, and he struck a match to the lamp upon the table and carried it through the back hallway. He frowned at first when he saw the furniture against the walls, turning toward the far end of the room where one couch still sat in front of the hearth.

Michael sat there with Lily, her black head nestled in the crook of his arm, and while Logan watched, Michael nuzzled her temple. Logan grinned slightly, thinking a lot had happened since he'd been away. He cleared his throat as the kiss deepened, and Michael jerked around.

"Logan, thank God," he said when he saw him. "We were afraid you wouldn't make it back for the ball."

"The devil himself couldn't make me miss that," Logan said as Michael rose to meet him. "Where is Elizabeth?"

"Upstairs. We spent the day in Central City, and she was very tired."

Logan started to turn, but Michael stopped him.

"We got your message about Parker. Is he all right?"

"His arm's broken where the beam hit him, but it's healing." Logan sighed, running tired fingers over his whiskered jaw. "The fire damaged the house, but we managed to save most of the furniture."

Lily spoke in concern. "Is Zack all right?"

"Yes, he's fine, but he stayed to help with the rebuilding. Half Denver's under construction."

"Would you like something to eat or drink?" Lily offered.

"No, I just need some sleep. I take it everything's in order for tomorrow night."

Michael looked at Lily with admiration. "Lily's done a wonderful job. Everything is ready."

The intimate look they shared told Logan their romance had progressed even further than he'd assumed. But he was glad. Both had been lonely, and if they could find happiness together, they had his blessing.

He bid them goodnight, then went straight to Elizabeth's room. He had to see her, assure himself that she was still there, before he could close his eyes. He opened the door quietly, not wishing to awaken her. The canopied bed lay empty, and he frowned until a splash of water sent him to the velvet screen beside the hearth. He drew the curtain aside with one hand.

The white porcelain hip bath had been drawn near the fire, and Elizabeth sat in the scented water, her back to him. Logan could not move when she lifted one shapely leg and squeezed her sponge upon it, the trickling rivulets leading his hungry eyes to where her thigh met the water. The glow of the fire haloed coils of fair hair, and his face relaxed in a slow, relieved smile.

Something innate made Elizabeth turn, and the sight of Logan brought an involuntary gasp from her lips. She watched as he moved closer and stood looking down at her. His face was grimy and bewhiskered, and his eyes glittered blue in the firelight. Pain started up deep inside her as she realized how much she'd missed him. She did love him, she could no longer deny it, but the sense of betrayal lay heavy on her heart at the thought of his being with Isabel. Neither spoke as his eyes scorched into the smooth shoulders above the water, and Elizabeth sank deeper as lean fingers brushed damp tendrils away from her face. When he ran his knuckles lightly across her cheekbone, she averted her face, and Logan withdrew his hand, his low sigh audible in the silent room.

"I've missed you," he said softly, and Elizabeth looked into the fire without answering. She wanted to believe him, wanted to forget the suffering she'd endured since she'd learned he loved Isabel. But how could she? Even now, her mind returned to the amethyst necklace upon Isabel's throat.

Logan stared down into her impassive face, unable to stop the disappointment that tortured his heart. He had hoped she would have missed him, but her eyes were cool and remote, as if she cared nothing for him.

Elizabeth watched him move to a chair on the other side of the hearth. He sat down, hidden by shadows, and Elizabeth sat self-consciously in the tub as the room grew very quiet.

She wanted to confront him, to ask him if he loved Isabel, if he wanted Elizabeth herself only for her money, but she could not bring herself to do it as Brent had suggested. What if he admitted his love for Brent's sister? How could she live with that? She knew she could not, that she'd have to leave with Brent. She remained silent, indecision and hurt raging inside her heart.

She was not sure he watched her until the logs shifted, revealing a gleam of blue in the darkness. The water gradually grew cold, but the towel lay warming by the fire, and Elizabeth could not bring herself to reach for it.

She shivered, and Logan's voice immediately spoke from the corner.

"Come, before you catch a chill."

He arose and came to her, holding the towel out for her. Elizabeth looked up into his face, still hesitant.

"Come, sweet, it grows late," he said, his voice very tired. "You have nothing to fear from me tonight."

She steeled her nerves, then slowly stood as his eyes

openly assessed her firm, rounded body. But the hot perusal lasted only an instant, then she found herself enfolded in the soft warmth of the towel. His strong hands lingered briefly upon her arms, then he slipped her gown over her head, watching with a certain degree of bittersweet pain as fine silk of the palest pink molded over her damp limbs. He slipped an arm beneath her knees and swooped her against his chest, and Elizabeth closed her eyes tightly, wishing she'd never gone to Central City with Michael, wishing she'd never seen Brent or his sister. Logan carried her to the bed, then drew the silken coverlet over her. He pressed a tender kiss upon her brow, his voice very low.

"Until tomorrow, my love, when you will be mine again."

She watched him pull the door closed behind him, and she stared at it, tears threatening to spill over as she wrestled with her desire to stay with Logan and the terrible sense of betrayal she felt. How could he really love Isabel and look at Elizabeth the way he did? How could he be so gentle and loving to her when he had just left another woman?

It was much, much later when her troubled, anxious thoughts allowed her long dark lashes to drift together and close out his azure-blue eyes.

SEVENTEEN

The guests began to arrive the next afternoon, and Elizabeth watched dully as an endless stream of carriages rolled into the valley. Invitations to the rare social events given by Logan Cord were eagerly sought after in Denver, but his wedding celebration was even more to be coveted. Despite the hardships brought about by the fire, everyone was eager to see the woman who'd finally claimed the rich and handsome landowner.

According to custom, the bride and groom were not to see each other until the ball, and it was a practice that Elizabeth welcomed wholeheartedly. She'd kept to herself, in the seclusion of her room. But most of her time was spent pacing the floor, as Brent and Isabel's words ran never-endingly through her mind. Just as often, she dwelt upon the shady glen far across the meadows, where Logan's hard body and gentle touch had sent exquisite pleasures racing through her blood. She looked out over the lake, shivering slightly as she turned from the window.

The gold amethyst ring lay upon her dressing table, bringing back Isabel Whitcomb's lovely face. Deep down, Elizabeth knew she did not want to leave Logan, and perhaps for that reason, she could not bring herself to believe everything that Isabel had told her. The way Logan looked at her said otherwise, and she had to admit that he'd had a chance for an annulment if he'd wanted it. And it was just as hard to believe he needed her money. Woodstone was much too opulent, and besides that, Michael was very wealthy. Perhaps he'd given Isabel the necklace long ago, before he'd even known he had a wife.

Amanda knocked, and Elizabeth watched, unsmiling, as

Rachel and Amanda entered, ready to assist her with her dressing. Amanda poured scented oil into the deep, warm water, drawing a deep, savoring whiff of its fragrance, then closing her eyes in ecstasy as Elizabeth stepped into the tub.

"This oil is from China. Logan brought it for you from Denver. Have you ever smelled anything so wonderful?"

Elizabeth nodded unenthusiastically and closed her eyes. She tried to clear her mind completely, block out the girls' excited chatter. But her thoughts could not stay away from Logan. Sometimes it seemed as if she'd known him forever, loved him forever. Her dreams about him mixed with reality until she could not separate them. Rachel spoke from close by, and when Elizabeth looked up at her, the young girl's expression was alight with excitement.

"Logan is nearly crazy with impatience, Miss Elizabeth." She giggled. "He paces even now at the bottom of the steps."

Rachel was only thirteen, and Elizabeth looked at her happy face surrounded by soft brown curls, envying her innocent exuberance. She remained silent as the two girls helped her wash her long, silvery hair. When it was dry, Rachel took a long time fashioning it into soft curls and ringlets that becomingly framed Elizabeth's small face, then draped over both her shoulders in artful abandon. By now, both girls had noticed Elizabeth's despondence and grown quiet themselves, but Amanda could not help but exclaim over the magnificent wedding gown as she lifted it from its trunk.

Elizabeth looked at the iridescent splendor of its long train without emotion. She'd not worn it, although her grandfather had paid a small fortune to have it made in Paris. It was the crowning achievement of the famous French couturier who had designed her trousseau.

Rachel joined Amanda at the bed and ran her fingers over the finest and sheerest of pure white silk with thousands of silvery threads sewn into the wide skirt. The fragile ivory lace was from Ireland, intricate intertwining swirls and flowers fashioned by hand into fine cobwebby delicacy. The bodice was clinched to fit Elizabeth's tiny waist, and the lacy transparent silk lay high upon the throat, the design teasing the eye with glimpses of the bare flesh beneath. It was a gown created to set a bridegroom aflame and make the wait for the wedding bed sheer torture.

The two girls helped Elizabeth step into it, both gasping at the sight of her diminutive beauty in the glittering gown. They hastened to fasten the tiny buttons at the back, then set about straightening the heavy skirts upon stiff satin petticoats. As a finishing touch, they wove wild daisies and glistening ropes of pearls into her fair hair. They stepped back, awed by their handiwork, and Elizabeth stared into the mirror, hardly recognizing herself in the silvery gown. She looked into her own eyes, something unknown triggering memories of the ring Logan had given her. She looked at it, thinking he had compared it to her eyes, but knowing he had not. It must have been another of her vivid dreams, and she shivered, thinking how thoroughly he'd invaded her life, filling every corner of her mind, dominating her thoughts.

The first lilting strains of violins floated upon the wings of the night breeze, and Elizabeth turned to the window, suddenly overcome by nervousness. After this night, she could not escape the confines of marriage. She had an alternative; Brent could take her away for good if she wished, but somehow the thought gave her no pleasure.

She jumped at a rap on the door, then relaxed as Lily's serene face smiled at her.

"Out with you, Rachel, and you, too, Amanda. You're to put on your new dresses and attend the party. Logan has requested it."

Both girls squealed in delight and veritably flew into the hall. Lily laughed as she closed the door, then set a tray with a bottle of champagne upon the table as her eyes swept over Elizabeth.

"You are a beautiful bride. Logan will be pleased."

Lily smiled slightly as Elizabeth turned away, looking miserable. Lily's voice was gentle.

"What is troubling you, Elizabeth? You should be happy. Surely you aren't still afraid of Logan."

Elizabeth forced a small smile. "I'm a little nervous, I suppose."

Lily smiled wickedly as she glanced at the wine.

"Michael sent this up for you and Logan to share later, but perhaps the two of us should have a private toast, just to calm our nerves. I'm a bit shaky myself. I've never attended a ball."

Elizabeth agreed, hoping the wine would melt the hard icy knots of indecision in her stomach. Lily poured the bubbly liquid into tall crystal goblets, and her dark beauty seemed to glow against the pale yellow gown trimmed with blue satin.

"Your dress is lovely, Lily. It was kind of Michael to order them for you and the girls."

"He is very thoughtful," Lily said, a special glow in her dark eyes.

Elizabeth took the champagne, wishing for the happiness Lily and Michael shared when they were together. She sipped her drink, welcoming the path it burned into her stomach. She looked up, wondering if Lily was acquainted with Brent's beautiful sister.

"I met a woman in Central City yesterday," she said slowly. "Her name was Isabel Whitcomb. Do you know her?"

Lily immediately dropped her eyes, and Elizabeth's heart fell. "Yes, she has visited here before."

"Have she and Logan been lovers?" Elizabeth asked bluntly, and at Lily's reluctance, she persisted. "I want to know. Please tell me."

"At one time they were, but never have I seen him look at her as he looks at you."

It was somewhat reassuring, but tonight Elizabeth would find out for sure. Isabel would be in attendance, and if Logan loved her, it would surely show in his eyes. Then and only then would she leave with Brent. She looked up as Lily stood.

"You must come down soon. Logan is very anxious to see you."

After Lily left, Elizabeth sat silently, then, taking a deep breath, slid the amethyst ring upon her finger and walked resolutely to the door. The music grew louder as she approached the open stairwell, and she stopped to take a deep, fortifying breath, then moved to the wide landing that looked out over the assemblage.

The great room was filled to capacity with hundreds of

formally dressed guests, laughing and chatting as they waited for the dancing to begin, but Elizabeth's eyes fell solely to Logan where he stood at the foot of the steps, his hands clasped behind his back as he scanned the gathering. He wore a superbly tailored coat of the purest white, and the color emphasized his deeply bronzed skin and blond hair. His waistcoat was silver-gray, his long legs encased in black breeches that fit snugly over his powerfully muscled thighs.

The orchestra leader saw Elizabeth, and as the musicians ended their song, Logan turned and looked up at her. His breath caught at the exquisite silver-and-white vision at the top of the stairs, and he realized in awe that the name Starfire had never fit Elizabeth as it now did, with the glow of hundreds of candles reflecting upon her white dress and silvery hair. Their gaze locked, the crowd becoming hushed as all eyes turned to watch the bride and groom. Her black-fringed eyes glowed their unique violet beauty, and Logan smiled as he slowly ascended the stairs to meet his love.

He took her hand, bowing low as he pressed it to his lips. Applause rippled over the crowd below, and Elizabeth tore her eyes from her husband, for the first time becoming totally aware of the people below. Her fingers tensed inside the warmth of Logan's lean fingers.

"There is nothing to fear," he whispered softly. "I'll be with you the whole time."

Elizabeth jerked startled eyes to him, her mind whirling in a vortex of flashing white lights as submerged memories fought to rise to the surface.

"You have said that to me before," she said slowly. "I am certain of it."

Logan's eyes became wary, almost watchful, but she had no time to ponder the strangeness of it as he smiled.

"You are right, but this time nothing will take you from me."

Elizabeth allowed him to lead her down the steps, puzzling over his words. The wedding guests separated, and Logan led her to the middle of the floor.

"We must start the first dance," he told her, smiling down at her from his great height as he took her in his arms. A slow waltz began, and Logan never once took his eyes off his wife as he expertly led her in a graceful circuit of the floor.

Neither noticed Brent Holloway and Isabel Whitcomb where they stood near one of the open doors that led to the veranda.

"Look at him fawning over her, as if she were some kind of goddess," Isabel hissed furiously, and Brent looked at Elizabeth's small, graceful beauty in the exquisite gown, thinking Isabel's description of her most appropriate.

"I hope he does want her—then it will give me greater pleasure to take her away from him."

"I don't give a damn what happens to her, as long as I get Logan back."

Brent glanced briefly at his sister. She was so disgustingly enamored of Cord that she didn't even care that he'd ruined her family name. But when Elizabeth humiliated Logan by leaving him on his wedding night in front of most of Denver, the Holloway vengeance would be complete. Brent watched the way Logan held Elizabeth, his green eyes narrowing at the possessive pride Logan displayed as he escorted his bride to the end of the room where they would greet their guests.

Elizabeth barely reached her husband's shoulder as she stood beside him, waiting as the long line of people congratulated Logan and wished her well. She tried to smile, grateful for Logan's hand upon her waist. He stood very close, and she looked up when she felt his arm tense against her back.

Isabel Whitcomb stood before them in a stunning gown of green chiffon, the décolletage plunging to show an indecent amount of bare flesh. The scalloped amethyst lay upon the creamy bosom as a painful reminder to Elizabeth.

Elizabeth's eyes went to Logan's face, and her worst fears were confirmed. He stared at Isabel's low-cut gown with an expression that Elizabeth could not bear to watch, and Isabel smiled up at him, enjoying his fascination with her breasts almost as much as she did Elizabeth's obvious distress over his interest.

Logan's first shock at seeing his grandmother's necklace upon Isabel's throat faded quickly, and his jaw clamped tight with fury. It was the very one he'd given to Starfire long ago, and he had to forcibly restrain the urge to rip it from Isabel's neck.

Brent took Logan's unexpected interest in Isabel as a godsend and moved near Elizabeth.

"Can you see now that what we told you is true?" he whispered, encouraged by the hurt look in her eyes.

Elizabeth tore her eyes off Logan and his lover as Brent took her hand in his. Before he could lift it to his mouth, Logan had her small hand clasped tightly in his own, his eyes like frozen blue ice.

"Sorry, Holloway, I'm particular about who touches my wife."

Brent's jaw clenched hard, his look as dark and ugly as Logan's.

"Elizabeth and I are old friends. Surely I'm allowed to wish her well."

Logan looked into Brent's false smile, thinking that if it took him the rest of his life, he'd prove to Elizabeth just how low Brent really was.

"Oh? How long have you known my wife?"

The unexpected question caught all of them off-guard, but Brent's answer was as smooth as oil.

"I first met her years ago, but as you probably know, we became very close since she came to live in St. Louis."

He ignored Logan then, looking steadily down at Elizabeth. "I hope you will honor me with a dance later tonight."

Aware of Logan's black scowl, Elizabeth gave a barely perceptible nod as Brent escorted Isabel away. A terrible resignation settled over her, followed by a gradually rising anger as her husband's eyes continually sought out the flame-haired beauty in green, even as he greeted his guests beside his wife.

When Michael requested a dance, Logan gave his permission reluctantly, watching uneasily as Michael whirled away with Elizabeth in his arms. The dance floor was very crowded, and he frowned when he lost sight of them. When they reappeared at the far side of the room, the tension on his face lessened momentarily.

"You don't seem to mind your marriage as much as you once did," said Isabel from close beside him, and Logan took his eyes from his wife, the warm, possessive look growing cold as it settled on the amethyst upon Isabel's heaving chest.

Isabel swelled with power as his eyes burned into her breasts again, thinking Brent had been wrong. Logan's little silver-haired wife had not completely won his heart. And she would not last long after Logan had sated his initial passion for her beauty. Even now, he looked down at Isabel as if he wanted to grab her. He had missed their wild and brutal lovemaking as much as she had.

"Your necklace is very unusual, Isabel. Where did you find it?"

Isabel tensed, wondering if Elizabeth had had the nerve to confront Logan about the story she and Brent had told her. She tried to read some meaning in Logan's words, but they remained totally inscrutable.

"Brent gave it to me. He bought it from his good friend Carl Rankin." she said. "He was my houseguest for a time."

Logan's face grew hard, and a muscle flexed, then relaxed in his lean cheek. So Brent knew Rankin. Pieces of the puzzle began to fall together as he realized Brent could very well have been the one who had engineered the plot to take Starfire away from him. He wondered if Isabel was involved as well. He lifted the heavy stone in his palm and looked into her eyes.

"I'd very much like to have this. It would look most lovely with my wife's eyes."

Isabel gave a low snarl, inflamed by his words.

"Don't waste your time. She won't be around long enough to wear it."

She realized at once that she'd said too much and tried to move away, but Logan's grip upon the necklace held her in place.

"And what do you mean by that, Isabel?"

Isabel shivered, having seen the cold, lethal anger in Logan's blue eyes before. She was suddenly more afraid of him than she was of facing Brent's wrath if she exposed his plans. Logan's grip tightened as he pulled her forward with the golden chain, and Isabel spoke breathlessly.

"Because she intends to run away with Brent this very night."

Logan's face closed into a blank mask, and he gave a

quick jerk, breaking the clasp at the back of her neck. He squeezed the necklace in his palm and went in search of Brent Holloway.

Across the room, Elizabeth moved mechanically, unaware of Michael or the music as she watched Isabel and her husband. She turned her head when Logan held the amethyst in his palm and looked deeply into Isabel's eyes. She fought back the angry tears, knowing she would never live with a man who humiliated his wife by flaunting his mistress in her face.

She made her decision with swift finality. She would go with Brent, home to Missouri, where Thomas could dissolve the marriage. Logan was an insensitive womanizer, just as Brent had said. When the music ended, she excused herself from Michael and rapidly made her way through the crowd. Logan was nowhere in sight, and she jumped when Brent suddenly appeared at her side. She didn't give him time to speak, but whispered urgently.

"I've decided to go with you, but we must hurry. I'll pack and meet you behind the house."

Brent nodded once, then melted into the crowd again, and Elizabeth moved slowly through the milling people.

After Logan had left Isabel, he'd moved to a position near the front veranda, where he could scan the couples on the dance floor for Brent Holloway. The more he thought about it, the less inclined he was to believe Isabel had been telling the truth. It was more likely an attempt on her part to drive a wedge between Elizabeth and him. Elizabeth would not run away with another man, and in the last few weeks, he'd made progress with her. Her reticence with him the night before flashed into his mind, but he turned away from it. His eyes rested upon her as she danced with his father. She wouldn't leave him.

He searched for Brent again, wanting to confront him about Starfire's abduction. He was behind it, Logan had no doubt of that.

The music stopped, and Logan nodded at his guests as he slowly moved toward his wife, who had left Michael and was heading toward the back of the room. He stopped as Brent approached her, his jaw tightening as they whispered together a moment, then separated. He watched Elizabeth hurry away, then followed Brent.

Holloway left the room by the doors leading to the front veranda, and Logan stepped out into the cool night air moments later, his fists clenched, his eyes dark. Zack and Amanda stood at the banister near him, and both looked up, easily reading the coldly contained rage in his face. They looked at each other as Logan moved away without speaking to them, following Brent down the side porch.

The moon was full, and the bright light created stark black shadows as Logan stepped down to the grass and stood watching Brent pace impatiently in the back garden. Faraway music drifted on the air, but Logan concentrated on Brent Holloway. He was enraged enough at that moment to kill him with his bare hands.

Brent turned and looked up at the house, wishing Elizabeth would hurry. He wanted to get her as far away from Woodstone as he could before Logan learned of their plans. He didn't know what had convinced her to leave with him, but Logan's obvious fascination with Isabel probably had been a big part of it. Brent chuckled sardonically, thinking that Logan was a fool.

Someone moved behind him, and Brent smiled and turned, glad she'd finally come.

"Elizabeth?" he whispered, searching the shadows for her.

"Guess again, Holloway," Logan said, his voice low and deadly as he stepped into the moonlight.

Brent stiffened in surprise, then stared at Logan's grim face an instant before he gave a low, mocking laugh.

"Hello, Cord. If you're looking for your wife, she's upstairs packing. She's leaving with me."

Logan's face went white, but his voice remained deceptively calm. "Elizabeth isn't going anywhere tonight, or any other night."

"I hope you'll try to stop us."

Brent smiled coldly, his hand moving toward the small derringer in his vest. He knew Logan would not be armed, and since Brent was no match for Logan's strength, the pistol would even out the odds a bit.

"I wish I had time to give you the beating you deserve, Holloway," Logan said tightly. "But it's my wedding night, and I have guests in my house. So you're going to get on your horse and leave quietly."

He stepped toward Brent, and Brent went for his gun. Logan saw his intent, and he moved swiftly, hitting Brent's arm with enough force to send the gun flying out of his hand. Brent cursed and drew back, ready to slam his fist into Logan's jaw, but Logan caught his fist in midair, bending it backward with slow, relentless pressure until Brent was forced to his knees.

Logan stared down at him contemptuously, then leaned down and gritted into his face, "You're weak, Holloway, weak and cowardly. I ought to kill you now and have done with it. God knows I'd like to. But I won't ruin my own wedding, because you're not worth it. But be warned. Don't ever try to take what is mine. If you ever touch Elizabeth again, I'll kill you. I know you were involved in the abduction, you and Carl Rankin, and someday I'll take my pound of flesh for that. But not tonight, you bastard, not tonight."

Logan still had a painful grip on Brent's fist, and he gave a violent push that sent Brent sprawling backward into the dirt. Brent held his aching wrist against his chest, his eyes burning hatred, as Logan leaned down and picked up the derringer. He emptied the chambers and tossed the pistol to the ground beside Holloway.

"Now get the hell off my land."

Zack ran up behind them, leveling a rifle at Brent's chest. "I thought there might be some trouble out here," he said, and Logan turned away without looking at Brent.

"Get him out of my sight," he said, starting for the house. "And make sure he leaves the valley."

It had taken Elizabeth an eternity to reach the kitchen, and she'd fled up the back stairs, her heart like a drum. The upper hall had been deserted, and she'd entered her room quickly, going straight to the armoire and lifting down a small valise. Now as she pulled a riding habit from the closet and stuffed it inside the bag, she hesitated, as doubts began to nag at her. It was still hard for her to believe Isabel's story, despite the way Logan had looked at her downstairs. Logan had been good to her during the past weeks, had acted as if he really cared about her. Even though he'd first seemed cruel and cold when they had met, he no longer appeared that way. She'd seen him with the Winstead boys, easy and relaxed, and Lily had told her how good he'd been to her family over the years.

Elizabeth stared into space, realizing she'd come to respect him for his strength and kindness during all the days when he'd treated her as a cherished wife. Some innate wisdom she could not explain made her sure he had not faked the warmth in his eyes when he looked at her. Perhaps Isabel's story wasn't all true, she thought. Perhaps she should ask Logan about the other woman. She looked down at the ring upon her finger, biting her lip. How could she leave him, now that she'd grown to care? But what if Isabel spoke the truth? What if he kept Isabel in Denver as his mistress? Elizabeth could not bear that. She would be better off far away, where she wouldn't know.

"Going somewhere?"

She whirled around at the sudden noise, her heavy skirt rustling in the quiet room, gasping when she saw Logan. She had not heard him enter, but something in the set of his face made her raise her chin.

"I intend to leave with Brent for St. Louis."

Logan leaned against the door, his eyes unreadable.

"I'm afraid it's a little late for that. Brent's gone."

Elizabeth stared blankly at him.

"I don't believe you. He wouldn't leave without me."

Logan laughed without humor. "I'm afraid Zack and I were very persuasive."

Elizabeth's hopes plummeted, but her fury surpassed her disappointment.

"And what of Isabel? Did you persuade her to leave as well? To await you in Denver again? Until you tire of me?"

Logan's eyebrows drew together slightly under her blazing words.

"I have no idea where Isabel is and don't really care," he answered calmly, and Elizabeth's fury clicked up a notch.

"And I suppose you also deny having been her lover?"

"I don't deny it, but it happened long before I met you."

"Then how did she get the necklace she wore tonight?"

"She got this"—Logan opened his fist to show her the

amethyst, the long golden chain dangling from his fingers—"from a man named Carl Rankin, who stole it from me."

"And you expect me to believe that?" she said coldly.

Logan didn't answer, and Elizabeth picked up the valise.

"Please stand aside and let me pass. I will find Brent and leave here this night."

Logan's control slipped slightly, and he angrily sent the necklace scraping across a nearby table.

"Do you really expect me to stand by and let you run away with another man on our wedding night?"

"It makes no difference, because I will persuade Grandfather to annul this marriage, as I should have done long ago."

Logan's eyes were steady, and his voice was very quiet.

"I'm afraid that will be impossible. Annulments are not legal if the marriage has been consummated."

"I'll remind you," she said icily, "that it has not been."

"No, but it will be before you leave this room again."

Elizabeth froze, then looked at him contemptuously.

"You are going to force me?"

"I hope I won't have to, but I intend to put all talk of an annulment to rest forever this very night."

Elizabeth turned away, and Logan stepped toward her.

"We made a bargain three long weeks ago. I fulfilled my end of it, despite a good deal of difficulty, and now, my love, the time has come for you to pay the piper."

Elizabeth's look was scathing, but she knew he was deadly serious.

"And if I . . . pay the piper"—she emphasized it sarcastically—"will I finally be free of you?"

Logan smiled. "That, my love, I cannot say. All I know is that I intend to have you this night one way or another."

Their eyes fought a duel until Elizabeth moved across the floor to stand at the windows.

"I will not subject myself to the indignity of fighting you," she said in a low voice, "but neither will I ever forgive you for this."

Logan sighed, knowing he was taking a chance with her, as he removed his coat and unfolded his cravat.

Elizabeth braced herself as he moved behind her.

"All I've ever wanted is to love you," he muttered thickly, as he gently pulled the flowers from her hair until the heavy tresses fell to her shoulders in a glorious swirl. She quivered all over as Logan gathered it in both hands, the sheer essence of her reeling his senses, and she closed her eyes as his fingers went to the buttons at the back of her neck. She could hear the quick intake of his breath as he pushed the gown gently off her shoulders, and it fell with a whisper of silk to a pool of white at her feet.

His hand swept the softness of her hair off her nape, and she jerked spasmodically as his hot mouth touched her bare shoulder.

"I want you, I've wanted you so long," he said hoarsely as he turned her to face him.

She stood stiffly unresponsive as he slowly undressed her, his eyes burning blue coals, until she stood in only her sheer chemise. Her lips parted slightly as he slowly tugged at the satin ribbons between her breasts and eased the silken fabric over the curve of her hips.

Elizabeth closed her eyes and held her breath, and with a gentleness that belied his great strength, one powerful arm folded about her waist, bringing her tight against his hard chest. His hand was anchored firmly in her hair as he forced her to look at him. Then his lips were upon hers, warmly, softly, persuasively, until waves of heat radiated through her blood, making her entire body pulsate. Her will began to crumble as his lips continued to twist upon hers, ravaging her with a demanding hunger he could no longer withhold.

Elizabeth could not think, could only feel that it was meant to be, Logan was her destiny as sure as the sun would light the day and the stars would rise at night. She surrendered with a muffled moan, willingly offering to him the honeyed nectar of her mouth. Flaming currents brought wild and forgotten desires racing through her blood, and she slid her arms around his neck, pulling him to her, wanting to touch him, wanting him to touch her.

Logan groaned, one hand in the long silken tresses, the other sliding slowly down the warm velvet skin to cup her hip. Elizabeth gasped as she was lifted from the floor and lowered upon the bed, watching out of darkened eyes as his sunbrowned chest emerged from his shirt. Then his lips were upon hers, his arm beneath her back, lifting her against him, and Elizabeth's world dipped and careened as his hands began to move across her trembling flesh in an erotic search. The clean manly scent of him summoned sweet recollections of another time of love, but she could not think of it, did not want to remember. The only thing that was important to her was that Logan was her husband and she loved him.

Her lashes fluttered closed as his mouth skirted the satin angle of her jaw, dipping to the deep hollow of her fragile collarbone. His lips sought and found the hammering pulse in her throat, and Elizabeth lay in the mists of rapture as his fingers slid across the beloved hollows and curves of her naked flesh with slow expertise. Elizabeth felt as if she'd come home, as if they fit together, her softness molded into his hard strength, as if they'd both been created for this moment.

Each soft caress shredded already quivering nerve endings, and Elizabeth moaned as his tongue swirled a molten path to the pink crest of her breast. All inhibitions evaporated, and she responded to him, her palms moving over sinewy muscles, her slender fingers kneading the lean, hard-fleshed muscles of his waist. Nothing mattered, not anger, not distrust, not reason, as the fierce, long-forgotten needs of her body took command. She wanted him, and her mouth found his, greedily, hungrily, as her hands glided over the hard muscles of his hips until he rose above her, the heat of his body welcoming her embrace.

They moved together, limbs entwined, muscles flexing, their breaths mingling, ragged and hoarse, as they rode to the exquisite heights of their love.

"Tracker . . ." she breathed, without knowing what she said, and Logan barely heard her before the explosion of their union burst between them as all the love Logan had forcibly suppressed and all Elizabeth had forgotten came forth with a white-hot blast of pure ecstasy.

In the aftermath of their passion, both lay limp, realizing only love could create such a union; but it was later when their blood was calm that Logan's whisper was barely audible against her hair.

"Now are you free of me, my love? Or are you forever bound to me as I have been to you from the first moment I saw you?"

Elizabeth raised her face, and the soft look in her eyes was the answer Logan craved. He smiled as his lips closed over hers with a gentleness born of love.

EIGHTEEN

Logan came awake slowly, troubled by a vague sense of
unease. It was still dark, the fire burned down to a mere
glimmer, but the sweet fragrance that was Elizabeth
brought a drowsy smile to his lips. He thought of the night
they'd shared, reaching for her warm softness. His hand
touched cold and empty sheets, and the fear that she'd
gone to Brent sent the covers flying off him. Panic pinched
his heart with cruel fingers, and oblivious to his naked-
ness, he started for the door. Halfway there, he saw her,
standing at the window. The room had grown very cold,
and Logan went to her, drawing a coverlet from the bed as
he passed.

"Elizabeth?"

She did not turn as he wrapped the blanket around her
naked shoulders, and when he turned her to face him, he
saw that slow tears rolled down her cheeks. He pulled her
quickly into his embrace.

"What is it, my love?"

Elizabeth shivered, and his arms tightened reassuringly. She laid her wet cheek against the blond fur of his
chest, her voice muffled.

"I am ashamed."

A puzzled frown drew Logan's brows together.

"Whatever for?"

He felt her tense. "You are not disappointed in me?"

"Disappointed?" Logan repeated in amazement, disbelieving her question after their hours of exquisite lovemaking.

"You must think me terrible," she continued brokenly,
and it was so ridiculous that Logan couldn't stop his smile.

"I feel many things for you, love, but that certainly isn't one of them. Why would I think you terrible?"

She stood apart from him, her eyes downcast.

"Because now I know that I have lain with a man before. I do not remember when, or who he was, but I knew things that . . ." Her voice shook with shame. ". . . that a virgin could not possibly know."

Logan looked down at her, appalled at the guilt she harbored. Elizabeth shivered in the wake of his silence, and Logan made up his mind to do what he'd wanted to do since she'd come back into his life, and consequences be damned.

"Come, my sweet. It's time you knew the truth about us."

He took her easily into his arms, carrying her to the warmth of their bed. He slid his long length in beside her, then drew the downy comforter over them. She felt so small and soft in his arms and smelled so good that he almost forgot his intentions; but she'd suffered unfairly, and they had the rest of their lives to make love. That idea fascinated him, and he smiled as he gathered her silky head onto the hollow of his shoulder. He smoothed a wayward silver strand to press a gentle kiss upon her forehead, then raised one finger and tenderly wiped away all traces of her tears.

"Sweet," he whispered, "I've made love to you many times before last night."

In her surprise, Elizabeth could not move, and his softly uttered revelation hung in the air between them. Confusion clouded the wide lavender eyes when she finally raised herself on one elbow.

"I don't understand," she said haltingly.

Logan cupped her cheek in his palm, his eyes on her moist lips. "We were lovers, Elizabeth. Just weeks before you lost your memory."

Her mouth dropped agape, and she stared into his serious eyes.

"That is impossible," she breathed finally. "I lived in Boston then. With my aunt."

"No, you were with me. In a cave in the mountains north of here."

He watched her reaction carefully, wanting her to remember the rest on her own, but her expression remained skeptical. He suddenly decided that he'd help her remember. He wanted Starfire back once and for all. He'd tell her everything and to hell with the doctor's warning.

"You grew up with a tribe of Cheyenne Indians until I was sent to rescue you. We fell in love, but we were separated."

It was highly oversimplified, but it told the whole story.

"I was with savages," she repeated wonderingly, then her laugh tinkled in the air. She smiled, carving deep dimples in the softness of her cheeks, making it difficult for Logan not to kiss them.

"Why do you tease me with such ridiculous things?" she demanded, still amused.

"Because they are true. And I have scars to prove it."

Logan held up his arm, and Elizabeth's expression faded. The cold air forgotten, she sat upon her heels, examining the thin white line on his forearm.

"You stabbed me with my own knife," Logan commented, laughing as her lips parted in astonishment.

"But why?"

"You wanted to leave, and I preferred that you didn't."

A slight dart of guilt attacked his conscience as he remembered how he'd treated her that day. "I deserved it," he added, and Elizabeth's eyes narrowed.

"If all this is true, why didn't you tell me before? When I first met you?"

Logan was finding it increasingly difficult to concentrate on her questions with soft pink crests tantalizing him from beneath the gossamer gown. He smoothed her hair over her shoulders to give him a better view.

"I was afraid to tell you anything that would shock you. Father said your doctor insisted you should remember by yourself."

Elizabeth seemed to consider his story, then shook her head resolutely. "No, I don't believe a word of it."

She turned slightly, and Logan admired the thinly veiled curve of her hip before he forced his eyes back to her. She sat in profile now, and his eyes gleamed wickedly.

"Then how do I know that you'll gasp when I kiss you here?" He raised her gown, his lips burning into the small of her back.

The gasp came quickly.

"And shiver when I do this?" he continued with a smile, as he trailed one fingertip lightly up the back of her knee. Again the predicted response was immediate, and her black-lashed eyes turned to him in wonder.

"But how . . ." she murmured breathlessly, ". . . how could I have forgotten such a man as you, and the way you make me feel . . ."

She stopped, a revealing crimson hue rising to stain her cheekbones.

Logan laughed.

"In the long months I searched for you, Starfire, I often prayed for such forgetfulness."

Her eyes jerked to him. "Starfire?"

"That's your Indian name."

"I am Starfire?"

Logan nodded, and Elizabeth could not hide her relieved look. Logan looked puzzled, but Elizabeth explained.

"You called me that several times. I thought it was another woman."

Logan smiled, as Elizabeth insisted on more details.

"Tell me more. How were we separated?"

His eyes hardened, and his relaxed look gave over to a jaw tight with anger. "You were taken from me by three men. I didn't know why until I received a letter while I was in Denver last week. When I saw you again, Elizabeth, I wrote to Thomas asking him to confirm your identity. He finally wrote back and admitted he had paid a high ransom for your return."

She looked away in confusion, but Logan laid his fingers upon her small chin and turned her to face him.

"I know it's difficult now to accept these things, but someday you'll remember and everything will fall into place. You must trust me."

His gaze dropped to her soft red lips, and Elizabeth's eyes drifted closed as his mouth came against hers. His hands slid down her arms, taking the gossamer gown with them until it was a discarded heap upon the floor. She turned toward him and smiled, and the smoky seduction that darkened her violet eyes brought back to Logan visions of Starfire during their first days together in Denver. He smiled, for the first time seeing the essence of Starfire surface in Elizabeth. He sat very still as she reached out and smoothed her hands over his bare chest, her eyes following her fingers in a sensual caress that made his blood race.

She spread her fingers, enjoying the texture of his body, amazed by the hardness of the muscles beneath his smooth brown skin as she molded his bulging biceps. The blond fur of his chest was crisp beneath her search, and Logan's chest began to heave as she trailed her fingertips between the molded contours toward his lean waist.

Elizabeth raised her face, capturing his eyes. "I want to give you pleasure," she whispered huskily. "I want you to teach me."

Logan swallowed hard as her hand moved lower, thinking she was doing fine on her own. He lay back against the softness of the pillows, closing his eyes as she gently explored his body, her lips soft against his chest, her hair and skin like silk as she moved atop him. He groaned under her touch, and Elizabeth brought her mouth to his as Logan's arms crossed over her back, holding her satiny warmth tightly against him.

"I love you, Starfire, Elizabeth, beloved, you are my soul," he breathed against her lips.

"Logan, my love," Elizabeth murmured, but her words were stopped as Logan rolled until he was above her, his lips on the side of her throat. They became one—gently, lovingly, for all time.

It was long after dawn that Elizabeth slept again, curled peacefully against Logan's hard chest. A knock upon the door finally brought her to awareness, and she sat up, her long hair tumbling over her breasts in a wild disarray. Logan had been awake for some time, watching her sleep, and he reached for her, intending to draw her back into his arms. But she evaded his grasp, and he laughed as she scrambled in search of her gown.

Elizabeth had barely managed to wrap a sheet around her when Rachel and Amanda opened the door, giggling at the sight of Logan's sunbrowned chest clearly visible above the sheets. Elizabeth's cheeks burned as they eyed the rumpled bedcovers and exchanged looks, and she picked up the gown Logan had tossed away during the night and quickly thrust it behind her back.

Amanda laid the tray of hot chocolate and muffins upon

the table, and Elizabeth frowned threateningly at Logan's amused grin.

"I trust all my guests found their way home," Logan said to Rachel, and she nodded, her curls bouncing.

"Oh, yes sir. Mama's putting the house to rights again. She asked if you would be down for dinner."

Logan looked at Elizabeth, his eyes warm as he beheld her slender curves beneath the sheet. "No, I don't think we will."

Another blush crept into Elizabeth's cheeks at the way he looked at her, deepening to scarlet as he added, "Nor for supper, either."

The girls snickered behind their hands as they left, and Logan barely suppressed the laughter in his voice.

"It's not a secret what we've been doing in here, sweet. We are married, you know."

"Well, there's no need to show them, too," Elizabeth retorted tartly as she climbed back upon the bed, the sheet tucked firmly in place.

They sat across from each other with the tray between them, and the way Logan's eyes played upon her with warm, possessive pleasure made Elizabeth's skin burn self-consciously. But she found herself happy with him and the way things had turned out. Her husband's lovemaking was nothing like what Brent had led her to believe it would be, but tender and loving, awakening in her a response she'd never dreamed possible. Even the thought of his lips upon her flesh sent a slow, undulating shiver down her spine.

"Are you cold?" Logan asked at once, always sensitive to her needs, and Elizabeth shook her head. Logan's eyes played over her thinly draped figure with open desire.

"Too bad—I had in mind the most delectable way to warm you." His smile was tender, his eyes promising things that accelerated her pulse. She sipped her chocolate, watching him over the rim.

The sight of him stretched out, his hands laced behind his head, brought images winging through the draped corridors of her mind. Often she had felt things about him that she could not explain, but if they'd been lovers, she could now understand much that had bothered her. She was glad Logan had told her the truth, but she felt cheated, wanting to know every detail that had passed between them in their past together.

"It's not a bad idea taking all our meals here," Logan mused aloud, tugging at the sheet wrapped around her. It fell away, baring the petite perfection of her body, and Logan grinned. "The view is much to my liking."

Elizabeth blushed, still shy with him. But she hastened to set the tray aside. Logan smiled as he slid a warm palm over the silken warmth of her thigh.

"I see you no longer cringe away," he teased. "Have you lost your fear of me?"

Elizabeth leaned forward and placed a nibbling kiss upon his broad shoulder. "I have a different fear now," she confessed breathlessly, and Logan dipped his fingers through the rippling silver waves flowing over his chest.

"And what is that?"

His face dropped to her shoulder, and Elizabeth sighed, closing her eyes and moving her head to give him better access.

"That you will never let me out of this room again."

Logan raised startled eyes, then leaned back his head and laughed heartily.

"And would that displease you so much?" he asked, drawing her fingertips to his lips.

Elizabeth's body came alive as the warm male lips moved into her open palm, and she smiled dreamily as he pulled her bodily onto his hard chest.

"No, I do not think it would," she murmured before his lips took her words.

In the weeks that followed, Logan rarely let Elizabeth out of his sight. And his unflagging attention did much to rid her of the distrust she'd nurtured against him for so long. He continued to talk of their time together in a cave; and although his words continued to bring murky, indistinct images to mind, she could not remember anything about her childhood with the Cheyenne. She occasionally wondered what had happened to Brent, but her husband kept her much too content to worry about him long. The only shadow that ate at her tranquillity was the beautiful Isabel Whitcomb. Although Logan insisted she meant nothing to him, pain would surface in her eyes when she remembered the way Logan had sought out Brent's sister. Then Logan's touch would ignite her passion and make her forget everything but him.

The others in the household saw little of the lovers, and although they often joined Michael and Lily for supper, more often than not, blue eyes would rest upon Elizabeth with secret messages until she would plead fatigue and they would slip away hand in hand.

After one long and lazy afternoon lying together in the leafy bower that overlooked the falls, they returned to Woodstone. Aaron met them at the front gate, and Logan dismounted and lifted Elizabeth down, handing the boy their reins, before he draped one arm over Elizabeth's shoulders and led her across the grass to the veranda. He leaned down and whispered softly into her ear, and Elizabeth's seductive laugh floated across the veranda.

"Logan?"

They turned quickly to look at Michael where he sat with Lily on a low porch swing. Michael stood and spoke as he came toward them.

"There was news of Cassandra today."

"What has that sister of mine done now?" Logan laughed. "Run the Union Army out of New Orleans?"

Elizabeth smiled. She'd heard many stories of Logan's headstrong younger sister, and she longed to meet her.

"Has Cassie arrived in St. Louis?" she asked Michael, but his face remained creased with worry.

"No, the messenger was from some Union major named Connor. She's been placed under house arrest down there."

Logan sobered at once. "On what charge? She's a civilian."

"She's accused of being some sort of spy."

Elizabeth gasped in dismay, and Logan snorted in disgust.

"That's ridiculous. She's just a child."

"She's Elizabeth's age," Michael reminded him, drawing an odd look from Logan. "But apparently it isn't as bad as it sounds. It seems this fellow Connor has taken an interest in her. She's been placed in his custody, and he says if I come down he'll release her into my protection."

Michael sighed, running worried fingers through his

hair, and Lily moved up behind him, placing a comforting hand on his arm. He smiled at her, but his annoyance showed in his next words.

"If Cassie had stayed in London as I told her to do, this would never have happened. That girl's going to be the death of me yet."

"Do you want me to go with you?" Logan offered, and Michael shook his head.

"No, you have Elizabeth to think of now. I'm sure I can handle it with the help of Major Connor."

"When will you leave?"

"Tomorrow, and Lily and Rachel are going with me. Jacob and Aaron prefer to stay here until the wedding."

His calm pronouncement brought startled expressions to both Logan and Elizabeth, but Michael smiled at them as he slipped his arm around Lily's waist. "Lily has consented to become my wife, so she'll need to meet Cassie. And I want her to see my house in St. Louis."

Elizabeth's smile was quick and delighted, and she threw her arms around Lily, as Logan stretched his hand out to Michael.

"I wondered when you'd get around to asking her. I know you'll be happy."

"I'm already happy," Michael said. "And I want you to bring Elizabeth to St. Louis for the wedding. She could visit Thomas while you're there."

Logan looked down at Elizabeth's eager face and nodded.

"As soon as my house in Denver is rebuilt, we'll come for a long visit, I promise. And if you need my help with Cassie before that, send word to me."

They left the next morning with tearful partings on both sides, and Woodstone settled into a strange quiet with the twins staying in the bunkhouse and Amanda with Maria in the rear servants' quarters. That evening, Logan and Elizabeth shared an intimate meal before the fireplace in Logan's den, and long after Maria had gone off to bed, Elizabeth sat upon the floor near the hearth with Logan's head nestled comfortably in her lap, his long legs stretched out toward the fire. Elizabeth lifted a sun-whitened strand of his hair and fingered it idly.

"It is strange to be here alone with you."

Logan turned his head, blue eyes glinting up at her.

"I prefer to have you to myself," he returned, his fingers releasing the pins, shimmering the long softness around his face. He raised a lock, watching the thick silver curl itself around his wrist. He tugged it gently, drawing her down until his mouth spoke against her parted lips.

"With no interruptions, maybe I can get enough of you."

"We can only try," Elizabeth murmured as he pulled her down upon her back. He propped his head on one open palm, smiling into deep violet pools, and traced her full lower lip with his forefinger. The moistness of her lips closed over his fingertip, and the totally wanton look in her eyes sent molten lava into his loins. He rolled upon his back, pulling her full length upon his chest, her hair swirling over them both in a bright cascade.

"You're a witch, Elizabeth, a beautiful, adorable witch. Do you have any idea what you've done to me?" he breathed into her ear, sweeping her hair aside so that his tongue could taste the hollow beneath her ear.

"I fear I cannot help but know," she said wickedly, as the position in which he held her did little to hide his arousal. He laughed and took her lips, rolling again until his long body covered hers. His hand found entrance beneath the silken folds of her skirt, and Elizabeth moaned as he stroked her bare knee. Her response was total, and she slid her arms around his hard-muscled waist, barely realizing it when Logan lifted his face to search the crouching shadows of the room. Elizabeth lay beneath him, opening dreamy eyes as he rose to his knees. The flickering fire carved hollows and planes in his handsome face, and his blue eyes glowed with an expression that made her follow his gaze.

A tall Indian stood in the doorway, and his fierce appearance brought a gasp from Elizabeth, but Logan laid a reassuring hand on her shoulder.

"It's all right," he whispered. "Two Bears is my friend."

He stood, smiling, and walked to meet the Sioux, wondering what had brought him to Woodstone. He'd last seen Two Bears in Denver after the fire when he'd told him he'd found Starfire. Elizabeth sat upright, watching as the two men clasped wrists.

"I am glad to see you," Logan said, as the Sioux glanced at Elizabeth.

"You are happy with your woman?"

Logan's teeth flashed white. "Yes, very happy. But what brings my blood brother to my house?"

"Little Doe is dead."

Logan stared at him in shock, reading the pain in his friend's dark eyes. Images of Two Bears' daughter flickered in his mind, the small and beautiful twelve-year-old with her warm eyes and lovely smile.

"How?" Logan said, his voice clogged with emotion.

"She was violated and beaten to death by a white man."

Logan tensed, his eyes narrow with fury.

"What white man?"

"One who came to our village to sell bullets for our guns. He called himself Holloway."

Logan's eyes darkened into hard, lethal rage. For years, he'd heard that Brent enjoyed hurting women. Now he'd murdered a child. He should have killed him when he had the chance.

"I will find this Holloway and kill him," Two Bears said calmly.

"He was here several weeks ago, but he's probably in Denver now."

"There is much unrest in our camp. Many of the young warriors are very angry. I am needed there, but afterward I will find the white devil."

"Come for me when you are ready," Logan said. "I want to help you." He glanced at Elizabeth. "I believe he hired the men who took Elizabeth from me."

Elizabeth sat quietly, watching Logan and the tall, lean savage as the firelight glinted coppery tints off the Indian's impassive face. They spoke together quietly in a strange, guttural language, and she studied Logan's face, wondering what they said. He looked very angry, his face set in hard, inflexible lines, a look she had not seen since the night of the wedding ball.

She frowned slightly as strange, disembodied shapes began to crowd into her mind, floating like wispy ghouls just out of her grasp. Intense dread took her in its possession, her heart thumping erratically, and she sat very still, watching mind images erupt one after another, rising and bursting like bubbles in a boiling caldron. When it happened, it was quick and total, as if a long shutter had been thrust apart at the back of her mind. Bright light flooded her memory, and total recall revealed every scene from her past.

Shock overwhelmed her, and she was unaware that she'd jumped to her feet. Her heart palpitated wildly, her eyes on Logan.

"Tracker!"

Both Logan and Two Bears heard her gasp the word, turning as Elizabeth backed away from them. Logan stepped toward her, but Elizabeth darted away from him and ran into the back hall, pausing at the banister lamp to see if he followed. He was not in sight, and she ran up the steps and down the darkness of the upstairs hall. A bar of light slanted from Logan's room, and she slammed the door and locked it.

Tears streamed from her eyes as she leaned her back against the wood. Her chest ached as if a heavy stone lay upon it, and she slid downward into a miserable huddle upon the floor. The memories continued to flow, all curtains of forgetfulness rent apart, but one was like a hot poker held against her flesh. The shabby hotel room, the cruel men. Her tears came faster, her heart bursting with pain at the memory of Tracker calmly receiving his payment from Rankin. Logan, whom she loved so much, who had professed to love her, had sold her to them without so much as a second thought.

Elizabeth sobbed, burying her face in her palms, her shoulders heaving with agony. She'd trusted him, loved him, left her people for him, and he'd heartlessly betrayed her. She wept harder, gnashing her teeth, clenching her fists, her misery total and horrible. Long moments passed as the first tide of grief wrenched her body and soul, eventually dissipating into low moans of despair.

She finally got to her feet, feeling drained, the hurt still there but the tears spent. She wiped the wetness from her cheeks with the back of her hand as anger came in swift, powerful strides that burned into her aching heart. Her fingers curled into her palms, her fragile jaw hardening and angling up dangerously. She hated him! He was a filthy wasichu, a lying, deceitful white man who had used her!

She inhaled deeply, then walked to the standing mirror upon her dresser. She stared at her reflection dispassionately, hating the way she looked, the clothes she wore. She moved with sudden rage, tearing the ribbons from her hair, snarling as she jerked her bodice loose and ripped the dress away from her body. She was not white, not a wife to the man who'd betrayed her! She was Cheyenne!

NINETEEN

Logan took the steps at a run, the look he'd seen upon Elizabeth's face chilling him to the bone. He rattled the doorknob of the room, frowning when she refused to answer. He was sure she'd regained her memory, and he had to get to her, had to know what she was feeling.

"Elizabeth, please, let me in."

The dark, silent house mocked his burgeoning anxiety, and he tried the knob again, calling her name. She didn't answer, and he gritted his teeth, then stepped back and gave the door one vicious kick that sent it splintering off its hinges to hang askew.

He stepped through the threshold into the dimness of the room. It took him a moment to see her where she stood by the bed, half hidden in the deep shadows. A shudder ran down his spine as he looked at the chemise she wore, belted to fit like a Cheyenne shift. Her feet were bare, her hair braided over her shoulders. Her face was shrouded in the darkness, and he spoke warily.

"Elizabeth?"

His mouth dropped as she stepped out where he could see her.

Streaks of rouge coursed down each cheek in jagged, angry lines, and Logan found he could not move, as an icy crust solidified over his heart. Her violet eyes were frozen with hatred, and she moved with a quickness that stunned him.

Air waved beside his ear, followed by a dull thud, and he jerked his face toward it. His nose almost touched the small dagger still quivering from impact. It stunned him for the space of an instant, but he knew it was from his knife collection upon the wall, and others were within her reach.

He moved as swiftly as she had, jerking it from the doorframe, two immense strides taking him to her. She did not flinch or run, and he grabbed her by the shoulders.

"Starfire, listen to me!"

She twisted away viciously, teeth clenched with fury.

"Do not touch me, white dog!" she spat.

There was no doubt now that his wild and beautiful Starfire had come back, and his grin infuriated Elizabeth. Cursing, she flew at him, her nails spread like sharp talons, and Logan barely managed to catch her wrists before they reached his face. His grip was firm but gentle as he turned her and clamped her back against his chest. He lifted her bodily, ignoring her wild struggling.

"Elizabeth, stop it, and listen to me!"

Cheyenne curses answered him, and he pinned her arms to her sides, dropping her upon the bed, where he half lay upon her, holding down her kicking legs with his knee. He held her wrists pinned beside her head, and Elizabeth glared at him, trying to wrench free. He was much too strong, and she finally lay still, panting from exertion.

"Now will you listen to me?"

"I hate you," she said in Cheyenne. Logan frowned. And to think he'd looked forward to the return of her memory, he berated himself. He released her abruptly, at a loss for the cause of her rage. He kept his arms braced on either side of her to prevent her escape. Elizabeth stared up at him, fighting the hot tears prickling behind her eyelids. How could he have done it? How could he have been so cold and unfeeling? He'd won her love, treated her with tender care all the weeks in the mountains, in his house in Denver, then he'd sold her like a horse, given her into the hands of cruel men. She swallowed hard, hurt hardening again into rage.

"You will not live to sell me again, wasichu," she gritted out in a hissed whisper.

Realization dawned in Logan's eyes, and he took her by the shoulders, his voice urgent.

"I didn't sell you. You must believe that."

"I believe only my eyes," she said coldly, sneering into his face. "What was I worth, Tracker? Fifty gold pieces? One hundred? Do you plan to do it again when you tire of me?"

The absurdity of her words was dwarfed by his fear that she really believed them.

"They knocked me unconscious and took you by force," he said with quiet desperation. "I swear it."

Elizabeth's laugh was bitter. "I will find a way to kill you for what you've done to me, then I will return to my people."

At that moment, it was all she wanted. The whites with their easy, comfortable life were full of deceit and lies. She preferred the honest, hard life of the Indians. She was ashamed that she was a white woman, ashamed she'd left her people willingly.

Her last threat had been much more frightening to Logan, and his frown grew blacker.

"You will go nowhere. You are my wife," he snapped.

"I am not your wife! I hate you!"

Logan made the mistake of raising his hand to touch her, and she knocked it away and was halfway to the door before he reached her. He knew Starfire's temperament enough to know nothing less than physical restraint would keep her in the room, and he tossed her over his shoulder, one arm against the back of her knees, then dumped her unceremoniously on the bed. Elizabeth sputtered her rage, grabbing the nearest object. Logan saw the candlestick coming at his head and dodged it, but her aim was good enough for it to glance painfully off his shoulder.

His own temper rising, Logan grabbed the towel beside the pitcher and wet it, blocking her attempt to scramble off the bed with his other hand. He frowned darkly as he held her down and rubbed off the jagged lines of rouge. Ignoring her furious threats, he gritted out harshly, "You are my wife, and you will stay here."

He slung the cloth into a far corner, his own anger rapidly gaining momentum. "You're white, and you're going to act like it! And if I have to, I'll keep you under lock and key until you do!"

Elizabeth snarled as he threw a leg over her, getting his

palms on either side of her head to force her to look at him.
He glared at her.

"Damn it, woman, you're going to listen to me! Do you
really think I'd let you go? Do you? Much less sell you to
another man? God knows I nearly went insane after
Rankin took you from me. I searched for you for months
without giving up. Think, Elizabeth, think about our
time in the cave, in Denver. Think about the last few
weeks. I love you, damn it, I've always loved you! And
I'd rather die than turn you over to another man. Can't
you see that?"

Elizabeth had stopped fighting halfway through his
words, and his hands fell to his sides as they stared at each
other. Elizabeth's eyes slowly filled with tears, and she
sobbed, turning her face into the pillows. Logan stared
down at her, his anger dissolving; her tears affected him as
her anger never could.

Her weeping was a terrible, silent despair, and Logan
watched helplessly, aching to comfort her. He reached out
and touched her hair, and when she didn't protest, he
turned her unresisting body to lie across his lap. He closed
his eyes in relief, clutching her tightly as she wept into his
shirt.

"Elizabeth, please, don't cry. I can't bear to see you suffer. . . ."

His words brought up dark lashes, spiky with tears, and
her voice trembled.

"Then take me home," she begged. "Take me back to my
people where I belong."

"This is your home now," Logan said stubbornly, trying
to ignore the tears tracking down her cheeks. "You belong
here with me."

The despair deepened in her eyes.

"But I hate it here! I hate the ways of the whites," she
cried. "And you promised! You promised me you'd take me
home if I was unhappy."

The vow he'd made to her the day they'd left the cave
came back to Logan with ominous clarity, but it was the
one thing he could never do. Now that he'd found her
again, he couldn't risk taking her back. He sighed and
shook his head, and Elizabeth broke away from him,
flinging herself facedown on the bed. Logan stood,

bleak eyes on her small form huddled upon the bed, each of her heartbroken sobs raking his heart like sharp claws.

The next day they left for Denver. Elizabeth sat beside Amanda in the carriage, her face carved in stone, while Logan bid goodbye to Aaron and Maria. Elizabeth was sick at heart, wan and weak from crying herself to sleep. Despair tore at her heart as she struggled with her thoughts. She loved Logan, loved him with every fiber of her being. She believed now that he had had no part in her abduction, but it didn't lessen her need to return to the security of her tribe. She could not bear the thought of leaving him, but neither could she contemplate a life among the whites. She did not belong with them, even with Logan at her side. She could never be happy until she went home to her people. Her heart began to ache again, and she fiercely blinked away tears.

Jacob sat waiting on the driver's box, his rifle across his knees, as Logan mounted Zeus. Two Bears had warned him of the smoldering resentment among the Sioux, and several homesteads around Central City had been burned by the Cheyenne. Logan was on friendly terms with most of the tribes nearby, but nevertheless he'd take no chances when Elizabeth was with him.

He reined up beside the window, but Elizabeth refused to look at him, so he signaled Jacob to proceed, glancing again at Elizabeth's grim face. He'd hoped to be able to reason with her, but after her weeping had subsided the night before, he'd tried to make her understand the dangers of going back to the Cheyenne. She'd only stared at him with accusing eyes. Her stony silence was hard to bear, but he worried more about what went on behind her beautiful, impassive face. Starfire was more than capable of concocting an escape plan, and it was that fear which had prompted his decision to leave Woodstone.

Living in Denver, it would be more difficult for her to find her way back to them. Especially with the Parkers to help him watch her. So Logan's thoughts ran as he rode beside the carriage, his eyes intent upon the terrain, but Elizabeth was much more miserable as she stared dully at the mountains rising like imposing sentinels against the blue of the sky.

She gazed at the smoky crowns of mists hugging the peaks, wishing she were where the clean winds could blow against her face and clear her mind. Pain constricted her throat. All she wanted was to go home, to be free again. Why couldn't Logan understand how she felt? Her life with the Cheyenne had been simple and uncomplicated. But all she'd known since Logan brought her to the whites was pain and hatred.

She glanced at Amanda, who dozed on the seat beside her, then squeezed her eyes shut, thinking of Rankin's cold black eyes when he'd pawed at her that first night. And the fat man who'd jerked away her amethyst ring and necklace. She shuddered. There were some things she did not want to remember, now that her memory had completely returned. She was mixed up and confused, and worst of all she longed for the comfort of Logan's strong arms and comforting touch. She loved him so much it hurt inside.

She took a deep breath, refusing to weaken toward him. He'd made a promise to her. How could he love her if he refused her the only thing that would make her happy? Her resolve hardened. She would not rest until she returned to her people, and if Logan would not take her, she'd find someone who would.

Understanding green eyes came unheralded into her mind, and her hopelessness took wing. If Logan really loved her, he too would agree to stay with the Indians. They could be happy together living the simple life of her people. Why couldn't he see that?

They made good time, stopping only once at a small settlement, and Logan tried to be understanding as Elizabeth remained silent and remote. Eventually he'd convince her of the folly of returning to her village, but for the present, the important thing was that she was safely with him.

When they reached Denver, Logan was amazed at how much had been accomplished since he'd left a month before. The downtown had been the worst hit by the fire, but now as they rode past, the new brick buildings were near completion, and the city appeared to be booming. He hoped his own property had fared as well, and he smiled in satisfaction when Jacob turned the carriage into the red brick drive beside the house.

Zack appeared in the doorway of the carriage house, grinning in delight when he saw them. He ran forward and took Logan's bridle.

"We didn't expect you, sir, but it's sure nice to see some familiar faces!"

Logan nodded and dismounted. "The house looks good."

Zack's serious brown eyes lit up. "We've worked hard on it, but I missed Woodstone something fierce." His eyes were on Amanda as he spoke, and her eyes shone with pleasure.

"Hello, Miss Elizabeth," Zach said eagerly as Logan lifted her down, then looked to Amanda questioningly when she only nodded slightly.

The porch door banged, and Elizabeth looked up at Agatha Parker, who greeted her with a beaming smile.

"So you've finally brought our little lass back to us. And high time it is, too."

Her eyes were warm with sincere pleasure, and Elizabeth thought of how good the Parkers had been to her when everything was new and strange.

Emotion overwhelmed her and she ran up the back steps into the housekeeper's arms, sobbing out her unhappiness upon her matronly shoulder. Mrs. Parker's arms came around her comfortingly, and she murmured soothingly as she directed mildly accusing eyes at Logan.

Logan frowned and walked away, pulling his horse behind him, and Mrs. Parker led Elizabeth into the house, followed by an unusually solemn Amanda.

Logan talked with Zack for a time, then left him with his brother to discuss their mother's forthcoming marriage. He entered the kitchen, where both the Parkers awaited him. James wore a splint from shoulder to wrist, and Logan sank wearily across the table from him.

"Is Elizabeth upstairs?"

"Yes, I put her to bed and gave her some laudanum. The child was very upset, and exhausted, too, if I could tell right."

Logan sighed, rubbing his fingers over tired eyes. He looked at Aggie.

"What did she tell you?"

"Only that she wants to go home, and you won't let her."

Logan heard the accusation in her voice.

"It's too dangerous to take her back. A faction of the Cheyenne have been raiding, and you know as well as I do that the anti-Indian sentiment is growing here in Denver. Trouble's brewing, and I won't take her back into that."

Both agreed with him, but Mrs. Parker's voice was pitying.

"But she is so very unhappy. Perhaps just a short visit would help. She wants to see her mother."

"She'd never return with me if I took her back," Logan said. Lone Wolf's hard, handsome features burned into his mind, and he shook his head obstinately. "I can't do it, not even for a visit. Is she in my rooms?"

"No, she wouldn't let me put her things there. She's next to you."

Logan stood, suddenly feeling drained. He needed rest. He'd not closed his eyes for the last two nights, afraid Elizabeth would be gone when he awoke.

"I'm going upstairs for a while. Keep an eye on her, will you?"

Mrs. Parker nodded. "A letter arrived from St. Louis three days ago. It's on the hall table."

Logan walked to the front hall, admiring the job the Parkers and Zack had done on the interior of the house. The letter lay on a silver tray, and he picked it up and broke the seal. It took several minutes to read through it, and when he was finished, he folded it carefully. It was the last thing Elizabeth needed right now, but he knew he'd have to tell her. He climbed the stairs wearily, pausing before her closed door, then took a deep breath and entered.

Elizabeth lay sleeping on the bed, her blond hair loose and spread out over the dark pillows. Violet shadows smudged her cheeks, and Logan stood silently, staring down at her innocent beauty. He regretted what she'd been through, but no matter what happened, he could not lose her again. His sigh was loud as he leaned over and kissed her forehead.

Elizabeth felt Logan's warm lips upon her temple before she was completely awake, and she smiled contentedly as they caressed her closed eyelids. She sleepily slipped her arms around his neck, and one strong arm slid beneath her back, lifting her against him. Elizabeth savored the tight embrace, making no objection as his firm lips finally tasted the sweetness of her mouth.

"Believe me, sweet, we can be happy here. As long as we're together."

It took her a moment to comprehend the husky words, then the events of the past few days came barreling back to her.

"No!" she cried, pushing urgently against his chest with both palms, but her frail strength did little against that immense barrier, until his hands voluntarily dropped away from her. She scrambled away, and Logan watched with grim eyes as she slid from the bed and put a good distance between them.

"Why must you do this to us?" he said woodenly, and Elizabeth's hands trembled as she held her dressing gown tightly together.

"I have done nothing. You have broken your word to me."

"What of your vows to me? The vows you took when you became my wife?"

"White man's words!" she spat out contemptuously, as she turned away.

"Elizabeth, look at me."

Something in his voice made her turn, and the sorrow in his eyes brought fear into her heart. Her eyes dropped to the letter he held in his hand.

"It's Thomas, sweet. Your grandfather is dead."

She did not move, her violet eyes wide with shock, and it took everything Logan possessed to keep from going to her.

"He died peacefully in his sleep."

Elizabeth listened dry-eyed, her face stiff and expressionless. It was Thomas who'd arranged to have Logan steal her away from her tribe. It was he who was responsible for all her suffering.

"He was not my grandfather. He was a white man."

Bitterness turned her voice caustic.

"He loved you," Logan said quietly. "Everything he did was because he loved you."

Elizabeth did not answer, and Logan went on relentlessly, "There was no accident that caused you to lose your memory. You were made to forget by a scientific process called mesmerism."

Elizabeth jerked her eyes to him, and he held up the letter.

"It's all in here. He wrote out the whole story to be sent to me after his death."

Elizabeth stared at him, Logan's eyes still holding hers.

"And do you know why he did it, Elizabeth? Because he couldn't bear your unhappiness. It broke his heart that his beloved granddaughter hated him. He agreed so he'd have a chance to love you before he died."

Elizabeth remembered the last time she'd seen her grandfather, when he'd worried that she'd hate him someday. And now he was gone, and she'd never see him again. Her teeth caught at her lower lip as a great wave of grief rolled over her. Tears welled, glittering in her eyes, and when a broken sob escaped her, Logan could stand it no longer. He went to her, ignoring her half-hearted attempts to free herself, clamping her to him until her struggles stopped. Long, racking sobs shook her slender body, and Logan held her tightly, murmuring soothing words, until the torrent of grief settled into exhausted sniffling. She lay limply against him, all fight gone, all feeling deadened. Too much had happened; it was too much to bear.

Logan gathered her into his arms and laid her gently on the bed.

"Try to sleep, my love," he whispered, brushing a tear-dampened strand from her cheek.

"He was good to me," Elizabeth murmured, and Logan nodded. Her long lashes drifted closed, and he barely heard her last words before she slept.

"I loved him."

Two weeks passed, and Logan tried to bear up under her continued cold withdrawal by concentrating on his business concerns. Zack and Jacob had returned to Woodstone to bring a herd of horses to replace those lost during the fire. The army agent was ready to buy, and Logan did the negotiating for the new contract himself, wanting to get his mind off Elizabeth. It rarely worked, and he often left work half finished in the hope she would relent and greet him with a smile. But as of yet, it had not happened. A cold silence usually prevailed between them, as it did now, as they sat alone at either end of the polished dining-room table.

Mrs. Parker served supper, her worried eyes going from one to the other. She'd never in her life seen two such miserable people, and Logan had worn the same dark, forbidding look since he'd arrived. She looked at him, where he leaned back in his chair, staring broodingly down the length of the table to where a pale Elizabeth picked without interest at her meal. Mrs. Parker shook her head, wishing there were something she could do to help solve their problems. She sighed, knowing they could only do it themselves, and Logan barely noticed when she silently glided from the room.

His eyes ranged appreciatively over the lush curves mounding above the royal blue fabric of his wife's gown. Her hair was pinned up with a cascade of curls over one side of her pearl-studded collar, and Logan resisted with difficulty his temptation to stride down the table and press his mouth on the tantalizingly exposed throat.

"How long will you keep this up?" he said suddenly, his voice louder than he'd intended.

Elizabeth raised determined eyes. "Until you take me home."

"You are home, damn it!" he shouted with sudden anger, bringing his fist down on the table hard enough to rattle the cutlery.

Elizabeth looked down at her plate and was silent, frustrating Logan further. He struggled with his own simmering temper. He could not blame her for the way she felt. She'd been through more than any woman should have to experience. And he could understand how she could blame him. He had taken her away from a life she remembered as happy and without problems. With effort, he managed to control his annoyance enough to speak normally.

"The Olympia Opera House will open next week, and I'd like you to accompany me to the first performance." His smile was stiff. "I donated quite a lot of money to build it, and I have a private box. I think you would enjoy it. It's an operatic entourage from London."

"Since I am your prisoner here," Elizabeth said dully, "I suppose I have no choice in the matter."

Her words ignited Logan like flame to a fuse, and he thrust back his chair, hurling his napkin to the table as his lean jaw worked furiously.

"Damn it, Elizabeth, you are not a prisoner in this house, and you know it! Anything you wish will be provided for you. All you have to do is ask for it."

"I have asked, but you refuse my only desire."

Logan paced to the sideboard, angrily splashing brandy into a glass. His patience was being tried unmercifully, and he tried again to remember how she must feel.

"We've been over this a dozen times. You belong here with me, and besides that, it's too dangerous," he tried to explain.

"I am not afraid. My people will fight their enemies bravely and win."

Logan turned, his voice softening. "Don't you see, Elizabeth, the Cheyenne don't have a chance to win against the government. Numbers alone will be their downfall, not to mention guns and weapons. There are ten or twenty white men for every warrior, and after the war's over with the South, the army won't stop until every Indian in this territory is either dead or on a reservation like the Cherokee."

"No! That is not true!" Elizabeth stood and threw her own napkin down, her temper out of control. "And I will go back to them! If you don't care enough to help me, then Brent will! He wants to see me happy, even if you don't!"

Logan froze, his drink halfway to his mouth, and when he turned slowly to look at her, Elizabeth quailed back beneath eyes that glinted the icy blue of mountain lakes. His words were harsh, gritted between set teeth.

"You'll ask nothing of that bastard. You'll stay away from him, is that clear?"

Elizabeth steeled her nerve and glared at him.

"He is my friend. You cannot stop me from seeing him."

Black wrath took over Logan's face.

"This is one time you're going to listen to me. Brent is a

dangerous man. One who gets some kind of pleasure from hurting other people."

Elizabeth stared at him, hesitating slightly before she spoke. "Brent was kind to me when I needed a friend. He wouldn't hurt anyone intentionally."

Logan's fists clenched until muscles ridged in his arms. "Remember the night Two Bears came to Woodstone, Elizabeth? Do you know what he told me? That Brent Holloway had raped and killed his twelve-year-old daughter."

Elizabeth gasped, her eyes horrified, but she could not believe Brent capable of such a terrible thing. "I can't believe that," she said slowly, "Two Bears must be wrong."

Her defense of Holloway infuriated Logan. Rage rose like a red haze over his eyes.

"And what's more, he's the bloody bastard who hired Rankin to take you away from me! He's behind all your suffering, if you really want someone to blame! None of it would have happened if I could have kept you with me from the beginning!"

"You only wish to turn me against him so that I will not go to him for help," Elizabeth returned evenly.

Their wills clashed angrily, until Logan spun furiously, sending his glass to smash against the hearth, then turned and left the room with immense, infuriated strides.

Elizabeth sank weakly into her chair, trembling under his rage, as he shouted angrily for his horse. Moments later, a clatter of hooves on the brick drive marked his departure, and Elizabeth dropped her face in her hands. She clenched her teeth, fighting against tears, as she looked around the lavishly decorated dining room with its red velvet wallcovering and elegant gilded furniture. Why couldn't he take her back where no one had ever hurt her or demanded things of her? she thought in despair. Why was he so stubborn?

She wandered through the large, silent rooms, lonely and upset. Isabel Whitcomb was in Denver now. Would Logan turn to her? Was he with her now? Visions of Logan's lean and virile body atop the beautiful coppery-haired woman made her totally wretched, and she sought refuge in the sanctuary of her bedchamber. She stared morosely into space as Amanda brushed out the coiled thickness of her hair until it lay long and shimmering down her back.

All the servants had heard the shouting between Logan and his wife, and all were stunned at Logan's burst of temper. Even Amanda had lost her fear of him during the summer at Woodstone, and she knew it was a terrible quarrel indeed to make him yell at Miss Elizabeth.

"May I speak, ma'am?" she said hesitantly, fidgeting with the brush as Elizabeth looked up and nodded.

"I know I am not one to know, but I cannot help but think the reason Master Logan will not let you go is that he loves you and wants you here with him."

Amanda's eyes were earnest, and as Elizabeth looked down, she added quickly, "And I would miss you sorely if you were to leave. And so would Zack and Rachel and all of us."

The last came in a hurry, and Elizabeth smiled.

"And I would miss you. But I do not belong here. I know it's hard for you to understand, but I'm not like other white women. I am Cheyenne."

"But they are savages!" Amanda interjected, with horrified eyes.

"No, they are good, honorable people. I belong with them."

Amanda looked so sad that Elizabeth forced another smile.

"Go now. I know Zack waits for you."

After Amanda left, Elizabeth walked to the bed, one hand upon the bedpost. She was not eager to slide between the sheets, knowing it would be as cold and lonely as it was every night when Logan wasn't with her. She shivered, remembering Logan's muscular arms around her, and the moans his kisses forced from her lips.

She loved him so desperately, but she could never go to him again. She climbed into bed, realizing she was caught in her own trap. If she went to him and declared her love as she yearned to do, he would never take her back to her people. But each night spent without him was torture. She pulled the satin comforter to her chin, her gaze unseeingly on the heavy velvet above her.

It was very late when she heard the sound of his horse beneath her window, and she lay tensely waiting until heavy footsteps approached her door. She held her breath as they paused there for a long moment, then moved on. It was then that tears began anew, and she buried her face in her pillow to muffle them.

TWENTY

In the week that followed, Logan remained aloof, his manner stiff and courteous as he held his pride in firm leash. He spent more and more time at the corrals with the Winstead boys or in his mining offices downtown, becoming more involved in his work than he had been in years. Elizabeth fought the desire to go to him and forget the idea of rejoining her tribe, but when such weakness shook her resolve, she would call upon her inner strength. She had but one weapon against him, and a feeble one it was, because she knew only too well that it was only effective as long as Logan allowed it to be. She dreaded and anticipated the day when he'd disregard her wishes and take her into his arms, because despite her resistance, she knew very little force would be needed. When his lips came to hers, all defenses crumbled, and he would win.

Her fear was not to be tested, however, for Logan did not attempt to touch her. But the forced estrangement from the woman he loved etched grim lines on his face, and the frequency of his long, solitary rides at night bore witness to his own brand of hell.

The evening of the opera arrived, and Elizabeth dreaded the occasion, knowing a night spent in close proximity with her husband would weaken her will to keep him at bay should he decide to claim her. But as much as she dreaded it, she also entertained hope. The more she'd thought about it, the more she'd decided that Brent Holloway was her only hope to return to the Cheyenne. No one else she knew would dare defy Logan's wishes, and she could not make it back alone. She'd taken a drastic step, sending a reluctant Amanda to Brent's house with a sealed note, hoping it would be passed to him, requesting that he meet her at the opera. It was something she'd had to do, but she found herself aflutter with nerves as she sat before her dressing table.

Logan had purchased a new gown for her to wear at the social event, and she turned to look at it where it lay across her bed. The very simplicity of the black velvet gown made it more stunning than any of the extravagant creations in her closet. It plunged deeply to lie just off her shoulders, revealing a delectable amount of soft white flesh, and its bodice cinched her small waist to best advantage before flaring with graceful flattery over her slim hips.

Elizabeth adamantly refused to let Amanda weave her hair into the elaborate coiffure preferred by Denver's society, but instead allowed the glowing silver tresses to ripple to her waist unadorned. Twin combs of ebony held the soft silver away from her face, Indian-fashion, and Mrs. Parker clicked her tongue as she helped Elizabeth into the soft black gown.

"The high dames will sputter behind their fans when they see you, my dear."

"I do not care what they say," Elizabeth said offhandedly, and Agatha Parker's eyes twinkled wickedly as she stepped back and looked at her small charge. If she was right, it would take only one look at Elizabeth in this gown before Logan would be obliged to give her anything she might ask of him. And when that happened, perhaps the awful silence and grim tension would leave their house forever.

Later, Elizabeth descended the steps, her soft velvet cape over one arm. She stopped when she saw Logan where he stood motionlessly in the foyer, staring into space. He was dressed immaculately in formal attire, the rich sheen of fine black fabric glowing against the sun-kissed blond of his hair.

He turned slowly as if he sensed her presence, and he let his eyes move over her with a slow, thorough scrutiny that set her hands to trembling. Logan looked at her, unable to stop the emotion that welled against his chest, stopping his breath. She was so unbelievably beautiful. It had been so long since she'd given him a kind word or a warm look. He missed her as much as if they'd been physically sepa-

rated. Not just in the dark of the night when he would
groan when he reached for her to find empty sheets, but in
every way. A vast void had opened in his life the day she'd
withdrawn from him. He missed her laughter, her humor,
he missed the myriad of looks, and actions, and emotions
that made Elizabeth the only woman he would ever love.

Their eyes met, naked hunger flaring between them,
and Elizabeth quickly averted her gaze. Logan walked
slowly to her, standing very close, and Elizabeth picked up
the manly scent that robbed her composure and flushed
her cheeks as it brought back intimate memories.

"You are lovelier than I can say," he breathed, and the
way his eyes caressed her shredded at her resistance. He
traced the fragile line of her jaw with a gentle finger, and
Elizabeth's knees went weak, her heart lurching out of cadence. She turned away, but Logan followed, resting his
palms lightly on her bare shoulders, before he swept away
her hair. When his warm lips touched the sensitive nape of
her neck, Elizabeth could barely suppress the breathless
pleasure it started deep inside her.

"I want you more than anything," he whispered. "I
want to hold you and kiss you. I want to make love to you."

Elizabeth's eyes closed and she weaved slightly, re-
laxing against his chest. The slight unbending was enough
to give Logan encouragement, and his mouth moved to her
ear.

"Please, let me love you. It's what we both want."

She pulled away from him, her wide eyes telling Logan
just how close she'd been to the sweet response he needed
from her.

"Take me home," she said breathlessly. "We can love
each other there. We can be happy again."

His face closed into an impassive mask, and without
speaking, he took the velvet cloak from her hands. Her
flesh still quivered from the heat of his lips as he placed
the heavy cape around her shoulders and led her to the
door.

Parker waited outside with the carriage, and Logan
handed her up, then settled across from her. Elizabeth sat
uncomfortably during the short ride as his eyes shone
upon her like blue flames, not realizing how the flickering
light from the interior lantern turned her skin a soft,

warm honey that tore at Logan's rigidly imposed self-control.

The Olympia was the cultural achievement of the frontier city, and its opulence was not to be bested anywhere west of St. Louis. The intricate woodwork had been carved by the finest craftsmen of New Orleans and shipped across the prairie, its gilt flowers and leaves resplendent against the white flocked walls.

Its magnificence did not fail to impress Elizabeth, and she shed some of her contempt for white ways as she gazed in awe at the huge chandeliers said to have graced the country palace of Napoleon himself. The lobby was very crowded, as every affluent member of the city was in attendance, and Logan led Elizabeth toward the curving staircase, his fingers firmly gripping her elbow. He nodded and smiled at acquaintances in the milling throng, but did not pause to chat, inwardly annoyed by the obvious stares his wife drew from any masculine eyes that fell upon her. Among the lavishly dressed women with their jewels and vibrant colors, Elizabeth's fair beauty gleamed like a flawless diamond displayed upon black velvet.

Logan led her along the upper balcony, then held back the heavy velvet drapery so she could enter his private box. Despite her initial reluctance to attend, Elizabeth looked with delight across the vast interior of the theater as she sat upon one of the velvet-tufted chairs. The audience below them buzzed with muted conversation as people observed each other through long-stemmed opera glasses. Fascinated, Elizabeth took in everything eagerly, while Logan's eyes stayed upon her, his lips curved in a slight smile.

The lights dimmed, and Elizabeth leaned forward as the curtains were slowly drawn apart. The opéra was *La Traviata*, by Verdi, and when the singers appeared, Elizabeth followed every movement of the fair Violetta and her Alfredo with awed wonder, delighted by their elaborate costumes and exaggerated gestures.

By the time the lamps flared for the intermission, she was totally caught up in the opera, and she turned shining eyes upon Logan.

"Do you like it?" he asked, his teeth a brief gleam of

white, and she could never remember him looking so handsome.

"Yes, very much," she admitted, but his eyes did not leave hers, the burning look making time its slave. The feeling flowing between them was so intense, so incredibly intimate, that Elizabeth was assailed by a wave of dizziness that sent her head spinning. She blanched, shutting her eyes, and Logan sat forward in concern.

"What is it, sweet? Are you ill?"

She leaned back, grateful for his supporting arm.

"No, I suddenly became dizzy."

She opened her fan and waved it back and forth, not wanting him to know it had happened several times in the last month.

"Perhaps a drink would help. Refreshments are served in the lobby."

Elizabeth smiled weakly. "Yes, Logan, please."

He left at once, and Elizabeth leaned back, smiling wryly as she realized that Logan's eyes upon her had brought about the spell. Surely she was weakening toward him, if only a look could cause such a reaction.

She turned as Brent Holloway entered their box. He moved close to her, smiling.

"Elizabeth, darling, I got your note. I was so glad that you wanted me to come."

Elizabeth stared at his handsome face, realizing she felt nothing at the sight of him, not even pleasure. It was hard to understand how she could have thought herself in love with him.

"I'm so sorry about the night of the ball," he continued. "But Logan forced me to leave. I had no choice."

He put his hand upon her bare shoulder with open familiarity, and Elizabeth's first impulse was to cringe away. But he was her only hope to return to Raging Buffalo and Gentle Reed.

"I have regained my memory," she said bluntly, and noted how his green eyes seemed to close into themselves.

"Why, Elizabeth, that's wonderful."

His carefully controlled expression did not match his sincere words, and Elizabeth did not have time to dwell upon it. Logan would be back soon, and she had to gain Brent's assistance.

"Brent, please, you must help me to get home to my tribe. Logan refuses to take me, and you are my last hope."

Her voice had grown urgent as she looked to the doorway, afraid Logan would appear.

Brent's mind raced, disbelieving his luck. After all his plots and plans had gone awry, here was the lovely Elizabeth begging him to take her away from Logan. And there was no doubt, being the hothead he was, Logan would follow them in a lethal rage, giving Brent a most opportune time to get rid of him for good.

Brent smiled and took Elizabeth's hand. "I will take you anywhere you wish. I still love you, you know."

Elizabeth stared at him, a vague uneasiness touching her mind as she remembered Logan's warnings. But she had no choice. Before Elizabeth could protest, Brent had pressed her hand against his lips.

"Meet me tonight at midnight, and I'll take you away."

"I'll be ready," Elizabeth said, gasping as she saw Logan behind Brent, a glass of champagne in his hand.

His face was the personification of cold deadly rage, but before anyone could move, a female voice carved its way into the draped alcove.

"Logan, darling, I heard you were here," Isabel Whitcomb said as she stepped into sight behind Logan. "Oh, and there you are, Brent. A friend of yours dropped by as I was leaving, and I persuaded him to be my escort."

Isabel looked at Logan as she drew her handsome new lover into the room, hoping to make him jealous, but Logan ignored Isabel and rigidly watched Brent.

Elizabeth's eyes went to the man with Isabel, and she sat transfixed as she stared into the small black eyes of the man who had taken her from Tracker. She gasped in horror, and Logan looked down at her white face, then followed her frightened eyes.

Logan's movement was so swift and decisive that neither Holloway nor Carl Rankin had time to react. Isabel screamed as Logan shoved past her, his eyes dark and murderous, and slammed Rankin against the wall, his thumbs like steel bars against his throat. Isabel backed away and Elizabeth's hands rose to her mouth as Rankin's hands clawed desperately to break Logan's grip.

"Tell her who hired you," Logan growled harshly.

The altercation had drawn the attention of the other boxes now, and many trained their glasses upon the excitement in Logan Cord's box.

Rankin gasped, trying to choke an answer from his constricted throat, and Logan loosened his hold and stepped away.

"It was Brent, Brent did—"

A sharp crack exploded, and blood appeared against Rankin's white shirtfront as Brent's double-barreled derringer ripped a hole through his heart. Elizabeth arose in terror, but Brent grabbed her as Logan whirled to face him. Brent smiled, aiming the gun at Logan's chest, his finger moving against the trigger.

"No, Brent, don't!" Isabel screamed, throwing herself in front of Logan. It was too late for Brent to change his course, and the bullet struck her, knocking her backward into Logan's chest. She crumpled to the floor in a tangled heap of yellow and white silk, and Brent looked in horror at the blood streaming from her dress, the gun still smoking in his hand.

Several men burst into the box, and Brent hurled the gun at Logan, then pushed Elizabeth into the others, before he leaped to the railing. Women in the next box shrieked and scrambled frantically to get out of his way as he jumped into their midst. He overturned chairs in his frenzied attempt to escape, and Logan helped Elizabeth into a chair as the other men went in pursuit of Holloway. Elizabeth watched as Logan moved back to Isabel and supported her back as he yelled for someone to summon a doctor.

"Is she dead?" Elizabeth whispered.

Logan shook his head. "No, but she's losing a lot of blood. He got her in the shoulder."

Elizabeth watched dazedly as a doctor appeared, and he and Logan leaned over the prone woman, working to stanch the flow of blood. Several men entered and hoisted Carl Rankin's corpse and carried him out, and Elizabeth stared at the bloodstains upon the floor. She couldn't deny the truth; Logan had been right. Brent was the one behind her abduction. His friendship, his gentle understanding, all that had been lies. Every white man she'd trusted had rewarded her with betrayal. As she watched Logan lift Isabel carefully to a makeshift stretcher, her resolve to return to the Cheyenne increased tenfold. There she could find trust and loyalty. But there was no honor among the white man.

It was very late when they finally reached home, and Logan preceded her into the hall, where a single lamp burned for their return. He did not wait for her, but walked into his library. Elizabeth stood in the doorway as he poured himself a drink and tossed it down, then jerked off his stiff collar and slung his coat into a chair. She tugged her cape from her shoulders, watching as he sank into a chair.

"I am glad Isabel will be all right," she said, and Logan looked up at her out of angry blue eyes.

"Now do you believe your precious Brent was involved?" he asked bitterly. "Now that he killed a man in front of you and shot his own sister? Or will you still run away with him as planned?"

Elizabeth met his contemptuous eyes steadfastly.

"He is a monster, and I was a fool ever to trust him. I only wanted him to take me home, since you would not."

Logan closed his eyes and laid his head against the chair. His jaw remained clenched, and Elizabeth suddenly wanted to comfort him, to erase the hatred seething in his veins. She walked slowly toward him, sinking to her knees at his feet.

Logan opened his eyes in surprise, and Elizabeth searched his face with great beseeching violet eyes, as she placed a gentle palm against the rigid set of his jaw.

"Please, Tracker, please . . . if you still love me, if you've ever loved me . . . take me to my people as you promised me. I beg you."

Her voice was softly imploring, her red lips parted and moist, and Logan shut his eyes and groaned as he caught her hand tightly against his cheek. He turned his face until his lips pressed into her small palm, wanting her in that moment with a desperation that plunged like a steel spike into his soul. He wavered on the brink of agreement, wanting to give her anything she desired, do anything she wished to gain the sweet moment when she melted into his arms freely, her lips eager beneath his own.

But reason returned quickly. He'd experienced life without her, and the thought of losing her again was inconceivable. Her face was very close, her lips inches from his mouth, and he could not stop himself as he gathered her onto his lap, their lips meeting with a hunger that consumed every other thought.

When he could speak, his words were a gruff whisper.

"I would do anything on this earth for you, my love, but I cannot willingly let you go. I cannot."

Elizabeth sobbed with disappointment, pushing away from him.

"Then surely everything I have ever felt for you will slowly wither into the blackest of hatred, until I cannot bear even the sight of you!"

Logan jumped to his feet as she ran from the room, her words turning his blood cold. He wanted to yell in frustration, to kick a hole in the wall, anything to vent the terrible, helpless rage. He began to pace the floor, fists clenched hard at his sides, his lean cheek flexed tight. He picked up the bottle of whiskey upon the sideboard, tilting it high as he drank great, deep drafts, craving the oblivion it would provide. A stupor that would make him forget red lips and violet eyes filled with hatred.

Hours later, Logan raised a different bottle and squinted at it with one eye closed, then let it drop, turning dull eyes into the orange flames. Vivid memories of the bedchamber at Woodstone welled up with astonishing clarity, and a drunken smile played about his lips as he watched mind pictures of Elizabeth, her silky hair flowing over his chest, her soft, warm body atop him, her red lips upon his jaw, then his shoulder. He groaned as his loins began to throb, passing one hand over liquor-blurred eyes. But the vivid images would not fade, and the thought of her upstairs in her bed drove him unmercifully.

He suddenly sat up straight and looked toward the door. She was his wife, damn it, and it was high time she acted like it! He stood, trying to right his spinning head with a tight grip on the back of the chair. His eyes fell to the last bottle of whiskey, and he tucked it carefully in the crook of his arm. He swore softly as he staggered into a table in the darkness, tinkling several porcelain figurines into millions of shards upon the carpet. He peered into the darkness at the top of the steps, then stumbled upward, clutching the bottle protectively.

His mind was fuzzy, his thought on one thing alone, as he grasped the doorknob to Elizabeth's room. The residual glow of embers revealed her small form huddled upon the bed, and Logan smiled blearily. He dropped the bottle, forgetting everything but the desire that raged inside him.

From deep within her troubled dreams, Elizabeth heard a thudding noise. She sat up, alarmed, gasping at the sight of Logan careening toward her. She grasped the quilted coverlet tightly, and he stopped at the foot of the bed, hugging the post for support, grinning drunkenly at her. Elizabeth frowned as his blue eyes tried to sear through the blanket that hid her body from him.

"What do you want?" she said hesitantly, and Logan dragged his eyes from the rise and fall of her breasts beneath the comforter. He gave a short bark of laughter.

"I want you! What else would I want?"

He moved jerkily to the side of the bed, and Elizabeth watched him warily, knowing he was very drunk. She inched toward the other side, but with amazing quickness, his arm caught her about the waist and pulled her close. She could not fight his immense strength, and she lay still as his face dropped to her shoulder, nuzzling aside her hair. The hot kiss sent fire streaking through her limbs, and she quivered as his mouth sought her lips. Logan's near stupor did not prevent him the ecstasy of the moment, and his lips moved up the slender column of her throat to rest upon her ear.

"You'll always be mine, always: I'll never let you go."

The words awoke Elizabeth, and she dipped into her strength enough to twist away. Logan frowned in confusion as the sweet softness suddenly deserted him and stood like a pale apparition beside the bed. He lunged at her, and the swift movement was his undoing. He grunted, grabbing his reeling head, and Elizabeth watched his heavy body keel backward upon the bed and lie still.

She grasped the bedpost for support, staring down at his handsome face. She wanted to touch him, to slip her fingers beneath the tousled blond hair, but she did not. She did not trust herself. She must not give in to her desire, not until he agreed to take her to her village. He lay spraddled half off the bed, and she struggled to lift his long legs. It took several minutes to accomplish it, and when she reached across his chest for the blanket, Logan stirred, sensing her nearness. His arms imprisoned her against him, and he became vaguely aware of her soft hair upon his cheek.

"Starfire, Starfire," he murmured, as he sank again into dark dreams.

Elizabeth tried to move, but his arms tightened instinctively, barring her escape. She lay still for a moment, Logan's heartbeat a strong, steady rhythm beneath her ear, then relaxed, deciding to enjoy the quiet captivity for just a little while, until his arm loosened and she could slip away.

She closed her eyes, warm in the circle of his arms, and when her eyes fluttered open again, the gray dawn filtered hazy, indistinct light through the draperies, misting the room with hovering shadows. She was so sleepy and warm, nestled close to Logan, that she did not stir until a muffled groan pierced her drowsiness. Completely awake, she found herself in a most compromising position with her nightdress twisted around her waist, and one arm and leg thrown over Logan's body. She cautiously sought to remove the offending limbs, knowing a sober Logan to be much different from a drunken one. She slowly inched her leg across him, finding him quite aroused by her presence, asleep or not.

Logan struggled up from the thick, clinging arms of unconsciousness, Elizabeth's hasty departure forcing his bleary eyes open. He raised his head, and pain hit his head like an anvil dropped from above. Elizabeth winced at the pain on his face, as he pressed his palm upon the top of his head to stop the pounding. When he was finally able to bring the room into focus, he saw Elizabeth where she stood beside the bed, her hair tumbling around her shoulders in a mass of shining waves.

"What . . ." he grumbled, as he struggled to sit up.

He still wore the clothes of the night before, but his white dress shirt was unbuttoned, his breeches wrinkled and stained with wine. It was such a radical departure from his usual immaculate appearance that Elizabeth had a sudden, irresistible urge to laugh.

She did, bringing Logan's brows together. Elizabeth hid her smile as he hoisted himself up, supporting himself with one hand on the mattress. Without a word, he moved away from the bed, and Elizabeth glided silently out of his way as he walked stiffly to the door. After he passed through the portal, she slammed it after him, smiling wickedly at the painful groan that came from the hall.

Elizabeth dressed and spent the morning in the garden, where Mrs. Parker was trying to restart her flowers in the aftermath of the fire. Logan did not appear for the noon meal, and Elizabeth ate in lonely solitude. Afterward, she wandered aimlessly about the house, thinking of her tribe. They'd be preparing for the coming winter now, and if she didn't persuade Logan to take her back soon, the snows would make traveling very difficult. She sank down on a chair in the small parlor at the front of the house, gloomily watching Zack and Amanda as they talked together at the front gate. She raised her head as she heard Logan descend the stairs and listened as his slow footsteps moved toward his library. Perhaps he intended to repeat his performance of the night before, she thought, then discounted it as unlikely in light of the suffering he'd endured upon awakening. It was the only time she'd ever seen him in such a condition, and judging from the number of bottles she and Mrs. Parker had found in front of the fire, it had taken an impressive amount of spirits to put him in such a state.

"I've been looking for you."

Logan stood ramrod-straight in the doorway, faultlessly groomed in dark breeches and a white shirt. His blue eyes looked strained, and when she didn't answer, he walked past her to stare into the grate. Elizabeth looked at his broad back and the inflexible set of his shoulders until he spoke without looking at her.

"All I remember is that I was very angry. I trust I didn't hurt you in any way."

He turned suddenly and met her eyes.

"No, I am fine."

The ensuing silence was awkward, and Elizabeth transferred her eyes to the hazy blue mountains in the far distance. She heard him move until he stood directly behind her.

"I cannot live like this any longer, Elizabeth," he said quietly.

Elizabeth turned to him in surprise.

"I've decided to do as you want. It's against my better judgment, but I'll take you home, if that's what you really want."

Elizabeth stared at him in shock until happiness forged sparkling amethysts of her eyes, and she ran into his arms. Logan gathered her close, one hand tangled in soft blond hair, but his eyes were bleak as he stared over her head, hoping he had the strength to go through with it.

TWENTY-ONE

The Cheyenne village was almost a hundred miles north of Denver, and it took them nearly four days to reach the southern branch of the Crow Creek.

Elizabeth's excitement increased as they traversed the familiar terrain of her childhood. It was late summer now, a bright cool day, and unless trouble with the white man had driven her tribe north, they would still be camped along the wide river.

It was hard to believe that Logan had taken her from the Indian village almost a year ago, and when the sweeping plain finally came into sight, Elizabeth reined up, staring at the dozens of tipis spread out along the bend in the river. Smoke streamed from cookfires, and tears of joy filled her eyes. She spurred her horse, galloping ahead of Logan, and he followed, watching the wind whip her hair away from her shoulders in a silvery swirl.

When she reached the river, she turned and looked back at Logan, but the deep sorrow in his eyes could not dampen her happiness. She splashed her horse across the shallows, knowing Logan's horse was close behind her. They galloped across the meadow, her eyes riveted on the Indians now visible as they moved among the tipis. They were sighted quickly, and half a dozen warriors hastily swung atop painted ponies.

Logan watched warily, realizing his danger. He had stolen one of their prize possessions, and although he now returned with her, he would be considered their enemy. He kept his right hand near his holster, as the fierce-looking braves thundered toward them. Elizabeth laughed with eagerness as they surrounded Logan and her, reverting easily to her Indian language and calling them by name. They looked suspiciously at her white woman's riding attire, but it did not take them long to recognize the fair hair of the daughter of Raging Buffalo. Their grim expressions left them, and they greeted her with excited yelps, wheeling their steeds to escort her into the camp.

Logan rode at Elizabeth's side, tough, wiry warriors on either side of them, all his senses on alert. Women and small children gathered around, as they walked their horses through the camp, smiles splitting one face after another as the Cheyenne recognized Starfire. Logan searched the people for Lone Wolf's dark features, knowing Lone Wolf could no more forget Elizabeth than Logan could. The Indian would be enraged to find her married to a white man, and Logan feared a confrontation between them could not be avoided.

Elizabeth greeted each by name, sometimes leaning down to hug a child, and Logan watched her, never having seen her so happy. For the first time, he appreciated just how much she'd given up when she'd willingly agreed to leave her people to go with him.

They stopped near the center of the village, and Elizabeth slid to the ground in front of a large central tipi. A tall chieftain ducked through the flap almost at once, wearing the full feathered regalia of his position. Logan watched his stern countenance pale as he saw Elizabeth.

"Starfire," he whispered, and Elizabeth ran to him.

The Cheyenne around him grew still, and Logan sat quietly upon his horse, touched by the emotional reunion. After a moment, Raging Buffalo stepped back and held his daughter at arm's length.

"We had mourned you for dead, and now you have come back to us," he said gruffly, but Elizabeth did not have time to answer, as a small woman pushed her way through the onlookers. She carried wood for the fire, but on sight of Elizabeth, she let it fall to the ground. Elizabeth held out her arms to her mother, and they clung together in wordless joy, until Gentle Reed led her inside the tipi for a more private reunion.

Raging Buffalo turned hard black eyes upon the white man upon the big stallion. The wasichu was very strong, with massive muscles bulging under his fringed garments, and the strange blue eyes met his unwaveringly, without fear. The chattering throng quieted as their chief spoke to Logan.

"Who brings my daughter to me?"

He spoke in Cheyenne, and Logan answered in kind.

"I am Tracker. Starfire's husband."

A gasp of dismay went up from those near enough to hear, and hostility emanated from the young warriors guarding Logan.

"Are you he who stole Starfire from us?"

Logan tensed, knowing how quickly he could be subdued if Raging Buffalo ordered it. He gave a short nod, his hand resting on his pistol, and the chief's eyes darkened.

"And Tracker is the one who brings me back to you."

Elizabeth's clear voice spoke from the flap of the tipi, and Logan turned to look at her. She'd doffed the gray riding skirt and white blouse and stood proudly in a fringed shift of soft tan doeskin. Her hair flowed to her waist, a beaded band of red and blue encircled her forehead. Her appearance brought back the first time he'd looked upon her face, when her beauty had stunned him. A great fear arose in his heart, fear that he'd lost her forever, that she would never return to Denver with him. He could not imagine going back without her, nor could he resign himself to live the rest of his life with the Cheyenne. He watched as Elizabeth stepped forward and placed her hand upon Raging Buffalo's arm. "He has been good to me, my father. He is not our enemy."

Raging Buffalo looked down into her eyes for a long moment, and Elizabeth held her breath as he walked to Logan's horse. He raised his arm, and Logan gripped his wrist.

"You are welcome as a friend."

Elizabeth's tense face relaxed into a breathtaking smile, and she hugged Gentle Reed as Logan dismounted. Never had she been so happy. The affection of those around her was like a soothing mantle over shoulders tired from many burdens. Her fears and worries dissolved. She was with her parents, with Logan. She was home where she belonged.

Cries came from afar, causing Elizabeth to turn, as people parted to make a wide corridor to the back of the crowd.

She gasped as her eyes met Lone Wolf's where he stood at the opening, feet braced apart, a rifle gripped tightly in one hand. His eyes glittered upon Elizabeth, and his tribesmen backed away as he moved with swift, silent footsteps to stand before her.

Elizabeth looked up into his dark face, shivering under the unreadable black depths of his eyes. She could not speak, and Logan's whole body tensed to stone as Lone Wolf raised one fair lock.

"You have come back to me," the warrior muttered, and Elizabeth opened her mouth in denial, but Logan's hand closed over her shoulder, thrusting her behind him.

"She is mine," he said in a loud voice, and a hush fell over the Indians surrounding them. Lone Wolf's teeth clamped hard.

"You took her from me in the dark of night like a skulking coward. She is my woman."

His words were harsh and clipped, gritted out with hatred grown poisonous with the thirst for vengeance.

Elizabeth's heart seemed to stop as she realized the danger Logan was in. For weeks she'd thought of nothing but returning to her tribe, but not once had it occurred to her that Lone Wolf might claim her. She stared at the hard lines etched in Lone Wolf's face, then slid one arm around Logan's waist before she stepped from behind him, ignoring Logan's restraining hand, as she lifted defiant eyes to her father.

"I carry the white man's child," she said proudly.

Logan's face went white, his fingers tightening convulsively on her arm. Lone Wolf's face blackened with rage, and he raised his rifle over his head, his dark, spiteful eyes upon Raging Buffalo.

"By the law of our people, Starfire is mine. I demand justice."

Raging Buffalo stepped forward, without looking at his daughter.

"The council of chiefs must decide."

Several men followed Raging Buffalo into the tipi, and Logan drew Elizabeth close beside him, his hand protectively on her waist. Lone Wolf's eyes burned into them with unbridled fury. His followers gathered in a tight knot around him, each armed with a new rifle, all staring at the big white man, and the hatred in their eyes was cold and deadly.

Elizabeth shivered as she looked at them, the vicious look in Lone Wolf's eyes chilling her blood. He wanted to kill Logan, and Elizabeth's fear for her husband increased as time passed and the chiefs did not emerge.

Logan held Elizabeth securely in the circle of his arm, his eyes never leaving Lone Wolf. But his thoughts were on the child Elizabeth carried, his child. He had inadvertently brought them both into danger, and the very thought of Lone Wolf's making Elizabeth his wife made Logan rigid with anger. He'd die before he let the Indian touch her.

The flap lifted, and Logan turned his attention to Raging Buffalo, as he and the other chiefs filed outside. Raging Buffalo stood between Logan and Lone Wolf, and Elizabeth searched his face, praying that Lone Wolf's demand would be denied.

"Starfire belongs to Lone Wolf," Raging Buffalo said. "She was taken from him by force. By the sacred law, she is his woman."

Elizabeth cried out in dismay, not understanding the events which were happening so quickly. Logan pulled her closer as Lone Wolf's eyes turned to her, glinting triumph. He stepped forward, ready to claim her, but Logan moved between them, blocking his path. He jerked the knife from the sheath on his thigh, his eyes locked with Lone Wolf's, and hurled it to the ground between the Indian's feet.

"I challenge Lone Wolf for the woman."

His words rang out, and Lone Wolf's black eyes glittered.

"To the death," the Cheyenne gritted, and Elizabeth grabbed Logan's arm in alarm.

"No, no, Logan, please," she whispered, but Logan didn't look at her, his eyes still hard upon the Indian.

"To the death," he agreed, and Elizabeth bit back a sob of fear. Lone Wolf whirled and stalked away, followed by his men.

The challenge was set for the following day, and Elizabeth was not allowed to stay with Logan, as a great feast of celebration was prepared in honor of her homecoming. All her happiness at seeing her parents again had died beneath her fear for Logan. She had put him in terrible danger by forcing him to bring her back. If he died, it would be her fault, but she was helpless now to stop the fight. She tried to talk to her father, but although his eyes were pitying, she knew there was nothing he could do to stop the death challenge.

By the time the festivities began, it was dark, the night cold and clear. She wanted so desperately to be with Logan, to tell him how sorry she was. She wanted him to hold her in the security of his arms. She trembled as she was led to where the tribe had assembled around a roaring fire. Drums beat in a furious din as dancers twisted and shrieked in front of it, and she finally saw Logan. He could not touch her or speak to her as she sat down between Lone Wolf and him, but his eyes were warm with reassurance.

Elizabeth sat through the dance, her muscles tense, aware of the strength of the men on either side of her. Lone Wolf's courage as a warrior was famous in their tribe, but although she knew Logan possessed the same strength and confidence, her love for him precluded a relief to her anxiety. She looked at his carved profile against the glow of the leaping flames, her heart clutching in panic. She could not bear the thought of losing him. She put her hand against her belly, her eyes filled with tears. What if he never saw his child? What if he died knowing that Lone Wolf would be father to it? Her eyes brimmed with tears that rolled down her cheeks as she contemplated for the first time the horror of living without Logan. She sat sick with dread about the coming battle, and was barely able to walk back to her father's tipi after the ceremony.

She made plans as she lay upon her buffalo robes. She must go to Logan after the village slept. They must leave during the night, leave before the unthinkable could happen. She waited until she heard the even breathing of Raging Buffalo and Gentle Reed, then rose quietly and moved toward the flap. She paused, looking at them a moment, realizing she would probably never see them again. She ducked out the flap, shivering in the cool night air, then crept away from the tent.

Logan lay upon a bedroll near Elizabeth's tipi. His hands were behind his head as he stared at the sparkling stars scattered across the vast dark heavens. He had been a fool to bring Elizabeth back. Now he faced losing her forever, and at the same time sentencing his wife and child to a dangerous life of hardship among an endangered people. He shuddered. He could not, would not lose to Lone Wolf.

A sound brought the cold steel of his gun into his palm, and he lay still, searching the darkness with alert eyes. Lone Wolf had loyal friends who would like the honor of killing his enemy.

He relaxed when he saw Elizabeth's slender silhouette against the starry night sky. He sat up and slid his gun back into the holster as she dropped to her knees in front of him.

"You should not be here, sweet, it is forbidden," he whispered. He could not see her face in the darkness, only the starfire glinting off her hair. She reached out and touched his cheek with gentle fingertips.

"How can you ever forgive me for what I have done? I have been so foolish."

Her voice trembled with fear and regret, and Logan reached out and pulled her close. She came willingly, resting her cheek against his soft buckskin shirt.

"I'm so afraid for you, Logan. I love you so much."

Logan smiled, pressing his lips against the top of her head.

"I would fight a hundred men to hear those words from your lips."

Elizabeth clutched him to her, her voice an urgent whisper. "Please, Logan, please don't fight him. We can leave now while they sleep."

Logan tightened his arms around her comfortingly, his voice very gentle.

"We cannot. Your people would shun me for a coward, and you'd never be able to return here."

"I don't care." Elizabeth was sobbing softly now. "I thought I'd be happy if I came back here. I thought everything would be the same, but it isn't the same. Nothing is the same. All I want is to be with you. I don't care where we go. I'll go anywhere with you."

"Ssssh, my love, please," Logan said, tenderly wiping away her tears. "Everything will be all right. I promise you."

Elizabeth raised her face, her voice breaking. "But I cannot bear the thought of your being hurt, or of Lone Wolf being my . . ."

She choked on the word and was unable to finish, and behind the cloak of night, Logan's face hardened, the very thought piercing him like a blade. He swallowed, his voice low and gruff.

"I will win, because you are mine, and you will always be mine."

Elizabeth pressed herself closer, wanting to believe him, having to believe him, and Logan held her tightly, his palm smoothing the satin of her hair.

"Why didn't you tell me about our child?" he said, after a long silence.

Elizabeth's voice was low and regretful. "I was afraid that if you knew, you would never bring me here."

"You were right, sweet," Logan answered softly. "I would never have taken any chances with you if I'd known, but I am most pleased by the news."

Tears welled in Elizabeth's eyes and coursed down her cheeks.

"What will happen to us, Logan?" she murmured, and Logan was quiet for a moment before he spoke softly, his eyes on the stars.

"Nothing will ever come between us again. We will be happy together, and our child will grow and give us joy. We will come back here often, so Raging Buffalo and Gentle Reed can teach their grandchild the wisdom of Cheyenne ways."

"And will we have other children?" Elizabeth asked, and Logan nodded and squeezed her to him.

"Many others."

"I love you, Logan," Elizabeth said, as their lips melded together in a tender kiss, salted by her tears. They lay together, content to hold each other tightly, until the first light of dawn forced Elizabeth to return to her tipi.

She did not sleep again, pacing endlessly in front of her father's tent, wringing her hands with anxiety. The day was clear, the sky blue and unbroken over the yellow grasses of the plain, but its beauty was lost upon Elizabeth. Her only thoughts were of Logan, and she continued to move about restlessly, while Gentle Reed watched her quietly, aware her daughter's love for the blue-eyed one rivaled her love for Raging Buffalo. There were no words that would comfort Starfire now; only her Tracker's victory could erase the fear in her eyes.

The challenge was to begin when the sun burned directly overhead, and the drums had begun before the sun had risen, a long, slow beat that grated on Elizabeth's nerves and rattled her composure. The wait was interminable, and when Elizabeth was finally summoned to the field of combat, she walked white-faced beside her father.

The tribe had gathered in a meadow close to the river and stood in a wide circle, waiting silently as Elizabeth was led to a buffalo skin spread upon the ground. She sat there alone, searching for Logan, wanting to cover her ears against the wild frenzy of the drums that had now joined the lone beat. The cacophony was deafening, until all stopped at once as if controlled by the same hand. The abrupt silence was unnerving, and Elizabeth jerked her head around as Logan appeared.

The circle parted to give him entrance, and he rode to the center of the ring, his spirited stallion stepping high and proud. He wore only a loincloth, his broad, sun-browned shoulders held erect, his sinewy muscles rippling as he handled the reins with one hand. His head was bare, wind from the river ruffling the blond hair away from his forehead. She stared at the beloved face, the handsome, carved features that meant everything to her. Straight black arrows of paint slanted across his cheekbone with a streak of white just beneath. It was the mask of death, and Elizabeth held her breath as he jerked his horse's head toward her, the clear penetrating blue of his eyes stopping her heart.

Lone Wolf entered from the opposite direction, his tightly muscled physique rigid with controlled anger. The death paint covered his dark, vengeful features. His stern eyes did not seek Elizabeth but watched his foe with deadly intent.

Slowly rising horror spread through Elizabeth as Raging Buffalo bound their left wrists together with a cord of rawhide, then gave each a long hunting knife. The two men stood facing each other, muscles tensed, faces hard, as Raging Buffalo stepped back.

They watched the chief as he raised his arms to the sky, each nerve quivering in readiness. Raging Buffalo dropped his arms abruptly, and Logan moved, slamming his back against the ground as he jerked savagely on Lone Wolf's arm. His feet thudded into the Indian's hard chest and flipped him to the ground behind him. Logan scrambled to his knees, but Lone Wolf wrenched away from Logan's thrust, aiming a vicious kick at Logan's throat.

Logan dodged him, then both men recovered their footing and began to circle each other warily. Lone Wolf jabbed at Logan's legs and Logan evaded it, but the Cheyenne's blade streaked up and hit its mark. Elizabeth cried out as a crimson slash appeared upon the tanned skin of Logan's bare chest, but Logan ignored the wound, knocking Lone Wolf's feet from beneath him. They rolled desperately in the dirt, locked in a lethal embrace. Elizabeth covered her mouth as Logan's knife was knocked from his grasp and Lone Wolf raised his bloodstained blade high over Logan's heart.

Logan clamped his fingers like a steel band around Lone Wolf's wrist as the Indian pushed the blade downward with all his strength. Logan held him, every muscle straining, face contorted with effort, until he pushed violently against him with his knee, sending Lone Wolf sprawling upon his back. Before he could regain his breath, Logan had his blade in hand and pointed into the vulnerable hollow of the warrior's throat.

Elizabeth's heart stood still as Logan held the knife poised there, his chest still heaving with exertion.

"Kill me, wasichu, kill me," Lone Wolf gritted through bloodied lips, and Logan stared down at him for an instant, then relaxed his hold, one quick upward jerk severing the rawhide rope that bound them together.

He stood and hurled the knife into the ground inches from Lone Wolf's face. He wanted to kill no one. He'd seen enough killing and hatred in his life. Lone Wolf was not his enemy. His only crime was wanting Elizabeth, and Logan knew what that could do to a man. He'd won his wife fairly and with honor, and that was all that mattered to him. He turned and started toward her, and Elizabeth laughed in joy and ran to meet him.

Lone Wolf jumped to his feet, his face raw and vicious,

and jerked the knife out of the ground. Elizabeth drew up in terror and screamed as she divined his intention.

"Logan, behind you!"

Logan's quick reflexes saved his life as he lunged to one side, causing the razorlike steel to slice into the meat of his shoulder instead of his spine. He staggered backward on impact, then jerked the blade out, ready to defend himself with it. But the other Cheyenne warriors had already subdued Lone Wolf. With his action, the brave had lost all honor.

Elizabeth ran to Logan where he stood, one hand over his wound, his fingers spread apart to stop the blood. The field of combat had grown very quiet, and Raging Buffalo's voice drifted across the field to them.

"You must decide the fate of Lone Wolf."

"I have no wish for his death," Logan said. "I have what is mine. Show him mercy."

Raging Buffalo turned to where the braves held Lone Wolf spread-eagled upon the ground.

"You are no longer worthy of our people. You will leave our camp forever, and you will wear the brand of a coward."

Another Indian knelt beside Lone Wolf, knife in hand, and one quick slice of the sharp blade severed Lone Wolf's right ear. Elizabeth turned her face into Logan's chest as a terrible shriek of agony rent the air and echoed far out over the river.

High upon a hill overlooking the camp, Brent Holloway steadied his spyglass on the scene below as Lone Wolf's scream died away. Two warriors hoisted the half-conscious man onto his pony and sent it galloping out of the camp. Several of his friends mounted quickly and followed him, and Brent lowered the glass. He frowned, raising it again until he brought Logan into focus as Elizabeth helped him to a nearby tipi.

"Damn him to hell," Brent said hoarsely, his face contorted with hatred. Cord had survived, but he would only live to pay for what he'd done to Brent. It was Cord's fault he'd hurt Isabel. It was his fault that Elizabeth hated him. He'd seen her face when Rankin had said his name.

But he'd repay him. He'd hurt Logan where he was the

most vulnerable. Elizabeth would be the instrument for Brent's revenge. He would kill Logan, to be sure, but first, before he died, Cord would know that Elizabeth was at Brent's mercy.

He trained his spyglass upon the retreating figures of Lone Wolf and his men. The maimed Indian would be a formidable ally now, and the wagonload of rifles that Brent drove would be enough to gain his cooperation.

He smiled coldly, sliding the spyglass together as he climbed upon the wagon seat and turned the horses in the direction that Lone Wolf had disappeared.

TWENTY-TWO

Logan and Elizabeth stayed in the Cheyenne camp for a fortnight, while Logan's wounds slowly healed. But as the nights grew cold and the surrounding aspen trees melted into the yellow and crimson hues of fall, Logan began to think of their departure. He often worried about the simmering unrest between the Indians and the whites, and above all, he wanted Elizabeth and their child safe in Denver.

It was late one warm afternoon, after a day filled with idle pleasures, that Logan watched Elizabeth where she waded in the river. They'd chosen a spot far from the camp, where low-hanging branches veiled their presence on the riverbank. He smiled, at peace with his life. At last, things were as they should be. Months of distrust and anger were over, and he basked in the contentment he felt.

Much of their time had been spent in the sun and fresh air, and Elizabeth's skin had taken on a soft apricot glow that emphasized her light eyes and blond hair. He chuckled to himself as he watched her where she stood in the stream. She was trying to catch a trout with her hands, and her lovely face was bent in concentration as she peered intently down into the water. She wore only her chemise, and the current had wetted the front, making the thin, transparent shift cling to her breasts as the skirt floated around her bare legs. His loins ached as his eyes searched her trim waist for any sign of the babe, but her belly was still flat.

She suddenly lunged into the still water, then triumphantly brought out a small trout in one hand. She looked up at him where he leaned against a tree in the shade, giv-

ing him a brilliant smile. He smiled back and stood, and
Elizabeth watched as he walked out into the water toward
her, fully dressed, a look in his blue eyes that made her
give her hard-earned fish a careless backward toss into the
water. His good arm folded about her waist and lifted her
off her feet.

"I want you."

"But I'm all wet," she protested, nevertheless wrapping
willing arms around his strong neck as he sloshed out of
the water with her. He lowered her gently to the blanket,
then dropped to his knees beside her. Elizabeth's fingers
slid inside his shirt and touched the bandage with gentle
fingertips.

"But your shoulder . . ."

"It hasn't bothered us before, has it?" he murmured, his
fingers teasing loose the laces of her bodice. His blond head
dropped to her shoulder as he pushed the damp shift away.
Her skin tasted warm and sweet, and he gave a soft groan
as her fingers went to work on his laces. Their clothes were
soon in a wet heap beside them, and Elizabeth lay atop Logan, his palm sliding over her velvety back, her hair
encasing them in a silken tent.

She suddenly sat up, straddling his hard waist as her
open hands caressed the molded muscles of his hard chest,
her fingers running across the crisp blond mat. She smiled
seductively and shook the silver silk away from her face as
she moved lower, exploring his leanly fleshed ribs. He
groaned, shutting his eyes as her breasts came against
him, her soft red lips pressing hot kisses along his collarbone.

His hands encircled her waist, fingers meeting front and
back, and lifted her easily, bringing her down upon him.
The exquisite sensation forced a strangled gasp from Elizabeth. She moaned weakly, her eyes closed in pleasure,
her fingers sliding into the thick blond waves at his neck.

"I love you," she whispered, then all words were forgotten as their lovemaking rose to the quivering, brilliant
starburst that left them weak and sated.

Afterward, they lay limply entwined, bound by silken
silver, and after a time, Logan lifted her chin to look
searchingly into her violet eyes.

"It is time for us to go, my sweet love."

A fleeting regret passed over her face, but she smiled. She had only been waiting for his signal.

"If I am with you, my husband, I will be content."

"Then you will be content forever."

Their lips met gently and the kiss was long and leisurely, until the fire once again took them in its grasp.

Their leavetaking was difficult for Elizabeth, but she knew Logan was anxious for news of his sister, and Elizabeth looked forward to seeing Amanda and Lily and her family. She hugged Raging Buffalo and Gentle Reed, promising to return after the child was born. She looked back often to wave at Gentle Reed where she stood at the edge of the village. But Elizabeth was not really sad, not with the tiny babe in her body, and Logan's love to warm her.

The last weeks had taught her much, made her realize that she did not have to make a choice between her white and Cheyenne heritage. She had experienced both ways of life and knew both were good in some ways. She put her hand upon the flatness of her stomach and smiled to herself. She and Logan would teach this wisdom to their children, and they would grow up with deeper knowledge and understanding because of it.

A tide of love warmed her skin, and Elizabeth smiled at Logan's broad back on the stallion in front of her as they picked their way over the rocky trail amid the breathtaking autumn splendor. She shivered slightly, wickedly wishing they did not have to endure the long day's ride before she could snuggle into his strong arms beneath the stars.

But Logan was eager to be home, and it was late in the afternoon when they stopped to make camp. Logan unsaddled the horses and started a fire, and Elizabeth frowned as he continued to favor his good arm. She would insist that he see a white doctor when they returned, she decided, as she walked through the trees toward the stream.

She'd donned her riding skirt and blouse for the journey, but she still wore the knee-high moccasins of the Cheyenne, preferring their soft comfort to the stiff leather boots. She knelt at the riverbank and dipped water over her face and neck. She felt grimy and hot, and she unbuttoned the front of her blouse and slipped her chemise off her shoulders. Later she would bathe, perhaps with Logan, she thought with a secret smile, but now the water would cool and revive her.

Brent Holloway stood motionless, watching Elizabeth where she knelt by the river. He raised his eyes, searching the trees behind her for Lone Wolf and his men. He could not see them, but he knew they were in position, waiting for Brent to make his move.

He smiled coldly as Elizabeth loosened her blouse and began to splash water upon her arms. She would be his soon, after a very long wait. He'd found Lone Wolf's campsite on a hill overlooking the Cheyenne village. As he'd thought, Lone Wolf had been eager to help him wreak vengeance on Logan. The Cheyenne hated Cord almost as much as Brent did. Logan would die very soon.

Their plan was very simple, but it would work. They would surprise the couple,. Brent capturing Elizabeth while Lone Wolf and his friends took care of Logan. The only thing Brent regretted was that Lone Wolf would get the pleasure of killing Cord. But first, Logan would see his wife in Brent's hands. It was important to Brent that Logan Cord know before he died that Elizabeth was at his mercy.

And with Logan's life at stake, Elizabeth would be cooperative enough. He would take her to Mexico until Rankin's murder was forgotten. Logan would be dead by then, and he would marry her and control her fortune. And if she refused, he would beat her into submission. It would be interesting to see how long it would take to break her Cheyenne spirit.

But now it was time to move. He mounted quickly and walked his horse into the open. Elizabeth did not hear him, and he stopped his horse at the opposite edge of the water.

"Hello, sweet Elizabeth," he said, his eyes on her bare breasts.

The deep, familiar voice startled Elizabeth, and she jerked up her eyes, quickly crossing her arms over her torso as she stared up at Brent Holloway astride his horse.

For the first instant, she could not move, then awareness of danger shot through her, and she began to run. She ducked through the undergrowth and bushes, desperately pulling on her blouse, as Brent's horse splashed through the stream behind her. She screamed for Logan as Brent caught her by her hair, laughing as he jerked her to a standstill. Elizabeth cried out in pain, striking at him and kicking as he slid off his saddle.

Logan heard Elizabeth's scream, and he snatched up his rifle, heading for the river at a dead run. He stopped and raised his rifle when he saw her struggling violently with Brent Holloway.

"Let her go, Holloway, or you're a dead man," he yelled, and Brent wrenched Elizabeth's back against his chest, covering her mouth with his hand. Elizabeth tried to scream a warning to Logan as Lone Wolf drifted out of the trees behind him.

Logan spun, but Lone Wolf's gun butt slammed into his bandaged shoulder, then came back in a swift uppercut that connected under Logan's chin with a horrible crack.

Logan's head jerked backward, and Elizabeth screamed as he crumpled at the Indian's feet.

Elizabeth fought against Brent's tight hold, but he held her securely.

"Unless you want him dead, you'll do exactly as I say. Lone Wolf wants to kill him very badly."

Elizabeth turned her eyes to Lone Wolf. His mutilated ear was uncovered, still a hideous, oozing raw wound. She stilled, watching as three of Lone Wolf's men joined him beside her husband's prone body. Brent released his hold, and Elizabeth ran to Logan, horrified to see the crimson stain darkening his shirt.

"His shoulder is bleeding!"

She tore frantically at her petticoat, managing to press some of the fabric against Logan's chest before Brent jerked her to her feet.

"Very touching, Elizabeth, your last loving gesture for your husband. Because now you're mine. You and your money."

"You can have my money. All of it. I'll give you anything you want if you'll let us go," she begged.

Brent laughed coldly. "You miss the point, my dear. I already have everything I want."

"I'll never leave Logan for you," Elizabeth said bitterly, pulling her arm free.

Brent's face compressed into a malignant grimace.

"Don't you see, love? You will do exactly as I say."

Elizabeth's eyes were frozen with hatred as he continued.

"Because all I have to do is give the sign, and our friend Lone Wolf will kill dear Logan in a very slow and painful way. Look at him, if you don't believe me. He's dying to finish him off."

Elizabeth looked at Lone Wolf's black eyes, obsessed with a hatred close to madness. A great calm settled over her as she resigned herself to her fate. Logan was helpless against them. She must protect him.

"How do I know you speak the truth?" she said coldly. "If I go with you, what will keep Lone Wolf from killing him?"

"Lone Wolf hates the white man. He intends to make war, but he needs more guns to do it. And I can get them for him. He wants the rifles even more than he wants to kill Logan."

Elizabeth hesitated, not trusting him, and Brent's voice grew ugly.

"Get on your horse, or I'll shoot him myself."

"He'll find us," Elizabeth said, and Brent's smile was lethal.

"You'd better hope he doesn't."

Elizabeth climbed into the saddle, realizing there was no escape, not now. Tears glistened as she watched Lone Wolf and the others roughly sling Logan over his saddle.

"Where are they taking him?" she cried, and Brent laughed.

"They're going to detain him for a few days, so that he can't pick up our trail."

He left her and walked to Lone Wolf, but Elizabeth's eyes stayed on Logan, her heart breaking as blood ran down his arm and dripped upon the ground.

"He's all yours," Brent said in low tones to Lone Wolf. "Do whatever you want to him. Just make sure he's dead when you get finished." He paused, his eyes on Elizabeth. "I'm just sorry I won't get to watch."

Lone Wolf's black eyes glowed with anticipation. "He

will plead for death before we finish with him. And what of the guns?"

"Don't worry, you'll get them. Wait for my message," he ordered.

Brent mounted his horse and took Elizabeth's reins away from her.

"Come, my love, we have a very long ride."

Elizabeth looked back at Logan, holding tightly to the saddle horn as Brent spurred his horse forward.

They rode hard until it was too dark to travel, then Brent stopped, jerking her down from the horse and pushing her to the ground. She sat silently as he built a roaring fire, trying to think how she could get his gun. She had to get away, get help from Raging Buffalo to save Logan.

Brent moved in front of her, and Elizabeth stared straight ahead. Brent smiled briefly, pulling leisurely on his mustache. She would fight like a cat out of hell. The idea excited him.

"Get up."

Elizabeth did not move, and he gave a short laugh.

"So Cord doesn't mean so much to you after all. It's but a short ride back to Lone Wolf and his friends."

Elizabeth got to her feet and stood stiffly as Brent's eyes raked over her appreciatively. He reached out suddenly, his hand closing cruelly over her breast. Elizabeth clenched her jaw to keep from crying out, and Brent smiled, dropping his hand.

"Unbutton your blouse."

Elizabeth shuddered, a long undulation that rippled coldly over her flesh. She unfastened her buttons slowly until the front hung apart.

"Now take it off," he ordered, and every fiber of Elizabeth's body rebelled as she slipped out of it, letting it fall to the ground.

"Now the skirt and petticoats."

She obeyed, her eyes burning with hatred, until she stood before him in her thin chemise.

"You are even more beautiful than I imagined," he murmured, fumbling at his belt.

"I despise you," Elizabeth gritted, but Brent smiled into her eyes.

"Good, that will make it all the better. Lie down."

Elizabeth stood still, her eyes on the rifle in the sheath of his saddle. He pushed her roughly to the ground, then jerked off his shirt and doubled his belt into a loop.

"Now I'll show you what Cord never could," he boasted, and Elizabeth shut her eyes as he dropped to his knees in front of her. She couldn't bear for him to touch her, she thought frantically, she couldn't. Her fingers found sand, and she squeezed it into her palm. When he leaned close, she threw it into his eyes, then rolled away from him and ran for the horse. She had to get the rifle, she had to kill him!

Just as she reached for it, Brent's hands swung her around, his open palm coming forcefully against the side of her head. Pain exploded in a white flash that numbed her, and she fell to the ground and lay looking up at him. He moved over her, slapping his belt against his palm, his mouth curved in a cruel smile.

"Now, Elizabeth, my dear, let's start over—"

The arrow struck him in the throat, severing the jugular vein. Elizabeth watched in horror as blood spurted in a pulsating stream, and his shocked eyes stared down at her, slowly glazing into an unseeing mask as he reeled backward to the ground.

Elizabeth jumped to her feet, sobbing with relief, as she searched the night for her savior. Two Bears materialized from the trees, his bow still in his hand, and she watched him gather her clothes and walk toward her. He handed them to her, and she put them on quickly. Two Bears looked down at Brent's corpse.

"I have avenged the death of Little Doe. Her spirit will soar free," he said, and Elizabeth glanced down at Brent's wide-open eyes and shuddered.

"How did you find me?"

"I went to the camp of your people, so Tracker could help me track the white devil. When I found you were already gone, I followed your trail. When other horses joined you at the river, I followed the tracks of the two horses."

"Thank God," Elizabeth said. Then she put her hand on his arm, her voice urgent.

"But we must go swiftly to help Logan. Lone Wolf has him!"

Two Bears listened intently as she told him what had

happened, his eyes inscrutable. When she finished, he leaped upon his pony. Elizabeth mounted and followed him without a backward look at the staring corpse.

Bright moonlight filtered through the forest, lighting their path, the trees long, hulking shadows all around them. It took them almost two hours to reach the stream where Logan had been taken, and Two Bears knelt upon the ground, his fingers touching the hoof-churned earth.

"They do not hide their tracks. Come."

They rode for another hour, Two Bears often dismounting to study the ground, and each minute that passed increased the cold fear inside Elizabeth's breast. Her heart pounded when Two Bears raised his hand to halt her and spoke low words to her.

"They are camped just ahead. I smell their fire."

He tied their horses, and Elizabeth gripped the pistol she'd taken from Brent as they climbed a small rise. Beneath them in a rocky clearing, two Cheyenne Indians lounged around a campfire, while Lone Wolf paced agitatedly not far away from them.

"I don't see Logan," Elizabeth whispered urgently, and Two Bears put a finger to his lips.

"He is there, in the pit," he said very low. "And another man guards the ponies."

Elizabeth's eyes found the gaping dark hole in the ground. It was perhaps five yards from the fire, and a faint glimmer showed a torch had been hung down inside it. Elizabeth went rigid with fear.

"We must get him out of there," she cried, lifting her gun, but Two Bears stopped her, both hands on her shoulders to calm her.

"No, little one, there are too many. If we fire from here, Tracker will surely die."

Elizabeth saw the wisdom in his words, but her eyes went again to the pit, terrified at what she'd find at the bottom.

"I will release their horses." Two Bears' whisper was quiet. "When they run to stop them, I will kill them one by one. You must free Tracker while I do this."

He faded away without a sound, and Elizabeth moved carefully down the rocky slope, remembering the many times she'd stalked deer with her father. Her moccasins were soundless, and she crept to within feet of the fire.

A fierce yell suddenly rent the air, followed by the wild neighing of panicked horses, and the Cheyenne left the fire to run toward the noise. One fell almost immediately as an arrow pierced his chest, and Elizabeth waited only a moment before she ran toward the hole.

She stopped as Lone Wolf appeared before her, his gun in his hand. She did not hesitate but raised her pistol and fired. The bullet sent him sprawling backward, and Elizabeth clutched the smoking gun tightly as she fell to her knees at the rim of the pit. She peered into the dim reaches of the hole, her eyes horrified when she saw Logan.

He lay at the bottom, his hands and feet bound together behind his back. His shirt was red with blood, and his face was battered and bruised. His eyes were closed, and Elizabeth's heart stopped.

"Logan!" she cried frantically.

He stirred, only half conscious, and she sobbed her relief as he tried to open eyes swollen by the brutal beating.

"Logan, can you hear me? Are you all right?"

He squinted, trying to see her. His voice was a hoarse croak.

"Elizabeth?"

He seemed to realize then where he was, and his words came stronger.

"Elizabeth, go quickly, before Lone Wolf sees you."

"No, I won't leave you. Lone Wolf's dead, and so are the others. Two Bears killed them."

Logan shifted, groaning as his cramped muscles screamed in pain.

"Go, Elizabeth, please. They will get you."

"No, we're going to get you out. Two Bears will help me."

She looked around, growing panicky again, breathing in relief when she saw Two Bears running toward her.

"Hurry! Logan's hurt!"

Neither of them saw Lone Wolf lift his head and slowly aim his gun. A shot cracked in the night, and Two Bears fell. Elizabeth screamed, raising her gun and firing point-blank at Lone Wolf. He rolled over and lay still, and Elizabeth leaped up and ran to Two Bears. He had been hit by a bullet, and he lay unmoving on his back.

Elizabeth sobbed over the still form, then gathered her strength and ran back to the hole, knowing she had to get Logan out by herself. She found the rope that Lone Wolf had used to lower Logan into the pit and tied it with trembling fingers around a small pine tree, then tossed it over the side.

Logan heard it fall, his mind alert now to her danger. He called up to her, his voice hard with authority.

"Stop, Elizabeth, and listen to me. You can't come down here. This is a snake pit."

Elizabeth froze, her eyes going in cold horror to the shadowy confines of the hole. Hairs rose on her neck, her phobia sending gooseflesh across her skin. Her hands shook as she saw thick coils piled together in the corner near Logan's feet.

"Did you hear me? There are rattlers in here with me." His voice was still quiet, but desperate to make her stay above.

She clutched the gun tighter.

"I have a gun, Logan. I can shoot them."

Her voice shook out of control.

"A bullet will ricochet or cave in the walls." Logan's voice came up calmly to her, trying to keep her from doing anything foolish.

"You must drop me a knife, sweet, so I can cut the ropes."

Elizabeth quickly fetched Two Bears' knife and leaned over the opening with it, her knuckles white around the handle.

"Drop it somewhere behind me, where I can reach it," Logan said softly.

Elizabeth moved, terrified she would hit him with the blade. She dropped it carefully, and it clattered loudly on the stones behind him. She cried out in dismay as it slid downward across the slanted pitch of the floor, disturbing a coiled rattler lying indolently in the shadows. The snake quickly wound itself into a writhing coil, its rattles clicking loud and angrily.

Logan kept his eyes glued to it as it whipped out of its corner, his fingers working desperately to loosen the cords on his wrists. A second snake slid out of the darkness behind Logan's head, and Elizabeth waited no longer. She had to help him. She grasped the rope tightly in her hands and swung herself over the ledge.

Logan's eyes were horrified as he watched her descend slowly toward him.

"No, damn it, go back," he whispered hoarsely, and the deadly rattling grew louder as other serpents began to sense danger. Logan lay still then listening to their slight scrapings on the floor behind them.

Elizabeth looked around cautiously, moving downward one foot at a time. She forced herself to move, her fear for Logan overruling all else.

Logan's forehead ran with sweat, knowing she'd come too far now to stop.

"Go slowly. Any quick movement will make them strike." His voice was barely audible above the sound of the snakes.

Her foot touched the bottom, and she let go of the rope, carefully edging toward the knife, her eyes on the vipers swarming together several feet away. She looked down at the knife and stood petrified as she saw the thick length that lay across the handle. She turned horrified eyes to Logan, helplessly bound, as one of the snakes slid over his boot.

Elizabeth could not bear it, and she looked around frantically, her eyes lighting upon the torch hanging upon a rope. She grabbed it quickly and thrust the flame at the viper atop the knife. It slid off and away, and she grabbed the knife, never even seeing the other rattler beside her. She cried out as fangs pierced her moccasin and sank painfully into her ankle. She scrabbled to Logan, cutting away the ropes, and Logan grabbed the knife from her shaking hands and cut his feet free.

Thrusting Elizabeth behind him, he got the torch she'd dropped, poking it at the agitated snakes.

"It bit me, on the ankle," Elizabeth said, then weaved on her feet as the venom began to affect her, and Logan pulled her limp body over one shoulder, his wounds forgotten as he fought for their lives. He got a hold on the rope, then threw the torch at the snakes as he began to pull himself up.

Elizabeth's cheek lay against Logan's back, feeling his muscles move as he brought them out of the hellish pit. Vaguely she felt the coolness of the night wind upon her face, and the last thing she knew was being cradled in Logan's arms, as his voice called her name from very far away.

A strange clicking sound entered her haunting dreams, and Elizabeth struggled to open her eyes, unable to think what it could be. Then her mind took her into the nightmare of the pit, and she jerked upright, her eyes wide and terrified, as she looked for the rattlers.

"Logan!"

Arms came around her at once, cool and gentle hands touching her brow tenderly, as Logan's voice soothed her terror.

"Shhh . . . my sweet, you're safe now."

She closed her eyes in relief and leaned weakly against him as he pushed damp hair from her temples.

"You've been very sick," he whispered. "But you are better now."

The clicking sound that had frightened her resumed, and Elizabeth opened her eyes to see the buffalo mask of her tribe's medicine man. He moved in a circle around the buffalo robes where she lay, chanting in a low, monotonous voice. Elizabeth sank back into Logan's arms.

A terrible thought jolted fear into her core, as she remembered she'd been bitten.

"My baby . . ."

"The moccasin stopped most of the venom. The baby will be fine."

Elizabeth looked down at her leg. Her foot was swollen to twice its normal size, but there was little pain. She raised her face to Logan as he lowered her carefully to the robe. His battered face was gray with exhaustion, his blue eyes haggard, a week's growth of dark beard covering his face.

"Are you all right?" she asked in concern. He nodded and smiled.

"But you look terrible," she said, reaching a finger to touch his whiskered cheek.

Gentle Reed's voice spoke from behind him. "Tracker

has not left your side since he brought you and the Sioux chief into our camp four days ago. He is a stubborn man."

Elizabeth looked quickly at him. "How is Two Bears?"

"He will survive, but he will be abed for many a month."

Elizabeth smiled at the welcome news, then shuddered as she thought how very close Logan had come to death.

"Hold me, Logan, please."

Logan complied with the greatest of pleasure, lying close beside her. Elizabeth sighed, and Gentle Reed laid down the ointment she had prepared for Starfire's foot. There would be time to apply it later. She motioned to the medicine man, then followed him out of the tipi, anxious to tell Raging Buffalo that their only daughter was awake.

"Never let me go," Elizabeth murmured softly, and Logan's voice was barely audible as exhaustion overtook him, but his low words warmed Elizabeth and filled her heart with peace.

"As long as I breathe, my sweet Elizabeth, you will be with me. . . ."

This is the special design logo that will call your attention to Avon authors who show exceptional promise in the romance

THE AVON ROMANCE

area. Each month a new novel—either historical or contemporary—will be featured.

HEART SONGS Laurel Winslow
Coming in April   **85365-5/$2.50**
Set against the breathtaking beauty of the canyons and deserts of Arizona, this is the passionate story of a young gallery owner who agrees to pose for a world-famous artist to find that he captures not only her portrait but her heart.

WILDSTAR Linda Ladd
Coming in May   **87171-8/$2.75**
The majestic Rockies and the old West of the 1800's are the setting for this sizzling story of a beautiful white girl raised by Indians and the virile frontiersman who kidnaps her back from the Cheyenne.

NOW & AGAIN Joan Cassity
Coming in June   **87353-2/$2.95**
When her father dies, a beautiful young woman inherits his failing landscape company and finds herself torn between the fast-paced world of business and the devouring attentions of a dynamic real estate tycoon.

FLEUR DE LIS Dorothy E. Taylor
Coming in July   **87619-1/$2.95**
The spellbinding story of a young beauty who, fleeing France in the turmoil of revolution, loses her memory and finds herself married to a dashing sea captain who is determined to win her heart and unlock the secret of her mysterious past.

A GALLANT PASSION Helene M. Lehr **86074-0/$2.95**
CHINA ROSE Marsha Canham   **85985-8/$2.95**
BOLD CONQUEST Virginia Henley   **84830-9/$2.95**
FOREVER, MY LOVE Jean Nash   **84780-9/$2.95**

Look for THE AVON ROMANCE wherever paperbacks are sold, or order directly from the publisher. Include $1.00 per copy for postage and handling: allow 6-8 weeks for delivery. Avon Books, Dept BP Box 767, Rte 2, Dresden, TN 38225.

Avon Rom 5-84

IT'S A NEW AVON ROMANCE LOVE IT!

A GENTLE FEUDING
87155-6/$3.95
Johanna Lindsey

A passionate saga set in the wilds of Scotland, in which a willful young woman is torn between tempestuous love and hate for the powerful lord of an enemy clan.

WILD BELLS TO THE WILD SKY
84343-9/$6.95
Laurie McBain   Trade Paperback

This is the spellbinding story of a ravishing young beauty and a sun-bronzed sea captain who are drawn into perilous adventure and intrigue in the court of Queen Elizabeth I.

FOR HONOR'S LADY
85480-5/$3.95
Rosanne Kohake

As the sounds of the Revolutionary War echo throughout the colonies, the beautiful, feisty daughter of a British loyalist and a bold American patriot must overcome danger and treachery before they are gloriously united in love.

DECEIVE NOT MY HEART
86033-3/$3.95
Shirlee Busbee

In New Orleans at the onset of the 19th century, a beautiful young heiress is tricked into marrying a dashing Mississippi planter's look-alike cousin—a rakish fortune hunter. But deceipt cannot separate the two who are destined to be together, and their love triumphs over all obstacles.

VELVET GLOVE

An exciting series of contemporary novels of love with a dangerous stranger.

Starting in July

THE VENUS SHOE Carla Neggers　　　　　　87999-9/$2.25
Working on an exclusive estate, Artemis Pendleton becomes embroiled in a thirteen-year-old murder, a million dollar jewel heist, and with a mysterious Boston publisher who ultimately claims her heart.

CAPTURED IMAGES Laurel Winslow　　　　　　87700-7/$2.25
Successful photographer Carolyn Daniels moves to a quiet New England town to complete a new book of her work, but her peace is interrupted by mysterious threats and a handsome stranger who moves in next door.

LOVE'S SUSPECT Betty Henrichs　　　　　　88013-X/$2.25
A secret long buried rises to threaten Whitney Wakefield who longs to put the past behind her. Only the man she loves has the power to save—or destroy her.

DANGEROUS ENCHANTMENT Jean Hager　　　　88252-3/$2.25
When Rachel Drake moves to a small town in Florida, she falls in love with the town's most handsome bachelor. Then she discovers he'd been suspected of murder, and suddenly she's running scared when another body turns up on the beach.

THE WILDFIRE TRACE Cathy Gillen Thacker　　　88620-4/$2.25
Dr. Maggie Connelly and attorney Jeff Rawlins fall in love while involved in a struggle to help a ten-year-old boy regain his memory and discover the truth about his mother's death.

IN THE DEAD OF THE NIGHT Rachel Scott　　　88278-7/$2.25
When attorney Julia Leighton is assigned to investigate the alleged illegal importing of cattle from Mexico by a local rancher, the last thing she expects is to fall in love with him.

AVON PAQERBACKS